Deape Woods

Deape Woods

⌘

Prudence O'Haire

Contagious Vision Publishing

Published by Contagious Vision Publishing
740 NE 3rd Street, Suite 3-96, Bend, OR 97701
http://contagiousvision.com
info@contagiousvision.com

Edited by Chelsey Young
Illustrations by Maggie Behnke
Cover design by Christopher Behnke

ISBN-13: 978-0692192580 (Contagious Vision)
ISBN-10: 0692192581

Bibliographic information for chapter epigraphs are available upon request.

Dedication

This book is dedicated to all generations of souls who value and never cease to search for the absolute truth. People in general tend to think they have it, but ultimately it is up to you alone to decide for yourself which direction is correct and what to do with it when it is found. Don't ever believe the lie that you're too old or too young to find it. And when you do uncover it, let yourself be an ambassador to share it with others.

PREFACE

I would like to inform my readers that—though this is a work of fiction—the content and information regarding occult activity and dialogue within this story are not based solely on my own willy-nilly imagination. I have spent the last five years researching both sides of the pendulum to verify and ask my own questions in regards to the power that lies within the occult. My own questions and curiosity began with ghost-hunting television shows. The shows fascinated me, but after watching them they left me with many questions that never were answered. They whet my appetite for more, but always left me feeling hollow. I began my research with one book, which led to web research and reading news articles. I asked questions of pastors—not just from my own church body—but also people around me. I read material written by specialists involved in ministry directly with those entrapped.

I think what discouraged me most was that the church and its leadership seemed to know very little about the dark dimension and the so-called enemy that we all are at odds with. How could we all have no idea what type of enemy we are up against? Why wasn't this subject more of a reality? Why were we only taking potshots at issues in church and not trying to understand more of why the issues were there in the first place? (At least in my own 38 years of experience with church culture.)

As I grew to understand more and more, I found that the very nature of the word "occult" means *secret* or *hidden*. I became wise to the fact that there were obvious reasons why it remained in the dark and why so many people were afraid to look it straight in the face. An ignorant Christian is unproductive. So, if the enemy can't steal our salvation, he will work to keep us uneducated and distracted and busy with other things, so as not to see so many things that hurt us and keep us from furthering the Kingdom of Christ. They want us to believe that things within the horror genre are not real and are only good for a thrill. The enemy works hard to desensitize the public. They work hard at breaking us down so we all accept nicely, those evil, little sugar pills designed to lull us all to sleep so we pay no attention. No, these things are real to those who are enslaved to the dark power. They are real to the victims of the occult—those who have seen it and experienced it, yet are called crazy for admitting it.

It often comes as an angel of light, because if it had no costume, perhaps more of us would be awake to its schemes. The occult is only the underground manifestation. It's where the ultimate dirty work is done. But make no mistake, it permeates everything and tries to hijack everything good. Its tentacles reach far and deep and the great majority of our world can't see it.

Every one of us knows, in various ways, there is more than just living and dying. We are spiritual beings. Given the amount of movies, music, books, and general entertainment and education on feelings, love, and heartache, and every other emotion—we desperately want to be loved and to feel something, even if it's pain. We all want to make sense out of why we are here. Unfortunately, we are also selfish. And while we want to make sense out of our lives, we also want to live it for ourselves. We want our cake and we want to eat it without getting fat. So we invent our own reasons for purpose and living. But when we find that our own invention of purpose is hollow and empty, we lose hope and death consumes us with laughter.

The ugliness of the dark is real. It's not a false thing. To understand the enemy is to understand the power of Christ and how vast His love for us is. Not everyone needs to know the gory details. For certain, not everyone is called to knowing more fully and researching continuously. But those of us that have been called to uncover and recover knowledge that has either been lost or stolen, have been given the task of informing or re-informing the troops about the mission at hand. I will never claim to have all the answers. Indeed, I've only scratched the tip of the iceberg. I will never know it all. You can never know it all. I will, however, not stop asking questions and marching towards a greater intimacy with God. I encourage everyone who has a question to, with prayer and petition, go look for the answer. You can't find something if you don't attempt to look for it. With God's wisdom and guidance He will take you to where you are called to be. This story—and others to come—is a vitamin in a cookie, education within entertainment. A way to convey what I believe is possible from my research of darker matters.

There is Hope—He's called Jesus Christ.

Prudence O'Haire
October 2018

ACKNOWLEDGMENTS

I would first like to express gratefulness to my best friend and husband Chris. You encouraged me every week to keep going on this project, you made meals, kept interruptions at bay and spent countless hours editing, reading, working on layout, and putting all the final pieces together. Without you, I'm not sure there would have been a finished book. I love that you're my biggest fan.

I would like to thank my four children who exercised great restraint by not knocking on my door while I was writing. You helped man the household when I was buried in my mind bringing the story to life. You guys, I love you more than french fries with fry sauce and my hope is this book in some way would ignite your Holy fires.

I would like to thank my oldest daughter Maggie for her contribution to this work. All the illustrations are a testimony of your skillset and I am thrilled you have been willing to devote your time to this project. I think, Maggie, that you are a glowing tulip in acres of tulips that have no shine. If we set aside your talents, I would still be very pleased to be called your mother. And my hope is one day I will be called your friend.

Thank you to all of you people who have pooled your time and minds in helping me edit or read for content, no matter the amount of time you donated. I appreciate every single one of you.

Chelsey Young. You came in last minute to this project but it was all in God's timing. You win the title of Editor-in-Chief for this book. You've spit and polished it till it shines and I am so thankful for your work and efforts.

And to finish my rounds of thankfulness, I give all the glory to You, God. It is You who have instilled and grown my creativity. You have and are taking me places I didn't know I could go. I asked You to fuel my imagination and You did just that. Thank you, Lord Jesus, for using me, I am Your humble servant. May any fame be Yours.

Contents

- One -

THE NEW TOWN

"Forever is composed of nows."

~Emily Dickinson

A VOLKSWAGEN BUS CLIMBED its way up logging road FS-33A at a slow speed, weaving its way around gaping potholes and wash-boarded rows along the knobbly gravel road. The engine revved up to gain some power as it backed into a cubby hole surrounded by young evergreens that enclosed the quiet forest land of Kingsman, Oregon.

The rig's motor shut down. The stout driver opened the door slowly. His feet swung out onto the slick, pine needle-covered dirt floor. His size thirteen black leather boots crunching the ground was the only sound heard as they took him around to the back of the bus.

Opening the back door, his rough-skinned hands sought a shovel and thrust it into the soft ground so it stood upright. Next, a sealed plastic barrel was pulled out and set on its end.

The man's dark, beady eyes squinted as they scanned his surroundings. Grabbing ahold of the metal-handled shovel, he traipsed a little deeper into the forest and selected a spot for burial right next to a buck-skinned tree. Tiny green strands of wild blackberries crawled along the ground like spider webbing wrapping around everything they could get ahold of.

The man dug for over an hour, pausing occasionally to rest. He was unable to think about his actions. There were no thoughts of empathy or regret. Penitence was not something he had ever practiced. The stubble from his unshaven face concealed wrinkles of disdain and the wear and tear from years of numbed actions.

Once he judged the hole to be deep enough, he rolled the barrel in, the contents inside thudding against the walls of its plastic prison. Again, the hands on the shovel worked hard, only this time they worked to fill in the empty space to hide the contents of the black plastic cylinder.

The man wiped his sweaty forehead with the back of his flannel glove. Not realizing he had a thorn stuck in the finger, he accidentally scraped it across his sun-beaten brow. A tiny line of blood dribbled down the side of his face like a sluggish waterfall. The look was appropriate. Yes, it was fitting. He was no stranger to bloody messes.

The predator hacked and snorted then spat a thick wad of saliva on the freshly turned earth. He was finished hiding his dark deed, the deed that wasn't his alone, but one he had shared with others. Using the shovel as a walking stick, the man slowly headed back to his van. A jet-black raven cawed loudly in a tree just above him. The August winds began to pick up and the roar of the trees hailed the rapacious human to leave.

Near the dirt crypt, a wild yellow daffodil hung its bell-shaped head in the memory of someone who was once loved, who now was lost.

◆ ◆ ◆

Nora Miller wrapped the blue knitted afghan around her father's lap and kissed him on the cheek. "Bye Dad, I will come and visit within a week, okay?"

Her father didn't reply. Instead he asked for a drink. Nora backed away, allowing his nurse to address his need, watching as the older man twiddled his thumbs and tapped his foot, oblivious to the presence and identity of his daughter. His mind was being ravaged by Alzheimer's and he was now just a shell of the man he once was.

Sweeping her long brown hair to the side, Nora walked to the nurse's station to wrap up any final details before leaving Green Acres Senior Living. It had taken a lot of energy to get her father moved here from Colorado, her family's home state. Nora had been running on adrenaline—as is normal during the process of moving—and she was starting to feel herself coming down from the high. It was just she and her father now. No siblings, aunts, uncles, cousins, or mother. Nora's mother Eleanor had lost her battle to breast cancer about three years ago when she was only fifty-six. The universe wouldn't wait any longer and requested the freeing of her mother's soul. The fight with cancer had been excruciating. In the end, cancer had won; the family had lost.

George Miller was in between stages five and six of the debilitating disease of Alzheimer's. He no longer recognized Nora. The disease had come on quickly for George after his beloved wife and soulmate had passed away. It was almost as if the stressful, passionate fraught of losing Eleanor had brought on the powerful impairment of Alzheimer's. Nora was in the process of losing her second parent to death's sting and she had no one for support. It was a lonely, scary place for a single girl of twenty-seven years.

"I think that's all I need from you, dear," said the nurse with the black mushroom-cut hair. "We'll make your dad comfortable, and we'll see you back within the week." Nora smiled and thanked the woman, and the fair-skinned nurse buzzed the steel-gray double doors open so Nora could exit the building.

The tall knob popped up as Nora twisted the key in the lock of the hefty door of her cobalt 1974 F-250. Double-checking that the items in the back were still firmly tied down, she climbed into the cabin, pulled the door shut, and immediately rolled down the window to let the warm air circulate throughout the cab. It was August and the heat in Astor, Oregon was at its season's highest temperatures. Sweat began to build on her dainty neck from the warmth as she backed out of the parking lot and pulled onto the highway, heading for her new hometown of Kingsman, Oregon. Glancing in her crooked rearview mirror, she watched as the care facility grew smaller and smaller.

Nora reached to turn up the volume of the radio. The words from the song didn't do their job of distracting her mind from replaying memories. Instead, they seemed to amplify them.

In a way, moving was causing Nora to grieve as she did her best to let go of the past and grab ahold of the future.

Nora was a fair-skinned young lady. She was slender and tall and owned thick straight brown hair that draped down the mid of her shoulder blades. Her facial features were dainty but chiseled, having acquired the best features from both of her parents. Her closet housed vintage apparel; she was usually decked out in something sophisticated and casual, simple, yet well put-together. Her heritage was strong in both Irish and German decent, with a splash of Viking bloodlines. Nora inherited her mother's long, thick eyelashes and nicely-framed brows—she needed no makeup to display her curious, kind brown eyes. She patted her heart-shaped lips together, tasting her peach chap stick while shoving her white sunglasses back up on the bridge of her slender nose.

The old blue Ford was now cruising along at a comfortable speed on the dry, cracked pavement. The high desert was producing speedy winds. Dried brown tumbleweeds of all sizes came to life, rolling across the hot pavement as if they were in a big hurry to get somewhere. Nora glanced at the picture taped to her dash. It seemed like that photo of her with her parents had been snapped during a whole different lifetime.

Nora's mind drifted to a memory from when she was sixteen years old. Mom had happily helped Nora shop for just the right dress for her violin recital with the local orchestra. Following the purchase of the dress, which was way too long, she had demonstrated how to do a blind hem on the sewing machine.

Nora's thoughts shifted again to envision her mom on her knees in the flowerbeds, so stiff that she had to roll over in the grass just to straighten up. Mom had been one of her best friends; her humor mixed with grace and wisdom were unmatched.

And Dad… he had taught her how to drive, how to balance her checkbook, and how to be an honest member of society. He had taught her how to defend herself, how to swim, and how to change the oil in her car. Most importantly, he had showed Nora what it was to be fully loved by a father.

Nora's brown eyes misted as the music paired with her memories, blurring the road. The mirage dancing on the asphalt rippled in the heat of the golden sun. Nora removed her sunglasses and wiped her eyes. Staring ahead, she squinted at a white blob in the distance. As she drove on, she removed her foot from the accelerator and let the truck coast to a slower speed—she saw what appeared to be a dog sitting in the middle of the hot highway.

Jiggling the gear shifter out of place, Nora released the clutch and rode the brakes until the rig lurched to a stop. There was no shoulder to pull onto, so she stopped in her lane and flipped on her hazard lights. She turned the engine off and slowly pushed open the squeaky door.

Getting out, she surveyed the area. She saw no houses, barns, or other cars for what seemed like miles in all directions. All she saw was desert, miles and miles of desert with the backdrop of faraway mountains. Coming around the front of her truck, the engine popping and gurgling, she stopped and stared at the animal in her lane.

It was indeed a dog. His back, tail, ears, and eye patches were black. His muzzle and chest were white. It had to be a border collie, with his one black paw, the other three white. The dog did nothing but sit upright and pant.

Nora held out her hand and cautiously walked towards the animal, talking sweetly and hoping it would understand she wasn't going to hurt it. When she was within sniffing distance of the dog's nose, it licked her hand.

Okay, this is a good sign. Licking hands is a sign that it's friendly.

As Nora stood there in the wind, her green linen skirt waved like a proud flag. The wind felt good, taking the edge off the intense heat of the sun's rays. The dog's long hair blew to and fro like her skirt, as Nora deliberated about what to do next.

"Do you have a collar?" she asked the dog. She walked back to the cab, leaned in, and grabbed her paper coffee cup. Ripping off the top half, she filled the cup with water from her water bottle and brought it back to the mysterious dog. The dog lapped it up greedily as if it hadn't had a drink in days. Nora patted the dog's head and slowly felt down the animal's shaggy-haired neck in search of a collar. She was hoping the dog would have some sort of tag to identify its owner, but her fingers found nothing but fur.

"Well, I can't just stay parked in the middle of the road, and you, my friend, can't just be left out here," Nora said. Walking to the back of the F-250, she let the tailgate fall with a bang. The dog sprang over and jumped up into the bed.

"Looks like you're familiar with the drop of a tailgate!" Nora chuckled. She pushed the gate up, then hoisted herself back into the driver's seat. After straightening her pink tank top, she turned off the hazard lights and eased the five-speed up to 65 mph once again. Checking her mirror, she could tell that the black and white collie seemed plenty happy with its head in the wind, tongue hanging out, soaking up the warm breeze. Nora smiled to herself. A dog in the back of her truck just felt right.

Nora passed the "Welcome to Kingsman" sign on which the population of 23,978 was posted, then slowed her speed to match the law. Her throat was feeling a little parched as she pulled into the first available gas station to refuel. Inside the convenience store, Nora bought a granola bar and a raspberry iced tea for herself, and some chicken strips for the dog.

Even though the town wasn't huge, trying to make a note of where things were was overwhelming for her as she rolled through downtown. Suddenly a realization hit her. She was on her way to an apartment with a dog, and she hadn't notified her landlord about it. Landlords—she had heard—could be very temperamental about pets.

I'll go to the dog pound tomorrow to find out about the dog's owner. There's a good chance that someone is missing their pet. But, on the flip side, it would be neat to own a dog like this. I kind of hope I can keep it.

Nora had never moved from the house she had grown up in until now. This was scary to her—a new environment and new people. The only large piece of furniture she brought with her was an old secretary desk which had been passed from her maternal grandmother to Eleanor, and on to Nora. Well, that and a red velvet wingback chair. Her thinking chair. She couldn't part with her thinking chair.

Dusk trailing behind her, Nora's GPS led her through town in about twenty minutes. Slowing down at the big, black, locked mailbox, she double-checked the name before turning in at the wide gravel driveway. The name on the box read "Deape Woods." The old truck's engine hummed softly as she edged her way slowly up the quarter-mile gravel lane. The narrow road snaked through a pine and fir forest to a clearing with a quaint two-story farmhouse, outbuildings, and a huge, classic red barn.

The gray, cedar-sided, weathered home looked enchanting with its wrap-around deck and black wooden porch swing. Black shutters framed the windows, which displayed faux candles glittering in the dimming light. Placed sporadically around the yard were many potted flowers.

Nora pulled into what looked like the parking area and let the dog out of the back. She watched as the animal ran over to a tree and lifted his leg to relieve himself. As Nora was lost in the revelation of the animal being a male, a petite older woman with light-gray hair came floating off the porch.

"Hello! You must be Nora then?" The older woman stuck out her hand for a handshake. Nora smiled in return.

"Yes, I'm Nora Miller. And you're Stella Deape, I'm assuming?"

"You're assuming right… though assumptions aren't *often* correct." Stella eyeballed the border collie.

"So, the dog…" Nora began. "I found him on the road on my way here and I'm planning on going to the pound tomorrow. I know I didn't ask about pets, and I don't know what your policy is about them, but if he doesn't have an owner, is it possible for me to keep him?" Nora asked, holding her breath.

"Oh, I don't care if he stays, but you'll have to put down a pet deposit, and if he starts getting annoying, I'm not going to be held responsible for his mysterious disappearance," the tiny woman said with a most serious face. "We are more cat people. Although, we do get a lot of wild dogs running through the property. Come, come! Let's get your paperwork out of the way so you can get settled. I'll bet you're thoroughly wiped out." The screen door banged shut behind the ladies as they entered the farmhouse.

Inside the home, Nora's nostrils were met with a sweet smell coming from the oven. Rough wooden floors spanned the kitchen and living room. Hues of old country were prominent about the home. A low-hanging cast-iron-and-wood candelabra hung over the dark, round wooden table. An excessive amount of seating options were available in the living room with random wooden chairs placed here and there. Bookshelves and cabinets with trinkets were aplenty. A big, rounded stone fireplace with softly glowing embers was the room's centerpiece.

In the kitchen area, a large, blue wooden china cabinet held an unfathomable amount of tea cups and saucers. Exploration of the dimly lit, cluttered knick-knack shelves would have to wait, as Nora was far too exhausted to even begin to closely examine her surroundings.

Stella bustled about in the kitchen and pulled a hot tray of peach scones out of the oven. She threw a few scones on a large plate, shuffled over to the table, and set them down. Stella quickly wrung her hands in the towel tucked into her apron and scratched her neck as she said, "Sit and eat a scone, and let me find the contract."

This lady is wound up. I wonder if she's always this tense?

Stella glided over to a desk which was stacked with papers and books and who knew what else. She hummed as she searched for and located the rental documents. She set the papers on the table in front of Nora and her thin, boney fingers crinkled the corners of the pages as she began explaining the policies of the lease.

"Now," Stella began, clearing her throat, "We already went over your payment and when it's due, and we have your deposit check. Do you understand that if you end up keeping the dog and he destroys property, you will be liable for that?"

At that very moment, a cool breeze blew through the pages on the table. Nora glanced around, but didn't see any open doors or windows.

That's strange. What's blowing the pages around?

"Jabon!" Stella screamed, somehow spewing her dentures onto the table, sliming the "sign here" spot on the paper with saliva.

Nora's eyebrows creased and she shifted in her chair.

Don't laugh, don't laugh! Be polite—don't laugh!

Stella quickly reached down, grabbed the false teeth, and slipped them back into her mouth, looking rather embarrassed by the incident.

"Do you remember from when we talked over the phone—the apartment is not inside this house, but around back near the barn in a little building that we also use for storage?" Stella questioned, tapping her sparkly, coffin-shaped nails on the table. Nora nodded yes, her brown bun wiggling at the top of her head. Just then, Nora felt something soft rub up against her leg and looked down to see a beautiful, steel-gray cat with magnificent green eyes purring at her.

"Oh, hello, Rastus," Stella said, reaching down to pick him up, and she began stroking the feline vigorously.

"Who is Jabon?" Nora asked.

"Jabon is Victor's late father," Stella replied. She set the cat on the table, hastily put away the rental paperwork, and then moved toward the door. Nora realized Stella wasn't going to comment any further about Jabon, so she decided to just let it go. Nora didn't believe in spirits or ghosts or any weird stuff.

That stuff just isn't real. Some people think they see things, but that's where it ends. Those people need medication to get their hallucinations under control. Science can explain away any claims of the supposed supernatural.

Walking out of the house, the ladies stopped as a khaki Volkswagen bus coasted to a stop near Nora's truck. A tall, beefy, balding man climbed out of the vehicle. He wore brown corduroy pants, a white tank top, and sandals with socks. Walking up to the ladies, he thrust out his hand and introduced himself without any hint of a smile.

"I'm Victor Woods," he said. "You must be Nora, the new tenant?" His countenance was cold and stiff.

My inkling is that he doesn't care much for people.

Nora introduced herself. His grasp on her hand lingered too long. As she began to loosen her hand, he held it tighter as he talked about showing her the apartment. Finally releasing his solid grip, he led the two ladies to the small outbuilding.

"Now, if you don't like the apartment, you have three days to terminate the agreement," Stella chirped.

"Oh! I forgot about the dog!" Nora said, with worry in her tone as she rapidly scanned the area.

"It looks like the dog is at your front door; he must've known where we're going," Stella pointed into the dusk. Sure enough, the dog was sitting at the door, waiting as if he knew exactly where he and Nora would be living. Following the humans, the dog trotted placidly through the door to explore his new home.

The apartment was on the second story of an outbuilding that matched the house in color. The downstairs was being used to store furniture and large boxes. An old, dark, wood piano was placed against one wall. Behind a door at the top of the stairs was Nora's new living space, already furnished. On a little table near the door was a small basket decorated by a big purple bow. The basket held boxes of crackers, canned fruit, and pickles, along with an apartment key attached to a rough-cut crystal keychain. The kitchen was ready for cooking and even included a coffee maker.

"Well," began Stella, as she opened the fridge and gestured toward the milk, bread, and eggs she had stocked for Nora, "let's go ahead and bring your things in, and then we'll let you get situated. You must be exhausted!"

Stella and Victor helped Nora move her secretary desk, red velvet thinking chair, and her boxes of clothes and other belongings. Then she turned in for the night.

Nora sat on the edge of the bed in her jammies, taking in her new home and adjusting her heart to something new. Clicking the lamp off, she stared at the crack of moonlight sneaking through the edge of the flower-print curtains until her eyelids felt too heavy to hold open and involuntarily closed shut.

Even in a strange bed and in a foreign place, Nora couldn't resist falling into dreams and sleeping soundly until dawn. She didn't know it, but she was going to need her rest, for the evil that would rob her of sleep in the coming weeks was biding its time, tapping its claws and waiting with black patience.

The dog who had been resting on the floor was unable to fully fall asleep. He decided that the thinking chair looked more comfortable. So he crept up on it and slept lightly through the night, hoping the soft chair might lessen his feelings of uneasiness.

- Two -

New Dog, New People, New Job

"Some angels choose fur instead of wings."

~Unknown

THE SUN CAME UP much too soon and Nora's alarm encouraged her to rise and shine. Nora opened her brown eyes and rolled over to see the dog sitting confidently in her red velvet chair.

"Oh no! No!" She admonished the dog. "No dogs in my thinking chair!" She got up out of bed and helped him step down. She had only had the animal for one day, and already it seemed as if he had been with her forever. "Ah, boy. We're going to have to drive into town today and see about finding your owner."

Nora tried not to focus on the strong possibility of losing the animal. She knew full well that if she kept him, and his previous owner ever did show up and take him away, how heartbroken she would be after becoming attached to him.

Nora slipped some black and purple tennis shoes on her slender feet. She slipped her Glock 42 into her weapon pocket tight on her hip and wound her brown hair in a loose knot.

"Hey pups, let's go out for a run and get some fresh air and exercise! What do you think?" The dog cocked his head to one side, ears perked, wagging his tail in agreement.

Nora may not have been a superstitious type of gal, but she did believe in common sense. A single 27-year-old girl was an easy target for a weirdo. Carrying a weapon gave her a sense of security.

I'm glad this dog is with me this morning. He can help me adjust to this new place.

The beautiful land split into all sorts of trails. It reminded Nora a little of home with its stones protruding plentifully and sprigs of green grass nestled around them.

Running down a narrow footpath, Nora remembered a phrase her mother had repeated to her during her childhood. "Home is where your heart is." Even though they had never moved around as a family, Mom had known that Nora was a homebody and would need encouragement to leave home someday.

Home is where my heart is. I just need to move my heart here.

Her memories of her mother were pushed aside as she cooled down to a walk, emerging from the woods behind the chicken house. Within the chicken yard, there seemed to be two or three chickens lying motionless. As she came nearer she realized that they weren't just dead—they were half-eaten. Nora scrunched up her face and went to tell Stella and Victor from the big house about what she saw. She climbed the steps and knocked on the door.

"Hey there," she started, as Victor opened the main door and stared at her from behind the closed screen door. "I was walking by the chicken yard, and it seems a few of the chickens were attacked and partly eaten."

"Yep," Victor cocked his head to one side and said, "I already know about that; I just haven't cleaned it up yet. Anything else?" Nora shook her head no and stepped back as he closed the door.

That man is strange, I think I don't like him.

◆ ◆ ◆

Nora and the dog drove into town as the sun rays gained strength. She parked in front of the city pound, a feeling of dread creeping into her heart. She really wanted to keep her new friend.

The clerk at the counter was a plump man with out-of-date, large, gold-framed glasses sitting at the end of his round red nose. His head remained stationary; only his eyes moved to peer over his glasses at Nora as she came quietly up to the blue counter. His name tag read BURT.

"Can I help you?" he asked.

Nora twisted her key ring, stammering and sputtering as she tried to explain the dog's situation. Finally, she said that she wanted to keep the dog if no owner was found.

"I see," Burt grunted. He then picked up his 32-ounce cola, shook the ice around in the nearly empty cup, rounded his lips over the straw, and slurped the last of the drink. He banged the empty paper cup on the counter and asked her to bring the dog around so that he could check him for a microchip. Waving the detection wand over the unclaimed animal, Burt found no chip. He then checked his computer for reports of a lost dog that fit the border collie's description. No report was found. Shuffling his feet, he rolled his chair over to a metal filing cabinet. Leaning over, he pulled out some papers and set them down in front of Nora. He patted his front shirt pocket and pulled out a pen, clicking the top several times as he explained the paperwork to her. She picked up the pen and began writing while the man picked up the cup and shook the ice around in it again. He told her that if a report came in that matched her dog, he would call her.

"If you don't hear from us in the next week, chances are nobody will report this dog," the stubby man said. He picked up a donut, took a huge bite, licked his fingers then signed off on the paperwork. Burt then plunked down a small metal tag with a license number on it.

"The dog needs a rabies shot, and I can do that quick." Burt went back to a storage room and brought back the rabies shot and injected it into the dog. Nora paid the man for the license and vaccine, picked up the tag, grabbed her paperwork, thanked the man, and felt grateful to finally be leaving.

On the way back to her truck, Nora grinned like a schoolgirl, excited to be a dog owner—even though she knew there was still a possibility of a previous master looking for him. In the meantime, the dog needed a name. He seemed like a gentleman of a dog, so she decided "Mr. Cooper" was fitting.

The dog also needed food and basic supplies. On her way to the pet store, Nora's stomach grumbled with hunger. As she completed her purchase, she asked the cashier about places to eat in town. She followed her recommendation and soon opened the door to a quaint little tea café called Tea and Me. Stepping up to the counter, she ordered a sandwich and a pastry to go. Nora loved baked treats. There was just something about homemade goods that made her all warm inside. The older lady behind the cash register smiled, revealing deep creases in her skin from years of repetitive motion.

"Are you new in town, or are you just visiting, hon?"

"I just moved here. I'm starting a new job at Sailing Media on Monday," Nora told her.

"Oh! My granddaughter Jessa works there. I think she has been really pleased with that company. Oh, by the way, my name's Joanna Shepherd." She reached out to shake Nora's small, pale hand. "I'm actually the owner of this teashop, so I'll throw in a few extra pastries for you to take home as a 'Welcome to Kingsman' gift!"

"Oh, thank you! I'm sure I'll be back in again soon, and I look forward to meeting your granddaughter," Nora replied with a smile.

Nora felt warm from Joanna's kindness and thanked the lovely gray-haired lady again as she stepped aside to wait for her food.

With her order in hand, Nora left the café. She and Mr. Cooper drove around town to get more familiar with the city and find out where her new job was located.

Mr. Cooper had been upgraded to sitting in the cab with her. Lucky dog. The animal's intense light-blue eyes didn't seem to miss anything. He appeared content and pleased with his front seat view.

A wave of lonesomeness swept over her from out of nowhere, a feeling of sadness that she had no one to talk to or share her life with.

I hope I can connect with people at work and find friends quickly. I'm a bit nervous about my new job starting and about figuring out this new life... I hope some of the people I meet are open to new relationships.

Among all the overwhelming aspects of moving to a new location, she also had her father to think about and take care of. It was painful to visit him. It hurt to feel like an imposter had stolen her dad's body. In a sense, her father had already died. There was always hope that he might be lucid while she was there with him, but the further the disease progressed, the more that hope diminished. While she could touch him—if he let her—she couldn't tap into his heart or have an intelligent conversation.

Before Nora realized it, she had driven all the way back to her new apartment in Deape Woods. Nora drove carefully into the wide parking area and discovered that several other vehicles were parked in and along the drive.

Stella, watching Nora from her front porch, walked briskly toward her truck. Stella's long, silver hair swished behind her as she approached the rig.

"Hey Nora, we're having a get-together with some friends tonight; we'll try and keep the noise down, but sometimes people drink way too much and get rowdy. We host a lot of parties, so when there are a bunch of people here, you'll know what's going on, okay?" Stella didn't wait for Nora to reply before she pivoted on her heel and scurried back to her company, her black cotton skirt billowing behind her like chimney smoke in the wind.

Nora opened her front door and called Mr. Cooper to follow her up the wooden stairs. After putting the groceries away, Nora made a pot of coffee and sifted through the coffee mugs in the cabinet.

"Let's see, we have Snow White, Wiccan Haven, Hard Rock Café Orlando… Let's go with Snow White!"

What is this Wiccan mug about? Maybe it's a Star Wars thing…

The party didn't disturb Nora that evening, but around 3:00 AM another disturbance arose. What sounded like a large pack of coyotes or wolves were howling and carrying on for what seemed like forever. The noise of it all was unsettling. Mr. Cooper nervously paced by her bedroom door, but Nora wasn't about to let him out.

Who knows what the dogs would do to you? Please don't pee on the floor.

Eventually, the animals outside settled down and quit their powwow, and Nora fell into a dreamless sleep.

◆ ◆ ◆

Nora spent the following day organizing, setting some goals for the coming months, journaling, and relaxing to settle her nerves. It was a cathartic way to prepare for her first day at a new job. Mr. Cooper watched her with one eye open and one eye closed as Nora shared her ideas out loud with the animal that she already considered her best friend.

Monday morning broke with dark-gray clouds low on the horizon, the belly of the sky grumbling a soft thunder every now and then. The clouds threatened rain. Nora sipped her creamer-sweetened coffee from the Wiccan Haven mug and decided against a jog. She was already cutting it close if she wanted to get to work early on her first day.

Nora remembered she now had a dog to care for.

Criminy—why didn't I think of this before now? What am I going to do with the dog while I'm at work?

Nora heaved a groan of frustration and decided to put the dog in the truck and figure it out once she got to work.

The old blue rig's tire hopped the curb as it pulled into Sailing Media. Nora found a shady spot and parked. Springing out of the truck, she straightened her blue dress, brushed back her brown, feathered bangs, pinned them into place, and checked her pink lipstick in the side mirror. She took a deep breath to settle her first-day jitters.

"You wait here a bit, Cooper. I'm going to find out where to get you settled for the day," she told the mutt, walking confidently toward the building. Until she tripped on a lip of cement. She caught herself before hitting the ground, and glanced around sheepishly.

"Oh, nice," she mumbled to herself. "Hope no one saw that." Blushing, she walked through the door and stopped at the secretary's desk.

A middle-aged woman with short, curly red hair, wearing a light-green jacket with wooden beads on it was seated at the cherry wood desk. She smiled as she said, "Good morning. How can I help you?" The woman had a large gap in between her two front teeth, which protruded slightly. Clearing her throat, Nora began, "I'm Nora Miller; I'm a new software developer here—today is my first day. I was told to ask for Randy?" Nora tapped her pale slender fingers on her brown leather bag nervously.

"Oh, yes. I was expecting you," the woman's voice chortled. She pulled out a manila file folder and then thrust her hand out to Nora for shaking. "My name is Patty. Welcome to Sailing Media!"

As Patty spoke, she whistled the letter "S" in "sailing." Nora decided she liked the full-figured lady already.

Picking up the receiver, her fingers flew over the numbers and her voice slowed a bit as she called over the intercom, "Randy, come to the front desk, please." While they were waiting for Randy to show, Patty casually mentioned, "You gotta watch that stone out front—it gets me every time I'm not looking for it!" Patty bobbed her red head as she cautioned the younger woman about the sneaky pavement. Nora turned red and nodded in agreement.

I wonder how many other people saw my grand entrance.

Randy appeared, introduced himself, and took Nora on a short tour of the office building. They ended up in her new workspace. Nora set her bag down on her new desk, then hesitantly brought up the dog sitting in her truck. She gave him the nutshell version and explained how he came to be with her. Randy nodded his balding head casually as she spoke.

"Well," Randy began, rubbing his unshaved chin, "If the dog is on a leash, I suppose he can sit at your desk with you. But if he starts causing problems, he will no longer be welcome here." Randy continued, "You will also need to sign a waiver for the dog, as the company cannot be liable for him."

"Oh, thank you so much!" Nora said. "Really, I can't thank you enough!"

After retrieving Mr. Cooper from the truck, Nora introduced herself to several new people, but of course, they were all a bit of an indistinctive blur (as is often the case when meeting a large group of folks at once).

I hate walking up to people I don't know and talking to them. It feels so unnatural for me... But I know I have to do it in order to make some friends.

She had been hired as a software developer and manager, and would be writing code for all sorts of projects. Nora was a computer nerd and an excellent programmer. She had never gone to college; instead, her skills had emerged from a passion to explore the computer world. Her talent and dexterity were what snagged this job, not a piece of paper from an institution. Her new boss had told Nora he often preferred to hire based on experience rather than education because those without degrees had to rely solely on their character and mastery. He felt that those who applied for these jobs right out of college tended to have a sense of entitlement and depended on their institutional affiliation to land them high-paying jobs. In Randy's line of work, however, the raw-born talent was more valuable than the institutionalized student.

Driving home from her first day at Sailing Media, Nora flipped through her mental directory of who she had met. Jessa Ritz was on her team; she was a younger gal close to Nora's age. Jessa was unnaturally blond, owned big, beautiful blue eyes and had a vintage flare to her. She was bubbly, and if a color were used to describe her, it would be pink. All different shades of pink. She wasn't a typical software developer. She talked a lot and was vivid and perky.

I bet that Jessa is the granddaughter of Joanna from Tea and Me. She sure seems nice; I hope we can connect.

From what Nora had derived, Jessa was dating a guy named Nolan Gao who worked in another department at Sailing Media.

Nora's reflection on her new acquaintances stalled when she pulled into Deape Woods. Nora drove slowly past a second Volkswagen bus parked in front of the house, this one black in color. Hopping out of her truck, she glanced over and saw Victor talking to another man in the driveway. Stella came running out of the house and waved Nora over. Nora didn't really feel up to socializing because she was tired and hungry; however, Nora relented and slowly strode over to Stella.

"Hey, I want you to meet Victor's brother, John. He's single, and you're single." Stella winked at Nora with a sly grin. Before Nora could say a word, Stella grabbed her and yanked her over to where the two men were standing, interrupting them to introduce her.

John was as tall and as beefy as his brother; however, he had more hair on the top of his head and was a few degrees warmer than Victor in personality. Nora couldn't have been less interested in the man.

Oh brother. I can't wait till I'm not single anymore and people don't just see me as someone that needs to be matched up.

"Nice to meet you," stammered Nora, feeling a little awkward. She looked around for a commonplace topic. "So, I see both of you drive Volkswagen buses?" she asked hoping her face wouldn't disclose her lack of actual interest.

"Oh, yeah. John is a Volkswagen mechanic, and so it ended up we both drive what he can fix," Victor explained.

"That's handy," Nora replied.

After enduring a little more small talk, Nora said, "Well, if you guys will excuse me, I think I'm going to retire early tonight; it has been a really long day." With that, she headed for the apartment. Mr. Cooper followed closely at her heels.

All three pairs of dark eyes silently followed her to the paint-chipped door of her building. Their gaze lingered long after she had closed and locked it behind her. Mr. Cooper paused halfway up the stairs and turned his black and white head around to look back at the door, and then resumed his trek to their room. Mr. Cooper sensed something. In his uneasiness, he wasn't quite sure what to look for, but this sense of foreboding carried the truth that this thing was adept in wicked conduct and would most certainly come in a fuddled mess of uninvited mystery.

- Three -

THE POND

"God did not create evil. Just as darkness is the absence of light, evil is the absence of God."

~Albert Einstein

THE WORK WEEK came and went quickly. Nora felt like she had secured a good start in her job. She was slowly procuring relationships with some of her coworkers—Jessa and Nolan had offered to line up a blind date for Nora, and they had plans to go on a double date on Sunday. Nora hadn't been thrilled about a blind date. In fact, she had never been on a date. Being the recluse that she was, she really didn't meet a lot of potential husbands.

Saturday morning arrived, bringing partial sun and the need for a jog. Nora chose her raspberry tennis shoes and whistled for Mr. Cooper. Plugging in her earphones to listen to her running tunes, she led her canine down a different trail this morning. It ended with a few more hills than the other trail she had been using during the past week. This one took them to a pond which

Nora judged might have been a half-mile around. The two of them stopped to stretch. Well, Nora stretched. Cooper just panted, lapped from the dirty water, and splashed around a bit, cooling his legs.

I wish I could just drink water from anywhere like a dog and not get sick. That sure would be handy.

The breeze picked up, and Nora breathed in deeply, taking in the warm mountain air. Opening her brown eyes, she became acutely aware of something moving through the thick green trees directly across the pond. It appeared to be a tall, black-robed figure with a pointy hood. Something like what the mythological Grim Reaper might wear. Nora popped out her earbuds, froze, and squinted harder, her eyes not leaving the strange, eerie form. Nora forgot about her tight calves, and her heart started beating a little faster. She didn't believe in fairytale nonsense outside of books and movies; they had their place to play in culture, but magical stuff was not of reality. She assumed it was a person, albeit a strange person. A person or no person, this was a little unnerving.

The dark frame moved slowly and smoothly, stopping not ten feet from the pond's edge, facing Nora. Mr. Cooper growled low, but he did not go after whatever it was.

Nora patted her hip for her gun.

I must have forgotten it back at the house! Of course, when I might need it, I don't have it. Of course.

She couldn't see skin under the dark hood, but it looked as if its eyes were giving off light. Nora strained to see better.

Are those eyes glowing? Or is this something I'm making up in my head?

Its hands extended from its long, bell-sleeved robe. The skin of the figure looked as if it had never seen the sun in the entirety of its existence. It was so pale and white, possibly albino. The figure held its palms flat and outward. The breeze picked up again, but this time on the veins of the wind came the sound of many whispering voices. Nora couldn't understand a word. The voices sounded like a different language and swirled around her as if she were in an amphitheater. She was more than a little nervous about what she saw, especially as the figure looked like it was floating.

Oh wait, my phone! I'll take a picture!

Without taking her eyes off the mysterious being, Nora took her phone out of her arm pocket. Her hands shaking, she unlocked her phone and opened the video app. Double-checking she was recording, she stood there for another ten seconds. With the sound of the voices growing louder and the wind getting stronger, the black robe form lifted its hands to the sky and from it a high-volume scream came forth. Nora winced from the loud noise and then felt a heavy pressure on her shoulders. Looking from side to side, she saw nothing and no one around her. She felt as if something ugly were weighing her down, and yet her heart was beating as if she were sprinting.

Then, as if someone pushed fast forward on a movie scene, the dark figure moved forward at an inhuman rate of speed, briefly levitated on top the muddy water and plummeted into the pond, and then disappeared under the murky, brown surface. Three seconds later, in the same ripple where the figure had melted into the water, what looked like the body of a huge, olive-green snake emerged once, exposing its back, and disappearing again under the murky water.

Mr. Cooper slowly backed away from the pond, his paws squishing in the softer mud. His hairline rose along the steep of his back as he barked warning. The dog was obviously worried as he put distance between himself and the murky water.

Nora felt the weight dissipate from her shoulders. She took a few steps back, tripping on a rotten log and landing on her rear.

Hustling back to her feet, she snatched up her phone and began questioning herself about what she had just seen and heard. But Nora wasn't going to stand around waiting for it to show up again.

Nora hastened to find the trail, called the dog, and started what wouldn't be classified as a slow jog. They were full-speed running. While her legs were moving as fast as they could go, her mind was processing what she just saw.

That thing couldn't have been a person; it floated off the ground and vanished in the water! Humans don't… no, humans can't do that. Maybe it was some sick joke someone rigged up… But the weight I felt and the huge snake in the water? How could those be tricks?

Nora needed a break in her jogging to catch her breath. She thought she was close to being back home, but this was the first time she had taken this trail. Maybe it would be her last if whatever that thing was caught up with her.

Nora stopped in a clump of trees and dared herself to turn around and look behind her. Out of breath, with her heartbeat pounding in her ears, plus the dog's panting, it was hard to make out any other sound within the woods. After standing there for about fifteen seconds, Mr. Cooper let out a low growl and started backing up again.

Nora was done with break time. She turned and ran all the way back home.

Slowing to a walk, sweat pouring down the sides of her face, Nora walked past the big house. Stella and Victor were sitting on their front porch drinking beers.

Ten in the morning is too early to be drinking, but whatever floats their boats. Their drinking in the morning is the least of my worries.

"Morning!" Stella hollered. "Want a beer? Come sit and talk to us a minute." Stella waved her over. Nora, still on edge, couldn't help but tell the couple about what she saw in the woods. Nora sat down and dug in her pocket for her phone, all the while describing what she saw. Victor looked amused, and Stella acted surprised.

"I think you just saw a figment of your imagination, young lady," chided Victor.

"No, no, I took a video of this thing; here look at this," Nora said, as she held out her phone for all three of them to see.

The three of them heard the dog growl, they heard Nora gasp, and they all saw a splash in the pond, but there was no creepy, black, floating figure in her video. No snake coil or screeching sound had been recorded.

I can't believe the thing didn't show up in my film! Wow. I look like a real idiot.

Stella reached out with her pale, bony hand and gaudily-ringed fingers and patted Nora on the back. "Oh honey, we all see things in these woods. Don't feel too crazy!" Victor and Stella started chuckling. Nora dropped the subject. It was plain they didn't believe her, and she couldn't prove what she saw.

After taking a hot shower, Nora still felt shaken up. She knew what she had witnessed had been real. She had seen that grim reaper. Why it wasn't in the video didn't make sense scientifically. She just hoped that whatever it was, it was gone and stayed gone.

◆ ◆ ◆

Sunday ushered in hope. While Nora couldn't forget about the grim reaper in the woods the day before, she did her best to focus on the day ahead and quit worrying about it. She put on a little extra makeup and did her hair in a loose bun at the base of her neck. She wore her mom's black pearl studs and a burnt orange sundress with shiny black patent leather short boots. She topped off her look with a vintage orange matte lipstick and called Mr. Cooper. He could sit in the cab with the windows rolled down. The weather today wasn't lava hot as it had been in the past days.

Nora felt jazzed to hang out with some new friends, even if it would be a blind date. Hiding behind the open truck door in the parking lot of mini golf venue, she reached down and adjusted her weapon on her thigh holster. Jessa and Nolan had made plans to play a game of mini golf, then go out to dinner. Nora wasn't a huge fan of golf, but if it meant making friends and letting her brain loose, then she welcomed the idea.

Nora walked through the mini golf entrance and waited near the cashier. She heard someone call her name and turned to see Jessa standing with two young men near a drinking fountain further in the building. Nora sauntered over to meet them. "I want you to meet Trey Silver. And Trey, meet Nora Miller!" Jessa introduced the two and backed away to let them get acquainted. Nora reached out and shook Trey's hand, and meeting his gaze, said hello.

Trey smiled a near-perfect-teeth smile and said, "Nice to meet you. Jessa was telling me you just moved here from Colorado?"

"Yes, I was born and raised in Colorado. This move is a huge deal for me!" Nora bit her orange lip lightly as she began a conversation about the difference between Oregon and Colorado with the poised and collected young man. Trey had a head of dark hair that had a natural wave to it, hazel-green eyes with thick, dark lashes, and freckled skin.

He is handsome.

She immediately felt comfortable with Trey, and that didn't happen very often with guys or girls.

Maybe it's a sign! Nah, I don't believe in that stuff. Horoscopes, lucky stars and lucky charms. All foolishness.

The two couples took their time mini-golfing, Nolan and Jessa cutting jokes and laughing their heads off. Nora and Trey were grinning and were generally amused by it all. It felt good to laugh and not think about life's problems, even if it only lasted for a little while.

"How long have you lived in Kingsman?" Nora questioned Trey.

"My folks moved here the year I started college. After I graduated there was a job opening at Sailing Media and so I followed them here about four years ago. I'm a manager on the second floor. I graduated with a degree in computer science, and I manage a team of about fifteen programmers. We are an unusual department and we do a lot of classified projects for the U.S. government," explained Trey.

"Oh, so you're also a genius!" Nora muttered.

"What do you mean, by also?" Nora blushed. She hadn't meant to say that aloud.

"Umm, ahh…" she stammered.

"I won! I won! And the winner gets a free dinner!" Jessa interrupted obnoxiously. Nora was grateful for Jessa's outburst.

"Well, Jessa; we're on a date, so I was already going to buy your dinner!" Nolan said pursing his lips and cocking his head sideways.

"Oh," Jessa, pretended to pout. "Well, how about dessert then?" Nolan grinned and played along with her, "Okay, dessert then. Because that wasn't a part of our date, that will suffice for your prize."

Jessa bounced her way over to return the golf clubs, and the four young adults drove to an Italian restaurant, continuing their evening.

During dinner Jessa exercised self-control in not dominating the conversation with everything she thought of. Picking up a cloth napkin, she rung and twisted it to keep herself busy. Jessa, being an extrovert, loved to be the center of attention. Thankfully, her folks helped her learn when she was young that she needed to shut her mouth occasionally to allow other people time to talk. Jessa and Nora weren't complete opposites, but Nora was the calmer of the two, and Trey seemed more chill than Nolan.

The subject of the supernatural was introduced when Nora brought up her experience with the grim reaper the day before. "Okay, I want to tell you guys about what happened to me yesterday, and I don't want you to think I'm nutso when I do," Nora said. The three new friends listened quietly as Nora nervously described her unsolved case. When she was done, each of them took a turn sharing their opinion on the matter.

Jessa was the first to share, and with her blond-haired head leaning sideways and hands under her fair-skinned chin, she began, "I don't really know what I think about ghosts and stuff, but as far as the supernatural, I, like, think God exists. I think He is a loving Being who wants us all to just be happy and feel good, you know? I mean, why would He want us to be miserable and demand we all follow the same rules and staunch regulations? Nah, I think He's a party Guy!" Jessa giggled a little too quickly.

Jessa had been raised in the Baptist church. Her parents still went to church, and she went too sometimes. However, no one would have guessed that Jessa was a Christ-follower. She didn't appear much different than any other Jessa out there. The way Jessa saw it, God was basically there when she needed Him—like a God on a shelf. She just took Him down if she needed Him for something.

Nolan shifted in his chair and explained that, as a kid, he had occasionally attended the local Chinese Community Church with his parents. As an adult, he didn't have much use for organized religion. He believed in karma and the idea that if you're a bad person, the bad you do will come back around to you. He tried to be a decent human, and that was enough for him. He didn't like to think too deeply about spiritual things; it gave him a headache.

Trey, hazel eyes sparkling, explained that he was neither hot nor cold when it came to belief in the supernatural. He wasn't closed to the idea of different dimensions being real, but in all honesty, he had just never been in a predicament where he had to face any paranormal situations and so never bothered to explore it. "I can't say for sure if ghosts are real or if they are just our imagination playing games with us. It seems to me, many people claim to have these interactions with what they deem as dead people, spirits, and whatnot. But really, for me, if it isn't hurting me, I don't want to waste energy on understanding it. I have enough in my life to manage without inviting things that don't pertain to me."

Nora was the last to give her stance. "I don't believe in paranormal mumbo jumbo. I don't believe in what I can't see. I believe in science and hard evidence. What I saw yesterday has me a little concerned about myself. Maybe it was just my imagination. Maybe I'm under more stress than I realize." Nora did her best to talk herself and her friends into believing that the grim reaper in the woods had just been a figment of her imagination—at most, a sign of the imminent death of her father at the door.

The evening wrapped up with jokes about spooky things and a resounding desire from everyone to do this all again real soon.

Trey walked Nora out to the parking lot. As they reached her F-250, Trey said, "I had a fun time tonight. Can I take you out again sometime?"

"I think I would like that." Nora smiled sweetly and replied, "I should tell you, I've never dated or had a boyfriend before. Not even in grade school."

"Well, I guess that makes two of us," he said to her. "Who's this?" he said, reaching to pet Mr. Cooper. Nora told Trey the dog's story as Mr. Cooper sat enjoying plentiful scratches behind the ears.

"I have a dog named Joey, although Joey is a female with a boy's name. Maybe you two pups will have to go on a hiking date sometime!"

The two made small talk for another few minutes and then called it a night. The sky was dark now. Nora felt like the double date had scratched an itch. As she drove home, she reflected:

I don't feel like I'm the type of person that needs a lot of relationships to feel satisfied. But, I feel like maybe I don't recognize very well when I've gone too long without mingling with others my age. I think I've been depriving myself of people. I need to get better at not going so long without having some fun. It really felt good to laugh and talk tonight.

- Four -

THE PIANO PLAYER

"A man that flies from his fear may find that he has only taken a shortcut to meet it."

~J. R. R. Tolkien

IT WAS FRIDAY again. Nora loved Fridays. Friday meant the last day of work and hope for the weekend. Nora had been jogging in the mornings but hadn't taken the Trail of the Grim Reaper again, not yet. Every time she thought of the troubling event, she told herself it was just stress, but she couldn't convince her psyche to try that particular trail again.

Jessa invited Nora to go see a chick flick. The two young ladies enjoyed some bonding at the small-town movie theater over buttered popcorn and gummy candies which were Nora's favorite sweet.

The two new girlfriends enjoyed casual conversation as they walked to a local burger joint for a bite to eat after the movie.

"So, what do you think of Trey?" Jessa bubbled out with a big smirk.

"I like him. He seems like a nice guy, and he asked me to dinner on Sunday." Nora breathed deep and smiled. She swept the bangs out of her face and continued with her clear glossy lips. "I've never dated anyone, and I'm twenty-seven! This dating stuff is new territory for me, and I'm a little nervous about it."

Jessa's mouth hung open and she pushed her wad of gum to the other side of her cheeks while staying focused on Nora. "Wow! You *are* a newbie! Good for you! I can help you with anything you need to know!"

"Thanks, Jessa." Nora smiled at her friend. "So, how long have you been dating Nolan?"

"Um… let's see here… I think it's almost been a year now. Which, my relationships don't ever make it past a year. God only knows why." Jessa looked a little doleful after making the statement. "But," her eyes brightened, "I think Nolan could be the one. We get along like tea and crumpets!"

"Speaking of tea and crumpets, I've been getting a few lunches at your grandma's teashop lately," Nora told her charming blond friend.

"Oh yeah, grandma Joanna is fabulous! So is her café. I used to spend a lot of time working there when I was in high school. She used to have these weeks where she would get sick, and the doctors couldn't figure it out. She claims she had to pray hard and that cured her illness. I just dunno. She's always yapping to me about Jesus this, Holy Ghost that, and I'm just like, 'Oh my God, Grandma, take a chill pill!' And then she gets mad at me for 'using the Lord's name in vain'… She's, like, really into this spiritual stuff. I'm just like, 'Whatever Grandma. Whatever frosts your cake.' I believe in God, but I'm just not ready to go crazy over Him like she does. Anyways, I still work at the café a few times a week, and I've always enjoyed it."

Nora was thinking of making tally marks for every time Jessa used the word "like," but she didn't have a convenient way to track it.

Maybe next time. Is that mean or innocent amusement?

The evening with Jessa now over, Nora found herself walking in the front door of her apartment building. Nora stopped briefly, laying her eyes on the old, scratched piano sitting next to the wall. Its rich, dark, cherry stain looked dulled from years of wear and tear. The small, faded white lettering spelled the patented word "Chickering" on its breast. Nora lifted the narrow lid on the top and found the protected veneer shiny. A chalk date was scribbled by the piano's pins and strings. It read 1893. She ran her fingers over the old-fashioned detail and pushed down a couple of the ivory keys.

Nora's mother had played the piano. The violin was Nora's instrument. When Nora was a little girl, her mother would play songs for her to sing along to. At other times she would play aimlessly, and the sound was always relaxing to all who heard.

"I miss you, Mom," she whispered in a soft voice and closed the key cover.

Nora fussed about in her tiny living space and eventually fell sound asleep in her bed. A sleepy Nora woke to the faint sound of the piano's out-of-tune noise slowly plunking out what she made out to be the lullaby, "Twinkle, Twinkle, Little Star." She awoke in the dark room and lay in bed trying to decipher whether she was dreaming or if the music coming from the stairwell was indeed reality. Nora was awake long enough to make the judgment that someone was playing the old piano. Now the question was, *who?*

Nora turned on the lamp on her nightstand. Sitting on her bed with her feet on the floor, she creased her brows and her heartbeat quickened. The music slowed. She grabbed her handgun, put on her bathrobe, and wondered if it was a bad idea to go down the stairs.

I don't believe in spooks, I don't believe in spooks, I don't believe in spooks!

She *had* to find out who was playing this piece of music, as this wasn't just a cat roaming the keys. Plus, she remembered putting the flap back down over the keys when she stopped to touch the instrument a few hours ago. She checked the time. It was just after three in the morning.

Nora opened the door and gingerly flipped the light switch at the top of the staircase. Her knees and her voice both shaky with fear, Nora yelled, "Who's down there?" The music slowed even more, then banged randomly, which made it sound like some horror movie. Then the music stopped in an abrupt manner.

This can't be happening. Someone is trying to play me for a fool.

She inched her way down the stairwell slowly, her gun pointed out in front of her, and she looked through the rough wooden railing to see the piano.

No one there; how is this possible?

There were brown boxes stacked all around and random pieces of old furniture in the storage room. Nora's heart was beating so loud she could hear it pounding in her ears.

What is going on here?

She decided against looking for the perpetrator herself. Instead she backed up the stairs and called Mr. Cooper.

If there is someone down there, the dog won't be afraid to find them.

"Go get 'em!" she told the animal. "Sic 'em!" she commanded him again, pointing at the doorway. Mr. Cooper wouldn't budge. There he sat on the chair, looking intently at Nora and panting unusually fast and loud.

Usually he's ready to be let out, but the one time I need him to go and be a scout for me, he decides he doesn't want to go.

"Some guard dog you are!" she mumbled to him.

What should I do? I could call Stella and Victor. It's late, but it seems as if they never sleep anyway.

She dialed the big house. Stella picked up the phone as if it was the middle of the day. "Hello?"

"Um, hi, Stella? I'm sorry to call so late, but I heard the piano playing downstairs. I can't see anyone down there, but I'm scared to go and look myself. Can Victor come and search it for me?" Nora blurted in her shaky voice.

"He's sleeping. I'll come over and look for you," Stella responded with a noticeable sigh, and she hung up the phone.

It seemed time took longer than normal before Nora's phone finally rang. "I didn't find anyone in your apartment, Nora. I think you must be hearing things. A bad dream maybe?"

Nora thanked Stella, apologizing for calling so late. She made a cup of decaf tea, then pulled her laptop onto her bed, watching her favorite old movie to take her mind off the eerie piano. Eventually she drifted back to an uneasy, light sleep.

Meanwhile, back at the big house, Stella pushed open the door to Victor's bedroom. The couple did not share a bedroom and were not married, at least not in a religious sense. Their relationship stretched far into the past with a deep connection. They were partners for sure and acted like a married couple living with each other. Husband and wife, though, not officially married. Marriage was a religious thing, a Christian-type thing, and they wanted no part of anything religious.

Stella strode across the scuffed wood floor. She halted in front of an old-fashioned, matte black coffin raised up on a wooden platform. Above the lidless coffin on the wall hung a huge painting that depicted a war of angelic beings. A soft spotlight pointed upwards onto the painting; Victor loved to lay and meditate upon the artwork. Inside the satin-lined box lay Victor. Standing quietly, clutching her bony hands, she broke the dim silence and began talking as if the man were awake.

"I think Jabon is starting to stake his claim on Nora. She just complained about the piano playing downstairs in the storage building, and I know it wasn't a cat on the keys."

Victor's dark eyes fluttered and opened mechanically. He moved no other muscles. Then he closed them again. "Was it you, Victor? Were you in there tickling the ivories from the comfort of your coffin? You have probably been astral projecting yourself into Nora's apartment, you sick bastard." Stella said with a twinge of nasty sarcasm in her voice. She heaved a chest full of air and realized he was in no talking mood. Stopping for just a moment to trim a candle wick, she walked noisily on purpose back out of the room.

Stella sat down at the big kitchen table and stared into the darkened window, her reflection peering back at her. A tiny, tarnished silver spoon clinked around in her blue flowered tea cup. Stella thought about many things, but mostly, she thought about the weekend ahead. They were planning to host a large party for their people. Stella and Victor normally were the hosts. It was best not to move their meetings around too much. Plus Deape Woods was the perfect location—exclusive, secluded, and safe.

Maybe she could get Nora to visit a bit tomorrow and probe her to see if she would be a good fit for joining their party. Then again, maybe it was still a bit too early.

Stella swallowed the last of the enchanted tea, sitting in the still of the room, and allowed the tea to slowly bring her to a state of tranquility.

Tomorrow. Yes. Stella would invite her in tomorrow. Her dark, sparkly blue fingernails tapped on the table in curious rhythm with her sinister thoughts.

◆ ◆ ◆

Nora awoke early to a sky of orange autumn brilliance. Rays of warmth filtered through the maple, pine, and fir trees like highlights in hair. The trees were well on their way to putting themselves into winter hibernation, full of vivid red, green, and yellow hues which edged their way onto the leaves like paint on a canvas.

It's kind of amazing that the natural part of our world knows how to put itself to sleep for the winter. All by itself, it falls asleep and awakens again, as if it was created on purpose, knowing what to do. I don't know how it could have been created on purpose, but it seems like it would make more sense if it had been.

After having seen the strange being in the woods, Nora still couldn't quite shake the feeling that someone menacing was out there amongst the trees, watching. Nora finished her morning jog with a soft, warm breeze chasing her home. While stretching outside the big house and taking some time to pet Rastus, Stella approached her with a slower-than-normal stride, hands behind her back.

Stella, appearing relaxed, had her long gray hair brushed down and pulled to one side of her face. "Morning," she said to Nora with a pleasant smile. "I'm about to whip up some brunch.

Care to join me? Victor is working with his brother this morning, so he isn't around to annoy us."

Stella stood still and then bent to pick up the cat, stroking his steel-gray short fur. Rastus was stating his agreement by purring heavily.

"Sure, but do you mind if I shower really quick, then come over? I'm visiting my father in Astor this afternoon, so I won't be able to stay too long," Nora replied pleasantly.

"That's no problem. I'll get started on the grub!" said Stella.

◆ ◆ ◆

Nora zipped up her favorite, floral-print blue sundress and fluffed her vintage lace scarf.

I wonder how many more times this year I'll get to wear this.

She tucked her Denver Broncos cap into her bag to wear when she visited her father. He loved football. For some reason, he still remembered past games and the team he loved most of all. When she visited, she always wore the cap. They would talk about football for hours. He might not recognize her, but he did remember the Broncos logo. The fact that he seemed to remember something so trivial—but not her—caused a familiar ache.

Football… At least we have something to talk about.

She tried not to think too deeply into it.

She and Mr. Cooper walked over to the farmhouse. The dog sat himself down on the porch as if he knew he would not be invited into the house. Nora knocked lightly on the white screen door. Stella called for her to come inside.

"Make yourself at home. I'm almost finished here in the kitchen," Stella called, as tribal drum music and the smell of blueberry scones floated through the room.

Nora sauntered into the large living room, adjusting to the busy decor. This was only the second time Nora had been inside the lovely farmhouse. Now, in the daylight, she could take in a little more of what these two odd people considered home. A large crystal rock that had been turned into a lamp lit up a dark corner containing stacks of old books. Sitting down in a big rocking chair, she noticed a basket of knitting items and an old rag doll with needles stuck in its head and neck.

Nora picked up the figure and looked it over. She pursed her lips and her brows creased.

Wow, this doll is just a tad creepy.

On the back of the doll the initials J. S. were sewn in red thread. Nora carried the doll into the kitchen where Stella was setting some freshly baked scones neatly on a platter next to a pot of tea.

"What is this?" Nora questioned Stella, as they sat down at the table.

"Oh! That's just an old doll that was my mother's. I use her as a pincushion, so she's useful."

"Huh," Nora grunted. "I would have guessed it as some sort of voodoo doll."

Stella lit up. "Are you into voodoo?" she asked Nora.

"Nope, I don't believe in that hogwash. But, I've seen those silly dolls in novelty shops and movies." Nora replied.

"Why do you think it's hogwash?" Stella questioned with a quick and certain tone.

"I believe in what I can see and touch. I don't think curses, spirits, and things like that exist. I think people who believe in the paranormal are just seeing things from their own imaginations," Nora stated.

"So, the thing you saw in the woods, the piano playing in the middle of the night, those were just your imagination?" Stella asked slowly.

Nora bit her lip and rolled it around before answering. "I guess it was. I can't make any sense out of it, and I can't prove to anyone that it happened. I suppose it must be in my head."

"You don't believe there is a spirit inside you that you can't see operating your body?" Stella asked.

"I don't know. I guess I haven't thought of it like that," said Nora.

"Well, I think it's foolish of you to not believe in spirits just because you can't see them. You put faith in a lot of things you can't see without even realizing you do. Like the wind and the air you breathe. You must believe that if your body dies, your mind goes somewhere, right? It doesn't just dissipate into nothing. Or do you believe that you are just no more after you die?" Stella probed. "Are both of your parents still alive?" Stella squinted at Nora.

"No, my mother died of cancer a few years back. My dad isn't doing so well; he has Alzheimer's disease," said Nora with a downtrodden voice. She fiddled with her napkin.

I don't like where this is going. She's trying to corner me on something.

"So, are you telling me that you believe your mother's spirit just vanished and is nowhere now? That you don't ever pretend like she's still with you or went to some better place?" Stella was getting a little excited and kept pressing with her questions, her beady eyes widening at Nora in disbelief. "When your dad passes on, you won't believe that they are together again?" Stella asked her.

Nora straightened her back and sighed. She took a bite of her blueberry scone and swallowed it down with a swig of tea before answering. "Well, those are all good questions, I suppose.

I've never thought of it like that. I suppose I do think my mom is with me sometimes. I do like to think my parents will be with each other again. I guess what I believe might have some holes in it," Nora laughed uncomfortably.

Stella grinned and put her boney white hand on Nora's and said, "Honey, you have a lot to learn about the spirit world. I would be happy to help you understand some of it, if you're ever up to it."

Nora pursed her glossy lips. "So, you don't think these scary experiences I've had were just my imagination?"

Stella moved one eyebrow into a different position and swallowed the last of her tea. "They very well may have been just your imagination playing games." She set down her cup a little too hard and the handle broke off. Stella didn't skip a beat. "Or, it may be a spirit trying to talk to you. If something else happens where you think it might be supernatural, I suggest you try to talk to it." Stella leaned in and touched Nora's arm with her cold white hand. "Invite it to conversation and see what happens. Maybe your mother is trying to connect with you via the piano," said Stella. "You said yourself, you have no idea about any of this, whether it's the truth. So, don't be telling me I don't know what I'm talking about!" Stella said sharply.

A chill ran down Nora's spine. "My mother did play the piano very well. Maybe it was her!"

I shouldn't have voiced that out loud. Now she's going to say it was my mother. But what if she's right?

Stella stood up and straightened her blouse. "We're having a get-together with some friends this Sunday. Come join us! We talk about a lot of spirit-type things, and you could learn a lot about how to communicate better with the spirit world!" Stella said with enthusiasm.

"Okay, okay," Nora said waving her hands in front of her and shaking her head. "I think that sounds like a little too much all at once here. But out of curiosity, exactly what religion do you practice?" Nora inquired, her head tilted in a question.

Stella turned slightly as she walked to the sink, "We started as Wiccans, but we have progressed to a different level now. I don't know what you would call us. We are deeper into the spirit world and are enjoying the discovery of finding our inner powers and depth. We worship the universe and powers that come from the energy of a different dimension." Stella was busy with her hands in the sink now.

Yikes. This sounds like a glass of classic hippie cocktail. I don't run in that circle.

Nora decided it was time to end the increasingly uncomfortable conversation. She checked the time on her silver wristwatch. "I need to get moving. I didn't realize how late it was getting. Thank you for the brunch and the invite. I'm going to have to think about things before jumping into anything, and I may actually have a date Sunday!" Adjusting her hair tie, she asked, "Do you mind if I use the bathroom real quick?"

Stella silently pointed her in the direction of the bathroom.

Inside the bathroom, Nora noticed an upside-down crucifix on the wall behind the toilet. It meant nothing to Nora, as the cross in an upright position meant nothing to her.

I know an upside down cross means something, probably an opposition to Christians or something. I just don't care. No one is right or wrong. They're all just playing a game of politics amongst their religious ideas.

On her way back through to the kitchen, Nora's lacy scarf snagged on something sharp. She turned to see a door layered with a chain link fence and locked with a big, silver padlock.

Of course, I have to get caught on the dumb door. Why is there a chain fence in the house covering this doorway anyways? Why is there crusty stuff on this fence? I'm wearing out the word "creepy" in my own mind. I need a new word for this place.

She got herself unstuck and asked Stella about the secured door on her way out. Stella laughed and waved it off, "Oh, that's where we put naughty boys and girls and fatten them up for the stew pot!" Nora grinned to be courteous, but she felt quite uneasy about the joke.

It's obvious she doesn't want me to know, but I'm not going to be blown over in shock if what she said isn't partly true.

Outside the house, Mr. Cooper was ready to go and needed no prodding to get into the old truck. Nora had a lot to think about on her drive to see her dad.

- Five -

THE FLAT TIRE

"If you're going through hell, keep going."

~Winston Churchill

VISITING WITH NORA'S DAD was becoming increasingly hard, and this visit was no exception. This visitation, her dad was as close to normal as he could get… well, for his "normal." He didn't recognize her as they shared small talk about his favorite sports team, and he consistently circled back to the same few phrases.

She had brought him his favorite candy, Milk Duds. Nora watched him as he spent some time opening up the box of candy then stuffing a large handful into his thin, stubble-skinned cheeks. He offered her some several times. His eyes were happy and content with the sugary taste of the chocolate in his mouth.

"No thank you, Dad. Those are for you!" Nora said to him each time.

Well at least I can help him gain some simple happiness. Amazing what a box of Milk Duds can do for Dad. I think his hair is whiter since the last time I saw him. He needs his fingernails trimmed. I need to get an update from the nurse.

Nora rose to leave. She was faced again with the painful reminder that he didn't know her. As usual, he didn't want to be hugged or touched, and he was confused by who she was.

I think I'm pretty tough emotionally, but this has to be the hardest thing I've ever had to work through since Mom dying. It feels like I'm experiencing a death that is just never going to have an end to it. I don't want him to die. What I want is to have him back mentally. I need to stop wishing that. It's never going to be reality, and I just torture myself with my thoughts.

She stopped at the door and turned to watch the shadow of the man who once knew her. He was standing near the window excitedly pointing at a bird.

He is so much like a little boy who is seeing the feathered creature for the first time.

Nora smiled at the man in his innocent excitement. It was all she could do to not break down in tears. Biting her lip, she turned away and left his room. She talked to the nurse in charge briefly and then headed back home to Kingsman. Mr. Cooper sat on the leather bench seat and panted lightly as they cruised down the cracked cement road.

The skies were growing dark from the shadows of rain clouds rolling in. The wind blew the old pickup around on the road.

Nora thought about her conversation with Stella, about believing in things she couldn't see. She felt herself wrestling with truth. In every other area of life, Nora sought to uncover the truth. But for some reason, this subject was one she purposely avoided.

Why? Why do I not want to go there?

Nora's long, straight hair was pulled back into a ponytail, and the little wispy hairs around her face were being set loose by the wind from the cracked hand-cranked window. She reached over to Cooper and scratched his back, and he moved closer to her for more. Nora was really beginning to love this dirty, hairy dog.

Nora shifted and coasted into a slower, more comfortable speed to accompany the darkening sky. Rubbing the knot in her neck with one hand while the other manned the wheel, she kept thinking about what had formed her thoughts about the supernatural world.

The truth about death and what happens to us... how could anyone know for certain? It is uncomfortable. It's taboo, depending on who you talk to. It wasn't ever talked about in my house when I was growing up, which makes thinking about it worse. There seems to be a lot of folks out there who believe in something. So many different religions, church sects each with their own ideas about what is truth. If they are all different, who is right?

Nora sneezed, the power of the sneeze temporarily jerking the wheel close to the edge of the pavement. She sipped from her water bottle and set it back down. Classical piano music from the radio filled the truck cabin with a staccato beat of thought-inducing sound.

I suppose we all die. That's obviously true. But, couldn't we just dissipate? Who do I believe? Where do I start? This is a rabbit hole. If I start going down it, who knows where it will end up?

The thought was overwhelming. She had heard of the Bible, of course. Who hadn't? However, she had never opened a Bible, nor had she ever desired to do so. It was just another religious book. One of many worthless religious books.

I have no desire to be put under rules and regulations of some constrictive religion. I'm not a bad person. I'm a responsible citizen who only sometimes *breaks the speed limit. I always put the trash in the garbage can, and I pay my taxes. I'm the kind of person who would help an old lady across the road and give money to a person in need. I support taking care of the earth, and I believe in practicing kindness. "Be the change you want to see in the world." Gandhi said that. I believe in that. Our lives are just a karma path. That is all. Why do I need anything else? Yes, there is bad in the world. Anyone living in it can see that. Why is there horror and ugliness and injustice?*

Those last few questions hung around for a bit longer then she wanted them to. Nora became frustrated because she didn't have an answer to them.

Nora arrived home and wearily climbed the stairs to the apartment, greatly anticipating settling into her bed. It had been an exhausting day. Preparing some Sleepytime tea, she sat and sipped, welcoming a quiet night with no weird activity.

◆ ◆ ◆

Nora awoke in a state of panic—she couldn't find her gun. She usually slept with it next to her bed. After searching for about ten minutes, high and low, Nora discovered it in the bathroom drawer.

Did I sleepwalk and put it there? There is no way I would have put it in that drawer.

She had no history of sleepwalking, but she had no history of a lot of things that seemed to be happening recently.

Has someone been in my apartment? I think it's time to change the locks on my doors. Well, now that I'm up I may as well get ready for my day.

Sunday morning brought thick rain, the kind where you can't seem to stay dry, even under a tarp. Nora slipped into some skinny jeans and a soft orange sweater that sat nicely on her hips. A date with Trey was in the plans for the evening. Nora set her novel down on the table. She had almost consumed the entire thing that afternoon. When it was time to leave for town, she felt rested and ready to share conversation with someone intelligent and handsome.

Nora was fashionably late for the date, but only by five minutes. Sitting with Trey at a table, Nora thanked the waiter for the water and felt a few butterflies floating in her stomach.

Trey seemed calm and collected as he sat watching Nora get adjusted to her surroundings. The two adults shared small talk, and suddenly Nora found herself talking about her recent experiences at Deape Woods. Trey listened attentively, his hazel eyes much greener tonight. "I guess I don't know what to think about all this spirit nonsense. I don't even want to think about it, but the last few weeks, it has been in my face whether I like it or not." Trey couldn't give her any real helpful advice, but it felt good to be able to talk to someone about the issue.

They shared a dessert after stuffing themselves with Italian food. Work and history were the main topics of the evening. Nora came away from the date feeling that she liked him a bit more than she had before. She hoped he felt the same.

Driving home alone in the dark, the truck started pulling to the right. Nora guessed maybe she had a flat tire. She immediately checked her phone and NO SERVICE flashed on the screen. There seemed to be a dead zone between town and home. Of course she landed in that zone with a flat tire. Of course it just had to be pouring rain.

She dug in the glove box for the flashlight. She found it; it wouldn't stay lit. She smacked it to adjust the batteries. The light flickered into a constant beam.

Nora knew how to change a flat. Her dad had insisted she learn how to do it. He was all for a gentleman helping a lady, but a girl never knew when a predicament like this would show up and there would be no gentleman to help.

Okay, changing a flat isn't a pleasant job, but it won't get fixed with me sitting here twiddling my thumbs.

She tightened the strings in her hood around her face and opened the door, stepping into a three-inch-deep puddle.

I'm not sure how long my leather boots are going to stay water-tight. Maybe I should go barefoot? Gross. It's the pits that my boots might get ruined! What other choice do I have, though?

She reached under the seat and pulled a lever. The bench seat reluctantly slid forward. Mr. Cooper ended up doing a strange leg split with the bench sandwiching him against the dash, and he gave her a desperate look. Nora found the sight mildly amusing. She located the jack from behind the seat, pulled it out, and carried it around the truck, setting it on the bed.

What am I forgetting here? It's been a while since I've done this.

The spare tire was bolted under the very back of the tailgate area. She went back to the cab to find the right tool to get the tire loose. After locating the wrench, she remembered the only way to get it off was to lay upside down to unscrew it. She removed Mr. Cooper's rag blanket from underneath him. "Sorry, buddy. I just need to borrow this for a second. I'll wash it when I'm done," she told the animal.

Laying the blanket down on the wet pavement and gravel, she slid herself under the pickup and went to work getting the spare loose. The pouring rain was a lonesome sound as she held the flashlight in her mouth. Remembering her handgun in its hip holster, she couldn't imagine having to use it. There wasn't anyone out here.

Man, I hope I can get this loose! I guess I'll be walking home if I can't. So freaking glad I carry a gun. Ugh. I'm not a fan of laying in mud in the dark.

Just as she had reached a point of complete confidence that she was all alone, her flashlight beam caught the legs of a huge, dark animal slowly sauntering past her truck. Nora's muscles froze and her throat instantaneously went dry. She purposely pointed the light out from underneath the truck. Steam from the animal's breath formed a foggy trail as it stopped briefly, snorted, and then kept moving. She couldn't see its head, only the enormous paws padding on the wet pavement, splashing through the puddles.

What. Is. That? The paws look like a dog's paws, but they are huge! Is that a wolf? Are there wolves in this part of the country? Maybe it's a neighbor dog from somewhere.

Nora realized she was holding her breath in fear, hoping the animal wouldn't discover her.

Oh, okay, like a dog would know you were here, Nora!

Nora waited for it to pass, then refocused as best as she could on her task. She finished removing the last bolt, and the tire fell towards her, finally loose from its position. She slid out before the tire dropped down with a big thunk, splattering water everywhere. It didn't matter. She was soaked and muddy now anyway. Standing up, she heard a wolf howl—or at least what she guessed might be a wolf.

It has to be that animal that just snuck past.

She pointed the now-flickering flashlight out into the dark. She had to hit its side every few seconds to get it to light back up. Beginning to shiver and unsure if it was safe to continue the tire change or not, she stood there in the rain, debating in her mind.

Nope, can't dwell here. Ignore the howl, Nora. This tire needs to get changed so we can get out of here.

Mr. Cooper was beginning to wind himself up inside the cab. His anxiety was evidenced by his whining and panting which was fogging up the windows.

"Settle down, buddy. There's no way I'm letting you out with that thing waiting to eat you," she told the antsy dog.

Nora propped the spare against the back tire. She paused and scanned the darkness with the weak light streaming into the dripping sky. Trusting that the goose bumps raised on her arms were a natural warning, she unlatched her weapon and waited. It sure felt like she needed to point the pocket pistol a lot lately—a disconcerting feeling.

The creature howled again, but this time it sounded closer. Nora went to the cab and turned on the truck and its headlights. Nora glanced at the fuel gage, noticing only a quarter-of-a-tank left.

Well, if we decide to stay here in the truck till dawn, there isn't enough fuel to keep the truck running. But we don't need heat; its barely September! I also just can't leave the truck's headlights on without the engine running, or the battery will go dead. Oh crumb. We don't need to sit here all night—we can do this!

Nora climbed in and sat in the cab for a few minutes to get warm and squinted through the wet windshield. She pushed now-soaked strands of hair out of her face. From a distance, she saw what appeared to be a huge black dog with glowing eyes. She guessed it was standing about two hundred feet away. The wolf, if that's what it was, looked strange, its back arched like a hyena. As a kid, she had loved to go to the zoo and read through animal books. Wolves were fascinating animals to her, but also quite scary. This beast looked beefier than the wolves she had learned about. It didn't stay long in the light before trotting into the forest.

Nora was concentrating, transfixed upon the spot where she had seen the wolf, for about five minutes, looking hard for the creature to show itself again.

I just want to be sure that thing is gone before I get out again.

She jumped in fright, nearly hitting her head on the ceiling, at the sound of a sudden rapping on her window. With her hand on her pistol, she turned fearfully to look at the source of the sound. There, standing in the rain in a black tank top and spandex pants, was Victor. His face was smeared with mud and scratches. He was completely drenched and barefoot.

Nora didn't feel any safer with this man here. He appeared out of nowhere and was wearing next to nothing in the pouring cold rain. Everything about this scene was strange.

She reluctantly rolled down her window, pointing the flashlight so she could see his face, causing the barefoot man to squint in the light.

"Uh—hi? What are you doing out here?" Nora asked in a cautious tone.

Victor wiped a finger across one of his dark, beady eyes and answered her, "We're playing party games in the woods with friends tonight. I saw your truck had a flat, so I stopped to see if you needed some help changing the tire."

Games in the dark, rainy night? These people are genuine freaks.

Despite her reluctant feelings about Victor's intentions, Nora accepted the man's help. As she got out of the truck, she told him about the wild dog she saw.

"Oh," Victor said. "That was probably just Hank."

"You *know* the wolf?" Nora questioned Victor.

"Yeah, he's a fascinating guy."

"How is the wolf a 'guy'?" Nora asked uneasily. "You know what, I don't want to know," Nora added quickly, throwing up her hands.

Victor kept working and said nothing more. He bent to finish up the last of the bolts and threw the flat tire in the back. "Okay, looks like you're ready to go," he said.

"Do you want a ride home?" Nora asked him

You can ride in the bed of the truck.

"Nope, not done playing in the woods." Victor grinned, "You go on ahead."

Oh good. You stay out here and creep out the poor trees and squirrels. I don't mind keeping my distance.

"Thank you for the help," Nora said to Victor. He nodded and began walking away.

She hopped in the cab, turned the key over, and the engine sputtered to life. Nora didn't waste time getting the truck in gear and starting down the road, watching in her rearview mirror.

The tail lights are messing with my eyes! I could swear that weird man just turned into a... a wolf? He was just walking away and then all of a sudden, his figure is bent over, and then a wolf is running off?

Goose bumps overtook her slender arms. If goose bumps promote hair growth, she was sure she had just sprouted a full logger's beard.

No. I can't believe that. I won't believe that. It's purely my imagination!

Nora wanted to believe something other than what she had just seen. But if she stuck by her own beliefs, she *only* believed in what she saw.

Driving to the apartment, she passed many parked vehicles of guests.

Oh, that's right, they're having a party tonight.

Nora parked, and got back out into the pouring, cold rain. She and Mr. Cooper quickly hopped out of the truck, and through the door. They didn't waste any time getting back into her personal space.

After taking a hot shower, she decided that she had to talk to someone. Not wanting to scare off Trey with all these strange happenings, she called Jessa.

Jessa picked up the phone after the third ring. The two young ladies spoke for about ten minutes. Jessa was certain that Nora was just stressed from seeing her father that day and that her mind was imagining extreme things. "Get some chamomile tea and chocolate, and then curl up with a good show. Nothing scary. You don't need more of that fed into your poor overloaded brain! Also—I know my mom was seeing a psychiatrist or a counselor or something for a bit last year to get some things ironed out. I'll get their phone number, and maybe you should start seeing someone to help you with this life transition. I fully believe that is what's going on with you," Jessa told her.

Feeling a little better, Nora finished up the call and hung up the phone. She sighed as she flipped on the radio to a classical music station. Mr. Cooper was resting on the floor with his head over one paw and both eyes looking up at Nora, ears perched at attention.

Before bed, Nora changed the lock on her apartment door. She didn't plan on telling the landlords about it until she moved out. Nora also wanted to swap the lock on the entry door downstairs, but Victor and Stella had to get in from time to time for some of the junk they were storing, so that wasn't an option.

She ran downstairs and locked the entry way door before calling it a night. As she came back into her space, she found that the radio was no longer tuned to classical music. Curiously, it was now partially tuned to some kind of heavy metal, the blaring, scratchy music filling the entire room with unnerving sounds.

Nora stared at it briefly before switching the radio completely off. Not even wanting to entertain the idea of another strange thing, she ignored her thoughts.

Sound asleep at 4:00 AM, Nora awoke to the radio blaring the same ugly sound that she had turned off earlier. It was pitch black in the room. She whipped her thin arm around in a hurry, almost knocking over the lamp, and switched on the light. Stumbling out of bed, she quickly went over to the radio and yanked the plug from the wall to cease the noise. Eyes still squinty, she rubbed her brows, and chalked it up as a bad dream. She got back in bed, but she left the lamp on.

As always, morning showed up just on time. The dark-gray clouds, however, indicated that the sun didn't get the memo. It had stayed in its cloudy gray bed. The morning was dimly lit and wet. The bossy September winds pushed drops of rain against the window panes.

Nora reluctantly pulled her legs from the warm bed and sat up with her feet planted on the floor. Thinking of the night's affairs, she got up to examine the radio.

If memory serves me right, I remember unplugging it.

Nora's hands followed the cord trail to the end of the plug. The black cord was found plugged firmly into the socket.

Ah! My memory isn't serving me right!

Nora turned the power button on. Classical music came flowing through the speakers. Nora sighed relief.

That had to have been a dream then!

She wasn't going to let herself believe any differently.

◆ ◆ ◆

Monday lived up to its no-good reputation. It offered a team meeting in the conference room about not getting projects done on time. Nora eyeballed the two culprits who were responsible for everyone getting bad marks on their evaluations—Jerry Stine and Joel Buckley. The boss called on Joel and addressed him as "Mr. Buckley…" just like in the movie *The Matrix* when the agent called on Mr. Anderson—stringing out his last name. The whole room was snickering and stifling laughter.

It feels so horrible to have to stifle laughter!

Nora covered her sneaky smirk with her fingers.

It feels like not being able to scratch something that itches really bad!

Monday also brought a broken coffee mug. Or rather, a *cracked* coffee mug. Nora set down the porcelain cup at her workstation, and it slowly relieved itself of its contents all over the desk, drenching her papers to the point of no return. Ironically, the mug was yellow with a plain Jane smiley face on it.

"You're happy you whizzed all over my desk, aren't ya?" Nora said to the mug, then lowered the offensive Monday crackpot of a cup into the trash can.

Nora ate lunch at Tea and Me with Jessa. The young ladies joked about Monday's atrocities and enjoyed tasty scones and sandwiches, washing them down with blueberry mint kombucha.

It feels good to have a friend.

On the way out the door, Nora stopped to look at the corkboard in the hallway. One of the flyers tacked to the board showed a picture of a 19-year-old girl. In bold black letters, it read **MISSING**.

The date read the last week of May. Jessa saw Nora pause at the board.

"I know that girl," Jessa said. "She's the sister of an old friend from high school. She's been missing for quite a while. Some say she left town with a guy she met through an online dating website, but her family said she wasn't the type to leave and never say anything or not contact them. It's a pretty big mystery. I hope she's okay," Jessa stated as she pursed her pink-lipsticked lips. "It's scary, but things like this happen sometimes."

"That's why I carry a gun," Nora said confidently. Jessa looked at her in surprise.

"You have a gun? Let me see!" she said, a little too loudly.

"Shh!" Nora shushed her. "I probably shouldn't have told you that! People aren't supposed to know when you're carrying a gun because it removes the element of surprise—which is bad."

"What?" Jessa questioned.

"If the bad guy knows I have a gun, he'll come after me first, maybe even just kill me outright because I'm a threat. If he thinks he's the only one with a weapon, I'll have an advantage because I can whip it out when he least expects it. If everyone else knows I have a weapon and we're faced with a scenario of needing my weapon, then everyone—in their desperation—will shout at me to 'get out my gun' in which case I'll probably get shot immediately. So, it's much safer all around if people don't know I pack. Plus, people get nervous if they know you have a gun on you," Nora explained and breathed deeply.

"Okay, that makes sense," Jessa replied. "My lips are now sealed with your life-saving secret!" and Jessa pretended to zip up her lips.

Nora gave half a grin. "Oh good. I thought you were the secret-leaker type!" Nora said to her blond friend.

"Secret leaker?" Jessa batted her blue eyes. "Well, I'm no secret leaker, unless the secret is worth leaking, and then I might leak it! I may not be completely secret-tight. You may be right about that. But, if it's life-saving information, I'll retain it, rest assured!" Jessa retorted.

"That's what I thought!" Nora said with an all-knowing smirk.

- Six -

The Invite

"Right is right, even if everyone is against it, and wrong is wrong, even if everyone is for it."

~Unknown

IT WAS THURSDAY NIGHT right around dinner time. Nora's old Ford engine puttered its way up the packed gravel lane of Deape Woods Drive. Mr. Cooper's head perched out the slightly cracked window; he was clearly enjoying the breeze. The setting sun weaved its rays through the thick forest of pines and firs. Things had been relatively quiet around the place since Sunday's episodes of weirdness. For that, Nora was glad.

Nora and the canine took their time getting out of the cab. She slammed the truck door shut, turned, and saw Stella heading in her direction. Nora smiled kindly at the older woman as she came nearer. Stella asked Nora if she would like to come over for dinner.

"Victor and I are having a Mexican food bar and always have plenty. I just saw you drive up… So, would you care to join us for a meal?" Stella stood there impatiently, awaiting her answer. "The dog can come too if you want to bring him," Stella added to sweeten the deal.

"Sure, that would be great! Let me get changed real quick and I'll come right over," Nora replied.

Stella grinned and massaged her thin-skinned hands together, her sparkly gray nail polish glittering in the sun. "Okay, great!" Stella quickly picked up the pace, her gray hair bun flopping to and fro as she walked back to the farmhouse.

Nora entered her apartment, pulled her laptop out of the leather briefcase, and set it on the tiny table, plugging it in to charge. Running her fingers over the stately detail, she paused for a moment to think about her father. This was his briefcase. He loved leather goods and always bought premium products when it came to bags. She couldn't bear to part with it when it came time to sell everything, so she had adopted it for herself. She called the bag "Andes."

I can't ever tell anyone I gave a leather bag a real name. I don't want people to think I'm a weirdo.

Her dad had always dreamt of visiting the magnificent Andes Mountains in South America. He never made it. She thought she would try to go in his stead someday. Giving the bag the name would remind her of that goal.

Nora changed her clothes from office attire to jeans and a slouchy green sweatshirt, tightening her holster underneath her clothing. She pulled her long, sandy brown hair back into a ponytail and reapplied her lipstick, reflecting on her day.

She had been working on a project at work and as it often goes, not all fellow employees were pulling their own weight as far as getting things done on time. Nora prided herself in her self-taught skills and great work ethic. If she was given an assignment to have finished by a certain time, she would get it done. Even if it meant staying late or working at home. And she made sure the work was cleaned up and without mistakes. She had a few coworkers who apparently didn't care about striving for excellence.

They just kind of drift through their work day and serve up sloppy work on a plastic platter, betting that someone else will clean up their mess if needed. Those types of people will never go very far professionally.

Trey had been a manager for a while. He had told Nora that it could be tricky finding good employees. "So many people offer their very best in an interview. Then they get the job, and the first few weeks are like a honeymoon. Once that starts to wear off, you begin to see their true self, and how they treat other people. Sometimes you have to deal with the problems of people dressing provocatively, or looking like they just came from shoveling cow manure, or—for Pete's sake—this isn't your bedroom! No sweatpants and clean up your desk! All we need to do is put a wooden fence around your area and hang a sign that says *Pig Pen*. At least that would give a reason for the mess. People's attitudes change, the more comfortable they get. If they aren't happy, then to rabbit stew with the rest of the world. It's all about me and what I can get, not about what I can give."

Nora sighed as she remembered their conversation. She agreed with him. Nora's eyes narrowed and her brow furrowed. She did see that attitude a lot with her coworkers. Many times, they would screw up because they didn't care enough or just didn't pay enough attention, and she would have to pull the weight of cleaning it up.

I've had to do damage control at least three times in the short time I've had this job already. Maybe I won't stay late at Stella's tonight so I can get back and finish this project.

Nora stepped out of her apartment and pulled the worn, metal knob toward her, shutting the door. She pushed on it to make sure it was latched. She didn't bother with locking it.

I'll only be over there for a little while.

Nora and the dog walked the short trek to the farmhouse. Both felt soothed by the soft breeze whipping their faces.

Nora rapped on the detailed, white screen door. Stella hollered for her to come on in. Inside, the savory smell of meat filled the air. Nora heard her stomach growl loudly, letting her know it was ready for food.

Heading into the kitchen, Nora saw Stella stirring something over the stove. "Can I help you prepare anything?"

"Nope! I pretty much have everything ready here. Go ahead and start dishing up," Stella said. Nora reached for a plain white plate and scooped up a spoonful of guacamole. Just then Victor came into the kitchen from the back hallway. He grunted hello and began fixing his own plate.

The three of them sat at the kitchen table making small talk about the town and its inhabitants, Stella and Victor reminiscing about the good old days.

"How long have you two been together?" Nora asked the couple.

Victor wiped his mouth with a napkin and sat back in the squeaky wooden chair, crossing his arms. His waxed, curled-up mustache held a small fragment of his dinner. Stella picked the food off his mustache; he pushed her hand away from him.

"You had a piece of something in your mustache; I was just getting it off!" Stella said in agitation. Nora sat still in her chair and waited for an answer. Stella rolled her eyes and tapped her fingers on the table, counting the years. "I suppose we have been together about forty years or so. Might be longer, I can't think straight. I think I have a migraine coming on."

Victor nodded. "Yeah, I suppose it's somewhere in there." He stood and stretched. "Hey, Nora, do you like the Dez Crosser books?" Nora watched with surprise as Victor's face lit up—she hadn't yet seen him excited about anything.

"Well, to be honest, I haven't read any of the books, but I've heard they're a good read. They're novels about a wizard kid, right? Kids learning magic and going on adventures or something? I guess I always assumed they were just for kids. I usually read more historical romance fiction. Do *you* like Dez Crosser?" Nora probed quizzically.

Stella laughed and said, "Does he like Dez Crosser? He has an entire room dedicated to Dez Crosser! He is a *huge* fan! Victor, you have to take her upstairs to see your Crosser room. I need to get myself a potion and lay down for a bit. This headache is becoming unbearable." Stella moved away from the table.

"Thank you for dinner, Stella. I'll see my way out after I look at Victor's collection," Nora said.

"Uh-huh…" Stella trailed off, as she mixed a concoction of something in a glass.

Victor proudly led the way to the Dez Crosser room, all the while giving her reason after reason for why she ought to read the series. He opened the door and flipped on the light; Nora—though only slightly familiar with Dez Crosser—was quite impressed with what she saw. It looked like a scene right out of a movie set, with an old desk and some wax figures that resembled real people. It was actually a little on the disturbing side.

This guy must worship this book series. I know some people who say they love the books, but wow.

"I even have a Dez Crosser tattoo," he told Nora. "You want to see it?" he asked as he started unbuckling the belt holding up his gray corduroy pants.

"Oh, no no, that's quite alright!" Nora waved her hands in front of her, gesturing for him to stop. She was more than a little concerned about where the tattoo was and had no desire to see it.

It was odd to see this normally pent-up man acting like a giddy school boy. He chattered away, picking up toy wands and weird-looking artifacts. He told Nora all about them and where he acquired them. An old broom sat encased in a glass box in the corner. Victor walked to the case and flipped on a soft light which highlighted the old stick. The broom was skinny and old-fashioned; it didn't look like a regular sweeper broom stick.

"So, Victor, why do brooms and witches go together? I have always wondered," Nora asked the tall man.

I actually haven't always wondered, but I bet this crackpot actually knows the answer.

Victor's beady eyes squinted as he played with his curled mustache. "Well, no one is certain how a witch riding on a broom became the icon that it has. But it has been told in folklore from the 15th century, when witches used the handle of the broom to transfer a blended ointment of herbs which were high in alkaloids. Basically, the ointment was a hallucinogen and when ingested orally, the side effects were way too powerful."

Victor removed the broom from the glass box with care; Nora could tell it was of great value to the man.

"The ointment worked much better when applied topically and to certain parts of the body where we absorb medicine and oils faster. Given the fact that clothing covered most of the body back then, a good spot to put the ointment was—"

"Wait! I do *not* want to know where they put the ointment! Stop there!" Nora cut him off, shaking her head vigorously. Victor looked at her in frustration as if she were juvenile, continuing his explanation without saying specifically where they put the ointment.

"So, they would take off their undergarments and put the ointment on the broomstick and ride around. As they got high, they would feel like they were flying!" Victor walked over with the broom and held it out to Nora. "You want to try it?" he said with a sleazy grin.

"Um, no," Nora responded with a disgusted look on her face. She pushed the broom away from her with the tip of her index finger.

Ew! Gross!

"This broom actually came from the set of the first Dez Crosser movie. I had to pay quite a bit for it. But it's such an amazing artifact, I just couldn't resist; it's worth every penny," he said as he carefully propped it back up in the glass box.

Nora thought it strange that a grown man was so in love with Dez Crosser, a fictional boy wizard. Cocking her head sideways, she asked the man why he, and frankly so many others, loved the books and movies so much.

Victor responded, "I would say, our passion for these books is so great because woven throughout these stories is a spiritual element that people feel a deep connection with. Whether they are Catholics, Baptists, or Mormons, or have no religion at all, people—young and old—reading these stories can almost envision themselves possessing the witchcraft power that the characters in the book discover. We all want power and authority. We crave it. The author beautifully mixes fantasy with reality, and he makes it so fun and easy to understand. Most people don't know that many things they read as simply fantasy can be, and most certainly *are*, in fact, real."

Nora held her breath and remembered the night she had gotten the flat tire, and the wild dog that, she thought, had changed into a man—who happened to be Victor.

No, I'm not accepting whatever I thought I saw as being reality. It was just a wild dog. No transformation. That's all.

"Shape-shifting for example, that's a real thing," Victor went on, as Nora coughed nervously. "Casting spells on and for people, that can happen too. Levitation, I've experienced that many times. Channeling spirits of the dead? Yes, I've witnessed that. The author of these books has masterfully painted what I have experienced to be valid and real to look like fun and games and pretend. Although, he may or may not believe in it himself." Victor's voice deepened in sound; it was evident he was completely enchanted by what he had seen and been involved with. His confident attitude was becoming increasingly uncomfortable to Nora. "Those of us who have seen things or actually practice witchcraft, we know the truth of it all." Nora shifted her feet uncomfortably, remembering Sunday's affairs.

"I would say Stella and I are into new spiritual ways of healing and finding our inner power. For so long, witchcraft has been something that our culture shunned, something that couldn't be touched with a ten-foot pole.

"These brilliant books have helped so many embrace pathways of enlightenment that have been frowned upon and been demonized for centuries! Witches used to be strung up and burnt to death. Did you know? And not only genuine witches, but anyone who was *suspected* of being a witch was killed. Witches have been outcasts in society for too long, but not anymore. We have movies, books, and TV shows all about some of these very cool and enlightened things, things that used to be so off limits.

"The series has helped many people, some of whom are my friends, with the acceptance of witches, Wiccans, and anyone who follows New Age enlightenment paths. We have become safer as we practice and channel the power we know is as real as the nose on your face. There really is power behind it all. We wouldn't be drawn to it if there wasn't.

"It was the communist revolutionary Lenin who once said something profound. 'Give me one generation of youth, and I will transform the entire world.' Thanks to excellent stories like

Dez Crosser, we are changing the world!" Victor inhaled and didn't skip a beat as he kept droning on.

Nora bit her lower lip and rolled it over and over between her teeth.

Apparently, Victor has an opinion on this. I need to get outta here!

Victor looked straight at her in a most intense way and told Nora, "The author made the books so lovable, funny, and creative that folks just can't help themselves. They must keep on reading! Witches, covens, occults, anyone who is delving into the energy of the earth, and within themselves, to find their god have only benefited from them. Nothing but benefits…

"Haters are always gonna hate, but those hypocritical religious folks are just soaking it in. It's quite amusing to watch really!" Victor was now ferociously twiddling his curly mustache while lost in a self-induced trance of his passionate monologue.

"If we can turn the tide on the lukewarm, warming up some of those religious bigots, too, I'd say the human race is on the road to freedom from the shackles of all the closed-minded weasel pukes who tout some absolute moral authority."

A groan and holler from Stella downstairs caused Victor to simmer down and end his tirade. Victor sucked in a deep breath and then released the air, spewing saliva in Nora's direction. Nora raised her eyebrows, blinked deep, and pursed her lips.

I just had to ask. I really did not want to know about any of this dark nonsense. With one question, I get a history lesson on the war on witchcraft and a creed about Victor's dedication in defending whatever mumbo jumbo he's into.

"Well, I guess you do have an opinion on that, don't you?" She laughed a little nervously. Victor picked up the first book in the series and carefully handed it to her.

"Here, take this and bring it back for the next one when you get done with it. It won't take you long to get through it."

Nora took the book and thanked him. "I had better get going, I have some work I still need to do tonight. Thank you for the tour and all of the interesting information on Dez Crosser! Oh, and dinner! I hope Stella feels better soon."

"Stella sometimes gets headaches that last a few days. I'll try some healing techniques and see if she can't get feeling better. We need to have someone running the kitchen and doing housework around here," Victor mumbled under his breath.

Nora rolled her eyes in the dimly lit hallway.

Oh, what a big, hairy jerk. Here Stella has a migraine and Victor is so caring *about his soulmate. He needs someone making his meals and washing his nasty, tasteless clothes? What an ingrate. I need to get out of here.*

Nora called Mr. Cooper and the two of them walked briskly back to the apartment in the dark, but not before tripping on a root and almost face-planting. Nora caught herself on the ground and saved her face from certain destruction, but in the process her wrist took a severe sprain.

I hope all I did to my wrist is sprain it. I don't need a hospital bill or a cast.

Nora made her way up the stairs and over to the sink, then washed her hands with warm soapy water and examined them for cuts. She found a big splinter and went into the bathroom to fish out the tweezers. "Nope, a needle is going to have to dig this puppy out," Nora spoke out loud. "Sheesh, what a class-act klutz I am! I shouldn't be allowed to walk in the dark." Mr. Cooper cocked his head at her and licked his dog lips as if to say, "I agree!"

Nora finished cleaning up her hand and slathered some ointment on the cut. The task brought to mind the whole witches' broomstick story and Nora shivered at the repulsive thought. "I wonder how much truth is in that tale. Probably nothing. I'm sure that man is a liar, and even if he's not a liar, he is for sure more than a little off his rocker," she muttered aloud.

Making a cup of mint tea and slipping into her jammies, Nora sat down to the computer to chip away at her work. Sitting there typing and thinking, she couldn't help but feel like something was missing. She got up and flipped on the stereo and then sat back down. Still something wasn't right. She got up and locked the doors and sat back down again, but the thought that something was lacking kept harassing her.

She realized that she needed a file she had brought home from work and went to retrieve the cherished leather case from where she had propped it up on the floor earlier.

The case wasn't there. She hesitated and stared at the spot where she was certain she had left it. She looked around in her small space but it was nowhere to be seen.

"What in the freaking world!" she shouted. "I know I brought Andes home! My computer was in it! This is ridiculous! I need the file, never mind the bag!" Nora bent to the ground and looked under the bed. She looked in the coat closet and in her kitchen, but it was just gone.

I knew I should have locked the door. I was with Victor the whole night, but Stella claimed she had a migraine. Maybe Stella lied. Maybe she snuck over here and raided my place when she thought I was busy. Why would the thief only take the case? Why wouldn't they take my computer too?

Nora had no answers, and she was upset.

Nora shut down her computer. She brushed her teeth and clicked off the radio. Climbing into bed, she reached into the nightstand drawer and set her gun on top of the nightstand. Someone had invaded her space tonight. She was sure it was some*one* and not some*thing*. Someone was much easier to deal with. A something would be worse.

That night, sleep was a hard train to catch.

- Seven -

The Office

"The measure of a man's real character is what he would do if he knew he would never be found out."

~Thomas Macaulay

MR. COOPER AWOKE his master by licking her arm. After realizing what was happening, Nora yanked her arm away from the dog's tongue.

"Ew," she groaned and rolled over to pat his head. "Oh buddy, your breath smells like a rotting carcass," she told Cooper. "Might have to see about a teeth cleaning."

The alarm went off, and Nora jumped.

I knew that was going to go off, and I still let it scare me!

Sitting upright in bed, she pushed back her black and white striped sheets and remembered that Andes was missing.

You know, if this strange business keeps happening, I may just look for another place to live.

On her way to the bathroom, Nora glanced at the kitchen table. There was her leather bag sitting exactly where she had left it the day before.

I must be going crazy! How can this be?

She grabbed up the bag. She checked it over, but nothing was missing or damaged. Nora was relieved the bag had returned, but the disappearing act was causing her to wonder if it was all in her head or if these things were truly happening. She had no proof and no other witnesses. "I think I may have to get an appointment with a doctor or something," Nora said out loud.

Hitting the "automatic brew" button on the coffee pot on her way out, Nora took Mr. Cooper out for a jog to wake up fully before the last work day of the week unfolded.

It was a partly cloudy day and felt like fall. Fall was her favorite season. The colors, the cozy things to wear, the promise of holidays, family, and friends.

Oh, hold it. I don't have any family members that can hold a conversation. What am I going to do for the holidays? This is kind of depressing to think about. I guess it will just be me and the dog?

Nora frowned. Her immediate family line was almost all gone. Nora did her best to not feel sorry for herself. It was hard not to.

She was a single woman adjusting to life without the family connection. No siblings, no grandparents, no cousins.

Dad said I have an aunt that lives back east somewhere, but he never wanted to talk much about her. How could a disagreement between Dad and his sister be so bad that they literally hate each other to the point of not talking for years? I have never understood that mess. It's crazy what arguing over money does to people. I don't even know if my aunt had children. That would be neat to have some cousins.

Nora found herself accelerating in her scrutiny of the issue.

Her dad never really said anything about her aunt and Nora never asked him pointed questions. She just figured it was his business and she didn't care to know about someone who apparently didn't care about her. Just because someone is blood-related doesn't mean you have to get to know them.

However, Nora did have a trace of regret about no family line. She sometimes wondered what it would have been like to have a sibling or cousins, or even a relationship with her grandparents. Nora's grandparents were only slightly involved during her childhood. One set of them sent cards and gifts instead of giving the gift of their time. She saw her maternal grandma a few times a year, but never knew her maternal grandpa. He was killed in a fishing accident when her mother was a teenager. Her mother never spoke much about her dad. Nora knew there had been a strained relationship between them and never really probed to find out why.

Why didn't I just ask her about him? What was I afraid of? Oh well. It is what it is. No amount of wishing things could have been different will change anything.

As Nora came over the last hill on her jog, she realized that thinking of fall, her favorite season, had brought out the bitter fragment of herself that was crammed into a closet space of her memory like a large wad of dirty laundry.

I can't dwell on this. I'm really drowning my positivity and I need to be present at work shortly, without bringing my emotional trash with me.

Coming back into her small home, she guzzled a glass of water and checked her mug for coffee. No coffee. The machine had apparently unplugged itself.

Wait a sec, machines don't unplug themselves. I know the thing was on right before I left. I pushed the button and the brewing light came on! Okay, that's it. I'm going to start locking my door even if I'm only going out to get something out of my truck and coming right back in!

Someone was pulling pranks here. Phone pranks, she could deal with those. Banana peels on her windshield, fine. Saran wraps over the toilet at work, that's pushing it. But, coming into her home for pranks, that was not okay.

The question remained in her mind:

Who is doing this? My small amount of money is on the Dez Crosser fanatic because Victor seems unpredictable and highly dubious. No one else lives around here except for those two characters who live in the town of Spooksville, the capital of Paranormal Lunacy Land. Maybe I should invest in an alarm system! Yes! That'll be my next step. I'll ask Trey if he'll help me with it.

Nora was feeling pretty good about her solution to the problem going on. Until she could get it in, she would place a glass coke bottle upside down on the knob, at least while she was sleeping. She had seen that in a movie once.

I wonder how hard it is to balance the bottle; it looked pretty easy.

Nora plugged in the coffee machine and pushed the button again and this time waited, watching the mug fill with delicious, dark brown elixir. She topped it off with hazelnut creamer. Not the cheap kind, this was all-natural creamer. Somehow the word "natural" on her creamer container made her feel more wholesome.

In a short time, she was ready to go conquer Friday. She cinched up Andes and called for Mr. Cooper who was always ready to go. The drive back into the heart of Kingsman was swallowed by her busy theorization, trying to make sense of nonsensical things.

Nora mumbled a hello and grinned slightly to the overly happy receptionist on her way into the office.

"Oh, say, Nora," Patty began, "I need to give you this—our policy on office relationships, also there is an all-office meeting this morning that starts in ten minutes in the big conference room." Nora took the paper hesitantly and looked at it with a furrowed brow. "It's because you're new here and it seems you're hanging out quite a bit with Trey Silver. So we just need to make sure you know the rules of dating coworkers," Patty explained, whistling through her teeth as she spoke.

Nora bit her lower lip and said, "Well, I really don't know that we are an item here. I mean we have been out to dinner a few times, but there is no romance happening."

Patty held up her hand and said, "Darling, I really don't care what happens on your dates. It's none of my business. I'm just here at the front desk doing my job. And part of my job is to give you the company policy!" Patti whistled, her head jiggling around like a bobble doll. Patty turned her attention back to her computer screen and began vigorously typing away. Her fingers moved so fast it seemed impossible she could be typing anything legible. Nora sighed and pulled Cooper along with her to her desk area.

The company meeting this morning was yawn-worthy. Groups of people were being assigned to teams to take turns doing dishes and taking out the trash. Everyone was being required to take a diversity class and an online class on how to use timeboxing to be the most efficient possible. More than half the employees were scrolling on their phones, prompting agitation from the boss, Randy. He then launched into a diatribe about how rude it was to not focus your attention on the person speaking, and he asked everyone to put away their phones. Lucky for Nora, she wasn't included in the group being reprimanded.

She eyed Trey across the room; he winked at her and smirked. Momentarily her phone vibrated, and she discreetly looked in her purse to find out what the message said. It was from Trey. It said,

> HEY, YOU'RE NOT SUPPOSED TO BE CHECKING YOUR PHONE DURING THE COMPANY MEETING!

Nora glanced back at Trey and narrowed her eyes at him.

What a turkey!

Trey just grinned.

"Trey Silver, is there something you think is funny?" Randy suddenly spotlighted him.

"Uh, no sir." Trey shook his head, straight-faced, and Randy moved on. Now it was Nora's turn to grin. She was smart about hiding hers.

The meeting concluded, and Nora passed a younger gal on the way back to her desk. A Latina with a bright smile, Camilla had long, thick, dark hair, brightened by one strand of fluorescent purple. Camilla was a part of the team Nora managed, but she mostly kept to herself. She seemed sure of herself and worked hard; however, in Nora's opinion, her clothing seemed distasteful. She wore things like thin stretch pants that showed the style and brand name of her undies and black bras that showed through her sheer white blouses. Sometimes she wore dresses that were so short, Nora anxiously hoped she wouldn't bend over. Her low-cut blouses often left little to the imagination. She didn't dress as though she was working in an office.

Nora typically didn't get involved with others' personal conversations in the office, but today her ears were drawn to a particularly gossipy discussion, a couple desks over. Two ladies were ranting about Camilla's sensual outfit with little reserve. Nora looked over at Camilla who was busy on her computer.

The ladies went on about her provocative attire and laughingly joked about what bar she might work at after hours. Nora didn't really know these two women and didn't disagree with them about Camilla's inappropriate attire; however, she did not believe in ripping people up in front of them.

She got up to refill her coffee and stopped by their gossip powwow, saying pointedly, "If you have a problem with another coworker, you should visit the HR office or talk directly to them. Otherwise, you need to shut your yappers and quit cheating your employer out of the time he's paying you for." The two young women's mouths hung open in disbelief as Nora strutted confidently in the other direction. Camilla smirked at her desk, her eyes shifting quickly in their direction, letting them know that she had heard every word.

Nora took Mr. Cooper out for a potty break. While he spent time reading dog news in the bushes, Camilla came outside and walked up to Nora.

"Hey, thanks for shutting down the loud-mouths in there; it was brave of you to do that. I would defend myself, but it wouldn't do any good. It seems as though office life can be just like high school life too often," the tan-skinned gal sighed.

Nora took a sip from her mug and smiled at Camilla. "Well, those two shouldn't be goofing off no matter who they are talking about. They can hate me if they want to. I'm not afraid of them," Nora stated. "How long have you worked here?"

"I think I've been here almost a year," Camilla replied. Camilla's toes fiddled with the grass strands, as she had taken off her sandals and was standing barefoot. "I've heard that being barefoot on the earth is actually good for you," Camilla interjected. "I think it's called 'grounding' or something?"

Nora murmured a "huh," as if she hadn't known that. "Do you have family here?" Nora questioned her.

Camilla replied, "I live with my dad and stepmom. I have two older siblings, but they live on the East Coast. We see them about once a year. I would like to get my own place, but I have college bills, a car payment, and medical bills I racked up from having appendicitis. At first I thought it was food poisoning making me sick. But I found out my appendix ruptured, and I nearly died. I was in the hospital for over a week and didn't have insurance. I'll probably be paying on that confounded bill till I die." The younger girl brushed long strands of hair away from her face, staring at her toes scrunched up in the grass. The breeze blew her hair loose again, and strands of it stuck to her lips. "This wind! Loose hair and lip gloss don't play well together!" she gushed.

"How long ago was your hospital visit?" Nora asked.

"I was in the hospital about two years ago. You know, you can't escape medical bills? A bankruptcy won't wipe out taxes, medical bills, and school loans, all of which I have. I suppose if I die, that might shut them down," Camilla replied. "You're new in town, right?"

"Yeah. I'm renting an apartment from a couple just outside of the city." Nora didn't care to give her any additional details.

Break time was over. The two ladies and the dog walked back into the office to finish out the work day. Neither Gossip Lady 1 nor Gossip Lady 2 would look at Nora or Camilla. Sitting back down at her desk, Nora scanned the area around her, noticing Camilla already glued to her computer.

Camilla seems a tad off. She's kind to me, but something about her feels a bit unpredictable.

As Nora came out of the office that evening, she saw Trey waiting for her in the parking lot. He had put her tailgate down, and he and his dog Joey were sitting there, swinging legs and tails. Nora greeted Trey with a big smile which she didn't give to just anyone. Trey's green eyes seemed extra green as he suggested they grab some dinner together. Nora accepted the invite without hesitation.

They picked a place where they could sit outside with their dogs at their feet. Nora had been wondering where their relationship was going, and decided to bring up the HR paperwork Patty had handed her this morning to nudge Trey down that conversational path.

"So, Patty gave me a handout on my way into the office today on office rules regarding dating coworkers." She stopped there and let him reply to that.

Trey took a sip of his drink and said, "Really?" His eyebrows raised and poised a sneaky smirk.

"I told her I didn't think we were actually an item… that we are just hanging out as two people getting to know each other. But she just waved it off and said that it looked like we were dating!"

Trey pursed his lips and folded his hands. "Well, I guess to everyone else, it probably looks like we *are* dating… I don't know what you're thinking—do you want to be in an exclusive relationship or do you want to just be two people getting to know each other?" Trey sipped from his water glass and set it back down on the table. Not waiting for her to reply, he picked up her dainty hand and he said to her, "I like you, Nora. I like you a lot, and I'm thinking my feelings might just turn into something more. I don't know how you feel about me, but I want to date you exclusively. How do you feel about that?"

Nora chewed on the corner of her lip and played with a strand of her brown hair, feeling a little unsure about her giddy feelings towards him and uncertain how to show them. She broke into a grin and replied, "I like you too and I've enjoyed spending time with you, Trey. I'm willing to commit to a dating relationship with you. I don't have a history with anyone else, no baggage to reveal, or secrets to hide. So, I guess that means this office paperwork applies to us now?"

They both laughed easily, then Trey lifted his glass to a toast. Over a small white candle and little vase of fresh yellow roses, the two of them toasted to building friendship, making wise choices, and living life to the fullest.

The sun was setting an exquisite array of orange, red, yellow, and purple. A gentle, warm breeze brushed them tenderly, and their well-mannered dogs roamed underfoot. The meal was expected to be set on the table anytime. Nora was enjoying conversation with this handsome man, who respected her and was willing to commit to her. Nora shoved away her fears and barred her doubts and worries throughout the rest of their time together that evening.

Right now, life is good. I'm happy here in this moment. I wish I could bag it up and save it for later. I suppose that's what my memories are. Reality, that we save for later.

Nora picked a rose out of the vase and inhaled its perfume. Catching Trey's eye, she blushed and put the flower back into its vase.

Life occasionally throws us batches of flawless moments here and there, and it's those memories that we live for. It's those times of undisturbed happiness where everything is right that we crave to be living in forever. We wade through all life's garbage, the chaos, the misery, the fear, and we search around looking for those perfect spots of joy and safekeeping that keep our hearts' fire burning. Nora found a place of pure joy that evening, and she would tuck away that memory in her formerly lonesome soul, perhaps forever.

- Eight -

THE HARVEST PARTY

"Go from knowing what others believe to knowing what you believe."

~Unknown

THE FOLLOWING WEEK, Nora's apartment remained quiet, except for the unnerving sound of the wild dogs howling occasionally. Victor and Stella seemed to be hiding, as she hadn't seen much of them.

On Friday, after a quick dinner with Trey, Nora asked him to help her install a security camera and an alarm system. They picked out what she wanted at a hardware store and drove out to Deape Woods. The sun was setting as the two cars slowly parked.

Nora opened her cab door and stepped out onto the gravel, turning her attention to a big black crow sitting in a tree over the vehicles. The dirty bird was just sitting there watching the humans, its greasy neck feathers ruffling with its twisted head. Trey retrieved the purchased items from the back of his 2000 matte black Ford Transit, pausing to look up at the crow. "It's odd that this bird is out this late," Trey mumbled. The black bird blurted out one loud screech and flew away.

"Have you ever seen the Alfred Hitchcock movie *The Birds*?" he asked Nora. Nora answered no.

"For an older movie, it's kinda freaky!" Trey said.

"So, you're saying the crow reminded you of a scary movie?" Nora smirked.

"Well, you know how memories work..." Trey replied.

The word "memory" was a tender topic these days for Nora. With her dad ill and his trouble with his own memories, each time she heard the word it stung a little. The thought of it must have worked its way to her face. Even in the dim light, Trey could see a wave of emotion pass over Nora.

"I'm sorry Nora, did I say something to upset you?" Trey asked his lady friend.

Nora hadn't realized she was wearing her thoughts on her sleeve. "Oh, you didn't say anything out-of-line. A lot of things cause me to think about my dad. I guess I don't have a poker face, so everything I think gets displayed on my face like a computer screen," Nora said.

"Well, I guess the positive side is that you won't be good at lying to me!" Trey laughed.

"Yep, that's the truth," Nora grinned and swept her feathered bangs back from her pale face.

The young adults got busy setting up the security system. There were two cameras, one trained on the first outbuilding door downstairs, the other capturing a view of the apartment door from inside her apartment. Then they installed an alarm buzzer for the apartment's front door and one for the sliding door to the little balcony by the kitchen. Trey and Nora spent a little time plugging in equipment and setting the software up on her computer, so she could see the captured footage and how it worked. The buzzer alarm would only go off for ten minutes before it shut itself off. This was to ensure it didn't alert the landlords or drive them bonkers. Nora really didn't want them to know she was setting this up. Nora and Trey did their best to hide the camera downstairs. Trey ran his slender, freckled fingers along the ivory keys of the piano in the little foyer. "Is this the infamous piano you had trouble with a few weeks back?" he asked Nora.

Nora scrunched her lips together, nodding a slow deep, yes. Sighing, she murmured, "Yep, this is it, a mind-boggling experience, for sure." Nora decided then to tell Trey about the missing leather bag and the unplugged coffee pot. Trey's eyebrows furrowed. He wrung and twiddled a plastic sack as she described the incident.

"I don't know, Nora. It sounds supernatural if you believe in that sort of thing. I guess time will tell if it's a person doing this or not. Hopefully, these cameras will help. Please make sure you keep your weapon near you. If this unsettling junk continues, I think we should look for another place for you to live. And keep your cell phone charged too. You never know when you will need that," Trey told her with a fatherly tone.

"Yeah, well, I'm a believer in what I can see, but I feel in my heart that something strange is going on here. I can never prove it. It just happens and then people think I've made it up. It's kind of a lonely, scary place to be, actually," Nora told the dark-haired young man.

"Call me anytime you need to. I'm not going to think you're out of your mind unless you start seeing gnomes walking around, talking unicorns, or glowing dogs!" Trey joked. Nora didn't find it quite as amusing as he did.

Nora thanked Trey for the evening and for his help, and she walked him down to the door. Locking it behind him, she waited for his van to leave the drive before walking back upstairs.

◆ ◆ ◆

The next morning, Nora jogged, showered, and chose a lovely brown lipstick to go with her bold pink sweater and blue jeans. She put her hair in a loose side braid, and then, with Mr. Cooper trailing behind her, took a grocery bag out to her truck to clean out the cab before driving to visit her father for the afternoon. She backed out of the cab with the full trash bag, and was startled to find Stella standing next to the cab with her hands on her tiny little hips.

"Oh, I didn't hear you walk up!" Nora gave a short smile. "Everything okay with you guys? I haven't seen you all week."

"We've had the flu and it wiped us out for a few days. Didn't you see the black spot on the front door?" Stella asked Nora.

Nora looked over to the house and tilted her head, "Uh, no. I guess I missed that," she said slowly.

"Well," Stella began with a straight face, "you missed it because there never was a black spot on the door."

"Oh, you're just messing with me then!" Nora grinned a bright white smile.

"No, I'm not messing with you, Nora," Stella again said with a sharp, straight face. By now Nora was thoroughly confused. "I wanted to invite you to a harvest get-together. We will also have a Halloween party," Stella said to Nora. "The harvest party will be tomorrow night at six in the garden. I have been working on some fun games and decorations. Will you come? You might meet some prospects for boyfriends or, if your door swings the other way, girlfriends."

Stella stood there blinking and waiting for Nora's reply, but Nora hesitated too long; Stella stamped her foot and said, "Great! We will expect you then, and you don't need to bring anything except your beautiful body and an open mind!" Then Stella did a 180 and floated back to the house, while Rastus, the gray kitty, sprang from a bush and trotted behind her, meowing the whole way.

Nora stood with her white trash bag in hand; she blinked her eyes and scratched her neck. "I guess the positive side to this is that we got invited to a party, right, Cooper?" she said under her breath. She was sure she could have found an excuse for why she couldn't attend, had she been given adequate time to respond. Something about Stella and Victor was amiss. She couldn't put her finger on it directly, but it was there.

The crow was back, sitting in the same spot it had been last night, staring and twisting its greasy, feathered head around like birds do. Nora ignored it and went back to her apartment to fetch her purse. She headed out to visit her ailing father.

Nora and the dog climbed into the truck cab, and she fired up the engine. As she started to back out, she remembered she had forgotten the sports cap and the caramel candies for her father. Nora put the truck in park and turned the engine back off. Unlocking the apartment door, she noticed the chandelier over the kitchen table swinging slightly.

That's odd.

She went over and reached up to stop it. She picked up her bag and headed back out the door, careful to lock up again.

There must be an explanation for that swinging lamp. Maybe an earthquake or a big squirrel or raccoon or something jumping around on the roof?

Nora inhaled deeply, then tried to put it out of her mind and focus on the day ahead. Mr. Cooper moved his hairy body next to her on the bench seat for a back rub. Nora honored his wish and scratched his back. The visit with her dad Saturday was uneventful, and the drive to and from was easy and without hindrance.

It's nice to have a day with no glaring obstacles to work through. Lately it feels like stress is becoming a part of my normal routine.

◆ ◆ ◆

Sunday morning was lazy and slow for Nora. She spent much of it texting back and forth with Trey about nonsensical things as well as jabs of quirky humor. As she stepped out onto her little balcony, the sun drew out her eyes like golden-brown raisins, highlighted by her oversized chocolate sweater. She held a hot cup in both hands, sipping chai tea carefully. Mr. Cooper sat upright peering through the railing and panting softly. From the chicken yard, the rooster was crowing his little chicken heart out to the world with all his might. A chilly breeze picked up and blew through the trees, a few of the loose browning leaves falling, the breeze sweeping them along the ground. Nora breathed deep and found comfort within her cozy sweater, slippers, and warm drink.

The long, cold winter was coming. The trees knew it, the animals were busy preparing, and Nora was thinking about getting out her box of fall clothing and swapping it with the spring and summer closet garb.

The unmistaken sound of an old Volkswagen interrupted her cozy moments as the bus buzzed up the lane and coasted into the parking area. Nora watched as Victor's brother John stepped out of the rig. Going around to the passenger side door, he helped a woman step down to the gravel. The woman had long, dark, straight hair that was so shiny that Nora wondered if it was real hair.

Ah! I almost need sunglasses to look at that lady's shiny hair!

The lady visitor wore an ankle-length gothic dress, black with a sky-blue bodice. The entire dress was made of velvet with eyelets and lace crisscrossing across her chest. She wore a long necklace with a large stone at the end that sparkled in the afternoon's soft sun. On almost every finger she wore huge, gaudy rings. Although Nora couldn't see her face up close, she appeared to be quite attractive. Nora watched the two walk slowly to the house. As they did, the woman paused and turned to look directly at Nora. John whispered something to her, then her gaze shifted back towards the house.

Nora sipped her drink again and sighed. "Uh, Cooper? I hope this isn't a costume party. I can't stand those." Mr. Cooper didn't know what she said but pretended he did and wagged his tail in reply. "You're a great dog, you know that? Why did I find you with no master? How could someone have just dumped you?" Nora questioned her canine companion. She knew he couldn't answer her questions, but this didn't stop her from talking to her furry friend.

Checking the time, she said aloud to herself, "Yep, I have a few hours before I need to get dressed. I think I'll mess around with some painting this afternoon." Nora pulled out a canvas from the storage closet, looking at the half-finished painting of her old home.

Why is it so hard to finish paintings once you start them?

Nora rummaged around until she found a bag of paints and brushes. She set up the portable easel and went back to the balcony. Plugging headphones into her ears, she squeezed the different colors of paint onto a pallete and went to work finishing the picture of her old home.

Much too quickly, it came time to clean up and brace herself mentally to meet new people.

Man, I do not want to go over there tonight.

Nora wasn't sure how to dress for the party that evening, so she just wore fall layers of orange, brown, and deep red. She pulled her brown hair into a high bun and loosened the roots. Adding a cranberry flower to her hair, she checked the mirror.

Lipstick… Where is my lipstick?

Nora was ten minutes fashionably late even though she lived so close. She figured if she weren't the first one there, she wouldn't be a huge target for the weirdies. But after she entered the house, it looked like ten minutes wasn't that late. Her plan was foiled. Stella was bustling around the kitchen and then went out the back door, and came back in again. Victor was his usual lazy self, lounging in an easy chair in the living room, not doing anything to help Stella. He was busy talking with his brother and the strange woman who had come in earlier that day.

In an effort to avoid participating in small talk with Victor and his tribe, Nora asked Stella, who was dressed in a floor-length black, velvet evening gown, if there was anything she could do to help. Stella put Nora to work in the kitchen stirring a caramel sauce meant for dipping apple slices.

Perfect. This way I can stay out of the way, be helpful, yet watch the door for all the interesting folks coming in.

And the interesting people came. Mostly middle-aged people, but there were a few younger people, Nora's age.

The smell of incense was beginning to fill the house, and it was getting so intense it was triggering a headache for Nora. "Hey Stella, why all the incense in the house?" Nora asked the older woman.

Stella stopped briefly and explained, "Well, the incensed air is very healing to our bodies, it purifies the air and it helps us all go into different states of consciousness if one of us wants to meditate or work our way into another realm for a bit. It can also help ward off bad spirits," Stella replied.

"Huh," Nora grunted. "Evil spirits indeed, it's giving me an evil headache."

Suddenly, Stella's face lit up. "Did you meet our special guest yet?" Nora shook her head slowly. "Oh come, let me introduce you. This will be so fun!" Stella yanked Nora over to the strange woman she saw getting out of the car earlier that day.

"Nora, this is Angelina Corte!" The woman did not offer a handshake as she was handling her large crystal at the end of her long silver necklace. But she did offer a small smile to Nora.

"Pleasure to meet you," Angelina said coolly to Nora. Nora, seeing her up close, guessed that she was probably in her forties. She was quite lovely with deep, dark eyes, long eyelashes, red lips, and pale skin. "You seem a little stressed. You don't like parties?" Angelina asked Nora.

"Not really. I'd rather be at home with a book or movie or with a smaller group of people," Nora replied.

"Let me guess, the show *Downton Abbey* is one of your favorites?" Angelina said with a grin.

"I do really like that show," Nora replied. "How'd you guess?"

"I'm gifted at knowing things. Watch… someone is about to spill their food or drink…" Angelina stated slowly and matter-of-factly and nodded in the direction of the back door.

Okay, people spill things at parties all the time. I wonder if this woman thinks herself some famous fortune teller. She kind of looks like one of those half-bodied dolls in those booths you put quarters into. I remember doing that once and frankly the plastic, mechanical doll robbed me of sleep for a few nights.

No sooner had Nora finished her thought than an older man tripped through the doorframe, his plastic cup of punch splattering all over the woman in front of him. Nora looked back at Angelina with big eyes.

"How did you… know…?" But as Nora looked back and forth, Angelina left the circle, nearly floating across the room, leaving Nora's question unanswered.

Well, that was more than eerie.

Candles were lit everywhere. Inside, outside, on the tables, and on the shelves. The candles sat on dishes and in vases. Puddles of rock salt surrounded their base. It looked as if someone had drizzled red food coloring over the salt.

It will be a miracle if this place isn't lit on fire by the night's end.

Nora sat in one of the many chairs placed randomly around the room and observed the crowd for a while. Sipping some punch, she looked into the cup, wondering what was in the purple drink.

I don't know why; but I don't trust these people to not spike the punch.

But Nora drank it anyway.

Some fellow with long, blond hair pulled into a man bun, wearing bell bottoms and a partially unbuttoned orange, plaid shirt began beating some drums set in tribal formation on the back porch. Two women in long, multi-colored, cotton skirts and skimpy tops started dancing with each other and singing some sort of chant. Another woman set some candle lanterns down in five different spots around the group dancing and then joined them. Nora noticed they all were wearing crystals somewhere on their bodies.

What was it with crystals anyways? Stella would know.

Nora walked back into the kitchen and asked Stella about the crystals she noticed everyone wearing. Stella was holding a bag of chips, refilling a bowl. She paused briefly as she explained it. "We believe the crystals carry vibrations and help us balance yin and yang. Crystals cannot only can be used to help heal our physical bodies, but can help us with emotional baggage as well." Stella shoved a chip in her mouth and closed her teeth down on it, then continued. "All the different stones have healing abilities to help with our unwanted symptoms. Does that make sense?" Stella's gray head bobbed slightly as she fingered her own stone hanging around her neck on a thick metal chain.

Nora nodded slowly as she said, "Uh huh," and she held the bowl steady while Stella refilled the chips.

"It takes some training and education to understand how some of these magical properties work, but crystal healing is a lot of fun!" Stella cackled.

"I bet it is," Nora responded. Inwardly, she was feeling sarcastic.

I bet it is fun, you cuckoo old bat!

Nora took a deep breath and added more purple punch to her cup. She wasn't sure what was in it, but it was kind of addicting, and she was extra thirsty that evening.

A middle-aged fellow with slicked-back black hair and extra white skin approached Nora. He had piercings on both ears that lined the rims, and four eyebrow rings. From the way his lisp sounded, it appeared he had a tongue ring as well. "My name is Marley," he said to Nora in a pinched sounding voice as he held out a limp hand to her for shaking. Nora, out of politeness took ahold of his gimpy, cold hand, and awkwardly shook it, as the man didn't move his hand at all.

I wonder if he actually meant to offer a handshake or if this is some secret code I don't know about. Maybe he thinks I should kiss his hand? Oh, this guy gives me the heebie-jeebies.

"I'm Nora," she said, feeling a little awkward, and definitely not wanting to divulge anything else about herself. Marley and Nora stood there for probably twenty minutes or so talking about meaningless and disjointed things like comic books, places to eat, and hair pieces. Then Marley checked his watch and eagerly dismissed himself for his psychic reading appointment with Angelina Corte.

"Have fun with that," Nora smirked as he left her standing alone. "Don't dis it till you try it," he quipped back at her in a cracked voice.

About an hour later, Stella asked Nora to come and sit in on a séance with Angelina Corte as the medium. Though Nora had never participated in these practices, she had definitely heard of a séance before. When Nora began pushing back on the invitation, Stella probed Nora.

"Okay, dearie, you say you don't believe in anything paranormal, yet you seem to be afraid of this. Why is it a problem if you don't believe in it? How about you try it, then make your judgment after your experience? It seems to me you have already been experiencing things you can't explain."

Nora tapped one finger nervously on her punch cup. She was caught and had no better rebuttal to Stella's request. Reluctantly, she finally just said yes.

Oh crumb, these people believe in so many silly things that hold no power or reality. What am I afraid of? I should just do it and find more proof that I'm correct in my assumptions.

But no matter what Nora told herself, she felt jittery about what to expect. All the people who filed into the darkened, cold room were given a small shot glass of some concoction to help open their minds and relax. Nora declined the drink.

- Nine -

THE MYSTERY MAN

"We don't always know it, but some people are angels in disguise."

~Unknown

THE EXPERIENCE SITTING in the séance was frightening, to say the least. Nora came out of it wondering if she still believed what she had before she went into it. Mostly, she was confused by what she had experienced. Someone was calling upon a dead father, wanting to know if the father knew a passcode to a locked file, where the safety deposit box key was, and what the number was for it. There were numbers revealed, but not from a human-sounding voice. There were little things picked up off the table and lifted in the air, and candles were blown out in a windless room. Nora thought maybe they could have been magic tricks, but the whole time she was sitting there, she had goose bumps galore.

Would my Spidey senses lie to me?

Nora left the room with the jitters and went to get another cup of the punch.

I need some air.

She went outside and wandered into a circle in the garden. It was surrounded by thick shrubs with strings of hops, making a crisscross-patterned ceiling. In the middle of the ring was a round, shiny, wood table and sitting at it were three people playing a board game. A chandelier holding tall white candles was strung up from the surrounding trees and lowered over the table for a soft light. Nora stopped in the shadows and sipped her drink, observing the players of the game. The chanting and drumming were still resounding from the back deck, although at a slower pace. One of the players waved Nora over to the table. Feeling a little tired and not wanting any more to think about, she reluctantly approached the game table.

"Hey," said one of the young ladies, "I know you! Nora, what are you doing here?" It was Camilla, the young lady that had recently been picked on by her coworkers. Nora wasn't sure she wanted to be recognized at this party, but she smiled warmly at the dark-haired girl anyway. "I didn't know you were into spirit-led enlightened parties!" Camilla said excitedly.

"Well, I'm not really. I just rent an apartment from the people who own this place, and they invited me tonight, so that's why I'm here," Nora said matter-of-factly.

"Oh, so you're still in the skeptic stage!" Camilla threw her head back and laughed sharply. "Let's help move you past that," and she patted the empty, heavy wooden chair next to her for Nora to sit down beside her. Nora sat and looked at the game in front of them. "This is called a Ouija board. You can buy this at most any department store or wherever a lot of board games are sold. Nothing to fear here! Just plain fun! Sometimes it works, and sometimes it doesn't," Camilla stated.

One of the girls across the table had a paper and pen and was silent as Camilla explained how the game worked. "So, on the board are the alphabet and numbers. And then we have the words 'Yes' and 'No' and 'Goodbye.' We'll all put our hands on the little pointer paddle and then ask it a question. Whatever it takes us to, Sandy will write it down on paper so we can read it as it spells out the reply. And of course, the 'Yes' and 'No' answers are self-explanatory."

Nora sighed and gulped down the last of her punch. She burped silently to herself and felt somewhat mentally fuzzy.

What could this hurt? It's just a dumb board game.

She sat both herself and her empty cup down for the next experience of the evening.

The three ladies piled their hands on the game piece. Camilla said she would go first to demonstrate. Camilla asked her first question: "Will the spirits discipline the nasty girls that picked on me in the office?"

The marker moved to "Yes." Camilla then asked what day would they get their punishment. The marker moved to the alphabet and spelled out the word "soon." Camilla giggled in delight and then asked Nora to ask it a question to which only she would know the answer.

That should be easy since I don't really know anyone here.

"Okay, what was my mother's first name?" The marker didn't move right away. And Nora was kind of relieved. In fact, she took her hands off the marker to prove to herself and everyone else that she was not moving the game pointer. Suddenly, it started moving.

Sandy wrote down the letters it stopped on and then read the name out loud. "Her name is Eleanor!"

Nora's throat went dry, goose bumps immediately returning to her arms and legs. With a furrowed brow, she managed to say, "Yes, that is correct."

"Ask it another question, Nora!"

Nora breathed big, "Alright, what is the name of my leather briefcase?" This was a real test because she was embarrassed to admit to anyone she had named her briefcase. Again, the paddle took its time and went to the alphabet and Sandy wrote out the letters. Nora fidgeted and felt sleepy and dreamy.

It's late, I don't know what was in the punch, but I'm wondering if they spiked it. This game can't be real.

"Okay, the answer is 'Andes'?" Sandy said loudly.

Nora's mouth dropped open.

Nope. this can't be real. How does this thing know the right answers?

One more test. Nora said, "Okay, one more, and then I'm out! How did the briefcase get its name?" Nora asked the board.

The board paddle moved to the word "No."

"It says 'no'? It doesn't know! Well, that is a relief." Nora pushed away from the table and grabbed her empty cup. "That's all I can do tonight. This stuff is weirding me out! I'm going home." Nora walked back into the house where much of the party was happening. She felt her head becoming increasingly blurred.

I'm drugged. I've never felt this way before, but I'm sure that's what's happening to me right now. Am I walking straight?

Her feet felt like lead weights and her legs were getting weaker. She knew she needed to sit soon or she was going to fall and black out.

Where's the nearest seat?

She saw a couch that was empty and stumbled her way over to it. She landed on it just before her mind went completely black and she fell into a deep sleep.

As the party continued to heat up, wicked things started to happen. People at the party began to do things they didn't know they were doing, nor would any of them remember they did them once they came to. If they were in a state of consciousness within normal behavior, they certainly would not have chosen to do the things they were doing. This was not a safe place for anyone—especially a woman, all alone—to fall asleep, incoherent to her surroundings.

Camilla tramped into the house, pausing at the couch where Nora was sprawled out. There, sitting upright on the couch, with his hands folded, was a large, elegantly dressed man of color. He looked quite alert and on-guard with dark eyes open wide and shifting back and forth as if he was worried. Camilla asked him his name. The man responded in sign language to answer her. Camilla assumed the well-built black man was deaf, and therefore she could not communicate with him, so she shrugged it off and went to find something else to do.

The psychic, Angelina Corte, entered the house and stood at the edge of the living room, exhausted from channeling a myriad of different spirits through her body. Her darkly made-up, blotched eyes were drawn to the couch where Nora lay. Angelina stopped to take in the man sitting next to a sleeping Nora. If daggers could shoot from eye sockets, they would have obliterated the strange man.

"He should not be here," she said in a strange, low voice that did not belong to her. It was followed by a strung-out, unnatural snarl. She was frozen in place and repeated herself several times over, pointing at the man with her sharp-tipped, shiny black fingernail. Eventually, her abnormal behavior drew some of the stoned party-goers to gather and watch. The unusually tall black man boosted his large body up off the low couch, his head almost reaching the ceiling. He towered over Nora, scooping her up as if she weighed nothing, and carried her out the back door away from Angelina. He glared through a window at Angelina in a silent, powerful stare-down as he packed Nora's limp body around the side of the house and out of sight.

Stella, sitting in a chair nearby, observed the whole exchange. She had not been drinking the punch that night as she was, in a sense, the "designated driver" for all the party-goers and felt it wasn't responsible for the host to be mentally out of it. Someone needed to make sure the place didn't burn to the ground. Victor certainly couldn't abstain, so the job got left to her. She would eventually drink the punch, so she wouldn't be entirely left out.

Stella got up and crept out the front door, silently following the strange, tall man as he carried Nora to her apartment. She waited for him to come back out, but he didn't reappear. She eventually got tired of waiting for him.

Inside the apartment, the dog never barked, the alarm system never went off, and the dark unknown man never reappeared.

Stella figured Nora would be fine. And if she wasn't, oh well. She was more curious about this man she didn't know and why the psychic was filled with so much distaste for him.

Coming back into the party house, she found Angelina and questioned her about the man. The most she could get from her was the sentence, "He doesn't belong here."

"Maybe she's racist. Maybe that's why she hates him," Stella mumbled under her breath. All the people in this group were Caucasian with a few Latino or Indian-looking skin tones. However she hadn't heard much talk on discrimination within this group. Angelina was from a big city, so she couldn't imagine that would be the case. The man was huge. She didn't remember ever seeing a man that big. Creatures, yes. Apparitions, yes. But not a real man. She decided she would ask Nora about him tomorrow. Obviously, Nora knew him.

◆ ◆ ◆

Monday morning, Nora stirred and awoke. Feeling disoriented and horribly groggy, she lay on her back trying to remember what had happened. Nora was at the party, and now she was in her apartment. She had no memory of getting to her apartment. The last thing Nora remembered was that she was walking towards the party house. Other than a sour stomach and a throbbing headache, she seemed to be in good condition. She was still wearing her clothing from yesterday except that her shoes were off. Mr. Cooper sat panting subtly near her.

"Oh, you need to go out, don't you, buddy?" Nora managed to pull herself upright, then felt her headache double in pain. She groaned and held her neck. "I don't know if I can go into work today. I feel so awful," she told the dog. Nora called in sick and felt embarrassed by the fact that it was because of a stupid party. She almost never went to parties. When she did, she never got drunk. She hated the idea of losing control. There must have been something in the punch she had been drinking.

Later that day, she sat out on her balcony. For a few moments everything was quiet and stationary. Stella came bustling out of the barn, long hair in a ponytail. She managed to spot Nora, even in her statue state-of-being.

Stella walked toward Nora's balcony and looked up. "Why aren't you at work today?" she asked Nora.

Nora held up a blue ice pack and said, "My head is throbbing. I can't see straight, and I feel like I might puke."

Stella pursed her lips and threw her boney hands on her tiny waist. "Maybe your hulk friend drugged you, huh?"

Nora's eyes squinted as she asked, a little concerned, "What hulk friend?"

Stella grinned slightly, "You couldn't have missed him; he was about nine feet tall and a beautiful shade of brown, dressed well, and I'm not sure that he wasn't deaf. Well, I don't know if he was nine feet tall, but he was huge, maybe the biggest man I've ever seen. Looked like he lifts weights, too!" Stella said in a hurry, with a wink.

Nora sighed and, scratching her face, told Stella she had no idea what she was talking about. She hadn't brought a friend to the party, and she didn't even know anyone by that description.

"He was sitting next to you on the couch as you were falling asleep. Then he carried you to your apartment and never came out… that I saw. So, I just figured you two were an item and that was that. I'll tell you one thing though; Angelina Corte didn't like him one bit!" Stella cackled. "I think she was still in a trance-type state because the only explanation I could get from her was that he didn't belong here. I guess she doesn't like black people or something. Must be a racist," Stella rattled away. "Did we make a believer out of you last night, or do you still need convincing?"

Nora really didn't feel well enough to have this conversation, but apparently, Stella didn't care. She gave a diplomatic answer. "Well, all I can say is, I definitely haven't been able to fully process yet what I saw and felt."

Stella stood there staring and blinking her dark, beady little eyes. "I'm going to whip up a little something for your headache. I'll be back in a bit," Stella told Nora.

Way to completely ignore my answer.

After a few minutes, Stella suddenly reappeared on the balcony, holding a little shot glass with something green in it. "This is going to taste really awful, but it will cure what ails you," the older woman told Nora.

"What's in it?" Nora asked her, not fully trusting.

"Don't worry about what's in it; just worry about feeling better!"

Nora's whole body ached, and she didn't have the energy to argue, so she downed it in one swallow. As Nora's face puckered and twisted badly, Stella must have laughed for ten straight seconds.

I'm glad I can provide her with some entertainment…

"Alright, I would lay down and take a little nap and then when you wake up, you will be as good as new!" Stella's thin bright-red lips sputtered.

"Thanks," Nora told her. Then Stella floated out the door, her black silk jumpsuit puffed from the gathered wind.

Nora laid down and slept like a baby, sprawled over the entire bed. When she awoke about an hour later, she felt no pain anywhere.

This is incredible! What did Stella put in that drink? I wonder if it's legal? Probably not. She probably just drugged me with something else.

Nora sat with a cup of tea, now able to think longer and more clearly about the party.

I'm a little concerned about this man Stella was talking about. This man carried me to my apartment and apparently knew where the key was and how to turn off the alarm and then managed to not get attacked by Mr. Cooper? Has this man been watching me? He could have done all sorts of devilish things to me while I was unconscious, but it seems like he didn't.

Nora tucked a long strand of brown hair behind her ear and sipped more tea.

Thanks so much, Stella, for making sure I was safe with a guy you were clearly *concerned about.*

Suddenly Nora had an idea. The security tapes would surely help her get a look at this guy! She pulled out her computer and sat for the longest time, drinking two more cups of tea while scrolling through security footage… and came up with nothing. Zilch. Not even a video of herself coming through the door late last night. She had footage of today, of Stella, coming up to give her the potion, and then of herself taking Mr. Cooper out today, but there was nothing from last night. Nora threw her hands up in the air in frustration.

Why do I even have this security stuff if it's not going to work when I need it most?! Wait a second. Maybe the guy erased it! If he knew how to turn everything else off, then maybe he took the footage off the tapes as well?

She sat back in her uncomfortable table chair and downed the last of the cold tea. Closing her laptop, she just sat for a minute and rubbed her brown eyebrows.

A growl from Nora's stomach alerted her to eat. Nora remembered she was supposed to have picked up groceries today after work, so there wasn't anything in her kitchen but a can of chicken and an apple. She showered, got dressed, and slipped on her black and white Sauconys. She grabbed her purse and called for Mr. Cooper.

Before she left, Nora called and asked Jessa if she wanted to join her at the teashop before it closed. Jessa happily agreed to meet her there.

The two young ladies ordered some food and sat and talked. Jessa's grandma joined them for a while, and they all shared a little small talk. Nora really liked Joanna, except for the fact that Joanna's mannerisms caused Nora to think about her late mother every once in a while.

Joanna shared some funny stories from her younger years, and they all laughed until they cried. Joanna was an excellent storyteller and could captivate anyone. She obviously had a lot of experience under her belt and was the type of woman Nora could feel good about asking for motherly advice. Nora hadn't met another woman who made her miss her own mother more until she was introduced to Joanna. Yes, it was sad, but she welcomed it too. She was hoping they would become great friends.

"How was your weekend, honey?" Joanna asked Nora.

"Pretty mellow; I visited my dad, chatted with a friend, and went for a jog near my apartment," Nora told the pretty, older woman.

Joanna nodded her silver-haired head pleasantly. "That sounds nice."

I'm not going to mention the crazy party that happened last night. I know Jessa mentioned her grandmother was a big Bible-Thumper. I don't want to get some guilt-laden lectures. I've had enough spirituality for one week. I'm pretty certain all these religions are basically the same gig anyway. They just stem from different veins. Plus, I don't want this older woman to think poorly of me for being involved in activities like last night.

Nora wasn't certain, but she assumed religious folks judged other people by their dirt, or what they referred to as "sin." Leaving some information out seemed like the best option for today.

Joanna gave each of the girls a hug goodbye and a few of her famous scones to take home.

The young ladies sat a while longer. Nora shared with Jessa about what happened the night before.

Jessa was also a little worried about the strange man. Turning her blond head sideways and twisting a strand of hair with her fingers she said, "You know, I wonder if… Nah, that's a dumb idea, silly…"

Nora's brows creased as she asked, "What is? Tell me."

Jessa snapped out of her daydream. "Well, what if the big black man is your guardian angel?"

Nora had her lower lip clamped and looked at Jessa like she was nuts. Then she started to laugh. "Yeah, that's a rational explanation, Jessa!" Nora scoffed.

Jessa grinned, her blue eyes sparkling and shrugged her little shoulders. "Well, it's my best guess at who he was! *You* don't know who he was!"

"How do we even know Stella was telling the truth about the man? I don't trust that woman as far as I can throw her. And that isn't very far. Feels like she's always working an angle somewhere, and I trust that Victor guy even less," Nora said.

"What have they done to cause you mistrust, Nora?" Jessa asked as she took a sip of her drink.

"I'm not sure, I can't put my finger on it. It's like I have this intuition about them that never sends me good vibes. They haven't done anything to me directly; it's just this aura about them. It's what they seem to be into that feels shady and unclear.

"I'm not comfortable with all this goose-bump-feeling spirit stuff. It's unknown to me. And unfortunately, I can now see that there is something to it. Some kind of power there. I suppose I must deal with the reality of that. What do I even do with my new conclusion that there *is* power in it? Do I leave it alone? Do I delve into it and embrace it? I have all these questions that I'm beginning to ask myself. I'm annoying myself. I need truth, Jessa. I'm a problem-solver. I have never believed in a supernatural realm. Last night really shook my little skeptic world. I think there was something in the punch we were all drinking, but I feel like what I experienced wasn't diluted. From the séance to the Ouija board, up until the unknown man, I was coherent. I remember everything, except for the man, if he even existed. I'm basically going off what Stella said to me," Nora explained.

"I haven't experienced anything supernatural. Not even with God," Jessa told Nora. "I'm not sure if that's my fault or just the way the cookie crumbled."

Nora asked Jessa, "So you've never experienced anything supernatural, but you still believe in a God?"

Jessa pondered the question and answered thoughtfully. "I was raised in church, so the idea of God is common to me. I have never experienced His power, at least that I know of. I guess you could say that I don't disbelieve in the 'idea' of God, but maybe that the idea of God is all that my religion is built on." Jessa sighed. "I don't really feel like God is physical or anything, just like, kind of this abstract support network. I pray sometimes when I need something or when I worry. But I don't really know what to think about the things you've been experiencing, since I haven't ever, like, seen anything like that," Jessa replied. "On a different note, because you weren't at work today, you didn't hear about the two ladies in our department."

Nora held her breath, remembering what Camilla had asked the game board the night before. "What two ladies?" Nora asked slowly.

"Nellie and Jamie, the gals you were telling me about that you chewed out for ripping on Camilla's clothes."

Nora's face went white. "What happened to them?"

"I guess they were out shopping together and got in a car accident. One of them smashed her face into the dash and broke a million bones, and then they both experienced burns on about twenty percent of their bodies. The police are trying to figure out what happened with the car. No drugs or alcohol were involved. They aren't going to be coming back to work for a while. I feel really bad for them. Maybe we should take them flowers or something?" Jessa asked.

"Yes, maybe we should…" Nora drifted off, lost in thought and concern.

"You okay?" Jessa asked Nora.

"Yes, I'm okay," Nora replied. Nora decided not to tell Jessa about Camilla and the game from the night before.

I don't have enough information on what else Camilla did last night. The game board was my only interaction with her. And how could a game board affect a car? I mean, what is this, Jumanji?

Nora and Jessa hugged goodbye and went their separate ways. Sitting in her truck, Nora texted Trey, and they made plans to meet up at the grocery store.

They took their time shopping. Trey was extra handsome in a sport coat, skinny jeans, and black Converse. In Nora's eyes, it wouldn't matter what Trey was dressed in; he was always handsome.

"So why weren't you at work today?" Trey asked.

Nora gave him a quick run-down of the night before, but left out the part about the big stranger. He was already worried enough about her being there, and that would have been the last straw for him. His eyes were wide as she told him about Camilla and the Ouija Board game. She wondered aloud whether there was a correlation between what had happened to Nellie and Jamie and what Camilla was messing with.

"Anyway, so this morning I wasn't feeling well. I'm not sure if I got bad food or if they spiked the punch, or what. Stella brought me over a nasty green concoction that made me feel better. Otherwise, I would still be at home in bed!" Nora told the young man.

They eventually finished their shopping and each returned to their own homes, the dark sky having enclosed the earth.

Later that night, Nora was grateful to be locked up in her little apartment for the evening. After taking some time to balance the glass soda bottle on the door handle, she got into her full-sized bed. Mr. Cooper looked content and licked his hairy lips several times over. Nora decided to leave the lamp light on—this was becoming a regular habit for her. Turning on her side, she stared at the black handgun sitting on the nightstand and mused about when she had crossed the line from fearless into a state of paranoia. Nora's eyelids morphed into lead weights and fell closed almost instantaneously.

- Ten -

THE BROKEN BOTTLE

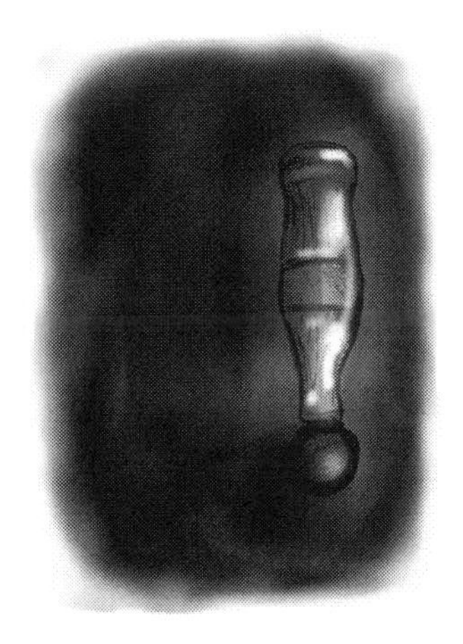

"Every obstacle introduces a person to himself."

~Unknown

BACK AT WORK the next morning, Mr. Cooper followed Nora toward her old brown desk. As Nora sat down and looked through her emails, she couldn't help but steal a glance at Camilla every once in a while.

I wonder if Camilla has some sort of power and actually did curse Nellie and Jamie with some voodoo nonsense. Should I tell the police? Oh this is dumb. What would I even say? So, officer, I think Camilla cursed these girls, and that's why this accident happened, so I believe she's guilty? Yeah, that would fly with the police like a blind, pink, wingless duck.

Later that morning, Nora entered the office kitchen for a coffee break and found Camilla loading up her own coffee with a fifth packet of sugar, a heap of wrappers piling up on the counter beside her.

Camilla looked up at Nora and smiled. "Hey, how are you, Nora?"

Nora returned the smile and replied, "I'm better than yesterday. That party nearly did me in!"

Camilla grinned revealing a tooth with lipstick smeared on it. "Ah, you had an enormous, beautiful man sitting next to you on the couch while you were passed out. I asked him a question, and he signed back to me as if he was deaf. Was he your friend?" Camilla asked.

"Um, I didn't know the guy and never saw him," Nora told the tan-skinned young woman.

"Oh," Camilla said with a frown. "Well that's unfortunate; if you do run into him again, will you introduce me? He looked like a real catch!" Camilla said, sweeping her pile of empty sugar packets into the trash can.

"Yeah, sure," Nora told the girl.

Camilla turned back to Nora and said, "It's unlucky for Nellie and Jamie to have gotten into that accident. Are we going to be replacing them soon, or do you know?"

Nora brushed her bangs behind her ears and said, "I don't know what the plans are for them yet. I haven't even heard how long they are expected to be out of work."

Camilla replied, "Hopefully we can just replace the wenches. They weren't any good at their jobs anyway."

Nora and Camilla sauntered back to their desks, both thinking different things left unsaid.

◆ ◆ ◆

Nora hadn't had a jog in three days and was feeling the need to exercise. It wasn't typical of Nora to jog in the evenings, but sometimes it had to happen that way or not at all. She packed her handgun in her tiny backpack, along with a water bottle and her phone, and she and Mr. Cooper headed out for a quick thirty-minute jog.

The shadows of the woods were different in the evenings. They were eerier. Nora wasn't sure if having headphones in both ears was more or less comforting as she both did—and did not—want to hear her surroundings. She went with one earbud and listened to both—her music *and* her environment. She spotted a coyote and several deer as she chugged through the wooded trail, the animals and human each spooking each other as she and Cooper went along.

Nora's footsteps were elegantly silent. Her mother had taught her to walk with grace, not to clomp her feet like an elephant. "Be graceful when you walk—don't stomp! You're a lady; walk like one." Nora could hear her mother's voice ringing in her ears. It took a while to learn, but eventually, she had trained herself to walk without sound when possible.

As Nora was walking up the gravel lane behind the barn, finishing her run, she made out faint voices through the cracked barn window. Removing her single earbud, Nora slowed to a stop, straining to hear what was being said. Nora scanned her surroundings to see if anyone would notice her standing there. She bent down to appear as if she was tying her shoe, listening intently.

She could make out two men talking. One sounded like Victor and the other sounded like it could be his brother. Nora glanced up at the drive and saw a black Volkswagen bus parked in front of the farmhouse.

"Look, you were in charge of the last gift and you almost screwed it up, John! There is no room for mistakes," Victor hissed at his brother. Nora inched a little closer to the barn window to hear better.

"It wasn't my fault last time. I disposed of the gift wrap after it was opened. No one will ever know it was us who gave it!" John's voice whimpered back. There was silence for a few seconds, and Nora held her breath and glanced down at the dog, hoping he wouldn't make a sound. "What gift do you have in mind for this next celebration?" John asked Victor.

No answer.

After a long pause, Nora heard a deep sigh.

"You know I can't say out loud, John. I will communicate to you in a way that is safer than words, as I always do with these things," Victor said in agitation. "I know what it is though. Trust me, you'll know soon."

Nora realized their conversation was coming to an end and they were about to exit the barn. She frantically looked for a spot to hide. Her best option was to flatten herself against the rough red wall and hold completely still until the sound of their footsteps faded. Eventually, amidst a darkening sky and howls of coyotes in the woods, she snuck into her apartment. Locking the door behind her, she breathed relief.

Okay. I don't know what that conversation was about, but they were definitely speaking in code. And that makes me uncomfortable. What did they mean by a gift or disposing of gift wrap?

Nora had no idea.

She had no clue that the gift they were speaking of was gruesome and dark. She couldn't have imagined it. Nora did not know how much her own soul was at stake just by dabbling in a séance and messing with Ouija boards. She didn't know about the doors that could be opened and the terror that could harass her from such a seemingly innocent interaction. Nora was ignorant to the powers that ran behind the veil of human living, and this made her a prime target.

She said she didn't believe. She didn't want to believe. But the swirl of spooky things that had happened to her recently either meant she was crazy, or that there was some force out there that she couldn't logically explain. She was on the fence in choosing what she knew to be truth. Her own desires wanted to keep her in the meadow of a safe, no-nonsense, boring life. She was forced to walk through the field of believing in things she couldn't see or even put her finger on—things she couldn't control. It was blisteringly uncomfortable and highly frustrating. But being one who can't ignore the truth of her reality, how could she not explore and uncover the whys of this weirdness?

Nora was brushing her teeth behind the closed bathroom door when the sound of breaking glass made her freeze, foamy toothbrush hanging from her wide-open mouth. Her heartbeat climbed instantly to a rapid pace as fear instantly washed over her entire body. Nora's mind switched gears, pulling herself into a rational explanatory space. Her subconscious grabbed at anything to help keep her sane.

I'm sure the bottle just fell off naturally, from gravity. It was a dumb idea to put it on the knob anyways! See, the alarm didn't even go off.

Setting down the toothbrush quietly on the counter, she swallowed her toothpaste without even realizing it was still in her mouth.

Opening the bathroom door a smidgen, Nora peered out into the kitchen area, then heard Mr. Cooper growling low and slow. She couldn't see the dog and pushed open the door further with a towel on her wet head bundled high. Spotting the dog in his focus on the doorway, she realized he sensed something behind the closed door. She felt the ugliness of fear continue to expand slowly throughout her body causing her to shake with growing panic.

Mr. Cooper was intensely focused on the wood door. Nora was out of the bathroom now and watched the silver knob as it began to turn slowly. It turned continuously in a slow, mechanical fashion. The dog didn't stop his growling. Nora didn't know what to do. Sweat beads broke out everywhere on her pale skin. She tiptoed over to the nightstand and grabbed her gun, pointing it at the door.

"Who's there?" she heard herself shout. She didn't know how many times she asked the door the question…

Eventually someone—or something—answered.

"It's me, sweetheart. Will you let me in?"

Nora heard the unmistakable voice of her mother. She was beyond confused and scared, and extreme fear pushed uncontrolled, warm tears down her cheeks. She had never known this level of distress.

My mother has been dead for over three years. How could it be Mom at the door? This doesn't make sense. Who is playing this sick trick on me?

"Who are you, you cruel person?" Nora asked the door again.

Again, the door replied, "I am your mother Nora. Won't you let me in?" This time the voice kind of sounded like her mother but turned into a deeper voice as it spoke, almost like a tape recorder with a dying battery.

Nora grabbed her cell phone, and her shaky fingers kept hitting the wrong numbers as she dialed Stella's number. The knob still turning, Nora couldn't peel her eyes off the doorway. The phone rang and rang and rang and rang, and she left a message hoping that Stella would get it before Nora was murdered.

"Stella, I'm scared. There is someone or something at my door, and I need help right away! Please hurry!"

Mr. Cooper wasn't letting up his growling chorus and it began to turn into barking. Nora called the dog to her and calmed him some as the two of them focused on the door neither of them wanted to go near.

Suddenly, a phone rang on the other side of the door. It rang four times, and then the message Nora had just left for Stella was played back to her loud and clear. Now Nora was *really* in angst.

"What is going on?!" Nora screamed. "Go away and quit this already!"

Is it Stella at the door? Is that how I heard the message replayed?

She looked at her phone to try dialing Trey for help.

"No service"—are you kidding me?

The words were like a bullet in her side.

How can this be? I have always had service here!

Nora was stuck. Imprisoned by terror in her apartment. The dog freaking out wasn't helping anything. It confirmed to Nora that she wasn't making it all up in her head.

She thought about putting a few bullets in the door to just scare the instigator, but whoever it was would be able to see her through the holes. She also knew if she shot a person and hurt or killed him she would be liable because he wasn't actually in her house. No, she was trapped.

I'm trapped in my apartment! I don't know what to do! What do I do?

Tears began to stream down her face again. She began to sob out loud, covering her mouth to muffle the noise. Suddenly the radio began blaring heavy metal music. It was so loud Nora wondered if the speaker might blow out. She ran over and unplugged the old stereo. A scratching on the door began along with a sort of inhuman, low, gravelly moan that was in sync with the knob twisting. Occasionally, the voice that had belonged to her deceased mother asked to be let in. Nora was up all night, sitting on her bed, her back to the brown wooden headboard, her red eyes dry from briny tears of agony. Mr. Cooper never fully relaxed, but sat next to her, never leaving Nora's side. Touching the dog gave her comfort.

The friction at the door stopped and was silent all at once. Nora checked the time, and the clock read 4:36 AM. She felt victimized and traumatized. Her emotions were nothing short of raw. She didn't know how to make sense of any of it, and her distress was over the top.

Nora stretched her stiff legs and stumbled into the bathroom. The light was still on. Gazing into the big bathroom mirror, she saw that her mug was a wreck. Puffy and dehydrated from the loss of her tears, she splashed water on her face and dressed for the day.

It was now Saturday, and she was supposed to visit her dad. She needed out of this place, even as exhausted as she felt.

Last night really did a number on me. I feel like I ran a marathon that I haven't trained for. I wish I could talk to Dad about what has been happening to me. I need him so bad! He surely could've helped me figure all this out.

Again, the warm tears began to dribble down her cheeks. She was sure she wouldn't have any tears left after that horrific night, but they came. The whole evening felt like a nightmare, like it had happened all at once. These weird things never seemed to happen when other people were around.

A knock at the door caused Nora to jump. This time the alarm system was buzzing as well. It was daylight now, and Nora walked to the door and asked who was there.

"It's Stella," said the voice.

Nora opened the door a crack to confirm the identity of her visitor, and there she stood, her gray hair wadded in a bun and her beady little eyes broad and real. In her hands there was a plastic shot glass holding a green concoction.

"I'm sorry. I didn't get your message till just a little while ago. Are you okay now?" Stella asked the wilted-looking Nora.

"No, I'm not okay." Nora, her swollen eyelids battling to hold in salty tears, explained what had happened to her during the last few hours.

"Sounds like your mom wants to talk to you, Nora. Maybe I should arrange for us to sit down with Angelina, and we can figure out why her spirit is knocking at your door? No pun intended," Stella said, as if what had happened was entirely reasonable.

Nora opened the door wide—then gasped and backed away into her apartment. She hadn't looked at the back of the door since last night, and now the two ladies stared at the message scrawled into the wood with sharp, pointed letters. It said,

LET ME IN.

Stella grinned and said to Nora, "I can have Victor sand that off today if it bothers you that much."

Nora nodded her head and followed it up with, "Yes, please."

The two ladies walked down the unfinished stairwell. Stella was doing her best to paint for Nora an unthreatening picture of the unknown identity behind the door.

"You need to just embrace the entity that seems to be following you. It might just be your mother, and she might be trying to tell you something important. This doesn't just happen to anyone, you know, only special people that have the gifting it takes to hear them." Stella paused on the stairs then continued to go down.

Stella knew full well that Nora knew nothing about paranormal pathways, but she did her best to draw her in, to help guide her down the path of captivation. Stella opened her bony white hand; in it lay a crystal pendant.

"Here, this is one of my necklaces. I thought you might find it healing to wear it. This will help give you clarity, especially as you're searching for some answers to questions you haven't even asked yet." Stella grabbed Nora's hand, pressed the crystal into her palm, and wrapped Nora's fingers around it.

"Thank you," Nora managed.

"I'm sorry I didn't get the message last night. Sometimes entities are powerful enough to intercept technology. Apparently, that's what happened here. The important part for you is to not be afraid and instead welcome whatever's trying to communicate."

"Don't you believe there can be entities that are evil, Stella?" Nora asked the tiny old woman.

"I believe some bodies are stronger than others and that they can have a strange sense of humor. I don't know that I believe in an inherent evil," Stella replied. "Well, I best get back to the house; Victor will want some breakfast!"

Nora watched Stella waltz back to the big farmhouse, climbed into her F-250, and closed the heavy door with a creak. She felt ready to drop; she was so fatigued and she hadn't even actually started her day. Before her drive to Astor, coffee was in order, along with a nap in her truck if necessary.

- Eleven -

The Gas Line

"Morality, like art, means drawing a line someplace."

~Oscar Wilde

NORA PULLED OUT OF THE GRAVEL road and onto the paved highway. Picking up some speed, the steady sound of the truck's engine was soothing to her. Nora's mind was filled to the brim with all sorts of thoughts and nonsensical ideas, but her growing exhaustion blurred them all together to the point where Nora made the choice to just ignore it all. She slowed and parked along the curb near Tea and Me Café and sat quietly for a minute in the cab.

I feel like my legs are made out of lead. I'm just going to rest my eyes for a minute. I really shouldn't drive this tired.

And Nora fell asleep without any effort getting there.

The sound of someone banging on the window woke her with a startling jerk.

Phew, it's just Jessa!

Nora hand-cranked the window down as Jessa covered her ears from the high-pitched squeal of the old window. "Wow, Nora, you need to grease that thing!"

"Good morning to you too, Jessa!" Nora told the young woman as she rubbed her crusty eyes.

"Morning? It's nearly one in the afternoon! How long have you been sleeping here? And *why*, may I ask, are you sleeping here?" Jessa's blond head tilted sideways as she questioned Nora.

Nora's brown eyes widened. "It's almost one? Oh, no, I'm going to miss visiting hours with my dad! I thought I would just take a ten-minute nap; I didn't mean to sleep for several hours! Oh, why does everything have to go so wrong lately?" Nora set her face in her hands.

Jessa put a concerned hand on Nora's shoulder. "Why are you so tired? What's going wrong? I was just on my way in for an afternoon shift to fill in for my grandma, and I saw your truck."

Nora sighed deeply and put both hands on the worn leather steering wheel. "I was kept up all night by something I can't explain. The nutshell version is, I may be looking for a new place to live, so please let me know if you hear about anything opening up."

Jessa twisted her red lips in weird formations and then said, "Okay, so you can't explain it to me?"

Nora blinked her long lashes and wasn't sure she wanted to go into detail right now.

I don't know if Jessa will take me seriously about this. And do I want to talk about this right now? I really need to get going.

Re-making her long brown hair into a tighter ponytail, she told Jessa, "Let's rain check and I'll tell you about it later. For now, I'm going to come in, use the restroom, and get a latte with a triple shot of espresso. I'm starving, and this little café has some of the best-tasting food around."

"Alright, I can help you with that! But, I still want to know what happened to you last night. So we definitely need to make sure to get together when you do have time to talk."

Nora looked her petite, bubbly friend straight in the eye and said, "You got it. Thank you for being interested in what's happening in my life!"

Jessa adjusted one eyebrow above the other and said, "Of course! We girls gotta stick together!"

◆ ◆ ◆

Back in the driver's seat of her truck, Nora stepped on the gas and hoped to make it for at least an hour of visiting time with her dad. The windows were cracked, and the dog was enjoying the crisp fall breeze. The road seemed to disappear as her mind drifted to her reality and the terror of the unknown. So many strange things had been occurring lately, and none of it made any sense.

Stella insists she knows what these occurrences are, but I have a hard time trusting her, particularly because Stella doesn't think spirits—if they are real entities—can be evil. But then, why do I even believe in good and evil if I don't even know where the two opposites originate from? What in the world am I basing my moral code on? Who comes up with all the rules for our society, and what are they basing their choices on? Fiddlesticks. I don't want to face these questions.

Nora found herself biting her inner cheek and gripping the worn steering wheel tighter than need be.

She had definitely made up her mind that she wanted to find another place to live.

Maybe the location is the problem. Who hasn't heard of haunted houses and graveyards and pieces of land that caused people grief? The stories are everywhere of haunted this and haunted that—so much so that they have TV shows about them. I, for one, never used to believe in this nonsense. But now, I'm more than half way leaning toward changing my mind on all my preconceptions about the supernatural.

At mile thirty-one, Nora's truck's engine began to hesitate…

What now?

Brows furrowed, she looked down at the dials in the dash. It didn't seem to be overheated, and the oil gauge was where it was supposed to be.

Wait, the fuel gauge is showing empty? How could that be possible? I just filled it up yesterday!

She pulled over to the side of the road, and the truck's body sputtered as it shut itself off and coasted to a stop. Nora rummaged around in her purse for her phone but couldn't find it.

"You've got to be kidding me! Of all the days I lose my phone, it has to be today!" she hissed aloud.

Mr. Cooper began panting. Nora looked under the bench seat and the floor carpets, checked in the cup holder and map pockets, but no phone was to be found.

She pushed open the creaky door and stepped out, adjusting her black sports sunglasses to her fair-skinned face. Fingering her wispy hairs, she walked over to the front of the blue Ford and popped the latch to the partly rusty hood. She pushed up the heavy hood and propped it up with its skinny metal rod. The truck's engine was hot, but she didn't see any smoke or steam, and she didn't smell anything strange.

I guess I'll leave the hood up; maybe someone will stop and give me a ride back to town.

Nora looked at her surroundings. Farm plains and desert as far as she could see. No houses or barns.

This is a pretty well-traveled road. It shouldn't take long for someone to show up.

Nora walked behind the blue truck and traced back along the road for a few hundred feet. She noticed a line of small, shiny drops that looked like they followed her vehicle. She bent down and touched a spot with her finger and smelled it. Diesel.

I wonder if my fuel line broke or if there's a hole in my gas tank? This weekend just keeps getting better and better. At least I know I'm out of gas. I'm not sure it's safe to drive if I'm leaking fuel everywhere. I'll have to call Triple A when I get ahold of a phone.

Nora looked to the left of her and noticed a big brown buzzard sitting in a lone, sparsely-branched fir tree. The huge bird was still, except for its bald red head, which swiveled as Nora walked back to the parked rig.

Unnerving. That dirty buzzard is watching me…

Nora and Mr. Cooper waited for about twenty minutes before a car slowed to a stop on the other side of the road in the direction which headed back into Kingsman. There were a few cars that had passed by but didn't stop, and Nora had shook her fist in pretend anger at them, assuming they wouldn't see her in their rearview mirror.

I might as well find some humor in this.

A single girl stranded on the side of the road was probably not ideal in the way of safety. She had her weapon in its holster under her knee-length, orange corduroy skirt, and it gave her the confidence she needed to protect herself.

The driver's window rolled down on the red minivan, and a woman stuck her head out.

"You need a lift, hon?" the middle-aged lady hollered with a southern drawl.

Nora shouted back, "Yes! My truck apparently has a fuel leak. Even if I had gas to put in it, I don't know that it is safe to drive. I think I left my phone back at a café in town. If you can drop me off there, I can pay you!" Nora said hopefully. "Also—I have a dog. Is it okay if he comes in the van?"

The van lady replied, "Sure, he can come, but he might have to sit on the floorboard with you in the front seat because I have a few kids in the car."

Nora retrieved Mr. Cooper, closed the hood, and locked the old Ford's doors. She planted a kiss with her finger on its side and said to it, "I'll be back to get you soon. Be safe!"

Nora and Mr. Cooper got themselves situated in the front passenger seat of the van, then Nora looked back at the seats behind her. Every seat was occupied by a small child under the age of ten. After they started driving, the quiet in the back began to fade into children's voices both happy and sad. The noise from all the kids in the van was loud. Nora had a hard time holding a conversation with the lovely woman who had rescued her.

"My name is Georgia, and I'm from Georgia, in case you couldn't tell by my accent. I have this many kidlets because my husband doesn't believe in birth control. He doesn't know I had my tubes tied after the last child I birthed, and he isn't going to find out if I can help it. This isn't even all of our kids; there are two more with a total of seven, all under the age of ten—plus we have two sets of twins. Honey, my sanity has been lost for about eight years now. I did put out some lost posters with a reward, but so far nobody has found it." Georgia laughed lightheartedly.

This lady is quite amusing and actually quite beautiful with her curly bright-red hair, freckles, and blue eyes.

Nora guessed her age to be around forty, but Georgia shared her age without any prompting. "I'm thirty-seven years old. My birthday is next Friday. It'll probably be forgotten till last minute.

That's how every year works. The kids have no idea it's their momma's birthday till it's the day of, and what am I supposed to do about it? Shouldn't their dad oversee helping the kids prepare for that? I'm not saying I need a big ole party, but, sheesh, every kid always makes a big deal about their birthday months in advance, so why can't their daddy train 'em to think of their momma?"

Nora wasn't sure if Georgia was taking the time to breathe while she was talking.

"I love my kids, but wow, if I had my druthers, the husband would give me a few more breaks by myself. I get worn slap out. Joey, that's my husband's name, he comes home from working—he works real hard—and sets himself up with football and beer. It makes me kinda mad. He wanted all the kids and doesn't mind the making them part of it, but then he can't lift a finger to grow them once they are out into the world? I love my husband, I really do, but that man is bit of a potbellied stallion. I'll be darned if I have any more children with such a lazy feller. There is more to a father than just paying the bills and grunting, you know? "

Nora's eyes were big.

I wonder if poor Georgia ever talks to other women.

"Uh huh," Nora managed before Georgia's next thought.

"So that's what I did. I tied the ole tubes. I feel a little rebellious about that, but shucks, darlin', I've never done anything super sinful, and I already asked the priest's forgiveness in confession. So, I'm good! I'm good," she concluded in her southern drawl.

"You know, that priest at the Catholic church needs to talk to the doctor about his breath. I think his breath singed my facial hair last time I was in there. No need to get my mustache lasered off—he already did that for me! It's not a sin to be talking about his halitosis, is it? 'Cause I can't go and confess to him about talking about his rancid breath, that wouldn't go over well," She laughed.

Nora chuckled. "I won't tell your priest that we were discussing his breath, Georgia. Don't worry!"

Georgia's eyes sparkled and she smiled at Nora. "I like you, honey! I have a really good intuition about people, and you're a sweet girl. You remind me of my sister back home. She married a man who doesn't amount to a hill of beans. Makes my husband look like Saint Paul! Poor thang. I'm trying to convince her to just leave him and come out west with us. She doesn't have any kids with him yet, thank the Lord. Yeah, divorce is a sin, except under a few circumstances. But that nasty man hits her and comes home drunk all the time. Not only that, but he has a porn problem. I wouldn't be surprised if he has a few other women on the side, if you know what I mean?" Georgia's head turned to Nora while her eyes stayed on the road.

The van pulled up to the teashop and Georgia put it in park. "Well, shucks, girl, looks like I did all the talking. Hopefully, we will see you around town sometime?" The southern-born, red-headed woman smiled sweetly.

"Thank you so much for the lift, I'm sure I'll see you around town. You're a lovely lady and hard to miss! Can I pay you for the ride?" Nora asked Georgia, opening her wallet.

"Oh, heavens to Betsy, no! I need to get one good deed in today. Use your money to hire a big ole tow truck!" Georgia replied.

Ah, I forgot to introduce myself.

"Oh, by the way, my name's Nora. I really enjoyed our conversation. Thank you again, Georgia," Nora smiled. She waved goodbye to the van full of kids and shut the van's passenger door.

Nora turned and walked into the café. When Jessa saw her, she immediately bent under the cupboard and came back up with Nora's sparkly, gold-cased phone, waving it around in the air as if Nora might miss it somehow. Nora sighed relief, walked up to the counter and took the phone from Jessa.

"Well," said Nora, "A crummy day to lose my phone! My truck ran out of fuel about thirty miles out of town. Something is wrong with the fuel line or the tank. I think it emptied itself all over the road, and I don't know for how long. I just filled up the tank yesterday!" Nora caught her breath after heaving out the trouble to Jessa.

Jessa stood there with her hands on her little hips, dressed in a purple and pink vintage apron with kitties embroidered on it. "Sounds like someone could use a cup of tea on the house—and a tow truck! I have a cousin who happens to own one. Do you have Triple A? I know he does business with them," Jessa told Nora, as she brushed a blond strand away from her eyes.

"A single woman, old truck, no family? You bet I have Triple A!" Nora practically shouted.

"Awesome, I'll call him!" Jessa acted quickly, recruiting her cousin to the rescue, and he was happy to help out.

Nora rode with Jessa's cousin James out to where her truck broke down. James wore his hair in dreads and didn't have a lot to say—which was very different from her last car ride. They chatted about Jessa and their families a little, and then about cars and how busy work was.

"So, the big question for you is, where do you want this towed?" James asked.

Nora hadn't thought about that.

"Oh blast, I completely forgot about needing a mechanic. Do you have any recommendations?" she asked in a worried tone.

"Well," James began. He thought a minute, as he played with a long strand of grass he had picked and was now chewing on.

How could he be this slow in recommending a mechanic? Doesn't he do this on a daily basis?

"I might recommend..." he stopped again. Nora stared at James, squinted her eyes, and folded her arms. She was just short of tapping her foot in impatience.

"I might recommend either Dewey's Automotive... or we could just take it back to the tow truck shop. We have some mechanics there that charge a reasonable price," James finally said.

"Okay, let's take it to your shop then," Nora replied.

"Do you have a ride back to your place then? Or, I have an extra little junker you can borrow if you want? I'd loan it to you, 'cause you're Jessa's friend, free of charge!" James told Nora.

"Sure! That would be great!" Nora felt relieved.

◆ ◆ ◆

They finally returned to the mechanic shop with the F-250, and Nora stood in front of the building, waiting for James to drive around with the loaner car. This day just wouldn't seem to quit, but she had met a few new people, and she was getting through the problems that had come up.

She decided to text Trey.

> CAN YOU MEET UP FOR DINNER? I'VE HAD A ROTTEN DAY AND NEED TO WHINE TO SOMEONE!

Trey texted back,

> WHERE DO YOU WANT TO EAT? I HAVEN'T HEARD ENOUGH WHINING YET TODAY AND NEED TO FILL MY QUOTA.

Nora smiled.

This guy, he shares my quirky humor! I love that about him. Well, amongst other things, that's just one thing I'm coming to love about him.

Her mom had always said, "You find a man you can laugh with, and you can make it through anything!" Nora's mom knew that sharing the same kind of humor with your spouse was incredibly important. "Life is rough enough," she would say, "so we need to make some of our unfortunate events into funniness. We should pull laughter out of life whenever possible."

Mom always had good advice.

The car Nora borrowed from James was a tiny, light-blue dented-up Datsun. It was dirty inside, bubble gum wrappers littering the cab, large wads of pink, chewed-up gum stuck on the dash.

"I didn't chew all that gum," James said with a straight face.

"Okay," Nora replied. She didn't ask any questions about it; she was just grateful for the car to borrow.

Yeah, right, you didn't chew all that gum…

"We call this car the Pez Runner. I don't know why, but we do," James added.

Nora bit her lower lip to stop herself from laughing out loud. "Thank you for letting me borrow the Pez Runner, James. I'll take good care of it and call in on Monday about my truck's diagnosis."

Nora turned the key and the little diesel engine awoke to life. She ground the gear shift a bit as she found first, and the tiny truck lurched out of the yard and toward her dinner date.

Trey was waiting at a table for Nora at their favorite Italian place. Nora welcomed the sight of his grinning face and slicked-back hair as he got up to pull the chair out for her.

Sitting back down, he said, "Nora, not to be critical, but you look exhausted. What happened today?" Nora didn't know where to begin. Her day had actually begun the night before when the bottle had fallen off the door knob.

"Well, first of all, do you think I'm crazy when I tell you about this paranormal stuff? I actually don't even know if that's what it all is," Nora asked as she picked up her napkin and began twisting it in frustration.

Trey's eyes sparkled as he looked adoringly at Nora. Folding his hands, he said, "No, I don't think you're crazy. I've never said that paranormal stuff couldn't exist. I just have never had any personal interaction with it, so it doesn't feel real to me. At least not yet."

Nora told him her story about the night before. About the radio, the familiar voice of her late mother, the door knob twisting, and the scratched message on the door. She told him about her immense fear and the phone message replayed back to her.

"I'm telling you Trey, I have never felt so much fright of something I couldn't see. It was so intense. And then I told Stella about it this morning, and she assured me everything is just hunky dory and that I just need to invite whatever it is in to talk. I think she's crazy! Besides, whatever it is doesn't seem to need an invitation. On top of that, I fell asleep for a few hours on the curb outside the teashop. I forgot my cell phone on the counter, and I'm certain that's the reason why my truck ran out of gas in the middle of nowhere on my drive to see Dad. No sarcasm implied." Nora breathed deep. "I really am not wanting to go back to my apartment. It doesn't feel safe."

Trey sipped his drink, then set it back on the table and waited for Nora to continue spilling her emotions. She was really wound up and obviously growing more paranoid of the seemingly paranormal experiences.

"It's just when these weird things are happening, I don't know what to do with myself. I don't know how to talk to it. I'm not sure if it's safe. I'm not sure if Stella is right or wrong, and I don't know if it's even real. I don't want to be crazy, but then again, maybe telling myself that I'm crazy is safer than thinking it's real? Will it physically hurt me? I think I want to move out of the apartment and then, hopefully, it will all end," Nora told the young man.

Trey folded his hands on the table and leaned in toward Nora, his hazel eyes watching her intently.

"I want some answers, and I'm not sure where to even begin or who to talk to. I don't fully trust Stella and I especially don't trust Victor or his brother John. Those two creep me out to no end. Did I tell you about the conversation they were having in the barn? It was like they were speaking in code or something. Something about getting and giving a gift. I don't know. I'm just thinking that if I move away from the property, maybe it will all cease and my nights can return to normal, not paranormal."

Trey sat still for a few moments, making sure it was his turn to talk, then responded to Nora. "You're right, you do need some answers. I can help you look for those for sure. Of course, I'm sure it'll take some time to find the answers you need. In the meantime, what can I do to help you not fear where you live? Do you want me to come and sleep on the floor for a while? I don't mind doing that if you would feel safer."

"I might like it if you stayed with me for a few nights, just until I feel okay again. Do you have a camping cot or a mat you can bring?" Nora asked Trey.

"I do. I'll go home and get my things, and Joey, then I will be right over, unless you want me to follow you out to the apartment?"

"Yeah, I'd like that. I'll wait for you, and we can drive together," Nora replied. Trey asked for the check, and the two young adults left the restaurant.

- Twelve -

The Visit With Dad

"A good father is one of the most unsung, unpraised, unnoticed, and yet one of the most valuable assets in our society."

~Billy Graham

NORA CALLED THE MECHANIC Monday afternoon and discovered that the fuel line had been slit, but not cut entirely. "It's almost as if someone wanted the leak to happen slowly so it would die on you while you were out driving somewhere. This was definitely deliberate. If I were you, I would let the police know about it. Sometimes really strange things happen around here. The only way to get to the bottom of these mysteries is to report it so the authorities know when and where strange things are happening. I've fixed two other rigs with this same problem in the last year. At any rate, your truck is ready to be picked up!" the mechanic told Nora.

"Thank you, sir. I'll come by after I get off work to pick up my truck," Nora responded and ended the call.

Slit fuel line indeed.

After work, Nora did exactly that. She came by the mechanic's shop, paid her bill, and exchanged the bubblegum-filled Pez Runner for her truck. Then Nora drove over to the police station and filled out a report about the sliced fuel line.

After stopping at the police station, Nora made her way across town to tour an apartment that was available for rent. She had found it in an online advertisement last week, submitted a rental application, and made a viewing appointment with the owner. Nora was seriously considering moving out of Deape Woods. The new place was on the outskirts of town; it was a duplex that was shared by an older woman. According to the owner, the older woman was deaf and a very easygoing neighbor.

"So, if you want it, I'll need first and last month's rent and then rent will be due on the date you choose, with an extra deposit for the dog," said the short, balding man with a handlebar mustache.

I don't know if I should do this or not. Am I being too hasty about this? Should I think about this longer? What if someone else rents it before I make a choice? This place seems nice enough for the price. Oh, I hate making decisions quickly.

Nora stalled for time by pacing in and out of the two rooms and the one bathroom. Thinking about her growing apprehension regarding her current apartment, she made a cut-and-dried choice right then and there.

"When will it be move-in ready?" Nora asked.

The owner stroked his mustache and cocked his head to one side in thought. "About three weeks, possibly four. I'm having a few things updated. You never can tell when the contractors will be finished. I won't cash your check till you move in though," he answered.

Nora breathed in deep and said, "Okay, I'll take it." She filled out the paperwork and wrote the man a check.

"Why are you moving out of the place you're in now, if you don't mind me asking?"

Nora's eyes darted to and fro as she replied, "Um, I don't feel entirely safe where I am. I think the property might be haunted, and I need to leave that behind."

The man stacked the papers and slid them into a manila folder. He held the door open for the both of them to leave the apartment. "Well, don't be surprised if the haunting follows you. I have heard of that happening to people." He headed for his fluorescent green jeep with a wave of his hand. "I will be in touch as soon as it's ready!" Then the man drove off.

The man's words of caution made Nora feel uneasy. To go through all the effort of moving, only to have this haunting (or whatever it was) follow her to the new home? That would be futile. It was such a pain to move, and not only that, she didn't know what kind of wrath she might incur from the unpredictable landlords.

I feel like I'm making the right choice to leave Deape Woods, but this is going to be a real headache to make all the arrangements. I'm not looking forward to dealing with Stella and Victor. Hopefully, it won't be that bad of a transition.

◆ ◆ ◆

That entire week, Trey stayed each night in Nora's apartment, sleeping on a stiff cot. She slept like a baby every night, and nothing strange occurred that either of them recognized as such. Nora found herself slightly hoping something might happen to prove to Trey that her complaints were legitimate and that she wasn't making all of this up. It figured that whatever it was, it was apparently trying to make her out to be a nut.

Friday morning, Nora made both of them a cup of coffee and some scrambled eggs. They sat and ate mostly in silence, except for the sound of the dogs smacking their lips every once in a while, waiting for a drop of human food to come their way.

Trey broke the silence, "Well, I've been here almost a full week. My back is so screwed up from that camping cot, I might have to visit the chiropractor just to get it back in place!" Trey said with a grim smile.

She beamed and gave him a huge hug. "Thank you for doing this! It means a lot to me. I've felt so safe with you and Joey that I almost forgot about what happened! Well, actually, no, I don't think I could *really* forget about it. But sleeping on that cot has definitely been a sacrifice that is much appreciated," Nora said to Trey.

"I never actually saw Victor or Stella while I was out here. Are they on vacation or something?" Trey asked Nora.

"I have no idea. It seems that they often disappear like this. I don't know why, and I don't think they want people digging into their business without an invitation to do so. I can't wait to move out of here." Nora slumped over in her chair, a look of discouragement spreading across her face. "I have to break the news to Stella. I don't think I'm going to do it until the day before, though. I'm pretty sure it's not wise to make her angry. I don't want to live here longer than I have to, especially with her mad at me."

Trey absentmindedly tugged on the edge of his shirt, nodding his head in silent agreement.

◆ ◆ ◆

Saturday morning, the first of October, unrolled in various shades of orange hues.

"I'm going to visit my father today, as I missed last week. Do you want to come with me and meet him?" Nora asked Trey.

Trey pondered the thought and said, "Yeah! Yes, I would love to meet your dad."

"Oh, are you getting serious on me now? 'Meeting Dad' is a pretty big next step I hear!" Nora joked with him.

Trey blushed and changed the subject. "Hey, that's a beautiful crystal you're wearing. Did you find that and polish it yourself?"

"Nope, Stella gave it to me. She said it will protect me from harmful spirits, and now that I'm thinking about it, maybe she's right! We haven't had any trouble since she gave it to me last week! She can be very giving, you know. She isn't entirely a bad apple."

Trey and Nora piled into his van, along with the dogs and some coffee, for the drive to Green Acres Senior Living.

I wonder how today's visit with Dad will go. I hope Trey will be okay with it. I guess it will be a good test to see how he handles himself in an awkward situation.

As they checked into Green Acres, the nurse at the front counter informed Nora and Trey that Nora's father was in the large visiting room and said they could go in.

"I will notify his chief nurse to come and find you. She's working today so she can give you a report about the last two weeks," the shorter gal in green scrubs told Nora.

Nora nodded and thanked her as she and Trey turned to walk down the deep, multi-color carpeted hall to the visiting room.

Coming into the room, Nora spotted her dad sitting on a couch facing the big, arched window, where he had a view of the garden's many trees, flowering shrubs, and stone fixtures. The item holding George's attention was a beautiful, four-tiered water fountain featuring a stone angel holding a large, overflowing goblet. Little birds of all colors socialized and swam in the fancy bathtub. Many of the residents found amusement from watching the birds take a dip in the fountain, shake, and preen their feathers. Soft music could be heard from the speakers throughout the room, and a locked fireplace glowed with an orange flame. A few other patients were seated at tables, playing cards or coloring pictures, and spaced around the room were a few caretakers, keeping watch.

Trey was quiet as he observed the room and followed Nora, sitting on the couch next to her and her father. He had many mixed feelings as he watched her interact with her dad. This was the first time he had ever been close to a person with this disease. Nora obviously cared for her father. So many people left their loved ones to die alone, thinking that it wouldn't make a difference to the sick relative or friend if they were there or not. Nora's desire to still be close to her dad showed good character. Nora sat close to her father. George didn't seem to realize someone had sat next to him as he was quite focused on the little birds outside.

Trey thought George looked way too young to be in this condition. According to Nora, the disease attacked him right after Nora's mother passed away. Nora believed it was brought on by a broken heart. George had a full head of hair that only had a few silver strands mixed with the light brown. He had well-chiseled cheekbones and spectacles that were rounded like old-fashioned reading glasses. He was a good-looking man. Nora resembled him a little.

Nora sat still, watching the birds with her dad for a while. Periodically, George would spontaneously laugh with excited amusement. Suddenly, he realized that Nora was sitting next to him, and he looked at her intensely as if he was trying with great effort to remember if he knew this person.

Nora smiled and grabbed his hand and said, "Hi Dad! I brought a friend today. His name is Trey." She gestured toward the young man.

George grinned big and said over-enthusiastically, "Hello!" He put out his pale hand to shake Trey's. "What did you say your name was?" George asked Trey.

That was the trend of the afternoon. George would go back to watching the little birds for a few minutes, then notice Nora and Trey, beginning the same scenario again.

Nora had become used to the expectation that George would not want to be touched by her during their visits. But today he allowed her to hold his hand almost all through the visit. And that meant the world to Nora.

Nora looked at her father's hand closely, taking a mental picture of the precious moment of touching him, not knowing if this would be the last time. Trey watched the two, and his heart broke for Nora as he saw the conflicting emotions displayed before him. It occurred to him that he was taking his own father for granted. He made up his mind to re-evaluate his own relationships with each of his parents.

That afternoon went by slowly. The three of them sat for almost two hours together, mostly quiet with the occasional repetitive conversation. After visiting hours were over, Nora and Trey said goodbye to Nora's father, knowing full well that the goodbye was for Nora's benefit alone. Nora had a meeting with the nurse assigned to George. Not much had changed since he had been moved to the facility, there weren't any significant updates. Nora thanked the nurse, and they headed out the secure entrance toward Trey's black van.

Trey treated Nora to dinner at a little hole-in-the-wall diner before they left town to head back to Kingsman. Walking into the near-vacant café, they found a seat near a big window framed by white and yellow gingham curtains. While they waited for their burgers, they began talking about each of their family histories and childhoods. Between the two of them, they had over fifty or so years of memories to share and sift through.

In between stuffing French-fries in her mouth, Nora asked the young man, "What's your relationship with your dad like?"

Trey wiped his mouth with the red napkin. "It's okay. Dad was always buried in his work. We never had any hobbies we did together. Well, Dad never really had any hobbies at all. Life was all about working, eating, and sleeping. Sometimes I would help him work on projects like cars, or house projects like carpentry work, or yard stuff. He taught me many things in the way of fixing and repairing, but he never tapped in with me emotionally. I loved technology, and he didn't know the first thing about any of that. He still has no desire to know. In fact, texting is something he has a really hard time with. Mom got him a smartphone, but he felt so overwhelmed, he had to take it back to the store. He got a flip phone that is much simpler to use," Trey shook his head and grinned slightly. "We get along for the most part. I guess when I see my dad I don't see him as in touch with feelings or emotions. I know he loves me, but I don't think I've ever heard him say the words to me out loud. The words 'I love you' are tough for him. I also don't know a lot about his upbringing, but I do know it was a rough one," Trey told her.

"And your mom?" Nora asked.

Trey's freckled face softened as he talked about his mom. "My mother is a very sweet woman. I think you would like her quite a bit. She has a great sense of humor, and wisdom, and whatever my father lacks in emotion, she makes up for it! They are opposites in many ways. I have heard that it's common to marry your opposite, or opposites attract?" Trey replied.

Nora nodded slowly in contemplation, pulling out her phone to glance at the time. "Oh, it's getting really late. We still have a long drive back to Kingsman; we better get moving." They paid for their meal and headed for the van.

Trey fired up the vehicle and headed for the highway toward home. The hum of the engine was soothing, as was the presence of the two dogs sitting on the floor between Nora and Trey, staring out the front windshield as if they understood the concept of driving and where they were headed. Eventually, the dogs decided a nap was in order and laid down on the back bench seat.

"So, nothing against vans, but can I ask why you bought a huge, 15-passenger van for your choice of transportation?" Nora posed the question.

Trey grinned and bobbed his head while watching the dimly lit road. "Well, I really enjoy camping and going to different parks, and just traveling in general. I wanted a rig that could provide better cover than a wimpy little tent and that could also carry a bike or canoe and the dog comfortably," Trey told her.

"Well, why didn't you just get an RV or a camper van?" Nora asked him.

"One word: money. Those RVs cost a fortune in gas, the camper vans are pricey, and I really don't need two rigs. I'm planning on changing out this engine for a diesel one. I already have it, I just need to schedule the time and get my dad to help me change it out." Trey carried on about some of the details of his plans for upgrading his van, and as he was talking, Nora's mind drifted away from his van monologue and onto the apartment and its creepy issues.

Nora snapped back and returned to the conversation with Trey about his van, doing her best to recover what she missed while daydreaming. Eventually, she was successful in shifting the topic of conversation to solving the supernatural mess she was wound up in.

"I'm thinking of getting you, me, Jessa, and Nolan together at some point and having an Internet answers-to-weird-questions party," Nora told Trey.

"Alright, I'm not sure we'll find anything conclusive, but it sounds entertaining at least!" Trey said.

Trey's Ford Transit slowed down as it coasted down the gravel lane into Deape Woods.

I don't want to stay by myself. Why am I being such a weenie about this? I'm a big girl, with a weapon and a phone. I don't want to ask him to stay longer. But I wish he would. Get it together, Nora, just get it together!

They came to a stop near the entrance of the dark apartment. Nora opened the heavy door and hopped out, calling her dog to follow.

"You going to be okay? You want me to walk you in?" Trey asked Nora.

"No, it's alright, I got this. I have to face it sooner or later." Thanking Trey for the ride and his company and their dinner, she heaved the door shut and watched as his black van backed out and the red tail lights disappeared into the darkness.

She stood still in the dark, waiting for Mr. Cooper to relieve himself for the night and heard a faint sound of moaning. She didn't know where it was coming from. Maybe from deep within the farmhouse? She strained to hear. It almost sounded like someone wailing, but it was just wasn't clear. Maybe it was a cat. Sometimes cats could make noises like that.

A light breeze chased itself through the trees and blew Nora's hair over her eyes. Not desiring to find the source of the strange sound, she hurried in through the building's front door and up the stairs to her apartment. Reaching the top, she saw the scar on the door in the dim light of her phone, where Victor had sanded off the message left by someone or something unknown. Turning the key in the lock, she opened the door and stepped inside. Mr. Cooper followed close behind her, but before she shut the door, she turned and saw an old coffee can rolling across the floor at the bottom of the stairs. The can stopped, then moved slowly again. Nora watched carefully, wondering if a rodent might be pushing the coffee can around. Squinting in the dim light—in order to satisfy the sane part of her mind—she nervously walked back down the stairs to examine the can.

Reaching the bottom of the stairs, she walked across the room and flipped on the light downstairs. When she turned around, the light switch flipped back off. Nora reached out and turned it back on, this time staring at the switch. It stayed on until she turned to look at the can. This time the sound from the click of the switch raised the hairs on the back of her neck, and looking down at the big rusty can, she watched it slowly move another few inches in the dim light.

Somewhat frozen in her movement, her eyes moved to the top of the stairs, watching as the apartment door seemed to be slowly closing itself. Nora sprang into action, double-stepping the stairs as fast as her muscles would let her move. Nora sensed something was right behind her, and the door slammed closed just as she reached it, shutting out almost all light from the hallway. In fright, she grabbed the now-locked knob, twisting it vigorously and simultaneously pushing on the door. She broke out in a cold sweat, and even though Mr. Cooper was barking ferociously on the other side of the door, she barely heard him. All her thoughts were pounding in her ears, and fear was seeping out of her.

She reached for her weapon. Her clammy hands unsnapped the holster and gripped the butt of the cold handgun. Nora pointed it down the wood stairwell in the dark, unable to see any outline of an intruder.

"Who's there?" Nora yelled in a voice that didn't sound familiar. The bottom stair squeaked as if weight was being put on it, but she couldn't see the shape of a human body causing the noise.

The sound of a rattlesnake somewhere in the space was the last straw. Nora let out a scream so loud it most likely busted out light bulbs over in the next county. Within a few minutes, the lights were flipped on by Stella. The tiny, short woman walked to the bottom of the stairs and mindlessly kicked the can to the other side of the room. She looked up at Nora with a facial expression of "you've-got-to-be-kidding-me." Nora holstered her gun.

"What in the name of Sam Hill is going on here?" Stella demanded. Her dark brown, beady eyes almost blackened.

Nora felt as if she had just been experiencing a horrible nightmare. She was shaking as she stammered to explain. "I—I got locked out of my apartment, then there was a tin can rolling around, and it sounded like a rattlesnake was down here!"

Stella waltzed her way up the stairwell and twisted the knob on the door, and it opened effortlessly. She gave Nora a lightweight glare of disbelief, then told her to settle down and get some rest before she left the building.

Nothing has physically happened to me. I know someone or something is pulling these shenanigans on me, and sooner or later someone is going to get hurt! They're messing with me. If it isn't Victor and Stella, then who is it? Stella was right there after I started screaming like a blithering fool. Could she have been responsible for it?

Back in her apartment, Nora set down her weapon on her nightstand where the lamp was always lit. Just a few more weeks and then she could move. Tonight, she let Mr. Cooper sleep on the bed with her. He lay in between her and the thin wooden door that separated them from the hair-raising disturbances.

- Thirteen -

THE RESEARCH COMMITTEE

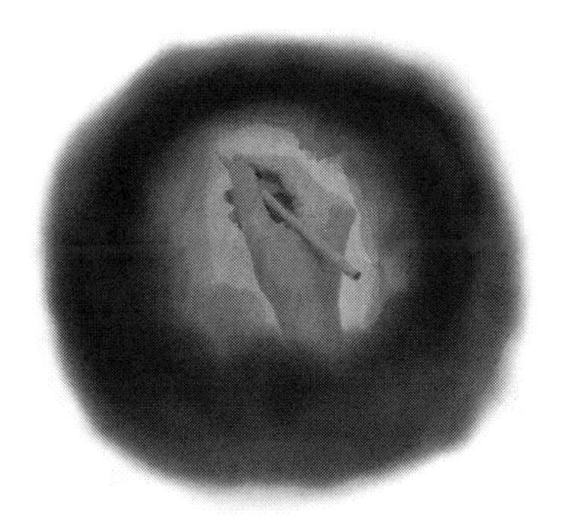

"Never lose a holy curiosity."

~Albert Einstein

ON SUNDAY, NORA TEXTED JESSA to ask if she and Nolan would like to meet with Trey and herself for lunch at Tea and Me. They met at about one that afternoon. Nolan and Jessa pulled up in Nolan's silver Toyota Tacoma, and the two jokers got out of the rig, laughing about something.

Nora was feeling somewhat melancholy from her scare the night before. She didn't want to dominate their double dates with her creepy stories, but somehow, they always leaked out. And really, it wasn't as if anyone else had anything exciting to share to top her crazy experiences.

The two couples sat down at a corner table after ordering from the front counter. Jessa looked extra cute today with her hair bundled up in a bright, multi-colored scarf and bright-orange lipstick, the epitome of her sassy, classy style.

"I went to church today!" Jessa exclaimed.

"Oh, yeah? Did you see the Holy Ghost anywhere?" Nolan jabbed.

"LOL, Nolan!" Jessa dramatized and laughed. Jessa and Nolan sobered up a little when they looked to Nora, who wasn't laughing.

"Oh, we didn't mean to make light of the ghost business happening at your apartment, Nora," Nolan said to her with a look of apology.

"Oh, yeah, I know you weren't. I'm not upset about your joke. It's just that some very scary things are happening to me. I don't know if I'm making up this stuff in my head, or if it's real. Or why this is happening to me at all..." Nora told the three young adults her latest story. Her friends listened patiently, waiting quietly during her frequent pauses for her to pick back up. Nora folded and refolded a gum wrapper as she weaved together the picture for them. No one had any promising answers and all agreed it was mystifying.

"Hey, maybe we should look for one of those ghost hunter groups, like on TV! Don't they show up and exterminate the ghosts or capture the entity in a can and take them away?" Jessa asked, her blue eyes batting.

Nolan looked at her with his mouth half open, "You aren't serious, are you?"

Jessa shrugged her shoulders and sipped through her straw. "Well, do you have a better suggestion, Mr. Gao?" she asked the young man still staring at her with wide eyes.

Trey chuckled low, smirked, and stuffed the last bite of pastry into his mouth.

"I've never seen any ghost hunter shows before, so I don't really know what you're talking about," Nora said to the young blond woman.

"Maybe we should all watch that *Ghostbuster* movie and see if it gives us any answers," Jessa suggested.

Nolan rolled his eyes and laughed. "Oh yeah! *That* will provide us with answers!"

Trey whipped out his laptop and set it on the table. "How about we just do a little research and see what we find on the internet?"

Trey typed in the search bar, HELP I HAVE A GHOST IN MY HOUSE, and clicked on the first link that popped up: HOW TO GET A GHOST OUT OF YOUR HOUSE.

"Okay, these are the steps *WikiHow* recommends. First: 'Make sure the haunting has not been caused by infrasound.' "

"Wait, what is that?" Jessa interjected.

"It says, 'These low frequency hums can cause nausea, feelings of fear and even manifest shadows at the corners of your vision. These are caused by the vibrations of the infrasound, depending on the intensity of the sound wave.' So, it appears that this has to do with sound waves that might make us a little crazy. It has some suggestions here for making or buying an infrasonic microphone," Trey explained.

"Okay, tip number two: 'Eliminate other non-supernatural factors. Check around where the house is situated. Is there a garbage dump nearby? Sometimes methane gas can seep up through the ground, giving a smell of brimstone or sudden bursts of fire.' "

Nolan's brows furrowed as he stated, "That sounds a little like Teenage Mutant Ninja Turtles territory! *Cowabunga dude!*" Everyone looked at Nolan, unimpressed by his witticism.

“ ‘Often ghost sightings are simply light bouncing off of a reflective surface in an unusual way. Human sight and senses are incredibly error prone, so it can be difficult to trust what your eyes might be telling you…’ ” Trey’s reading was interrupted by a spontaneous double sneeze, and then he continued. “Number three: ‘Get psychiatric evaluation. Often people who see “ghosts” are primed to do so because of their mental health. Before you start doing odd things to your home, seek out some professional help. This doesn’t mean that you don’t have a ghost, it is simply a way to rule out one outside possibility.’ And then it says ‘try to have someone confirm your experience. If you’re the only one seeing or sensing anything, that’s the best time to get psychiatric evaluation.’ ”

“Now see, that’s the problem. I’m the only one who has been experiencing this stuff, except for the scratches on the door, which I can’t prove to any of you because Victor sanded it off already. And who’s to say I didn’t do it myself?” Nora was exasperated.

“Well, I did give you the number to my mother’s therapist, didn’t I?” Jessa questioned Nora.

“Yes, you did,” Nora replied, rubbing her cold hands together. “What’s the next one?”

“ ‘Record your experiences. Once you’ve gotten rid of any natural causes, you will need to catalog your haunting to better understand how to deal with it…’ So, you need to record sound, by asking it questions, and also taking pictures.”

“I did record the first time something spooky happened at the pond. It didn’t show up in the recording,” Nora said with a frown. “But, I’m going to use my phone more and see if I can capture something for sure. I guess when you’re in the moment, you’re so freaked out, you can’t think straight.”

"The next step says, 'Have someone corroborate your findings. See if your family members, or roommates sense and see similar things to you… If you can find a reputable ghost hunter or psychic, talk to them about what you've discovered and see what they think. If you can afford it, have them to come to your house and see what they can find separate from your experiences."

"Oh, more of this psychic nonsense. I'm not sure I want to deal with them. That psychic at the party seemed really odd," Nora said.

"See! There *are* such things as ghost hunters!" Jessa burst out, nearly spitting on the keyboard. "And what's after that?"

Trey scrolled down on the screen, "Don't be disappointed if your haunting turns out to be nothing. As any reputable ghost hunter will tell you, most of the ghostly visitations turn out to have a natural explanation. That doesn't mean ghosts don't exist!"

Nora choked on her bite of scone and coughed. "Well that's dumb, why would anyone be disappointed their house *doesn't* have a ghost? And it's totally easy for these hunters and psychics to say nothing is there if they are fakes or if the spirits don't want to reveal themselves while they're there. Next please!" Nora snorted.

"Next," Trey read, " 'Be confident when dealing with your ghost. Like animals, ghosts are supposed to react and feed off of fear. Since there are very few (if any) true cases where someone was hurt by a ghost, mostly what you'll be dealing with is irritating and possibly unsettling. If you talk to the ghost, use a no-nonsense tone of voice, as you would with a misbehaving animal. Be stern, but not mean. Ghosts may be the left-over spirits of other people. The fact that they are dead might already be traumatizing to the ghost.' "

"How does anyone know accurately who has been hurt physically by a ghost? How do you prove that?" Nolan asked.

Trey shrugged, "I don't know how you would. Unless there was a witness there to see it... So then it says: 'Perform an exorcism. This is specifically for Christians, as an exorcism means casting out Satan and his minions. If you aren't Christian, this way will be unlikely to work for you. Check in your specific religion, as all religions have possibilities for dealing with a type of spirit world. If you are Christian, don't perform the exorcism yourself. Instead, contact a local church and see what they recommend.' "

"Oh, I have seen something like this in a movie once," Nolan said. "It was creepy."

Jessa snapped her fingers as a thought showed up, "I can ask my grandma about this one. She seems to know a lot about stuff in the way of churchy things."

"And lastly: 'Cleanse the house. Once your ghost has been banished, you must cleanse the space so that it doesn't return and to discourage other spiritual and ghostly visitors... there are as many ways to cleanse a physical space as there are religions in the world. The ones offered below are only some of the more common ones.

" 'Burn sage or cedar. This is said to clear negative energy and burning incense is considered a purifying force in many cultures...' Um, here's a real great idea," Trey scoffed, " 'Ring a bell in each corner of your home. This is said to break up the negative energy...' and you should do it more than once..." The whole table sat with their mouths hanging open. "Oh, I like this one a lot. 'Physically clean your home. This will help to create an atmosphere of cleanliness and to discourage negative energy from coming back...' And looks like that's all folks!"

Just then their food made it to the table, so Trey put away his laptop. The four were quiet as they began to eat, pondering the different tips Trey had just shared.

"Here's the thing." Nora's hands laid flat on the table in protest. "Whoever and whatever is harassing my apartment hasn't physically hurt me. At least not yet. It's all just been stuff I have heard or seen. My intuition says it's just a matter of time before it does hurt me," Nora stated.

"Well, how can we help you, Nora?" Jessa asked, her blue eyes fixed on Nora as she sipped her tea.

"I don't really know how you can help. Just listening to me share my experiences is actually really soothing to me. So, maybe just listening might be the best way for you to help me. I'll get to the bottom of this mystery eventually. I have to. Hopefully when I move to this new place in a few weeks, it'll all just go away, and I'll go back to my regular, boring life," Nora told the group.

"I know all this sounds silly and unreal to you all. I wouldn't believe it for a second if I wasn't directly involved. So, I won't hold it against you guys if you think I'm making it up or I'm just having mental problems. It's uncanny that one of the world's biggest skeptics of supernatural stuff (that would be me) is getting plagued by something from another dimension!" Nora pursed her lips and pushed her chair away from the table as she got up to buy some dog cookies for Mr. Cooper.

While Nora was away from the table, Jessa continued the conversation. "I believe in ghosts, I mean, the Bible throws around the word 'spirit' all the time. So how can you call yourself a Christian and not believe in them, right? I just don't know much about the topic, and frankly, I don't think I *want* to know. The church I attended didn't—and still doesn't—ever teach on the matter except to graze it occasionally, but it's never in depth. I suppose it would make sense for the church to help Christians understand a bit more about the supernatural world, given it's supposedly where our battles are fought. I guess it's scary to think about, even for church leaders. I'm a tad afraid that if I go researching it or messing with the subject, weird things will start happening to me! I don't want to invite something…"

"Okay, well that sounds a little off, Jessa," Trey began gently, "I'm not a Bible-believer, but aren't Satan and demons or whatever the enemies of the God you say you serve? I mean, shouldn't you want to know who you're battling here? Isn't that the simple outline of all the Bible stuff? From what I know about Christianity, you serve a God, and that God has an enemy called Satan. Isn't Satan always trying to create havoc for the followers of God? Aren't you supposed to be looking at it almost like you're in the middle of war? You don't want to know how your enemy operates and plays the game because of what, now?" Trey asked point-blank.

Jessa squirmed in her seat. "Well I guess I would just rather focus on God, 'cause that's more positive. Plus it's not me that does the battling. It's God."

"So, you're telling me that your God just does everything for you, and you don't have to lift a finger? You don't have to put in any effort or anything, huh?" Trey questioned her again with squinting eyes.

"I mean, I'm not an expert in Christianity, but aren't you supposed to be, like, a warrior in a sense? You sound like a wimpy one." Trey chuckled at the thought. "What kind of God doesn't care if you don't offer Him anything? Doesn't He want you to at least be doing something that shows you're affiliated with Him? I mean, there has to be more to Christianity than just saying you're a Christian. Anyone can tout that. Even Nolan can," Trey smiled and patted Nolan on the back. Nolan simply smirked back.

"No offense, Jessa, but you obviously don't know anything about your spiritual enemy, nor do you seem to care about it. I'm not trying to be a punk here. Don't misunderstand my questioning," Trey said doing his best to be honest with his friend without being a cold-hearted jerk.

"I don't actually care one way or the other. But I'm just wondering if you've thought about how you might come across to the rest of us who aren't Christians. Honestly, you don't seem to me to be any different than the rest of us. I'm wondering if you should do yourself a favor and quit lying to yourself and to everyone else. The word 'Christian' seems to only be a title you like to use and nothing more, because I don't see any evidence in your life of anything that is vastly different from any of us here at this table. Wouldn't it just be easier to drop the 'Christian' title than to pretend? Maybe I'm wrong; maybe you're not supposed to show any difference. I'm not a Christian critic, although it sounds a little like I might be in this rant," Trey rubbed his neck and his hand moved to scratch his head.

Jessa blinked intensely several times. She felt a little ashamed of the assessment Trey had just made of her. Biting her lower lip and shifting her gaze back and forth, Jessa knew she had to respond, but she didn't know how.

What could she say to that? He was giving his honest opinion of how he saw her. She knew he was pretty much spot-on. She was a wimpy warrior, if she was one at all. Her mouth was dry and she felt like someone had just slapped her upside the head. This was not a good feeling, and this was an uncomfortable moment. Possibly the longest awkward moment she had ever experienced. With Nolan sitting beside her, a guy she cared for, she felt that how she responded in the next few seconds would mean everything. Jessa wrung her hands, fidgeting, then cleared her throat.

"W-well," Jessa stammered, "it doesn't sound like I have done a good job of serving God when you put it all that way. I think you may be right about my wimpy faith. Typically, if someone says they are a believer in something, you can tell they are from the way they live their lives, the way they talk, and the way they want to grow in their faith. If you can't see that in me, obviously I'm doing something wrong, because if I do really believe Christianity, it makes sense that it would affect the way I live." Jessa blinked hard to keep the tears from falling.

"Geez, Jessa, I wasn't trying to upset you. I didn't mean for you to cry." Trey sounded a little worried as he handed her a napkin.

Jessa swallowed the lump in her throat and waved him off. "No, Trey, you're just making me think, and it's actually a good thing. I mean, don't get me wrong, I didn't really like hearing what you just said. But I think sometimes when we hear things we don't want to hear, it can change us for the better, if we let it. When I went to church today, the preacher talked about how when life is 'la dee da' and easy we don't grow. But it's when life gets hard that we look for God more and grow in our faith. That we end up reaching to Jesus most in times when we feel the most powerless, because when we are weak, he is strong. But deep down, I don't ever want to depend on the power of something I can't see… because I *am* wimpy and afraid." She sniffed and blew her nose into a napkin.

"I don't think any of us want to be in a powerless situation, Jessa. I think that's natural, human behavior," Nolan said.

"Yeah, I know what you mean, but what I'm saying is that, as a Christian, we are supposed to know that we don't control anything, except our own feelings and actions. We don't have any power except Jesus' power. So, when we come up against sticky problems and scary stuff, we lean into Jesus to pull us through it." Jessa took a sip of her drink and continued. "I need to remember that life's overwhelming tasks and unknowns are opportunities to grow my faith, instead of being afraid of everything and curling up in my warm little bed, unwilling to come out."

"You're telling me you took all that away from one sermon?" Nolan asked Jessa in surprise.

"Well, yeah, I guess I did. Amazing what you can learn when you show up and aren't surfing your phone the whole time." Jessa dabbed her running eye makeup and snorted into the napkin. "Trey, what you've shown me today is that living the life of a Christian should look different. It makes sense. You guys, you know what? I think I'm gonna make a U-turn in my spirituality." Jessa threw her palm flat on the table and shifted into a more sanguine demeanor.

"Look, I don't think poorly of you, Trey, for pointing out what you said. Actually—*thank you* for doing that. I wish I didn't agree with you, but I do. And with what Nora is going through right now, I should be of much more help than I have been. I've been avoiding it because I'm actually scared. *Really* scared." Jessa's running mascara made her look like an undead extra on the set of a horror movie.

Nora walked back to the table and sat next to Jessa. "Uh, I get up for like ten minutes, and now Jessa's crying? What happened?" Nora put an arm around the blond woman and stuffed a brown bag of dog biscuits into her purse.

Jessa smiled and blew her nose again into a napkin. "Oh, I'm just having a 'come-to-Jesus' moment. I want to apologize for being a horrible example of a Christ-follower. I haven't been doing a good job acting out my beliefs. And some of that could just be that I don't actually know *what* I believe. But I'm gonna buckle down and figure it out."

"You don't have to apologize to me; I'm not offended. If you want to apologize to someone, apologize to your God. He's the one I'd be worried about, not me," Nora smirked. "I just figured you were the standard Christian, since I've never known any others. However, if you're saying you're holding out on answers to my supernatural encounters, I will accept an apology on that."

Jessa rested her head to one side and breathed deep. Smiling, she arose from the little table, the tablecloth sticking to her skirt. "Trey can fill you in on our conversation, Nora. I need to get going. I have to babysit for a friend tonight," Jessa said as she peeled the tablecloth from her skirt.

They all stood, gathered their things, and followed Jessa toward the exit.

At the door, Jessa threw her arms around Nora and held her tight. "Nora, I'm so glad you're my friend, and we *will* resolve these issues in your home. Let me think about who I know who might be able to help us with these unexplained things that have been happening."

"Thank you, Jessa. That means a lot to me."

Just then, in walked Joanna. "Oh no, are you all leaving? I just got here and didn't have a chance to visit! Wait just one minute." And the little lady quickly moved back behind the kitchen counter and threw some pastries in four paper bags. She came back to the young people, thrust a sack toward each of them, and squeezed each hand, blessing them as she went.

"You all come back now, and have a great week!" she said with enthusiasm. They all thanked her and stepped out into the dimming daylight.

Trey turned to Jessa. "Hey—is your grandmother a Christian?"

"Yep! How can you tell? Is it her loving, Christlike personality or do the Bible verses give her away?" Jessa smiled and held up her pastry bag, displaying its handwritten message.

Trey winked at Jessa and grinned.

- *Fourteen* -

The Voodoo Doll

"A tremendous price is paid when there is hatred in the heart."

~Unknown

IT WAS A CRISP, sunny October morning. Nora had worked through three days of the work week already and was starting in on Thursday. Her apartment had been relatively quiet for the last few days. There had been a few quirky cases that remained a mystery, including the downstairs door that had been found wide open two out of three mornings. But those things could be attributed to natural causes that could take place anywhere.

This morning a big black bird had killed itself by running into the sliding glass door, so Nora put it in a paper sack and threw it in the woods. She hoped it was the creepy bird that seemed to stare her down every once in a while when she got in or out of her truck.

Walking out of the woods after her morning jog, Nora spotted Stella working in the chicken coop. The slight woman was wearing big mud boots and an oversized black jacket. Nora slowed her pace in case Stella wanted to talk. Upholding a good relationship with her landlords was important to Nora. This couple didn't seem like they would handle conflict very well.

Stella waved Nora over with gloved hands. "Do you like chickens, Nora?" Stella asked her as her large gray bun flopped around on her tiny head.

Nora came to a stop outside the giant chicken wire cage. "I like to eat chickens; I don't know that I like them other than that," Nora answered.

"Have you ever looked at a chicken's tongue?" Stella asked.

"I can't say that I have."

Stella brought around a chicken and forced its beak open. The poor bird didn't like it much, but what could it do? Nora stole a look into the chicken's mouth; its tongue was shaped sort of like a skinny arrowhead.

"Huh," Nora said. "I guess I can check seeing that off my bucket list."

"You had viewing a chicken's tongue on your bucket list? You're an odd one, dear," Stella responded, turning away.

Nora furtively rolled her eyes at the woman. She was just way too literal. Or was she? Sometimes, Nora thought Stella might be joking, but often her tone was entirely serious.

Stella dropped the chicken to the ground and looked at Nora. "Have you experienced your mother trying to communicate lately?"

Nora suddenly didn't want to stay and talk.

I don't think I can talk to Stella about this anymore. She just disagrees with me on what it is and keeps pushing the idea that it's my mom.

Nora wound her headphone cord into a tight circle and fingered it nervously.

"I don't think so. Since the last incident when I heard a rattlesnake in the storage room, it's been relatively quiet," Nora said.

"Yeah, I sensed some negative energy in that room last week. Was your mother ornery at all?" Stella asked Nora.

"No, she was the sweetest woman ever. Sometimes she might laugh at ornery things, but she wasn't a prankster," Nora said as she brushed a strand of brown hair away from her eyes.

"Maybe I'll go over there today after you leave for work and talk to whatever's in there. See if I can suss out something. Sometimes spirits respond and sometimes they don't. I used to be a practicing psychic many years ago, but then someone sued me when my prediction didn't turn out. So I decided to get out of the business. I still use my talents to help myself or family though." Stella obviously still held onto some bitterness from the ordeal.

"Um, sure. That would be all right I guess." Nora didn't think now was the time to tell Stella about moving out. "Sorry, but I need to get going, or I'm going to be late for work," Nora said.

"Yeah, well, we don't want that." Stella turned and walked back into the chicken coop. Nora headed back to her apartment, leaving the older woman to her task of collecting eggs, or so she thought.

Shortly after, Stella left the coop and walked quickly to the big farmhouse, holding a struggling chicken upside down, by its feet. Opening the screen door, in she went—directly to the usually chained door that led down to the dank, dimly lit basement. It was unusual for the door to be unlocked. She descended halfway down the flight of stairs and tossed the bird into the dark. There was the sound of a scuffle between the chicken and an unseen predator lurking in the shadows. Stella's feet zipped up the stairs as fast as they could take her. She pulled the door shut and locked it, swung the chain link fence closed, and then—to complete her measure of safety—clicked the padlock into place. Pausing for a moment in the hall to bask in the feeling of security, she took a breath, brushed herself off, and straightened her dress. Stella tightly held her crystal on its chain as she briskly walked to the sink to wash her hands. Victor should be up soon. She set a pot of water on for a cup of tea specially brewed to help calm her nerves.

Two hours or so later, a rap on the basement door startled Stella. She unlocked it and opened it, and out walked Victor. He said nothing as he sat down, looking comatose, at the wooden table. Stella and Victor sat at the breakfast table in silence for a while. Victor looked like he hadn't shaved or bathed in days and smelled like it too.

"How was your power session last night?"

"Fine. I'm wiped out," he responded as he lifted his teacup to his crusty lips.

"I told Nora I would go over to her apartment and see if I can figure out what is bothering her, but of course I have no intention of doing that. What story do you think I should give her?" Stella asked.

"Just tell her it's her mother and she needs to just accept it and give in already," Victor said.

The older woman pursed her lips and fumbled with her bracelet. "It's Jabon for sure. He can be quite sinister. I don't like dealing with him one bit. Your late father was a very ornery man. I never liked him when he was alive, and now in death, he's five times worse."

"I thought you didn't believe in evil, Stella," Victor said as he narrowed his eyes at the little woman.

"Yeah, well, I didn't consider your detestable father, I guess. Plus I don't want to be scaring Nora too much. She's already having a hard time accepting the spirit world." Stella's boney finger traced the floral pattern on her teacup. "Do you and John have the next gift figured out? Halloween is coming up fast, and we need to have a plan in place."

"Yes, we have it figured out. But that's all I'm telling you. You just do the inviting, and we will do the gift-wrapping," Victor replied with a smirk.

Stella got up and cleared the table. Stopping on her way to the sink, she turned back to Victor. "Are you cleaning up the chicken mess in the basement, or do I have to do that too?"

"I'm on my way to work on a wood statue in the shop. Besides, cleaning—I think that's your department anyways," Victor said with a sly grin.

Stella gave him a look, the one that says, "you're a real jerk," as she turned back toward the sink.

◆ ◆ ◆

Later that day, Stella sat reading in the front room. After a while, setting her book down on her lap, she looked into the woven basket next to her rocking chair and picked up the ugly rag doll with pins stuck in it. Flipping it over, she stared at the letters embroidered on the back:

J. S.

Stella's eyes darkened to an intense brown as she whispered the name of her old friend, pulled a needle out, then quickly plunged it back into the neck of the doll. Thoughts of the past came to Stella's mind. Memories of long ago when they had been the best of friends.

When life was simpler and more tangible, their parties of worship had been lighter in nature and not so dense and mordant.

Stella had never had a closer friend. They had shared everything, and their lives were intertwined, it seemed, at all angles.

Stella turned her wrinkled, worn face toward the window and envisioned memories of the past. She saw the two of them outside in the garden together, in sun hats and hippie braids, the smell of patchouli, lavender, and bonfire smoke wafting through the air. They were young, laughing to the point of tears and conniving jokes and pranks on Victor. The picture faded, and her memory morphed into the chapter when her friend had begun asking questions, when she just had to go searching for answers about their religion and lifestyle. That probing eventually caused her to leave Stella's world, creating a huge void. Pain beyond anything Stella had ever comprehended in a relationship. She had been closer than a blood sister to Stella.

Over time, Stella had allowed her hurt to transform into an ugly bitterness, a staunch resentment toward this woman. Forgiveness was not an option. It had never even entered her mind. Letting go would be admitting defeat, in a sense, and Stella was spitfire all the way through. If her friend wanted to leave, then there was not a thing Stella could do to stop it. But Stella *could* curse her. Somehow the voodoo doll and curses were a sick way of staying involved in her life. Stella had never fully thought of it in that way, but that pain was the reason she did what she continued to do after all these years.

Stella would not let her go. She could not let her go.

The bitterness had consumed Stella. For countless years, it was a cancer in her soul, rotting away any remaining bits of soft-heartedness. She had an addiction for hate and she had no desire to get rid of the drug. There was no reason for her to quit, none at all. Stella had once loved this woman with a deep friendship, beheld her closer than a sister. She couldn't love her anymore; the next strongest emotion was hate.

Stella's boney fingers twisted the silver needle deeper as she remembered the past; her eyes released warm tears. She tossed the doll with force back into the basket. Stella glared at it. She noticed herself weeping and wiped off her wet cheeks. Getting up, she left the creaky chair and the biting memories in the room.

◆ ◆ ◆

That afternoon, Jessa received an upsetting phone call from her mother. She had bad news about Jessa's grandmother. It seemed Joanna had fallen down a flight of stairs in her home and had broken her collarbone. She wasn't irreparably injured, but she was going to be using an arm sling for several weeks.

After ending the call with her mom, Jessa immediately called her grandmother. "What happened, Grandma? Are you okay?"

"Yes, I'm fine, Jessa. It wasn't too bad of a break! I don't know what happened. If I didn't know better, I'd say I was shoved down the stairs, but I'm pretty sure I left that dark past behind me."

"What past, Grandma?" Jessa questioned the older woman.

"Well, honey, let's sit and talk about that over scones and tea. It's not a great conversation to be had over the phone," Joanna replied.

"Sure, Grandma, sounds good. Do you need me to work extra hours at the tea shop for a while?" Jessa asked sweetly.

"That would be really nice, but I don't want you neglecting your other important responsibilities for my sake!" she cautioned Jessa.

"Don't worry, Grandma, I won't. Hey, I wanted to tell you that I'm rededicating myself to the Lord, as of last weekend. I decided this after a friend gave me an audit of how he saw my faith. It wasn't pleasant to hear, to say the least! Between that and the sermon I heard last Sunday, I know it's something I need to do, though I know it's not going to be easy."

"Well, that's fabulous news! I have been praying for you for a long time. I'm so pleased the Holy Spirit is pursuing you. You're right; it won't be easy. There are unseen forces that want to prevent you from following Christ in every way possible. We can sit down for lunch sometime and chat about all of this, if you'd like," Joanna said to her granddaughter.

"Yeah! I need to have that discussion sooner rather than later. There are some things I've been wanting to ask you about a friend who's having some supernatural trouble. Maybe you can help us with it? After you've had some more time to heal from your injury?" Jessa asked.

"Yes, honey, I do know a lot about that kind of thing, so yes, let's do get together to chat when you have a chance and when I'm feeling a little better!" Joanna replied.

The ladies ended their conversation with the promise to connect in the near future.

◆ ◆ ◆

Nora returned home from work, tired from the drama of people and everything her job demanded of her. She received a voicemail from a number she didn't recognize. It ended up being the owner of the duplex, her new landlord. He said the apartment would be ready to move into by the weekend.

Oh good, I'm ready to leave Deape Woods in the dust. But, now I have to break it to Stella... Not looking forward to that, at all. Ugh. Why do people have to be so difficult sometimes?

Unlocking her apartment door, Nora wondered if Stella had come over and done any research like she had said she would. Nora came into her living space, locking the door behind her, and set the glass bottle upside down on the door knob. She hadn't done the bottle thing since the last time the glass broke.

I'm just going to set up the bottle again as an extra precaution. Can't be too careful.

Pulling her hair back into a ponytail, Nora made her way into the kitchen. She brewed a cup of coffee, microwaved a burrito, and sat down at the table with the TV tuned in to a reality show. After finishing her dinner, which she decided was downright awful after the first few bites, Nora got out her fingernail polish and gel light to give herself a manicure. She chose a cream white and went to work on her nails.

About mid evening, Mr. Cooper began a little growl and stared at the door. Nora focused her attention on the door and was unpleasantly startled when a knock was heard. The motion from the knocking caused the bottle to fall to the floor, but it didn't break.

Nora cautiously asked who was at the door. A voice answered from the other side, "It's Stella!"

"Hold on a sec," Nora said. The "your-nails-are-dry" timer happened to go off just as she got up to let Stella in.

Stella, dressed in a purple, silky, one-piece jumper, stood in the doorway for a few seconds, wringing her hands as if she was putting on lotion, then said, "So, Nora, I think the entity is just your mother missing you. I talked to it for a while. It knows a lot about you, so it must be her. Just invite it in, maybe set up a cup of tea at the table, pretend like it's her sitting at the table with you. These spirits can be really helpful sometimes with information and such. Plus, it could be a source of comfort for you if you're missing your mother—and soon to be—your dad."

"I'm having a hard time just believing what I'm seeing. I really don't know that I'm ready to believe whatever is going on is actually my mother trying to communicate with me. But thank you for doing some digging for me anyway," Nora said to Stella.

Stella shrugged her shoulders, "Suit yourself young lady. I need to get back to the house; I have a pie to get out of the oven." With that, she swished her way down the stairs.

I don't know how she does that. It's as if she never touches the stairs, she's so quiet on them! I thought I was quiet with my footsteps, but I can't hold a candle to Stella.

Nora's freshly painted fingernails scratched her scalp in a nervous twitch. She locked the door, set the glass bottle back on top of the silver knob, and sat down in her thinking chair. Mr. Cooper sat down directly in front of Nora. She bent down and rubbed his ears, patting him. She softly told him that he was a good dog. And he was. He was a very good dog.

Later that night, when Mr. Cooper growled, it was not Stella at the door.

- Fifteen -

The Invisible Intruder

"The greatest prison people live in is the fear of what other people think."

~David Icke

THE MORNING, FOR NORA, came before the sun rose. Sometime after midnight, but before dawn, the dog's slow growl rattled Nora awake instantly. The feeling she had, sitting there in her bed, was similar to having the flu. You know you're going to vomit, but you're not sure when. Anxiety stabbed into her heart with full force as she silently reached for her weapon. Pulling her knees up to her chest, she set her other hand on Mr. Cooper's head, stroking him, hoping to calm him down, hoping he had just heard a rat downstairs somewhere or another dog outside.

The lamp was already on. Nora no longer slept without a light on in the room. It was security for her. The dark contained unknown things, unsettling things. Now it seemed the light also held things of mystery, but to her brown eyes, the light was more trustworthy than darkness.

Nora checked the little blue bedside clock. The red numbers glared 4:00 AM exactly. She hastily grabbed her phone and waited, this time with her camera ready. Nora waited, and she waited some more… and yet, nothing happened. No knob moving, no bottle dropping, no noise or scratches on the door.

How long should I wait? Maybe Cooper is wrong this time. I hope he is. I hope it's just a fluke.

Forty-five minutes felt like two hours to Nora. She had to use the bathroom. She got up and nearly fell as one of her legs gave out, having fallen asleep. Still clutching her Glock, she shuffled to the bathroom.

As she finished her business and washed her hands, she heard an unmistakable sound—a bottle dropping and breaking. Nora turned off the faucet. Trembling, she pointed her pistol around the corner of the bathroom towards the door. Déjà vu set in. Hadn't she just been in this position? In this same bathroom, peeking fearfully around this same doorway?

The dog was seated on the bed, his black ears cocked and alert, but he wasn't growling. He was focused on the closed door, not taking his eyes off of it. Suddenly, he began moving his head slowly as if he was following something in the room. Something Nora could not see with her eyes, but she fully knew it was there.

Nora felt goose bumps everywhere on her body. Her hands were now visibly shaking. Her phone was back on the nightstand; she wasn't feeling brave enough to come out of the bathroom yet.

Mr. Cooper began to lightly pant and then whimper, and then a low growl emerged from his throat. Nora knew the animal could see something she couldn't. The dog got off the bed, walked over to the doorframe, and lifted his leg, urinating all over the wall, the frame, and the door.

I don't even care about Cooper peeing on the floor, I have much bigger problems. But this isn't normal for Cooper—he must be really freaked!

Nora wondered how long she should wait before retrieving her phone from the nightstand. Watching the dog's actions told her a lot about the location of the invisible thing.

The animal jumped back up on the bed but did not sit down. Mr. Cooper was watching something near the front window. Nora finally gained enough courage and tiptoed over to the nightstand, swiping up her phone. Her entire body shivering in fright, she couldn't get the screen to unlock right away—first her fingerprint wouldn't work, and then she kept getting the key code wrong.

Of course, I can't get the phone to open when I need it the most.

Just as the camera app came up, something imperceptible came rushing through the room and socked Nora so hard it pummeled her to the floor and knocked her out cold. The lamp crashed to the ground; the bulb shattered. All at once Mr. Cooper began barking viciously and leaped off the bed in haste.

Nora awoke a few seconds later with her mind in disarray. Lying still, she felt something heavy on her. Straining her neck, she peered downward towards her feet. She saw the shadow of the black and white dog straddling her body as if he was protecting her. He was no longer barking but panting, his demeanor much calmer.

Nora looked to the side in the dim light and saw her phone laying among shards of sparkly glass remnants about three feet from her hands.

"What just happened?" she said out loud. Pulling herself to a sitting position, she found her head throbbing. Rubbing her neck, she repeated herself, "What just happened?" Mr. Cooper moved forward and licked her face. "Pleh!" Nora spit at the dog. "No licking my face!"

Nora's goose bumps had withdrawn from her arms and legs.

I think whatever that was is out of here… at least, for now.

Leaning over to pick up her phone, she wondered if she had managed to hit "record" on the camera before getting her lights knocked out.

Her phone opened in its normal fashion this time. She was upset to find that, once again, there was no evidence that these weird things were happening to her.

Setting her device back down, Nora pulled herself fully up. Her shoulder was in great pain. Walking into the bathroom, she saw in the mirror that her shoulder was dark red. There was going to be a major bruise. She entered the kitchen, brewed a cup of coffee, and opened the freezer. She used a zip lock bag and ice cubes to make an ice pack.

Sitting down at the table, sipping her coffee, Nora wondered if she might have dislocated her shoulder—it hurt that bad. Whatever rammed her was not a force to be reckoned with. Now what should she do? Would she go to the doctor and tell them she thought a ghost rammed her and body-slammed her onto the floor?

Oh yeah, that's believable. They would probably send me over for a psych evaluation and then give me a free trip to the loony bin when I get done getting my shoulder fixed up. Maybe I could concoct a story about slipping in the tub or falling down the stairs? Ehh, if that had happened, I wouldn't only have a shoulder injury, I would have other bruises to go with it.

Well, she could just tell them the truth… She didn't actually know what happened. Something rammed her and knocked her out. She didn't see it.

Nora called Trey and told him the news of the morning. "Do you have a doctor you can recommend? I don't want to go to the emergency room."

Trey gave Nora the name and number of a trusted doctor. "Okay, I'm a little worried now. You can't stay in that apartment another night. When did you say your new place would be ready?"

"This weekend, a few days out," Nora replied. "I'm going to talk to Stella today about moving. I'm not looking forward to it at all. So, wish me luck on that."

"Luck is wished. Do you need any help getting to the doctor? I can help you do that if you want," Trey offered.

"No, I think I'll manage it okay. Thank you, though. But maybe you can help me move my things this weekend?" Nora asked.

"Of course, I was planning on doing that all along. But I really think you shouldn't stay another night in that apartment," Trey said.

"Well, I'll think about it. Since these weird things have been happening, I've noticed that something big will occur, and then nothing for a while. But now that it's physical, this is a whole new ball game. I was afraid of it turning this direction… and now it has," Nora lamented.

"Well, I'm here for you, and so are Jessa and Nolan. Stay with one of us if you need to. We'll get this figured out." Trey promised he would check in with Nora later, and they hung up.

Nora dialed the number for the doctor, and later that day she checked into the physician's office.

The nurse checking her vitals, of course, popped the question. "How did your shoulder get such a nasty bruise?"

By this time, it was black and blue.

Nora didn't know what to say. "Um, someone ran into me, and I fell backward. It knocked me out for a bit."

"Were you playing football or something? This is an atrocious bruise for just a standard 'someone running into you,' " the nurse questioned further. "You sure someone didn't do this on purpose? Are you trying to cover for someone who is abusing you, hon?"

Nora hadn't anticipated the doctor diagnosing her injury as a result of abuse. "No, I'm not covering for anyone. I was just at a party, and someone came running through and bumped into me. I was just in the wrong place at the wrong time!" Nora responded to the petite brunette who looked like she didn't believe a word Nora was saying. And she shouldn't have. Nora was absolutely lying—and she was a horrible liar to boot.

As it turned out, Nora's shoulder was dislocated, and the doctor put it back into place. Oh, did that hurt! They put her arm in a sling, gave her a printout on how to care for her deep bruise, and sent her on her way.

As Nora came up the drive and coasted to a halt in front of her apartment building, she spotted Stella and Victor talking on the front porch of the farmhouse.

I don't want to talk to that man. I'm going to wait right here and see if he leaves first.

Nora waited until she saw the hefty man get into his Volkswagen bus and leave. Stella turned and walked back into the farmhouse.

Walking over to the house, Nora thought about what she was going to say. She knocked on the screen door, her bracelet jangling, and she heard Stella call out, "Come on in!"

Inside, Stella was seated at her crowded desk with a pen and a heap of paperwork. Her long fingernails were unable to pick up the edges of the papers.

"What do you need, Nora?" Stella asked without looking up.

Nora stammered over her words, not sure how to start the conversation well.

"I uh, need to talk to you about something," Nora gulped some air and then blurted, "I'm going to move out of my apartment this weekend." Nora held her breath and waited for Stella's response.

Stella set down her pen, removed her reading glasses, and turned her attention on Nora. "And, why is that?" she asked her a little coldly, taking notice of her arm in the sling. "And what did you do to your arm?"

Nora looked down at her shoulder and said, "Something was in my apartment last night, and it body-slammed me, knocking me out cold on the floor. I guess it must be a spirit, since I didn't see it, only felt it. It dislocated my shoulder, and the bruise is so epic, it could probably compete with world records. I can't do this ghost stuff anymore. It's now physically hurting me. This can't be my mother. She wouldn't act this way." Nora brushed her hair from her eyes and blinked hard, hoping Stella would react in a relaxed manner.

Stella sighed and thought for a few moments, tapping her fingers carefully on the stack of papers. "So, who have you told about this encounter?" Stella asked, unhurried.

Nora thought that an odd question, "Well, there's no way to tell the doctor what really happened, so I made up a story for him. I haven't been to work today, so I guess no one." Nora left out her conversation with Trey.

"Well, you can't just break your lease without any consequences, so here's what I'll do. You sign a legal paper that says you'll talk to no one about your spirit encounters here on this property, and I'll let you out of the lease early." Stella's brown eyes narrowed as she folded her hands and sat still, waiting for Nora's reply.

"Okay... Why do you need me to not talk about it? I thought you said it was normal and perfectly safe?" Nora questioned the older woman.

"Look, I want to rent out the apartment again. If it has a reputation for causing problems, then we won't get any renters. So, whether or not what has happened to you here is truth or not, we need your trap to stay shut about it," Stella said matter-of-factly.

Nora chewed on her lip, not certain whether she should agree, disagree, or ask more questions.

The gray-haired woman read the look on her face. "You've already been talking to your friends about all this, haven't you? Which is why you're hesitant to say you'll sign something?" Stella asked Nora.

"Well, I have talked some about it, but I don't think anyone believes me regardless of what I've said. It's not like it's a real believable topic," Nora managed to say.

"How about you just sign it and not talk any further about it," Stella snorted. "But, rest assured, if you *do* start talking about it, I will nail you to the wall. And I have my sources to find out about these things, so do not test me on it!" Stella hissed at Nora. She turned back to her desk. "I'll have the papers drawn up by this weekend when you turn over the key."

Nora decided she was being dismissed by Stella and politely said, "Okay, thank you." And she turned around and left.

Stepping down off the porch, Nora couldn't help but feel a burden lifted off her shoulders.

Rastus, the gorgeous gray kitty, sat off to the side of the porch and meowed. Nora stopped and bent down, motioning him to come to her for pets. He got up and meandered over to Nora as cats do, taking his own sweet time to get where he wanted to go. She stroked him and gazed out at the trees. This was a lovely piece of property, and she was going to miss it some, but it came with its own peculiar baggage that just wasn't worth the beauty of it all.

Now, to pack up her things. She hoped she wouldn't have any more metaphysical experiences before her final exit from Deape Woods. But hope, in many circumstances, can just be an elegant type of wish.

- Sixteen -

THE NEXT APARTMENT

"Reputation is what men and women think of us; character is what God and angels know of us."

~Thomas Paine

NORA DECIDED to stay at her apartment in Deape Woods for the next few days, against Trey's advice. If history were to repeat itself, there would be no paranormal activity for a while.

Retrieving her flattened boxes from storage and taping them back up, she thought about her short stay at Deape Woods and how it had begun to change the way she thought about the world and the supernatural. She had shown up here a skeptic, and now—she didn't know what she was—but she was definitely not a skeptic. Nor did she even hold the same basic beliefs she had before moving to Kingsman.

Nora wasn't a timid woman. She held her own when she needed to and, being single, that attitude came in handy on occasion. Beginning a relationship with Trey, her first time ever having a boyfriend, Nora sensed that she may have some trouble down the road with allowing him to be a hero for her. She had been single for a while and had adapted to being by herself and doing things for herself. She was independent. Not only that, she was an only child. Nora was not accustomed to sharing although she wasn't opposed to it. It just wasn't something that had often been required of her in life up till now.

Having the dog was right for her. He helped her think about someone other than herself, and he was a sense of security for her. In the predicaments she had been in during the last several weeks, Mr. Cooper was a huge source of comfort, especially since he saw things she could not. If nothing else, that comfort alone was worth every penny she spent on him. It was as if she was blind, and he helped her to see. Her attachment to him made her feel as though life hadn't existed before him.

Nora grabbed a framed photo off the shelf. As she paused to look at it, a rush of homesickness overcame her. Behind her folks in the picture was their old home, decorated by the climbing rose bush on the trellis, in full bloom with huge golden-yellow roses.

She had loved cutting those flowers as a girl and inhaling the scent from their soft velvet petals. Mom would get mad at her when she would trim all the blooming flowers off at once.

"Leave some on the bush, Nora. We want the outside to be pretty too!" her mother would say. Sometimes, Nora would have up to four vases of cut flowers in her room. She would hide some of them so as to avoid getting chastised for having "cut too many flowers."

She wrapped the frame and packed it in a box. Her thoughts lingered on her dad. She needed to get over to see him. She had missed last weekend, and now would miss this weekend because of moving. Looking around the apartment, she suddenly realized that most of this furniture did not belong to her. She was moving to a place where she would have to provide her own couch and table and everything else.

Rats. More money, more time. Oh well, at least I have my thinking chair, that's a start.

◆ ◆ ◆

On Saturday, moving day, Trey and Nolan showed up at 8:00 AM to help haul Nora's meager amount of stuff out of the spooky place. Jessa had to work at the teashop, as she had promised to step in for her recovering grandmother.

The day was wet and clammy. Yet, there on the front porch were Victor, Stella, and John sitting lazily, talking amongst themselves in hushed voices. Every once in a while, a cackling laugh would erupt from Stella. They just sat and watched the younger people empty out the apartment, never offering assistance. Their dark, cold eyes never strayed from the young folks, each of them busily crafting sinister ideas within their individual, malevolent minds.

I can't help but think those three are plotting something nasty. Why am I being so judgmental? I mean what have they ever done to me? At least that I know about. I just can't put my finger on it. It's only my bare assumptions and intuitions I'm working from. It's like smelling a dead rat but never finding it because it's in the wall. You smell it, and you know it's there because of the smell, but you can't see it because it's hidden from your eyesight. This is a dead rat in the wall. That's what this is.

After they had packed everything in their cars, Nora told Trey and Nolan about the document she was being forced to sign.

"Are you kidding me? That's the most ridiculous thing I've ever heard!" Trey said in disbelief. "They don't have any right to force you into signing any such thing. I'd skip it if I were you." Nolan nodded his head in agreement.

Nora sighed with exasperation. She wanted to keep a peaceful relationship with these people. If signing this silly contract was what they wanted, then so be it. But on the other hand, Trey, was probably right. They couldn't legally force her to sign a gag order. Nora lingered a little longer before heading over to the front porch to turn in her key.

Stepping up onto the porch, Nora's little leather boots clunked on the brown, wooden boards as she walked towards the devious-looking trio slouching in the deck's black wicker furniture.

"Hey there, here's your key," she said. setting it down on the little table. "And is there a deposit I could get back?" Nora asked timidly.

Victor spit out his drink, sputtering, "Deposit? You want your deposit back after you're the one breaking the lease? Uh no. You can sign this gag order and get the hell off my property!" And he continued muttering and complaining to his brother as Nora stood there in awkwardness.

Nora had no desire to argue with this man. Clearing her throat and avoiding eye contact, she quickly looked over the paper and signed her name on the line, knowing full well she might be missing something in her haste. After asking them if there were any other documents she needed to get—to which Stella sharply answered, "Nope!"—Nora pivoted and hurried off the porch.

Okay, time to fly! Ugh, I can't get out of here fast enough.

The vehicles left Deape Woods and headed for the highway. It took them only fifteen minutes to get to Nora's new apartment. The manager of the place met them there to make sure everything was to her liking. He also introduced her to the older lady next door, Francine Taylor—or "Fran," as her friends called her.

Standing at Fran's front door, Nora remembered that her new neighbor was deaf. Instead of an audible door bell, there was a blinking light within her home that signaled to her when someone was at the door. The property manager pushed a button, and they waited for just a few moments before Fran emerged. Nora smiled and shook Fran's hand. The older lady seemed jubilant to have a new neighbor.

Fran hadn't always been deaf. She had gotten ill when she was just twenty-one years old, and the nasty disease had stolen her hearing. She was able to say many things and could read lips as well. The manager gave Nora some printed information on sign language and told her to keep it handy in case she needed to communicate with Fran.

The manager added that Fran was his aunt and that he would be grateful if Nora would check in on her every once in a while, if she didn't mind.

"Of course, I would be happy to help out," Nora said as she shook the balding man's hand goodbye. The man pulled up his khaki high tide pants further and bid Nora and her friends farewell. He strutted to his neon-green jeep and drove away.

Back in the new apartment, Nora, Trey, and Nolan examined the new place before bringing in her things. The kitchen was spacious, with dark wooden cabinets and plenty of room in the center to place a small table. There was a wooden china cabinet built into the wall that would display dishes vertically. Nora was excited to make use of the cabinet, filling it with her prized, family heirloom china set.

There were two bedrooms, one bathroom, a little living area, and a short stairwell to extra storage space in a basement. In the living room, a large window faced out towards a grassy field—a perfect place to put her thinking chair.

While Nora fetched the smaller boxes, the young men brought in her mattress, box spring, secretary desk, and red velvet chair. They finished within a half hour.

"It looks like you could use some more furniture, Nora!" Nolan exclaimed. "Hey, my folks have a garage full of stuff they aren't using. I could see if they would be willing to give you a few things. I know there's *at least* one loveseat in there."

"Thanks, Nolan, that would be awesome. And thank you guys for helping me out today. There is no way I could have done it without you, especially with my shoulder the way that it is right now."

"Yeah, Jessa was saying you got a pretty bad bruise?" Nolan questioned her.

"Yes, it's really sore. It hurts something awful when I try and move too much." Nora pulled her sling off and showed the guys her trophy bruise. Both guys made a scrunched-up face.

"Ouch," Trey said. "You want me to kiss it and make it better?" he asked with doe eyes.

"Don't come near it. Just you guys looking at it makes me hurt!" Nora smirked back.

Nolan took off, promising her he would be back with some additional furniture. The rest of the day, Trey helped Nora get situated. They stocked the fridge with groceries and even made a trip to the local thrift shop, where they found a trendy, burgundy lamp—just right for her nightstand. They enjoyed chatting and goofing around as they worked to put things away in the new place. Nolan and his dad brought by a small kitchen table, and a green loveseat, which fit perfectly in the living room.

Nora and Mr. Cooper said goodnight to Trey and Joey. She locked the front door behind them and headed for bed. *Exhausted* was too weak of a word to describe how she felt. Pulling her hair out of her ponytail, she brushed it out in front of the mirror. She wasn't yet acclimated to this new place, and it would be a while before she was.

The duplex had been built in the eighties. It wasn't exceptionally elegant, but Nora didn't need a super nice place to be content. It was affordable and had more space than the last abode. There weren't many other houses close by, and Nora was grateful there wasn't a lot of noise from nearby traffic, similar to her last living situation.

Still, she had begun sleeping with a little fan next to her bed to help calm her nerves. Since all the unexplained chaos in Deape Woods, she found the white noise of the fan helpful in drowning out sounds that may or may not have been something to be worried about.

That night, Nora tried not to think about supernatural things. It was pretty hard to do when her shoulder was riding around in a sling. The sling was a constant reminder to her of why her shoulder was hurt in the first place. She didn't want to think about it for many reasons. The number one reason was that it was a source of great fear. She was a gun-toting woman, not afraid of much, but she couldn't use a physical weapon on villains she couldn't touch or see. That was quite an unsettling feeling.

I'm just hoping that whatever was going on in Deape Woods isn't going to follow me here. I need to be rid of that trepidation. People have always talked about some houses or buildings being haunted and such, but—of course—I've never believed in it till now. I'm doing my best to look at it logically! If there are such places that hold so-called ghosts in one spot, it would mean that when you left that place, the ghost would stay put and not follow people, right? I just hope the new landlord's comments about entities following people were untrue. Boy, do I hope he heard wrong.

Nora's thinking was only wishful thinking, nothing more. The shadowy roaming watchers from Deape Woods moved throughout the planet as they saw fit. They had their depthless eyes on Nora and wanted to break her into yielding to their powers. If nothing else, they would simply light the match of terror and abuse in her life. Just because she couldn't see them didn't mean that they weren't there.

◆ ◆ ◆

Nora awoke to her new residence and yet another Monday.

Why does Monday seem to get plagued with awfulness so often? Maybe we all just don't want another work week to start and so we exaggerate things that happen on Mondays. Or maybe Monday really does have an attitude problem.

The day started with a dead car battery. Fortunately Nora had a portable battery charger for cars, one of the few things she owned that belonged in a garage (if she'd had one). She used the handy little device to jump start her truck.

Once at the office, she opened her email to find several messages from unhappy clients, whose products were incomplete and past due. Since Nellie and Jamie were no longer playing for Nora's team due to their car accident injuries, the balls in several courts were getting dropped.

Nora walked over to Camilla's desk, assigned her three tasks, and asked her to report back to her when the tasks were accomplished. Camilla was wearing a pair of black jeans so ripped, they looked like they had been shredded in a cheese grater.

"Those ladies still out to lunch?" Camilla asked Nora. "I'm pretty sure they are eating at the 'Café of Never Coming Back.' We need to hire someone to take their place, or we're just going to have to work overtime our whole lives," the girl stated bluntly as she batted her dark, wing-tipped eyelids.

Nora cocked her head sideways, chewing on her pen. "I don't do the hiring, so I don't have much control over that. Let's just focus on what we can do now."

"Hey, did you ever meet that black man from that harvest party again?" Camilla asked Nora.

"No… I haven't," Nora said slowly, doing her best to not open up this topic again.

"That's a shame," Camilla replied, as she re-focused on her computer screen.

"Oh, one more thing—you aren't going on vacation anytime soon, are you, Camilla?"

"Nope, I already went somewhere this spring, so I won't be taking another vacation until next year. In fact, if I disappear on you all, I'm either real sick or got abducted by aliens! Please send a search party for me right away if I'm not at home sick!" she said with a sinister laugh. "Why do you ask?"

"Well, we're already having a hard time fulfilling our commitments on this team, so I just want to make sure no surprises are coming up." Nora began to walk away, then paused and turned back around. "Do you actually believe in alien abductions?" She regretted asking the question as soon as it was out of her mouth.

"You bet, I believe it. Maybe over lunch, we could talk about it!" Camilla raised both eyebrows gleefully.

"Uh, I may have plans for lunch today… and tomorrow, and the day after that," Nora said with a sly grin.

Camilla smiled back, "Yeah, okay. I got you. But, if you ever want to hear about my beliefs, I'm open to talking."

"I'll keep it in mind," Nora replied.

The rest of the day was spent putting out fires and filling in holes that her coworkers couldn't manage to fill in themselves. Nora didn't leave work until much later than her normal quitting time.

After arriving home and reheating leftovers, she fell into a deep sleep built upon the false idea that she was safe from the portentous, invisible beast that lived at Deape Woods.

◆ ◆ ◆

A person must use discernment, or they will fall prey to predators. Predators love it when their potential victims have no common sense and no scruples about them. They overtake their prey in an easy feat when their catch is voluntarily witless and can't make a judgment because of the fear of being judgmental. No, they do not desire for humans to use smarts, to gain knowledge about their foes. To evil, ignorance is the tastiest topping on mortals. It devours those humans who are cloaked in stupidity and revel in foolish notions, those who desire not to look any further for truth and who bury their heads in a hole, thinking their entire body is hidden. How unchallenging it is for the dark to digest the defenseless.

And those who are fighting back? Yes, it will accept the dare. It will enjoy the game of cat and mouse, and it will sit upon them like a festering boil, hoping to wear them down to nothing. To wear them so thin, they pop like a child's bubble. Until a person can grasp the concept that the power to defeat evil lies not within themselves, but of a cleaner, holier, mightier power; then and only then will the evil spirits be more easily crushed and trampled over.

The vexed souls who do not perceive the thin veil between them and the unseen authority are harassed and egged into ugly despair. Blinded and pushed into mental cages of indoctrination and showered with the propaganda of the darkness, they are suffocating, yet still alive in their body.

Nora felt it. She saw symptoms of the authority she could not see. She had yet to come to a full conclusion as her search for answers was not nearly finished. In fact, it had only just begun.

- Seventeen -

THE FOLLOWER

"What you are afraid to do is a clear indication of the next thing you need to do."

~Ralph Waldo Emerson

NORA STIRRED UNEASILY in her bed, adjusting her red body pillow and purposely keeping her sleepy eyes shut. Determined to not wake herself up, she did her best to return to the dream she had just been enjoying. Mr. Cooper was a lead weight next to her and was pulling the sheets off her. In her half-slumbering grogginess, she reached over to push the shaggy dog out of her space. Her small hands found nothing but air.

Nora opened one crusty eye and boosted herself up a little in the bed. In the dim light of her maroon table lamp, she saw no animal on the bed next to her.

Hmm... that's odd. I guess I must be pulling on my own blankets. It's nothing. I'm going back to sleep.

She turned herself to the other side of the bed and shut her eyes, doing her best to not let her brain wake up. Nora drifted back off into sleep.

She stirred again because her feet were freezing.

Now what…? I hate my feet uncovered! Why are they uncovered? They feel like ice packs have been set on them—why are they so cold?

Nora threw the blankets back over them and rubbed them together to try and warm them up.

After a few minutes of foot warming, she got up out of bed to use the bathroom. She came back to her bedroom and, finding the door closed, tried the knob. It was locked. Nora's heartbeat quickened.

Did that thing follow me here?

Her phone was in the now-locked room, and it was the middle of the night. She knew she hadn't locked the bedroom door. Nora went back into the bathroom, dug around, and found a bobby pin.

She straightened the pin out, stuck it in the little keyhole in the gold knob, and twisted it around until the lock clicked open.

Hey, this is a new place. Maybe I accidentally locked it. Right? That's a possibility.

Entering her bedroom, she called for the dog, who was sleeping on the new loveseat in the living room. Mr. Cooper took his time in coming. Slowly getting up and stretching out his back legs on the green couch cushions, he continued dragging them around the corner and down the hall.

"Oh brother," Nora rolled her eyes, "can you walk any slower?"

Nora switched on the tall, skinny vintage lamp in the corner of the room. A low light streamed out from under the fringed purple shade. She had found it at a yard sale a few weeks ago. Jessa couldn't ever pass up a yard sale, so Nora had been going to plenty of them with her blond, bubbly friend. This was the second light on in her room tonight.

Nora called the dog to come up on the bed with her. She felt safer with his doggy senses nearby. If there was something weird going on, Mr. Cooper would know it. He was a paranormal-detector of a sort.

I don't know what he's been detecting exactly, but it sure feels good to have him close. I don't entirely believe in this ghost junk, but there isn't any way I can say it's complete hooey. Something is there—the question is what*?*

Nora lay in her bed, tossing and turning. She finally looked at the clock; it was almost 4:00 AM.

Was it only coincidence that she had been repeatedly awakened by either herself, or some unknown entity, at about 4:00 AM? Or was there a reason it tended to be that time? And what could the reason be?

Nora was too tired to pursue her thought path any further. The rest of the night was quiet, and she slept soundly.

In the morning, after making some toast, Nora thought back to her experiences during the night before. She hated the feeling of going down the road of what-if's and assumptions. She just couldn't stop her mind from going there. Her mind drifted to what could be significant about her waking up at 4:00 AM. Was something waking her up at this time on purpose? Did it correlate to some other event that had occurred at the same time? She thumbed through her mental rolodex.

Oh wait, Mom passed away early in the morning… I have the files, I should look at them, just out of curiosity.

Nora descended into her small basement storage area and found the little, gray, metal file box of important papers. The box contained documents from her folks' estate as well as papers from past medical history. She found the file labeled "Mom's medical."

Opening it up was tough. All those bills and reports and test results brought back a not-so-distant memory of heartache. She shuffled through the pile. At the back of the stack was the death certificate from Almost Home Hospice. Nora touched the page with her index finger and stopped right below the time of death.

She read it aloud, "4:07 AM."

Nora swallowed, put the certificate back into the manila folder, and closed it. Putting it back into the box, she clamped the lid on tight, clicked the light off, and exited the basement.

Stella had claimed the paranormal experiences were her mother trying to communicate with her. The time would line up with her mother's identity. But how could she know for sure?

Psychics are supposed to talk with spirits and know things about paranormal stuff. Like that séance with Angelina Corte. Maybe I should just take it with a grain of salt and go see one, just to see what they would say. Maybe they could help me.

Nora opened the kitchen drawer and pulled out a phone book.

It's been a while since I've used one of these.

She turned to the pages of listed psychics.

How do you choose one? Let's see, Leon J. Moot, Selma Boulevard, Don Beasley, MindTrek Psychics, Get It Right Club, The Know It All Psychic… Who comes up with these names?

Nora had a hearty laugh, then sobered up and picked one.

She decided to go with a woman, as it seemed more comfortable, somehow, than a man. Calling the psychic's office, Nora made an appointment for later that evening, then prepared for another day at work.

◆ ◆ ◆

After a typical day running on the hamster wheel, chugging along to complete numerous software projects, Nora drove up to a small building. It displayed a neon sign that read "psychic" in bright-purple letters with the word "open" in pink right below it. One of the letters was struggling to stay lit.

I can't believe I'm doing this. How am I here at a psychic?

As she opened the door, she heard a jingling from a little copper bell, attached to the knob. Sitting at a desk was a middle-aged woman whose long blond hair was partially pulled back by a copper comb. She wore a solid purple tank top, tribal-print gaucho pants, a beaded belt, and pink lipstick. She smiled pleasantly as she got up and walked around to shake Nora's hand and introduce herself.

"Hello, I'm Jenna Stoob! You must be Nora? I talked to you over the phone?"

She seems normal enough. She's dressed in decent attire. I guess my only interaction was with Angelina Corte, and she may have just been over the top.

"Yeah, that's me," she said with a quick, nervous smile.

"Why don't you come on back to our sitting area and we can begin our meeting there," the friendly woman said, as she led the way to a back room, where four black leather tulip seats sat around a small round table, adorned by a vase of flowers. A soft purple lighting shot up from the floor, illuminating the bamboo plants in the corners, and giving the walls a lavender glow. The aroma of incense permeated the air, immediately flooding Nora's head with memories of Stella and Victor's party.

That smell makes me nervous. My armpits are sweating. My back itches. I don't want to be here!

Jenna and Nora got situated with cups of tea, and then, as Jenna was smoothing out her billowy pants, she asked Nora why she had come to see her.

"Well, here's the story in a nutshell," Nora began as she fiddled with her hands. "I moved here about two months ago and rented an apartment from a couple," Nora cleared her throat and felt nervous. "Then I started having weird things happen to me, almost as if there was a ghost in my place. I didn't believe in spirits when I first moved here, and now I don't know what I think. But, whatever it is, it's real, and it's freaking me out."

Jenna stared at Nora for a few moments and said, "Anything I say today is not guaranteed to be one hundred percent accurate. If it has to do with health, you must check with your doctor to verify. I need you to sign this paper saying you will not hold me responsible for anything said in our session."

Okay, that's weird. What's all this fine print? I guess it's normal; Stella mentioned getting sued when she worked as a psychic... Oh, just sign it and be done with it.

Nora scrawled her signature on the line and handed it back to Ms. Stoob.

"And then, if you'll just move over here and let me connect with your spirit... I want to just touch your hand; is that okay?"

Nora switched chairs and sat closer to Jenna, and the woman took ahold of Nora's hand. Closing her eyes, Jenna breathed in deeply and exhaled. The sound of a small water fixture dribbled and echoed in the wooden-floored room. Nora watched the woman and waited. Jenna kept her eyes closed and began her reading.

After a few minutes, she began piecing together information. "You are alone, though not fully alone. There is another spirit in your life, but it's not human."

Nora swallowed. "Yes that's my dog. At least I think it is."

"You have a parent who is not quite out of the picture. Do you have a parent who is sick?"

Nora nodded and said yes.

"There is a life-changing event coming for you soon, but it doesn't feel like it's going to be fun going through it. You may or may not survive it. I can't tell for certain. Someone close to you is going to die."

Jenna went on for a while, and then stopped, listening carefully. "The spirit that is following you feels like your mother." Jenna scrunched her face and looked strained. "She wants you to know she misses you. She's waiting for your father to die so the two of them can go to heaven together. Until then, she's following you."

As Nora started tearing up, Jenna opened her eyes and let go of Nora's hand, handing her a tissue.

"It makes sense that she's waiting for my dad. They were inseparable. Never apart. I can only hope to have a love like that someday... Plus, if it is her, that would also make sense—I think she keeps waking me up at the same time that she died." Nora didn't tell Jenna about her experience of being knocked out by the invisible bull in her apartment. She didn't want to give her too much information; she wanted to see what kind of knowledge and power this woman truly had.

"Well, dear, I believe we never entirely die. We are spirits walking around in shells that we call bodies. When our bodies pass, our spirits have to go somewhere. So they either cross over to the other side, or they hang out among the spirits that are still using their body shells."

The two women talked a little longer and then Nora's time was up.

"So, you're saying that I'll just have to put up with this entity until my dad passes on?" Nora asked Jenna, as they stood to exit the room.

"Well, yes. Or maybe you could talk to it and ask it to stop bothering you. Be kind to it. I believe it has feelings just like us. I don't believe in evil in the spirit world. I believe we humans can be capable of a lot of bad things, but most of the time, spirits are just very misunderstood.

"And I don't do exorcisms or any of that religious mumbo-jumbo. You're already in tune with this entity, and that's not something everyone gets a chance at having. Just trust yourself and don't let it scare you. In most cases, it doesn't involve any physical harm, although they *can* suck a lot of energy from you. So, if you notice yourself getting sick a lot or feeling run down and depressed, come on back in, and we'll do another reading and see if we can help that."

Nora thanked Jenna, paid her at the front desk, and left, mentally processing their conversation as she walked to her truck.

"In most cases, it doesn't involve any physical harm." Why didn't Jenna read that about me? If she really had powers, why couldn't she see what happened to me? Maybe these fortune tellers can't see everything, only some things. What am I saying? Am I admitting they have power then? Ugh! I'm driving myself crazy.

After starting up her blue F-250, Nora decided to make a stop at the teashop to visit with Jessa for a few minutes.

Once she arrived, Jessa was helping a customer, so Nora waited at a table until her friend could take a break. Jessa brought over a cinnamon pastry and a cup of decaf coffee. Setting the treats on the table in front of Nora, she wiped her hands on her vintage embroidered apron and sat down with a sigh.

"I've been working on the weekends and in the evenings to try to help out while Grandma is recovering. It's been exhausting!

I've missed talking with you, though! How have you been?" Jessa asked, sweeping her hair up into a messy bun and pinning it down.

As Nora told her about the move to the new place and how she thought the unknown entity had followed her there, Jessa listened, bright-eyed and attentive.

"So, I went to see a psychic tonight." Nora paused and looked around the café for potential satellite ears, adjusted in her chair, and continued. "The woman said that she thinks it's the ghost of my dead mother and that the spirit will leave when my father dies because she's waiting to cross over with my dad!" Nora said with some question in her statement. "What are your thoughts on that?"

"Huh," Jessa said, as she picked up some wiry plastic sticks off the table and started twisting and reshaping the little mess of wires mindlessly. "My grandma said she knew a lot about supernatural things. I've actually been meaning to talk with her about all this stuff. Maybe that could be a start?"

Nora nodded and said, "Yeah, I need all the help I can get."

"What are these things anyway?" Jessa held up the plastic sticks she was twisting.

"Those are my earrings," Nora said with a straight face.

Jessa turned several shades of red and said, "You just let me screw up your earrings while you sat there and watched me?"

Nora shrugged, "Well, I wanted to watch and see what new shape you made—you're so creative, you know? I figured I would walk out of here with new earrings."

They both broke out laughing.

"It feels so good to laugh, Jessa. You're the friend who makes me laugh the most! And I need that," Nora told the young lady.

◆ ◆ ◆

Nora dreaded going home. (That is, if the duplex could be called "home" at all.) Having lived in only one location growing up, she wasn't used to moving around. These flats felt a little like she was just on vacation and that she should be going back to her home in Colorado once again soon.

Moving from Deape Woods, she had hoped that she would be freed from the plague that seemed to be finding enjoyment out of harassing her. Nothing huge had happened yet, but her gut and sore shoulder told her that it was only a matter of time before it did.

Pulling into her driveway, the F-250's headlights shown into the white curtains of the extra bedroom. One of the curtains was swinging slightly as if someone had just pushed them aside.

Lovely, it's beginning early tonight.

Nora checked the time. It was 9:33 PM. She sat in her truck, hands on the steering wheel, and thought about what level of bravery she wanted to have at this moment.

I should've left some lights on in the house. I hate coming home to the house pitch-black. Should I pretend this thing is my mother? Should I talk to it and act as if it's her? Would this be beneficial to me?

Nora decided that if it could help her overcome her fear of whatever was in her space, it might be worth a try. Jenna had seemed to know some things about her, though Nora hadn't given her much information, and that impressed Nora. Maybe Jenna did know what she was talking about. What could it hurt to try?

Nora shut off the rumbling engine and pushed open the heavy, squeaky door of her blue Ford. Hopping down, the dog following, she heaved the door shut with one loud bang. Swallowing hard, she unlocked the front door, reached around, and flipped on the lights before walking in.

Wait a second, what if that was a burglar in my house, that was moving the curtains?

What was she being reduced to? That she either had something she couldn't see walking around in her house, or possibly a madman in there? Nora drew her gun and cautiously walked through each room. After checking everything thoroughly, she holstered her weapon, and on high alert, began to get ready for bed.

My nerves are really getting spread thin. Why would my mother believe that it's fun to bring distress to me? She would never have dreamed of acting this way when she was walking around in her body. Never. She was the kindest, sweetest woman in the whole world.

Nora mulled it over. She still wasn't entirely convinced that this harasser was her mother.

However, there was that time when it did sound just like her on the other side of the door. How could it do that if it wasn't her? But, then there were other sounds it made too. And those sounds were not human in any way. But do people change when they die? Maybe we do become more animalistic, or maybe our personalities change. They do change when we get sick.

Nora thought of her dad.

Who knows the answers to these questions? There has to be truth. Someone has to have the truth.

Nora was determined to find answers, even if it meant a lifetime of looking for them.

Unbeknownst to Nora, the white curtains swished away in the bedroom next to her, back and forth like a cat twitching its tail. Evil was planning its next vile move.

- Eighteen -

The Cookies

"Yesterday is gone. Tomorrow has not yet come. We have only today."

~Mother Teresa

THE SECOND WEEK OF OCTOBER arrived with a thick, eerie mist. As the dawn began to glow brighter, Nora let Mr. Cooper out for his first potty break of the day, then sat in her red velvet chair next to the big front window with a hot cup of rich, creamer-sweetened coffee. Looking out into the white haze she imagined that maybe the ocean was just beyond the thick curtain of fog, that if she stepped out the door she would surely hear the constant roar of the ocean's big voice.

She had been to the sea a few times during her childhood. She remembered the pungent smell of fish and the salty wind whipping her hair in her eyes, sand that stayed in the car's carpeted floor mats for what seemed like years, and walking on the beach with her dad. He had held her bucket while she shouted with glee as she spotted another shell. Was she six or seven? She filled the bucket and requested to take all of those dirty pieces of ugly shell back home. She didn't know they were worthless to most people. She only knew that they were irreplaceable to her. Young Nora had found those unique treasures on the seashore with her strong daddy there to protect her from sneaky waves and stinging jellyfish—of which, like most children, she was oblivious. She saw him standing there in his khaki pants rolled up to his knees, white knit sweater with a blue collar, and brown fedora. He was patiently holding the plastic bucket, a piece of seaweed hanging off the side, smiling at his baby girl—exuding pure joy.

Far away, Nora saw her mother in a wide-brimmed white sun hat on a beach blanket. She was reading a book, lying on her stomach with her feet crisscrossed in the air. This memory was pleasant. It was pure and complete, and it made Nora smile unconsciously in her morning stupor.

Mr. Cooper broke through the mist and came within sight, dissipating her seashore memory, bringing her back to here and now. Nora let in the hairy, wet animal, drying off his paws with a towel as he came through the door.

Just after she had shut it behind her dog, a knock came at the door. Nora wasted no time in opening it for Trey.

"Oh great! You remembered to bring the flour and eggs! I was going to send a text to remind you, but I completely forgot," Nora said coyly to the handsome young man.

"Of course, I remembered. I'm a responsible type of man," he said, running his hands through his dark hair. "I even brushed my teeth and—gasp—*flossed them*!"

Nora laughed. "Well, I was worried about that; you know, many men aren't that responsible to be brushing and flossing…"

"Yes, I know. I work with a lot of those kinds of men." Trey rolled his eyes to match his comment.

Trey and Nora began working on two cookie recipes in the eighties-style kitchen. They joked around, tasting the raw cookie dough, then chiding one another for eating it. The dog sat and waited expectantly for his sample, which never came.

"No, Coop, this cookie dough isn't good for you! How about a milk bone?" Nora tossed him a dry dog biscuit. He sniffed it and left it on the floor for later.

Trey and Nora put some still-warm cookies on a plate and went next door to give them to Fran.

After they pushed the specialized door bell, it didn't take long before Fran opened the scratched-up wooden door and let the two younger people inside. Setting the plate on a little, yellow, metal, vintage table, Fran grinned a semi-toothless grin and signed *thank you* along with a slurred verbal "Thank you." The three of them stood there, smiling with uncertainty at each other, not sure how to communicate.

Fran motioned for them to sit down in the worn vintage chairs and bustled into the kitchen, setting some water to boil. She placed a stack of drawings in front of Nora. They were diagrams of different sign language phrases. Nora took forever to find the right signs to say, "How are you?"

Fran motioned with her arthritic fingers and verbally said, "I'm okay." They all did their best to talk through a simple small-talk conversation, but it wasn't easy.

Fran stood abruptly, retrieved a notepad, and drew out what looked like a ghost. She penned on it:

> IT SEEMS LIKE STRANGE THINGS HAVE BEEN HAPPENING SINCE YOU MOVED IN. DO YOU FEEL THE SAME?

Nora sat up taller and cleared her throat. Taking the pen, she replied:

> WHAT SORT OF THINGS HAVE YOU NOTICED?

Fran wrote again:

> LIGHTS ARE TURNING ON AND OFF, I GOT LOCKED OUT OF MY BEDROOM, MY FRIDGE DOOR WAS LEFT OPEN, AND MY CATS ARE RUNNING AROUND LIKE THEY ARE NUTS. MAYBE IT'S JUST ME AND I FORGET THINGS. IF YOU SAY YOU HAVEN'T NOTICED, THEN I MAY GET MYSELF EVALUATED FOR MEMORY LOSS.

Nora took a moment to think through how much she should share with her new neighbor, then wrote back on the scratch pad:

> IT'S NOT JUST YOU. I THINK MY MOM'S GHOST FOLLOWED ME FROM THE LAST APARTMENT.

Fran looked solemnly at Nora. The older woman slid her rickety wood chair back to stand, the worn metal feet scratching along the floor. She retrieved three dainty red china cups from the open cupboard, filled them to the brim and set the steaming tea down in front of Trey and Nora. She sat down with her own cup, then picked up the pen and began writing again:

> I THINK I NEED TO CALL A PREACHER OUT IF THIS GETS ANY WORSE. I HAVE NEVER DEALT WITH UNRULY SPIRITS BEFORE, BUT IT'S SCARING MY CATS AND ME. AND HONEY, I DOUBT IT'S YOUR DECEASED MOTHER...

Fran stared intently at Nora with sad but worried eyes.

Nora and Trey conversed a little longer with Fran using the written method. Finally, they got up from the table after promising that Nora would check on the older woman at least once a day.

Walking back to Nora's side of the duplex, Trey and Nora were a little surprised to find that all of the kitchen cupboards and drawers were wide open. Nora checked for the dog's whereabouts. She found him sitting on her bed, panting. Trey looked at Nora, wide-eyed as he began closing all the doors and drawers.

"Well, I guess, looking at this positively, you can now see I'm not crazy after all and I haven't been making all this up!" Nora stated.

"I never thought you were crazy. But Nora, you have to admit that things like this are never fully understood and grasped unless you experience it firsthand. That goes for anything, not just paranormal things..." He glanced around the kitchen again. "Do you think your food is safe?" he asked with an inquisitive look.

"It's never made me sick so far. Besides, if this is a spirit, I can imagine that they must be everywhere, right? So, how could you ever trust any food to be safe if you start going down that road? Besides," Nora continued, "I can't just start believing this thing is poisoning my food. That would push me over the edge for sure. According to the psychic I saw, this is my deceased mother haunting me, and she wouldn't poison me," Nora said.

"When did you go see a psychic?" Trey asked Nora his eyes narrowing in question.

"This last week... I didn't mention it to you?" Nora frowned and breathed in big. Clearing her throat nervously, she mumbled "Yes, I went and saw someone."

Great, now he's going to think I'm hiding stuff from him. How did I forget to tell him? What a birdbrain I am.

Nora pulled her hair back into a ponytail and proceeded to tell Trey all about the visit with the psychic and her most recent conversation with Jessa.

Trey and Nora lounged around for the rest of the day, chatting and munching on cookies and other snacks. It soon came time for him to head home.

"If you want me to stay overnight, I can. I don't know how I could be helpful, but you know I would do it," he said, his green eyes focused on Nora.

"I know you would. How about you just keep your phone charged and not get upset at me if I call you in the middle of the night?" she said with a sweet smile.

"I wouldn't get mad at you for that," Trey scoffed. "Just be careful with this spiritual stuff, Nora. I'm not fully on board with the 'it's your mom's ghost' theory."

She gave him a grateful smile and a quick hug. They parted, and the night passed uneventfully and without any emergency phone calls.

◆ ◆ ◆

The next day, Nora drove to visit her father in Astor. She had prepared a plate of freshly-baked cookies to take to him. Walking in the door, Nora was greeted by an awful shrieking coming from a room down the long hallway, paired with the smell of a sterile environment. Glancing to her right, she saw several nurses running towards a room—which, she supposed, was the source of the shrieking.

As she stepped up to the wooden receptionist's desk, a bushy-haired brunette seated behind her computer smiled and said, "How can I help you? Sorry about all that screaming. It's a resident who is now afraid of the toilet, and she has begun a habit of crying out in fear every time she flushes it. And I mean every time." The shorter gal adjusted her name tag; on it her name read RUTH.

"We have to tranquilize the poor thing sometimes just to get her to calm down! We might have to just lock the bathroom door to help stabilize her."

"Ah, that's really sad," Nora replied, adjusting her headband with a small frown. "Um, I'm here to visit my dad, George Miller."

The receptionist shifted in the squeaky black office chair and attacked her keyboard with quick fingers. Every once in a while, she paused to read, then her fingers flew over the keys again.

What on earth could she be typing? Is she still helping me here or what?

Glancing up at Nora, Ruth asked, "Now… has someone called you yet?" Ruth bit her lower lip and waited for Nora to respond.

"Um, no… what did I need to be called about?" Nora replied carefully.

The woman held up one finger to indicate that she wanted Nora to wait. She picked up a phone receiver and, with the butt of a pencil, punched three numbers into it.

"Hi, I have George Miller's daughter here; can I get the nurse on duty to come to the front desk, please?" Then she hung up the telephone. "He will be right up!" She smiled briefly, then left the desk and went into a back room.

Okay, that seemed a little secretive. Ruth isn't telling me much. That can't be good.

Nora stood there alone and waited. It took what seemed like forever for the nurse to finally get to the front desk. A thin man with a small mustache and a blond ponytail walked up to Nora, wearing light-green scrubs and carrying a clipboard. He introduced himself and stuck out his hand. Nora shifted the plate of cookies to her other hand and shook the man's hand. He suggested that they go sit at the little coffee table in front of the big stone fireplace in the entry way.

"So, I'm not the doctor—he isn't on duty today—but I have been apprised of your father's medical notes as I have been his nurse for the last week. I'm sorry you didn't get called sooner," the man said, adjusting his glasses on his nose. "It's been chaos around here." Nora held her hands tightly together and braced herself for the worst.

Would you just get to it already?

He began by clearing his throat. "Your dad has shown some decline this last week in his demeanor. On Tuesday, he got angry at another resident and threw his bowl of pudding at him. We restrained him and got him to calm down, but he has refused to eat anything since.

"It says in his records that he does not want to be resuscitated or kept alive by machines. We've been giving him IV fluids, but he rips out the needle after about five minutes of the treatment. He's withering away fast… it's a good thing you're here today."

"Well, I don't know why you guys didn't call me," Nora said in disbelief.

The nurse continued, "Our residents do a lot of shocking things, and we don't have total control sometimes. Our job is to keep them as comfortable and safe as best as we can. If we called you about every little thing, that could start to drive *you* mad. Now, sometimes patients will do things like your father where he refuses to eat and drink, but it will only last a day or two. We just never know. But you're here today, and I was about to call you."

Nora breathed in big and exhaled slowly. "So, is he in his room then? Can I see him?"

"Yes, of course, you can see him. In fact, many times a loved one can get a patient to snap out of their funk. So, by all means, let's go see him!" the nurse said.

While they headed in the direction of her father's room, Nora asked the man, "How long does he have if he refuses to eat and drink?"

The nurse slowed his pace and tapped on his clipboard. "I would say maybe a week, and this depends on if we can keep fluids in him, and a feeding tube. If he keeps rejecting the lines, it could be two days or less. Eventually, he will become so out of it that he will be too weak to even know if the IV is inserted.

"I would say we might already be there. Then, there is the waiver about keeping him alive. So I'm not sure that we aren't breaking a rule in hydrating him with the IV. You'll need to decide whether we should continue hydrating him before you go today."

Nora blinked, swallowed hard, and nodded.

They made it to George's room. He was resting in bed, sleeping. His graying hair was greasy from not showering. His skin looked ashen in color, dried up and thin.

The nurse stood there for a few moments and then told Nora, "I'll step out for a bit and go check on another resident. I'll be back shortly." He left the room.

Nora set the plate of homemade cookies on the bedside table, then she pulled up a light-weight fabric chair and moved it closer to the bed. Sitting down, she reached for her dad's hand. It was cold and bony feeling. It didn't feel or look like her father's hand. Looking around the dismal room, there wasn't much in the way of a sense of home. There was the mantle clock and a picture of her sitting on the dresser. The curtains were a floral brown color. The window framed a scene of evergreen shrubs along a gravel path. With as much as he seemed to enjoy the bird bath view in the common room, Nora regretted not having a bird bath put right outside his private room.

Looking back at her father in the bed, Nora began talking to him as if he could hear every word and might answer her back. She told him all about her paranormal experiences, her job, her friends, how she didn't know whether an afterlife or spirits or powers or God existed or not.

"Dad, I just don't know. I'm afraid of what I don't know. I'm scared for what that means for you and mom if I believe in any kind of existence after death. I just wish that I wasn't being plagued by mom's ghost—if that's even what it is. Do you know that the psychic said mom was waiting for you? It's a lovely thought, but who can know for sure? Do you like my new gray sweater?" Nora asked, looking down at her top and pulling on the detail. "It has a bird on it, 'cause I know how much you like birds, Dad." That was all she could say, as tears started to burn her eyes. She felt a lump in her throat and nasal congestion coming on. She knew her heart was starting to grieve the loss of her last parent. In all actuality, she had been grieving ever since he was diagnosed, but maybe this was a different stage of grief.

This really did feel like the last goodbye, and it was painful.

George's nurse came back to the room. Seeing Nora leaning over the bed and bawling her eyes out, he decided not to disturb her. He saw this scene often, spouses and children in extreme sorrow as they say their final farewells, but not as often as maybe he should have. Many patients wasted away, never seeing their loved ones, even for a single visit.

After Nora's sobs subsided, she glanced at the clock. It was past dinner time and time for Nora to leave.

She kissed her dad's cheek once more and said, "I love you, Dad. You can go and find Mom now; you belong with her. Don't worry about me. Just let go and rest in the spirit world, if that's the truth of it." As she turned towards the door, she heard her father's voice call her name. Whipping around, she walked back to his bed. His crusty eyes were barely open, and he weakly reached for her hand.

"Write this down," he told her in a weak voice. "Ephesians 6:12." He repeated himself a few more times before he slowly faded back into his sleep.

Nora jotted the message down, unsure how to spell the foreign word, squinting through her puffy red eyes. She was uncertain what it meant. Was it a code for something? Her dad had loved to do crosswords and puzzles, so maybe it meant nothing, maybe it was just something from his fading memory.

Nora left her father's room, and went to find the nurse to say, "I don't want any extra things for my dad to keep him alive any longer. He told me repeatedly he did not want to be on life support or any type of machine. However, I do want you to keep the IV in his arm. Can you please give me the consent papers if I need to sign anything? I need to get going."

Nora was done. She did not want to be here any longer.

The nurse gave Nora the paperwork, telling her he would call to give her updates and to let her know when her dad passed away. He assured her that they would keep him comfortable and watch him carefully for coherence.

Nora felt numb as she waited to be buzzed out of the building. Walking to her truck, she opened the door to let the dog out. Nora wasn't hungry at all, though she should have been; she hadn't eaten since breakfast. Her stomach was in knots. She wished that Trey was with her to drive her back home. Nora stopped for drive-thru coffee before leaving the town of Astor. She was in no mood to talk to the overly happy barista.

"And how has your day been?" the younger girl asked with a smile so big it made Texas look tiny.

"I was just visiting my dad in the nursing home; he's dying." Nora felt odd just saying it.

The girl's smile deflated, and her mood immediately shifted to empathy. "The drink is on us tonight, girl. I'm so sorry you're having a bad day."

Nora thanked the girl and her truck slowly crept out onto the highway for the long drive home.

A bad day? How about a bad several months? Oh, I'm being too hard on her. How could that coffee girl know what goes on in other people's lives?

Mr. Cooper sensed her wistful attitude and moved himself over next to her on the worn, leather bench seat. Staring at Nora intently, he leaned into her, slathering a big, wet, sloppy kiss across her salty, tear-ridden cheek. Nora didn't reprimand him.

"Thanks, Coop. I love you, too."

The crooning of Dolly Parton soothed Nora's exhausted heart as she surpassed the speed limit on more than one occasion without realizing it. The thought of bed was both a welcome and unwelcome thought. This time, she had remembered to leave a light on in the apartment. But, a fragile light bulb in a wooden-necked lamp could not hold its own to the concealed noxious scourge that was ready to expose itself fully to a mere human.

- Nineteen -

The Faux Mother

"Fear is pain arising from the anticipation of evil."

~Aristotle

DRAGGING HERSELF into bed that night, Nora stared off into space, thinking about her emotionally draining day, and—like so often happens—rabbit trails developed, splitting her thoughts. Her harried mind started running along to notion caves where she found herself unable to remember how she ever got there in the first place.

I need to turn my mind off. I'm so spent, yet here I am wide-awake.

Nora felt the black and white dog, whom she had invited up on the bed with her, lift his head up off the blankets. She held her breath as she turned her attention to him, hoping he wasn't detecting any strange phenomena.

There in the dim light, mere moments felt like minutes, and Nora's rabbit trail thoughts ended abruptly as she focused intently on her dog.

Mr. Cooper's deep brown eyes were fixed to the left corner of the bedroom. He didn't move a muscle for several minutes.

What… is he looking at?

The tall lamp in the opposite corner of the room flickered its tiny light.

Nora had a hard time sleeping in the lit bedroom. She could sleep better in the pure dark, but over the last several weeks, she hadn't been able to sleep in the dark because of the unknown messing with her. So, either way, she wasn't sleeping well.

Nora stroked the dog's head, mostly to comfort herself. He eventually laid his head back down. Nora fell into a light slumber, still shifting and tossing every now and then.

A few hours later she was awakened by the dog's slow, low growl. Anxiety grappled her awake; she abruptly sat up. Propping herself up with some pillows and rubbing her eyes, she followed the dog's gaze, which was now intent on the closed bedroom door.

Nora switched on her bedside lamp and grabbed her phone. Checking the battery, she saw that the phone was dead.

"What? I never plugged it in! Of course. Standard procedure," she mumbled. She reached down for the phone charger cord, trying to not move any closer to the door, and ended up falling out of bed onto the cold floor.

Boom!

"Ouch! That hurt!" she yelped.

Wincing from the stinging pain, Nora pulled herself up in haste, plugged the phone in and quickly got back into the warm bed.

Mr. Cooper broke into a pant, and in between that and the intermittent growling, she guessed trouble was there with them.

Here we go again. Be brave, Nora! Just be brave; you can do this!

She did her best to give herself a shot of encouragement, knowing in her heart that she was deathly afraid. Nora tried not to stare at the door. She told herself over and over she was not scared, but that was like eating a whole box of donuts and trying to believe it wouldn't make her sick. She was lying to herself to maintain calm.

Thus began the waiting game.

Nora's stomach twisted and burned. Its rumbling mimicked the sound of a fireworks factory in the process of exploding. A horrid smell was beginning to permeate the room. It smelled like something that had been dead for quite a while. Nora picked up a book and tried to take her mind off things. The sound of the gold knob turning was almost enough to make her vomit. The dog was up on all four legs now, erupting in vicious barking. Nora pulled him close and shushed him, trying to calm him. Picking up her gun, she checked to see if it was ready to fire, and waited with the barrel pointed at the door. The knob continued to twist. Slowly and mechanically it twisted.

"Mother, is that you?" Nora asked nervously towards the door. "Hello, Mother?" She repeated the question a few more times.

I'm nuts. I've gone mad. I'm actually hearing myself calling to this thing!

Suddenly, the knob-twisting stopped. Nora watched, her eyes trained on the door knob, her imagination working feverishly against logic. During the next ten minutes a thick, white, foggy substance began seeping into her bedroom from underneath the door. It appeared to be a purposefully slow-moving, tangible mist. Nora knew the fire detector in the hallway was working. She had watched the property manager check it when she moved in, so whatever this was wasn't a fire in the hall. All at once the door flew open with such force the knob punctured a hole in the wall. A chilled breeze blew around the entire room, noticeably lowering the temperature of the air by several degrees.

Nora was paralyzed in fear, unable to move. It was as if she was watching herself in her own horror movie. Then, mechanically and methodically, the door slowly shut itself, latching back in place. Something was now in the room with her. Something that was loitering in its translucent, foamy mist, intentionally taking its time to allow neurosis to build.

Nora backed off the bed towards the opposite wall and window, gun tight in one hand, pulling the dog by his leather collar with the other.

What is this?

The corner lamp was picked up by something unseen and flung with fury towards the wall. The bulb shattered, glass splinters littering the floor. Nora, fear pulsing through her entire body, still couldn't see what was behind the power. Shivers ran down her spine. The dog was now silent but alert. Somehow the animal knew he was no match for the unseen trespasser. Nora stood there, pinned in the corner in her oversized t-shirt and purple pajama pants, hair disheveled and jaw slightly ajar as she observed the milky white substance regroup itself and form into a pillar of humanlike physique.

The apparition's facial structure morphed into something that resembled her late mother. The grayish, glowing spirit formation said nothing but hovered still in the corner of the bedroom. It was taller than Nora by a foot or more and had no legs, just a draped, drippy bottom half.

Nora's eyes were huge.

Is this really Mom's spirit? It does look a little like her. What should I do now? My phone is on the nightstand and there is no way I'm walking near that thing to get it. Nope, no way. I'll just wait to see what it does. Maybe it will just go away.

The ghost's face was only somewhat human in nature, and its coloring was like the coloring of a corpse. Its hair was pulled up in a tight bun like her mother had worn her hair, its hair shone a tinge of red. But the thing's eyes were not her mother's eyes. In fact, she really couldn't see its eyes at all. Where its eyes should have been, there were piercing black pools of nothing. Someone once said that the eyes are the windows to the soul. These eyes were empty yet filled with an uncomfortable amount of confidence that was unequivocally married to evil.

Nora locked eyes with the spirit, feeling as if it was reading her mind, agonizingly unwrapping the very fabric of who she was. She could feel it sucking energy directly from her.

Nora looked away briefly, but her eyes were compelled to return to the unbelievable floating essence.

The dog held still but growled steadily. Nora had him by the collar, holding him close to her.

"What do you want from me?" Nora asked the ghost with a shaky voice. She waited. The ebony eyes never blinked and never took a break from their piercing stare. The translucent creature cocked its head sideways, as an animal does when it's listening carefully.

Who are you? Why are you here?

Maybe that was a better question.

Nora was cold and hot all at the same time. Her legs were shaking, and in her frightened hypnosis, she didn't notice it.

Oh, what am I doing? I don't know what to do! Don't show fear, Nora. Contain your fear!

The thing opened its mouth and out came a voice that sounded somewhat similar to her mother's. "I'm your mother,

Nora," the floating shape replied with an inhuman hiss. Its perverted smile revealed a set of white, razor-sharp teeth. Throwing back its head in obvious delight of the fear it was causing Nora, it began laughing in a most grotesque way. Within seconds the voice melted into another voice—sullen, wicked, and deep.

It lifted its hands towards Nora, its long skeletal fingers baring two-inch-long daggers where fingernails should be. Gradually, the facial structure of the spirit transformed into the most hideous, horrid, unrecognizable face. Its skin, if you could call it that, became wrinkled and flabby.

This is getting out of hand—it's going to kill us! How can I make it leave? I'm desperate!

"Leave!" she screamed in fear at the entity. Grabbing a book off the nightstand, she thrust it at the floating spirit. The book sailed over the bed, through the apparition, and landed on the floor

"Go away!" Over and over she screamed and then sank to the floor, pulling up her knees, curled up with the dog in a bar-less cage in the corner of her bedroom.

Peering up, she watched as the malevolent imposter called her name, beckoning her to come nearer with its slithery, lizardish voice. She was terrified—paralyzed—she couldn't move, but at the same time, she felt the desire to obey and move towards the spirit.

Should I just give into this? If I obey it, will it hurt me? Why does it want me?

She felt a tug of war inside herself—the presence of defeat against the desire to fight against the surrender to darkness.

Nora watched in a weary daze as the shape looked down toward its breast. Both its scaly, white, clawed hands grabbed ahold of its chest as if it was wearing a cloak. Slowly, it began to peel back its white, milky, plasma substance, which opened to a black cavern. Out came crawling hundreds of large, black, hairy-legged spiders. The spiders were as big as the palm of Nora's hand. They were scrambling down the ghost's form, plopping onto the floor, and scampering up the wall, covering it in complete blackness. Soon the entire room, including Nora and her dog, would be overtaken and suffocated by spiders if she didn't act fast.

Nora looked around the room at her escape options.

I could make a beeline for the door, but given its track record, it will be locked.

Nora looked to the window right next to her. The bottom of the window was at chest-height. Still, she decided that, no matter what, she was going out that window. She pulled the end table nearest her toward the window, but found the window itself was old and rusty, and—with the exception of an inch or so—was refusing to open. Nora's tears flowed as the sound of the spiders' clicking feet got louder and louder and the evil demon cackled, watching Nora writhe in its ugly vortex of fear.

With all her might, she pulled and pushed at the tiny opening of the stubborn metal window frame. The frame left gashes in her hands, rendering them torn and dripping profusely with blood. The desperation of escaping had shifted her into fight or flight mode.

Come on you stupid, dumb window! Open!

Finally, the window gave just as Nora felt sharp stings on her feet and legs. Spiders were now crawling up her pant leg, and Mr. Cooper was yelping and thrashing about crazily, trying to get rid of them. Nora pulled herself up into the narrow window opening and called for the dog to follow her up onto the makeshift step table.

Cooper needed no second prompting. After Nora jumped down away from the room, the dog clumsily found his way out as well. They ran as fast as they could from the open window and stopped next to an old shed, afraid to turn back towards the dark house. Both Nora and the dog had felt the spiders dissipate immediately after leaving the room.

It was dark and cold outside; a wild animal was rummaging around in a half-empty trash can nearby. Nora crossed her arms tightly to retain warmth and strained in the dark to see whatever was dumpster-diving.

I hope that's just a wild animal in the trash… There is no way I can wake up Fran; she can't hear anything. My keys are in the house… The truck cab. I don't think I locked it tonight.

Nora and Mr. Cooper climbed into the quiet cab parked in the wide, gravel driveway. Nora pushed down the tall knobs, locking them in the truck. Gazing in the dark towards the front of the house, she saw no movement nor strange light. Nora dozed lightly, only out of sheer exhaustion, off and on until dawn broke into the night sky.

Nora wished that what she had experienced the previous night had just been a nasty dream, but she knew it wasn't. It was as real as the cold truck cab she woke up in. The cuts on her hands and welts on her legs were a terrifying reminder of just how real it was.

I know without a shadow of a doubt, that thing is not my mother. The psychic is wrong and so is Stella.

Nora's whole body felt like it had been beaten. It ached as if she had the flu. She opened her creaky pickup door and sat up, rubbing her sore neck and back. From the looks of the sky, Nora could tell it was still quite early.

Nora wondered if she should call Trey so early in the morning. But, in all reality, he was only a source of comfort to her; he couldn't actually protect her from this evil thing. Nora cautiously tiptoed onto the front porch, then reached under the doormat for her spare key. Trying to be as inaudible as possible, she unlocked the front door and flipped on all her lights in her apartment. When she had gathered enough courage, she went back to her bed and climbed into it, pulling the soft blankets tightly around her. Mr. Cooper followed without prompting, laying down on the floor, between the door and the bed. With him in front of her and the door on the other side of him, she again drifted into a very light and troubled sleep.

Though she was both fearful of staying awake and afraid to go to sleep, she couldn't resist what her tired body was requesting. She slept and woke much later than she had intended.

Because she overslept, Nora was late getting to work. Her body throbbed. Mentally, she felt spent before even starting the work day. She had no excuse that was believable enough to use with her manager. The spider bites were now barely light-red bumps. Her bandaged hands hardly spoke of her night of terror. How trapped she felt. She had no one to understand the horror she had been enduring, no one to help her understand why this was happening to her. Stella and the psychic claimed to know what this poltergeist was, but they had been wrong in saying that the spirit meant no harm. Nora knew that this thing in her home was up to no good—in the worst way. She was feeling depressed, to say the least, and even around her friends, she felt somewhat alone.

Her cell phone rang as she was walking in through the door of the office building. It was the memory care facility. She answered it and held her breath.

"Hi there, this is George Miller's nurse checking in with you, just giving you an update on him. He seems the same as last night, no response to anything. We are giving him the IV as requested. I, or whoever is on duty, can give you a call later this evening as well."

"Okay," Nora said. "I'll take the day off work tomorrow and come sit with him," she replied to the nurse.

"I think that would be wise," said the man on the other end of the line, and he hung up the phone.

Nora sat down roughly in her chair, plopping her bag down on the desk in front of her. Scanning her work area, she breathed deeply and paused to adjust to work mode.

It's too much. All this at once is just way too much. Maybe work is good for me right now to take my mind off things.

Pulling up her pant leg, she rubbed the itchy red spider bites.

This happened to me. Now that I'm fully a believer in apparitions, the next step is figuring out the truth of what they are and how I get rid of them.

- Twenty -

The Witch at The Door

" 'Tis now the very witching time of night, When churchyards yawn and hell itself breathes out Contagion to this world..."

~William Shakespeare

THE MONTH OF OCTOBER was climbing quickly towards Halloween. The message spread through the office that the party-planning committee had decorated over the weekend in plastic toy skeletons and little sheet ghosts. Sitting down at her desk, Nora was greeted by a paper sign someone taped across her screen. BOO! it said.

Nora ripped it off without even blinking and threw it in the recycling bin. Nora's emotions were way too raw to interpret the sign as cute or funny. She had never liked Halloween, and now—after the last few weeks—she disliked it even more. Furthermore, why would anyone believe that some life-sized, nasty-looking witch that moves and cackles is fun? This very spectacle was set up by the front door with a black plastic witch's cauldron containing candy. It made no sense to Nora.

Getting herself a mug of hot tea, Nora chatted briefly with Camilla, who was also in the kitchen.

"So, do you think that fake witch by the door is fun, or cool in any way?" Nora asked, brow furrowed in question.

Camilla finished chewing, swallowing a mouthful of cookie, and said, "It doesn't bother me. I know that witches don't actually look like that in real life. Basically, the whole idea of witches looking like that was born from long ago when all those inquisitions and religious wars started. King James I of Scotland was a big instigator of it; he even wrote a book on demonology. Witches had struck fear into people. There was a period of time when people hunted down anyone they deemed was involved with witchcraft, hanging them and then burning them. They searched over the accused for any sort of spots on their skin like warts, moles, birthmarks, or deformities and claimed it was a mark of Satan."

Camilla paused briefly, then bit off another chunk of cookie, crumbs trailing down her black dress. Camilla swept them off, onto the floor for the cleaning crew to sweep up later. She continued her spiel.

"There was one guy—I can't remember his name—but he actually tried to make himself a career from hunting witches down and convicting the people who were accused of witchcraft. He used illegal interrogation and torture tactics. Sleep deprivation was his favorite to get them to confess they were a witch, whether or not they were one. These people literally wanted to die by the time he was done with them and probably, most gave a false confession just to end their torment. That guy watched more than one hundred people hang in the period of about two years and got paid well for doing it. Many of those people weren't witches at all. Most of the real witches hid their craft well so as to not get caught. I know a lot of this 'cause I watched a documentary about it a few months back."

Nora listened patiently, sipping her hot tea silently. Every once in a while, she absentmindedly used the top of one foot to rub the spider bites on the opposite leg.

Camilla knows a lot about this stuff; I feel somewhat ignorant.

Camilla kept jabbering away, encouraged by her awareness that Nora seemed genuinely interested in her knowledge.

"You know, many believe that the killings also could have been fueled by people who just didn't like certain people, and they started accusing whoever they didn't like, just to get rid of them. I think we have modern 'witch-hunting' government agencies that do stuff like that, but maybe not hunting actual witches, though."

Camilla briefly took a break and sipped her own drink. Sweeping her purple strand of hair behind her ear, she tilted her head and thought about her next round of speech.

"Personally, I think stories, folklore, and propaganda painted witches in a nasty, frightful way to scare people and to try to keep them away from witchcraft. So, to answer your question, the ugly witch dolls and pictures are just leftovers from the past. To me, they are just a symbol of a brutal time in history. Most people still associate the word 'witch' with some toothless hag with pointy fingers and a wart on her nose. I mean, come on, I get it that messing around with spirits and all that energy can take its toll on your body, but to think all witches look that way is preposterous!"

"That's an interesting take," Nora replied. "You know, what's strange is that you never see *male* witches in these pictures or decorations or in general."

"That's because the witches' Wiccan religion consists of mostly women. I don't know why. Maybe men just like to practice on their own more and not be a part of a coven. There is the term 'warlock' which is often used for male witches, but it's considered kind of derogatory within the Wiccan community. The word means *oath breaker*. Also, many from the Christian world called them warlocks long ago because it also meant *liar*. So, I'm guessing most male witches don't like to be called that," Camilla said.

"What's with the black robes?" Nora walked over to the counter, planning to add some sweet to her tea. She accidentally added way too much sugar.

Camilla answered, "I'm pretty sure that Wiccans believe that the color black is a mesh of all the colors and wearing it allows them to soak up all the vibes of nature and energy more wholly. But, the idea that witches wear all black all the time—this is another myth. Witches wear all colors of robes. Then, on the other hand, some more 'Goth' younger folk maybe just enjoy the shade of black because it fits how they feel and want to represent themselves." Camilla shoved in the last bite. "I have to be in the conference room in like two minutes."

"You know a lot about this subject!" Nora said.

"Yes, I do. I dabble in the art of it quite a bit. It's fascinating to me, and I feel like I belong in the esoteric society. It fits me like a glove," Camilla said, grabbing another snack out of the vending machine.

It fits her like a glove… I'm not sure if she completely understands the enormity of the power behind her esoteric society. But maybe she hasn't been shown the ugly parts of it? Maybe some people don't experience the ugly parts of it?

Nora thanked Camilla for the history lesson as the young ladies meandered down the hall and then went their separate ways.

Back at her desk, Nora texted Jessa to ask if she would come find her before she left from work. Jessa responded with a thumbs up emoji.

At the end of the work day, Jessa stopped by Nora's desk on her way out. Nora greeted her with a smile and a hello.

"Hey, I want to talk to your grandma and ask her about paranormal stuff, like we talked about. I'd also like to bring Trey along, if that's okay. When would be a good time to do that?" Nora asked the blond girl.

"Yeah! I'm meeting her down at the teashop to talk about business at seven. Come on down; we can sit and discuss it for a bit," Jessa said, a bobby pin poking out of her mouth as she smoothed and re-pinned a few stray hairs.

"Okay, that sounds good, thanks. Hey, that's a super cute jacket you're wearing, by the way. If you ever get tired of it, I want it next!" Nora told Jessa with a wink.

"Thanks, girl! It's one of my favorites, I may never get rid of it!" Jessa smiled back, zipping up the brown, faux leather coat decked out with strands of lace and random patches. "I'll see you guys down there!"

Nora used both hands to straighten a stack of files on her desk while watching Jessa walk toward the exit, past the old, ugly witch dummy. The mechanical thing came to life and made Jessa jump. Jessa jokingly slapped at the thing and then left the building. Nora continued to watch as Camilla walked past the witch doll. Camilla stopped, took some candy out of the cauldron, and unwrapped it while watching the thing cackle and move its limbs. She put the empty wrapper back in the pot, then walked out the door.

Camilla is a curious girl. I never see her with any friends. I suppose the workplace isn't a social event, but still, she seems likable enough. Maybe she's just the type who doesn't like or need people as much as others. I can understand that independence.

Nora met up with Trey for a quick bite to eat before heading over to Tea and Me. She told Trey about her most recent visit with her father and about his refusal to eat or drink. Nora hadn't yet told Trey about last night's events.

I'll tell him at the teashop. I have to tell him, but I just don't feel like it's the right moment.

A half hour later, Jessa, Nora, and Trey sat in mismatched chairs talking and laughing around a cute, little wooden table with a white lace tablecloth. Nora pulled her chartreuse wrap sweater tightly around her; the yellow made her hair look brighter. She couldn't fully relax, weary as she was from the prospect of having to rehash her terror over and over.

Joanna Shepherd came through the door a little after seven, wearing a soft, blue knit hat with a small, silver flower pin. She pulled off her coat and hung it on the dark, wooden coat rack. Waving at the younger adults, she carefully made her way toward their table and stopped halfway.

"Hey kiddos, I'm going to grab some decaf tea. Do you guys want any? It's on the house," she added.

All three eagerly accepted the offer, so she headed back behind the counter to collect a little tray of hot tea and some baked goods. It was just like Joanna to throw in extras. She loved to give and showed people her love for them through service. This was a trait she had gained from undergoing tragedy. Joanna's husband had died ten years ago. She had been a widow for a while now and found herself comfortable with it. She was certain she would never remarry.

Her late husband, Bennett, was a man who had spoiled her rotten. In her mind, no other man could measure up to him. She'd had a fulfilling marriage with Bennett and missed him almost every day. Joanna did her best to think positively when she missed him. Otherwise, it could cause her to become depressed and sad.

Bennett had passed away one winter, after slipping and hitting his head on the ice. Every time Joanna stepped onto the ice, she was reminded of that cold winter day that shut the door on the most sacred relationship she had ever experienced. She never got to say another word to her best friend, her lover, the man who adored her.

It had taught her that life should never be taken for granted, and that, at any given moment, she may never have another chance to say what she needed to say, to do what needed to be done, or to love who needed to be loved. To have the gift and privilege of carrying out the message of love in this world—this is something a person appreciates more fully after observing death's custom of jerking away our loved ones with one snap of its steely fingers.

Death changed Joanna. It always changes people. Sometimes it brings about unwanted change. Sometimes it opens our eyes and hearts to things of which we never knew we were capable. We adapt to it, or we die too, at least emotionally. We must go on in this dimension and carry on holding what was once a reality, now just a memory.

One can never fully know the deep pain of a lost loved one until they traipse through that uncut trail themselves. No one can take the journey for us. We must go alone, with only our machete, hacking away at the thick jungle vines of our minds, uncertain if our broken hearts will keep pumping, or just give up. The days of loneliness are long. The feeling of being locked up inside ourselves and wondering if anyone else understands and hating the world because we are pretty sure it doesn't—this is hard to overcome, but it's possible.

Joanna was never one to be dishonest or incapable of love and affection, but she had always been careful and comfortable. However, after the unexpected death of her husband—her best friend—anguish had changed her to become more raw and emboldened. And that rawness was united with a new clarity about the fragility of life. Sure, she grieved. It was difficult and painful working through a broken heart. But Joanna knew that it was a mistake to allow herself to halt in one emotional location. It was not wise to wallow within the depression and anger that could squeeze the life from her like a python and its prey. She had to keep moving forward to find the doorway out of her darkened, heavy soul.

Joanna set the tray down on the table. After passing out the cups of tea, she set the pastries in the middle of the table, then set herself down and breathed deeply. Looking around the table with a broad smile, Joanna touched the arms of Nora and Trey as she refreshed her memory regarding their names. Sprigs of gray hairs popped out from underneath her blue hat, and her eyes sparkled as she oozed acceptance and love to the young adults.

A person just couldn't help but instantly take a liking to this older woman. Nothing is more contagious than a soul that is on fire for the beautiful side of truth and echoes the sparkling gleam of hope. It's the authenticity that encapsulates a willingness to point out the fine-line cracks in our seemingly perfect surface and acknowledge the obviousness of the gaping holes from our mistakes. This soul is to whom we listen and from whom we learn.

The four shared small talk and laughter as they began a long conversation about their individual lives, their journey so far, and the reality of ghosts. Joanna—in all her wrinkles that told a story of maturity, experience, and wisdom—was about to introduce Nora to a life-changing way of living, thinking, and doing.

The young people had no idea where this older woman had been. Joanna was merely one woman on a planet of millions who had surrendered herself to the higher powers. Historically she had served two different higher powers, two different authorities. She had sold herself to the Most High, but not before she first saw, trusted, and believed. Joanna held treasure, and she was about to give it away.

- Twenty-One -

JOANNA'S STORY

"Yes and No are the two most important words that you will ever say. These are the two words that determine your destiny in life."

~Unknown

JOANNA ASKED THE YOUNG ADULTS about their jobs, families, and how long they had lived in the area. She listened with interest, and when the conversation drifted into silence, Joanna looked to Jessa.

"So, honey, you said you all had some questions about supernatural things? How can I help?" She lifted her cup to take a sip of tea.

"So, Grandma," Jessa began, tucking a strand of blond hair behind her ear with her orange fingernails, "I don't exactly know what experience you've had with ghosts and stuff. Mostly because the subject makes me nervous, I've always avoided talking to you about it. But Nora has been having some things happen to her that she can't really explain or understand. So we were wondering if you could give us some advice on how to get through this situation, and maybe give us your perspective on it, or share what kinds of things you've experienced?" Jessa asked, with honest blue eyes.

"Yes, of course. Where do you want me to begin?" Joanna asked. "Or would you rather start with your questions, Nora?"

Nora cleared her throat. "Why don't you give us a little background of your story, and then I'll tell you what I'm dealing with?" she suggested.

"Fair enough!" Joanna nodded and breathed deeply. "Okay. I feel that my story is best understood if I start at the beginning.

"I was born and raised here in Kingsman. I had one brother, Carl. (He died about fifteen years ago from a lung infection.) When I was about sixteen, our parents drowned in a boating accident. Life was really hard after that. Both my brother and I were taken in by a family that also had a girl my age, and she and I became best friends. After high school graduation, neither my friend nor I wanted to go to college, so we stayed in town. We both got jobs and basically just lived average, non-eventful, mediocre lives. We got an apartment together, and we were like sisters, sharing clothing, makeup, and secrets. We were best friends.

"When we were both about twenty or so, this was the early seventies, we went to the county fair together. Both of us dressed in flowy sundresses and cowgirl boots. Neither of us had many friends that were men. It wasn't that we were unattractive; it's just that we had each other and we weren't being chased by any young men. That changed for both of us when we went to the fair that day. We sat together, watching the rodeo, in the grandstands. Behind us, a couple rows up, there was a group of three boys that apparently found us interesting.

"They began bugging us by throwing popcorn at our backs. My friend turned around and gave them dirty looks, but that only fueled their sass more."

After a deep breath, Joanna continued, "After the rodeo was over, the boys came down, stood directly in front of us, and asked if we would go out to dinner with them. The look on my friend's face was comical—I knew she was thinking, *You've got to be kidding me!* But I knew how to handle her and calm her down. We knew each other well.

"We ended up eating at an outdoor burger joint in town. The boys paid for our meals. And my friend, being the feisty one, ordered more food than she could eat just to spite them for being stinkers at the fair. I think she ordered just about two of everything. She always had a hard time forgiving and letting things go.

"I assumed that as she got older, maybe she would get better at it. I later learned I was wrong about that, but I don't want to get ahead of myself here." Joanna wrung her hands and looked down at the table as she dug into her memories. She sipped her cup of tea and slowly set it back down, pondering her next thought.

"That day changed our lives forever. Sometimes, looking back at certain events or choices we made, I think to myself, what if we had just said no? Or in some cases, what if we had only said yes?

"The leader of the pack was tall and handsome and was a few years older than us. He didn't single out either of us girls but treated us both the same. He flirted with both of us. We ended up beginning a relationship with the boys, friendly and innocent enough at first.

"The guys lived together on a piece of property a little ways outside of town. They had a small house they all shared. The home wasn't great, but it was livable. They hosted parties and get-togethers often on the weekends, always inviting us girls. The parties started out as camping events with campfires and potlucks and such. Very much the hippie era. We girls loved our bell bottom jeans, and in those days we wore our hair long and straight."

Joanna coughed to the side, covering her mouth with her tight-fisted hand. Clearing her throat, she continued.

"Both my friend and I started falling for the same guy. Neither one of us would tell the other that we wanted him. We didn't want to have that problem or conversation. I think we just played a game to see which one of us he would choose. He ended up picking both of us." Joanna stopped and sipped her tea as Nora, Trey, and Jessa eagerly awaited the rest of her story.

"I know it sounds odd that one man would or could date two different women at the same time, but that's how it ended up happening. Over a period of a year, the parties sped rapidly down the slippery slope of drugs, drinking, and experimental sexual encounters. Things were being smoked and snorted that put us all out of our minds. We were all stoned and had no clue what we were doing most of the time.

"We thought we were all after peace and tranquility and free love given to all. Somewhere, things took a turn, and a veil began to lift to show us things from a deeper spiritual dimension. We all naturally want to worship someone or something. I know now What we were made to worship. But then, I thought I was a part of something that was going somewhere. Subconsciously, I wanted to be a part of something bigger."

Joanna's lips twisted as she paused, and the four young adults held their breath, waiting for her to continue her story.

"The following year, the boys built another, bigger house—and a barn—and invited us to come and live there with them, rent-free. Of course, we jumped at the opportunity and left our apartment. Both my friend and I shared the same man in and out of the bedroom. And we stayed the best of friends for another four years or so.

"As we all were busy experimenting with new things to try and open up the spiritual world, the man we both thought we loved became more and more enthralled with the Wiccan movement. It seemed so innocent and quite fun, actually, as my friend and I had never dabbled in such things, and in our drugged hippie minds, we embraced it wholeheartedly.

"Neither one of us knew anything about what we were getting into, but we had no guidance from any other sources that opposed it. And, thinking about it now, I really don't believe that an opposing view would've stopped us anyway.

"Eventually, our house began to turn into a coven, or a haven, of new age education and indoctrination. My friend and I ended up quitting our day jobs. We devoted ourselves to our new religion in worshipping creation and the various gods and goddesses. We believed there was no evil in the world. That's what we believed. There was only negative energy that needed to be pushed away.

"But, as time ticked away, life began to flicker in dark shadows. It was unsettling. The man we were both sleeping with delved deeper into vile matters, pressuring my friend and me to be people and to do deeds that we weren't thrilled about. He became abusive. It happens all too often when an abuser starts the abuse slowly… We couldn't see what was happening to us; our minds became warped and lines were blurred about what was right and wrong. We ended up believing that what was happening to us was normal.

"Our commune began to make sacrifices of animals. I don't know if we were still considered Wiccans by this time. We started from the basics of that religion and transformed into something much darker. The Wiccan religion was a doorway we opened to a way of life, a way of thinking that we never knew could be tangibly reached. Events were starting to happen that none of us could explain, to people who hadn't been there at our parties, things of supernatural power. Memories I wish I could erase out of my mind forever. I did things that I am too ashamed to utter aloud.

"We stayed at that commune for about six years in total. Gradually, both my friend and I slipped into numbing depression and eating disorders. The man we were dating insisted we stay trim, so we vomited up our food, to be able to eat and still stay very thin. We drugged ourselves with all sorts of things to try to feel something positive; being sober wasn't an option. Soberness brought with it overwhelming depression. I can't even remember significant portions of that time of my life because my mind was so gone so often."

Joanna picked up a croissant and began pulling it into little pieces, lining the rim of her plate with them. The three pairs of eyes watched her two aged hands work together on the pastry. Joanna took another deep breath and forged ahead in her story.

"Both my friend and I had several abortions. Honestly, I don't even know how many..." Joanna's eyes filled with tears, and her voice shook in remorse. "The abortion clinic knew us on a first-name basis. We didn't tell our partner about our pregnancies because we worried he would make us keep the babies. Both of us were afraid to be mothers—and, also, we didn't want him as our children's father. So, we made up stories about where we went and covered for each other while we recovered."

Joanna dabbed her eyes with a napkin and cleared her throat.

"About five years into this nightmare, both my friend and I attended her grandmother's funeral. Her grandmother was a Christ-follower, so her funeral was held in the large stone church here in town. My friend asked me to come with her for support, and so I did. We sobered ourselves up from being high for a short time and sat in a pew together, hoping it would get over quickly.

"The preacher who gave the eulogy that day combined it with a message of hope that led to my life being changed drastically again. This time, the change was for the better. It's customary to speak of the different realms and dimensions of our world at funerals. There we all are, facing the fact that sooner or later we're all going to be lying in a box with people standing around us, staring awkwardly. We're all going to perish, but the truth be told, most of us have an enormous amount of fear about death.

"The preacher talked for what seemed like forever. My girlfriend couldn't sit still for more than a few minutes. She grew abnormally fidgety almost immediately after the preacher began his speech. She began having heavy coughing fits, got up, then waited outside. I believe now the demons inside her were fearful, and that's why she couldn't stay in the service. They were refusing to listen to a gospel message. I know now that I had a demonic possession too, but for some reason, God's grace bound them while I sat there, and I was allowed to take in the message He wanted me to hear.

"As soon as the service was over, I found the preacher and asked him if I could meet with him and talk some more about questions that were beginning to build in my mind. Of course, he said yes, and I began secretly meeting with him and his wife once a week. It took a lot for me to get myself to the meetings. I was always late and sometimes even missed them entirely. There was so much opposition to making it to the meetings, from a car stalling, to me suddenly becoming sick. I felt the war internally too but didn't fully grasp what it was."

She felt at war... this sounds similar to what I felt with that nasty thing in my room. Joanna has been through a lot. I never knew that people lived this way. I'm beginning to think there is a lot *I don't know.*

Nora shifted in her seat, poured some more tea into her cup, and filled the cups of her companions.

Joanna kept her story going. "It took me several months to decide that Jesus was my answer out of the deep pit I had helped dig myself into. Throughout that time, I sobered up a bit and began to see things more clearly, to see them for what they were. I was procrastinating on talking to my girlfriend because I wasn't entirely sure of what I believed, and I didn't want to stir up unwanted attention from her or especially from our partner, who had anger issues.

"The preacher and his wife were kind and caring people. They were the type of people who knew their calling and answered it well. They loved people right where they were at, not just when people got to where they could or should be. When I was in the slums of the depths of despair, I felt their genuine, nonjudgmental love for me. They had no condemnation towards me. They simply cared for me and gently pointed me to the right path. They offered to arrange a place for me to live if I wanted out.

"After one night, a particularly nasty ceremony at our cult plantation, I felt terribly alone and utterly conflicted. The burden upon me was heavy. I wanted to drink and drug myself into oblivion. I was borderline suicidal.

"That night was the longest I remember ever having been through. I felt the spiritual war going on inside me. It was as if a rough-roped noose was tightening around my neck. I felt evil clawing at my mind and its poison stinging my soul. I was sure the choice to leave would be literal suicide. I had to weigh what I really wanted, but my drugged mind was unable to make logical choices.

"By midnight, I stopped using and drinking and allowed myself to come back into a slight state of sobriety. That night, as the drugs began to wear off, I found myself standing a few feet from the sacrificial altar with the remains of something or someone dripping onto the dirt floor.

"The scene was grotesque. My life was grotesque. Realization began to creep into my mind; I backed away slowly and then ran. I didn't know—and I didn't *want* to know—what I had been a part of. I didn't want the guilt to be something more I had to carry.

"I left the house very early the next morning. As tired as I was, I had packed a few personal things. I went to the preacher's house and knocked on the door around five in the morning. They opened the door in their bathrobes and messy hair and welcomed me inside, making me a cup of hot coffee. I sat at the kitchen table, tears streaming down my face. My hair was greasy in need of a wash, and I hadn't showered in a week. I was shaking and scared and wearing nothing but an oversized t-shirt and some flip flops. I was a complete wreck.

"Seeing me shivering something awful, the missus retrieved a warm bathrobe for me and some of her own slippers. She bent over and put my nasty, dirty feet in them.

"Through my tears, I told them that I wanted to accept Christ as Lord of my life and that I was scared to death of the choice. I could barely say the words. I had a hard time getting them out, as if something inside me was purposely holding them back. They prayed over me and while they did, I felt an internal disruption like I have never felt before. I couldn't sit still, I moved away from them, crawling into the corner of the kitchen like a scared wild animal. Yet they kept praying and commanded those demonic spirits to come out of me in the name of Jesus Christ.

"After several minutes, I came into a much calmer demeanor, and then they encouraged me to talk to Jesus for the first time. I did, and I told Jesus everything I felt at that moment. Then I confessed that I needed him and wanted the Holy Spirit to live in me. I remembered a talk we'd had about something important people do when they want to follow Jesus. I asked the preacher if I could get baptized. He said, 'You bet! I'll get my keys, and we'll go to the church now.' I asked if we could go to the lake, and they agreed.

"It was sometime in the late morning on a day in July; we drove to the lake. It was just me and the preacher and his wife standing there on the beach of the lake. The three of us stood there, him on one side of me, and her on the other. Their hands were on my shoulders, and I stood there bawling like a baby, salty tears streaming down my face while the cold, little pebbles on the bottom of the lake squished between my toes."

Joanna stopped, the lump in her throat rendering her unable to speak. The young people waited quietly. Jessa began to tear up. Joanna continued, sounding congested, while tears streamed slowly down her face.

"We slowly waded out into the cold water. The preacher prayed over me and dipped me into the clear lake and then brought me back up into the sun. That humble man helped me wash my sins away.

"When I came up out of that life-giving experience, his sweet wife was standing beside me in her wet jammies, messy hair going every which way, with a heart as big as the body of water we were standing in, singing Amazing Grace. As we waded back to the shore, we listened to her beautiful voice carry across the water.

"My tears were now of Joy. My burden was lifted. I felt lighter than I had in my entire life, right then. My shackles were gone.

"I knew that my life wasn't going to get any easier; from what the preacher had said, it would probably get a lot harder. But now, I had a power that was greater than he who is in the world, and I would learn to use that to fight on my behalf. The preacher said my biggest weapon was going to be prayer, and he was right."

Joanna took another sip of tea and looked into the faces of the young souls at the table. They all sat still and solemn, each one in awe of the story she was telling them.

"I decided to go back that same day to my commune. It was now or never. I had to tell my best friend that I was done, that I was leaving. I had to do my best to convince her to do the same. I cared a lot about her. Friendships like what we had don't come to us very often, if ever. I knew that I was possibly saying goodbye to her for the last time.

"Driving back, I was in complete dread. I wrestled with fear and sadness and over and over asked the Lord to protect me, to help me know what to do and what to say. I wasn't actually new to meditation and prayer-type things, but I was new to this God.

"I took my friend outside into the garden. I told her what I had decided, that I was leaving and wanted her to come with me. She broke down in tears for a few minutes, then suddenly a sharp look crept upon her face, her eyes darkened, and she backed away from me slowly. She screamed at me to leave, and started hurling insults and swearing at me. I knew she was hurt by my leaving, and I didn't know how to fix it. Her reaction to me was odd—she wouldn't come near me—as if I was, all of a sudden, unclean and unfit to even be near her. Her screaming didn't bring anyone else out of the house, but I could see them from the windows. They were watching me, and I wasn't sure if the faces in the windows were human or demonic.

"I knew then I couldn't go into the house to get anything else that had belonged to me. I was grateful I had taken the few things I had that morning when I left the first time. I saw that the house was heavy with evil. At that moment, I recognized it for what it was. Before, it was hidden from me, but no longer. I saw things with new eyes; I needed out of there. A new fear of the evil all around overcame me. With tears streaming down my cheeks, I turned, ran for my car, and left.

"Later that day, I was set up in an apartment with food and clothing and caring notes. Everyone in the entire church had pitched in something for me. I remember sitting there that first night, straddling doubts and fears.

"The preacher and his wife checked on me daily for the first month. I made some new friends within the church and eventually got a job.

"My life was fraught with strange things and hindrances. I came to realize that Satan's demons were still after me, doing their best to wreak havoc in my life. Satan doesn't like to lose, and he and his army will do anything to sabotage progress in Christ's kingdom.

"I never spoke to my girlfriend again, nor to our partner, the man we both shared. I thought about leaving town, but I felt the Holy Spirit telling me to stay put, that He would help fight for me, that I could be used here for good. And so I've spent the rest of my life so far, following Jesus, growing my prayer life, doing what I can to serve others, and trying to help those caught in the thicket of the occult." Joanna straightened her hat.

Nora took a deep breath and sat up straight. "Joanna, thank you for sharing your story. I… I don't even know how to describe how it's made me feel… I can't put these feelings and thoughts into words… I can't articulate how this is affecting me, but it *has*—I can feel that much. I'm sure there are many more details of your life that you haven't shared with us tonight. I hope that we can hear more," Nora said to Joanna with big-eyed interest.

Joanna smiled. "Yes, that *is* only the nutshell version. We might be here until next week if I told you everything! So," Joanna blew her reddened nose, "with all that in mind, my dear, what is troubling you? How can I help you?"

For the first time, Nora was eager to share about the evil that had been plaguing her since her arrival in Kingsman.

- Twenty-Two -

THE WAR OF THE GODS

"Do the best you can until you know better. Then when you know better, do better."

~Maya Angelou

NORA READJUSTED IN HER SEAT and began to tell Joanna her story about the ghost in her home during the last couple of months. Her three companions listened quietly, without interrupting. Nora gave them the details of her visit with the psychic and about last night's terror. Quickly reaching out to touch Trey's freckled hand, she let him know that she hadn't told anyone about last night's horror scene yet, because she had been certain she would share about it tonight.

She brought her hands back into her lap. Beginning to wring and twist them with apprehension, Nora explained to Joanna that she hadn't believed in spirits of any kind before moving to town, and now she was apparently being bombarded by something supernatural.

"It's evil. It's the very essence of evil." Nora went on to tell Joanna about her most recent visit with her ailing father and the "conversation" they'd had about her questions and unexplained experiences. She pulled a scribbled note from her wallet, straightening the paper as she set it in front of Joanna.

"My dad was sleeping almost the whole time I was there talking to him. But, after I told him about all the weird stuff that's been happening, he woke up and told me to write this down. I don't know what it is. I think it's some kind of code or something... You're so wise and have been through so much—do you have any idea what it might mean?"

Joanna picked up the note and read it aloud. "Ephesians 6:12. I know exactly what this means. This is a Bible verse." She reached down and pulled a little book out of her purse, and flipped through the worn pages, stopping at the book of Ephesians. Setting it down in front of Nora, she pointed to the verse as she quoted it from memory. "For we are not fighting against flesh-and-blood enemies, but against evil rulers and authorities of the unseen world, against evil spirits in the heavenly places."

Nora's face drained of color. Her mouth watered in shock. "My dad woke up from his Alzheimer's-induced stupor and gave me a Bible verse? About evil spirits? This is just getting weirder and weirder. The man never opened a Bible in his life as far as I know. What's going on here?" Nora said in desperation.

"Well, it's obvious to me; the Lord is sending you a message, Nora. This verse is telling you exactly what has been going on with your strange, scary experiences. I try not to ever put Jesus in a box. He speaks to us in many, many ways. And this way of getting a message across is no surprise." Joanna said calmly.

"Who is this Jesus?" Nora asked with sincerity.

Joanna wasted no time in responding. "Jesus 'Christ is the visible image of the invisible God. He existed before anything was created and is supreme over all creation, for through him God created everything in the heavenly realms and on earth. He made the things we see and things we can't see—such as thrones, kingdoms, rulers, and authorities in the unseen world. Everything was created through him and for him.' " Joanna paused and then continued, " 'He existed before anything else, and he holds all creation together.' You can find that in the book of Colossians in the Bible as well."

"So, what this sounds like," Nora said slowly, folding and refolding a napkin, "is that Christ is another supernatural being, but he is the bigger and better boss of planet earth? How many gods are there then?" She frowned. "Also, I've seen enough of Christian culture to know that Jesus died on a cross, but why would he allow that to happen if he's God? That doesn't sound like something a god would do. Is he not very powerful? He couldn't save himself?"

Joanna smiled and patted her hand on the table as she talked. "Christ is the original owner of the prime real estate which we know as the universe and everything in it. He made everything. He made all the angels that serve him, and he gave them a free choice to worship him, or not. He didn't want robots, he wanted real hearts loving him out of choice. But one of the head angels decided he no longer wanted to worship God, and he decided that he himself should be worshiped, and he was sure he could be just as great as God. So, this angel known as Satan was cast out of heaven and thrown down to earth, and he took many other angels with him.

"He basically claimed earth for himself and became a chief enemy of God. Since that day, he has hated and opposed everything God stands for, yet imitates everything possible about the power of Christ. He detests humans, who are God's beloved creations, desiring them to be destroyed. There is a major war going on that most of us cannot see visually. It's as if we are part of a chess game.

"This passage from Philippians 2:6-11 tells us about Jesus, God's Son," Joanna pointed to the passage for Nora to follow along. "It says, 'Though he was God, he did not think of equality with God as something to cling to. Instead, he gave up his divine privileges; he took the humble position of a slave and was born as a human being. When he appeared in human form, he humbled himself in obedience to God and died a criminal's death on a cross. Therefore, God elevated him to the place of highest honor and gave him the name above all other names, that at the name of Jesus every knee should bow, in heaven and on earth and under the earth, and every tongue declare that Jesus Christ is Lord, to the glory of God the Father.'

"That's the short version of Jesus' story. There was a purpose to his death on the cross. He could've stopped it, but he didn't. To answer your other question about how many gods there are—there is only one God. But God is made up of three persons. God the Father, Jesus the Son, and the Holy Spirit. Think of an egg and its three different parts; all have different names, but it's all an egg!" Joanna explained.

Nora rubbed her eyebrows and sighed.

"Honey, you've already seen the power of the dark side. You need no more convincing of that morbid reality. But only you can decide to believe in the truism of another power, a bigger power, one that can squelch and defeat that evil army.

"There are two sides to every story, and Satan and his demons—they don't want you to know the truth about them. They don't want you to figure out how to fend off attacks from them. In fact, much of the time they disguise themselves as good and light to entrap and ensnare us foolish, ignorant humans.

Satan imitates everything God does. His power is significant, but it's not as great as Christ's power."

Nora blinked hard, her body stiff from the intense information.

"Look, I understand what you're going through, I've seen many unnatural and awful things myself. But you've got to hear what I'm saying. You must believe in the all-powerful God to invoke the mighty name of Jesus Christ and send those evil beings running." Joanna breathed deep and cocked her head to the side. "Nora, I don't know you well, but I believe that God has a purpose planned for your life. The Lord allows us to go through unpleasant things to refine us, to build in us, to develop our characters. We become His messengers to the world. We are asked to spread the truth, to uncover the lies of the darkness, and to be a lighthouse for others when they're going through their own storms and cannot find their way.

"We are immortal spirits housed inside mortal, decaying bodies. When our bodies die, our souls remain intact. But the ghosts you're dealing with—they're not human souls. These are ancient fallen angels that are serving Satan, plain and simple. They are demons. You will hear many say that they are not demons, that maybe only a few are, but that the rest are just troubled old souls. This is not true. So many people have believed this fallacy and are headed for eternal destruction, roped in by these deceivers.

"Obviously, spirits can also be angelic and sent from the Lord, and that's where we Christians are told to test the spirits. Then we will know if the spirit we are dealing with is from Christ or Satan. I can tell you more about that later. But for now, you need to know that you're unguarded. You have felt this, haven't you? The helpless feeling of being at the mercy of something evil and unknown?"

Nora nodded, tears in her eyes now.

"The only power we have to fight is invoking the name of Jesus Christ to protect us. And that comes from the gift of the Holy Spirit. We fight fire with fire, spirit with Spirit. We humans are vessels, and we carry not only our own souls within us but also pack around other spirits as well."

"This doesn't make any sense. Why doesn't the bigger God just squash the nasty little one? Why does He let him carry on?" Nora asked through watery eyes.

"No one can know the mind of God. Our brains just can't understand past certain limits. We just aren't given that level of information. The Bible says a thousand of our years is like a day to Him. He is not concerned with our time limit because He has none. We all pick a side in this war, whether it's knowingly or unknowingly. It's incredibly mind-boggling, isn't it?" Joanna said. "Christ is coming back to this earth. We don't know when, but when it happens, Satan will be defeated forever. He will be cast into the lake of fire along with all of his evil angels and any humans that chose to play for his team. The great game of life—this war—will be over."

Nora dabbed her eyes with her napkin. "All this talk about Christ and Satan, I just can't believe I'm actually having this discussion. It all seems so surreal to me. I don't feel like I know enough to say that I believe in Christ. Then, on the other hand, I can't say that this entity in my apartment is not real because I know full well that it is. So what you're saying is the only way to get this troublemaking ghost out of my house is to believe in Christ? And then do what? Is it enough to just believe?"

Joanna swallowed the last of her tea. "Well, becoming a follower of Christ means a few things. It means how you see life, the way you live, the way you think—all that gets transformed by the renewing of our minds. This is something that we have to want, that we have to work on daily—and essentially, it's giving our lives away. It's hard to explain and to put everything into a short conversation. But, we have to start somewhere, and that starting point is believing in Christ and asking him for forgiveness of our dirty sin, all the times we've trusted or worshiped the wrong power. And we invite him to reign over us. We all start there.

"Then, the rest of your life is spent discovering who he is, and who you are in him. His Holy Spirit is given as a gift to you and dwells within you and is the only power you have over the darkness. The Holy Spirit is a gift given to us to help protect us, and He is always there.

"The life of an earnest Christian is not an easy road. We certainly aren't promised problem-free lives. In fact, the more you devote yourself to Christ and lean into what he's asking you to do, the more resistance you will get from evil. Now, not all problems are direct attacks from Satan. Sometimes we just do dumb things and receive the negative consequences of our actions. And not everyone has problems with poltergeist spirits in their homes."

Trey had been silent most of the time. He straightened from his slump, asking Joanna, "What do you believe happens to those of us who don't follow Christ when we die?"

Joanna was clearly uncomfortable with this question; she knew it wasn't good news, and she knew Trey was asking about himself.

She gently told the group what she believed. "Simply put, those who aren't living for Christ get sent to the same eternal fire as Satan will. Hell. And the reward for choosing Christ is eternal life in heaven with God, apart from pain and everything bad or evil."

Nora wrinkled her nose and played with her long ponytail. "This a lot of information. I'm going to have to take some time and think about it all. Thank you for talking to me about all of this. It's been really helpful to hear another side of the story other than that of a psychic."

Joanna set her hand on Nora's arm. "Honey, no one can make a choice to believe in Jesus for you. No one can force you to believe. I'll never try to prove Christ's existence to anyone. You either believe or you don't. But, for me, He has been the air I've breathed since the day I was pulled from the muck. He's what I live for, and nothing is more important to me than growing the faith I have in Him. I don't just love Him because I believe He will protect me from everything, because no one is guaranteed that.

"Only the Holy Spirit can change hearts. My job is merely to be His hands and feet and to ultimately be a servant and do whatever He asks me to do. One part of that is sharing the gospel truth. I'm the least of the least, a sinner just like everyone else. The only difference between me and a sinner without Christ is that I recognize that I am lost, and I have chosen to put my faith in Christ."

Jessa thanked her grandmother and gave her a long hug. The four of them moved towards the door.

Joanna turned and asked Nora, "Oh, hon, you mentioned you're on your second rental—can I ask where you lived the first time?"

Nora fiddled with the crystal pendant hanging around her neck. "A place called Deape Woods just outside of town. An older couple own the place; they're into some of the dark stuff we talked about. Stella Deape and Victor Woods. Quite creepy people and an eerie place to live… But it looks like moving didn't help me escape anything."

The color drained from Joanna's face and her mouth dropped open as she realized where Nora had been living.

"Are you okay, Grandma? No pun intended, but you look like you've seen a ghost!" Jessa placed a concerned hand on Joanna's arm.

"I'll be okay," Joanna responded.

But she wasn't okay. Stella was the girlfriend from her past; Victor had been her partner—their partner—from all those years ago.

The idea that Nora had been living on their property made Joanna's blood run cold. Joanna's tongue was tied up in anxiety. She wasn't sure whether she should divulge that the setting of the ugly story she had just relayed was exactly the location where Nora had lived during her first few months in town. And as wise women do, she waited to say something until she knew the time was right.

The evening's revelations would prove themselves relevant during Nora's next night alone in her contaminated house, where the ruthless haunt just wouldn't cease.

- Twenty-Three -

THE POWER IN THE NAME

"What wings are to a bird, and sails to a ship, so is prayer to the soul."

~Corrie Ten Boom

THAT NIGHT, as Nora was drying herself inside the shower, she heard a squeaking sound. The type of squeak that comes from fingers pressing on wet mirrors. Nora grabbed the curtain as if it was a source of protection and peeked around the cloth. On the fogged-up mirror she saw the name NORA scrawled in thin, tall, uneven letters. Glancing around before stepping out, she hastily used a hand towel to wipe the mirror dry. When the mirror fogged up again, she saw a new message facing her. This time it said:

DEATH IS COMING.

Nora paused and stared into the blurred glass, feeling as though this message should have been more shocking.

Oh, no… Here we go again. As freaky as this is, I suppose I should be expecting it.

Wiping it a second time, she did not allow the mirror to fog again. She opened the bathroom door and went to her room to put on her pajamas.

Nora's stomach felt uneasy. She began thinking about the solution that Joanna had offered to her as truth.

Is Joanna right? Does she have the answers to defeating this terror?

Nora wasn't sure. All of a sudden, she felt a pressure, a mind fog, come over her.

I feel a little strange… I can't focus on coming up with a strategy for a game plan. I can't think about this right now. I'm just too tired.

Getting into bed, she positioned the dog once again between the door and herself and fell asleep.

At midnight, Nora awoke suddenly, feeling an unfamiliar heaviness over her. She felt paralyzed. She could not move. Was she dreaming, or was this really happening? The room was dark. She had always the lights left on; the now-darkened room was not her doing. Nora couldn't breathe. She couldn't scream; she couldn't move. Only her fingers and her mind were working—but just barely. Nora assumed this must be what it felt like to drown.

A searing pain slowly dragged, like a claw, digging into the skin across her stomach. She couldn't see anything, but she felt it with every fiber of her being. Nora was trapped inside her own body. This went on for probably thirty minutes, though to Nora, it seemed like hours.

What about Jesus?

The question popped into her mind. Thinking about it caused her to utter his name aloud.

"Jesus Christ," she forcibly whispered to herself.

The pressure suddenly lifted from her. She gasped for air as if coming up from under water. Sputtering and grabbing her chest, she sat upright. She was shaking terribly, and tears fell without waiting for permission. Alone in her bed, she was tired of the fear that plagued her in the very place she should feel the least afraid.

She couldn't prove it, but she wondered if the name of Jesus Christ had caused relief from the oppression she had just experienced.

Is Joanna right? Is the name of Joanna's God so powerful, it could cause this unseen evil to leave? Will Joanna's God protect me even if I don't accept Him as my Savior?

Again, Nora felt that she couldn't think clearly. Her mind was scrambled, and she felt dizzy.

Nora got out of bed to flip on the lights in her bedroom, but the light switch didn't work. Stepping into the hallway, she was shoved against the wall hard enough to cause pain.

"You nasty bully!" she screamed—at what, she didn't know.

Mr. Cooper came bounding into the hall, whining and stepping on Nora's feet to get as close to her as possible. Nora felt along the wall to switch on the hall light. The lights in the hall weren't working either.

Did the electricity go out? It is *pretty windy out there.*

She heard the fridge running; it wasn't the electricity.

She attempted to go back to her room to fetch her phone and found that the now-closed door wouldn't budge. The knob wouldn't even turn. As Nora stared at the door, the knob began to glow red. Nora backed away.

She walked into the living room and sat down on the couch. Tucking her feet under her and pulling the couch blanket up over her shoulders, Nora sat quiet and still in the dark. A rushing breeze came through the room, bringing with it what sounded like a myriad of voices whispering words she couldn't understand. The dog began to whimper, shaking his head to rid himself of the cluttered noise.

"Come here, Cooper. I hear it too, buddy." She patted the cushion and the dog climbed up on the couch with her. He was panting now, occasionally releasing a worried whine that revealed his fear. Nora stroked his head and ears to help him settle down.

I don't know how much more of this I can handle. The intensity seems to be growing. I'm certain this thing wants me dead. This is like a cat playing with a mouse before slaughtering it. That's what I am. A mouse being tortured before death.

Nora sat there on the couch for the rest of the night, eventually falling into a light slumber made up of anxious dreams.

Nora woke when the sun's rays illuminated the sparsely decorated front room. Her legs were asleep and her neck was sore from being in the same position for too long. Nora stood carefully, swinging her tingly legs to push the blood through them.

She pulled up her t-shirt to view her stinging abdomen. Three red lines had been scraped across her belly, each about eight inches in length. They weren't bleeding, but the welts were raised and noticeable.

Nora walked into the kitchen and saw that all the cabinet doors had been flung wide open again. She retrieved a water glass and filled it. Turning around to lean against the counter, facing the island with the plate cabinets above it, she watched as one of the plates sprang out of its place. It was flung with force into the opposite cabinet, shattering into a million pieces, narrowly missing Nora. These were her mother's dishes, the precious inheritance that had been passed down from her mother's mother.

"No! No! No! You stop that!" Nora screamed. Nora's emotions were now jumping back and forth between fear and anger.

Nora ran to stop the other plates from facing the same fate. But as she was reaching up to pull them down to safety, all of them began to roll at once. They came rapidly and with force out of their place in the cupboard as if someone was throwing them like a Frisbee. The plates were being pelted at her and breaking all over the kitchen.

The plates started taking aim for her head—one of them managed to make contact with her forehead, leaving a huge, open gash. Warm blood gushed down through her eyebrows and into her eyes. Nora covered her head and fled the kitchen, cutting her bare feet on the shards scattered on the floor. She ran to her room—the door opened this time—and jumped into her bed, covering herself with the blankets. The blood from her gash soaked into her sheets. Shaking in fear, she uncovered her head just long enough to grab her phone from the nightstand. As she was dialing Jessa, something heavy jumped on the bed, and she yelped in fear. Pulling the covers from her head, she was relieved to see it was only the dog who had joined her.

Jessa answered the phone in a sleepy voice. It was early, way too soon to be calling people.

"Jessa?" Nora said in a shaky tone. "I'm scared, I don't know what to do! Can you and your grandma come to my place and help me?"

"Where are you, Nora?" Jessa asked her friend.

"I'm in my bed," Nora almost whispered. "This evil spirit has been torturing me since the middle of the night and locked me out of my room and broke all my dishes. Your grandma will know what to do. Can you bring her here?" Nora asked in desperation.

"I'll be over right away, and I'll try and bring her too. Do you need me to call the police?" Jessa asked.

"No. The police can't do anything. No one can even see what this thing is. They'll assume I'm a mental case," Nora replied miserably.

Forty-five minutes later, Nora heard a cautious rapping on her locked front door. She slowly got out of her bed, slipped on slippers, and let the women inside. Coming into the kitchen area, they surveyed the broken plates strewn about the floor and the cabinet doors wide open, the drawers pulled out as well.

Jessa walked over to Nora and hugged her tightly. Joanna began praying over Nora, who was trembling. Joanna took a brief walk around the apartment and came back to the younger ladies, who were talking about what happened the night before.

"More than likely you have several demons in this home that need to be cleaned out. But, in order to clear them out and keep them out, you're going to need to shut some doorways that were opened. Unknowingly, you have given them permission to be here. Only the power of the Holy Spirit can order them out. So, do you want to use that power?"

Nora looked at Joanna with red-rimmed, puffy eyes. "Yes, I want it. I don't know entirely what I'm saying I believe in yet, but I'm going out on a limb here and just jumping into it. I can't live this way anymore. This thing is violent and excruciatingly real." She swallowed and took a deep breath. "And I want to get baptized this morning. I know it's cold and breezy out there, but I want to go to the same lake where you were baptized all those years ago," Nora pleaded to Joanna.

I'm afraid to do this, but I have more apprehension about not *doing it.*

"Let's go. Put on something you can get wet in. I'll get some towels—and Jessa, while she's getting dressed, get a broom and let's start sweeping this house."

The three ladies didn't waste a lot of time before leaving the apartment. Within a few minutes, Joanna and Jessa led the way out. As Nora approached the doorway, the front door slammed shut in her face, locking her in the house. Nora banged on the door with one fist, the other hand twisting fiercely on the inexplicably locked knob. Her gashed face peered out through the door's small window.

Joanna, beginning to get into her car, turned and saw Nora stuck behind the closed door. Joanna marched over to the front porch and firmly declared, "I rebuke you in the name of Jesus, you evil spirit; turn loose of that door!"

The door knob twisted almost immediately, allowing a frightened Nora to escape.

"I don't think whatever's in the house wants me to claim Jesus," Nora stated as she rubbed her sore abdomen.

On their way to the lake, Nora called Trey. She told him about her most recent encounter with the paranormal, her injuries, and Joanna's intervention. She told him she had decided to get baptized, and asked if he, and maybe Nolan, would like to meet them at the lake.

"Yes, please wait for me. I want to be there," Trey told Nora.

The three women stood overlooking the beautiful lake in the wee morning hours. The sun's glow was opening the horizon and revealing the colored details of the surrounding trees. As Joanna described the spiritual death and new life represented by the symbolic act, Trey's van pulled up. Both he and Nolan hopped out and walked briskly down the rocky terrain to meet the girls.

Trey gave Nora a warm, short hug and told Joanna, "I'm next after her."

Joanna grinned and nodded, and she and Nora waded into the cold water. It was crystal clear; they could see every rock and creature below. But Nora couldn't feel the cold. She felt all at once way too excited and conflicted about what she was about to do.

And just like that, Joanna baptized her in the name of the Father, the Son, and the Holy Spirit. When Nora came up out of the water, she threw her fists up in the air and yelled "Yes! Evil, you are and will be defeated by the power of Christ!"

The young adults watching from the bank whooped and whistled and clapped in agreement. Then, true to his word, Trey was next. He slowly waded out to the smiling older woman, hugged and thanked her, and was dunked into the freezing lake.

No one knew that Nolan too had been considering giving his life to the Lord. To their surprised delight, Nolan stepped into the water and made the choice to take the gift of salvation. With his olive skin and shiny black hair drenched with the cleansing water, he beamed in satisfaction of beginning this new life.

Jessa watched in awe, tears in her eyes, as her friends made the life-changing choice. At this point in her life, when she was making a turnaround in her faith—to have three of her good friends join her on this journey all at once was wondrous.

Nora cleaned up and changed into dry clothes at Joanna's. Her three friends had gone to their own homes to prepare for another workday. Nora had taken the day off to sit with her dying father, and before she left, Joanna talked with Nora over a hot breakfast.

"You've made an important decision this morning. But I don't want you to think that life is going to be a piece of cake from here on out. You will have much resistance. The darkness does not want a Christian's life to be fruitful. It will throw everything it's got to discourage you, to prevent you from carrying out the Lord's will.

"Being a Christian does not guarantee easiness. In fact, it's quite the contrary. But, young lady, you have to know that the hard things are usually the things most worth doing. And we need each other to help us through the trials. We need each other for encouragement; we need each other to spur us on. If you isolate yourself from other Christians, if you don't continue to seek a relationship with God, you will wither and become useless and ineffective as a Christian.

"You will, and should always, have questions. I still have questions, and I have been following Christ for years. There's nothing wrong with questions. Ask them! Be curious! Get some answers! And dear, don't think that you can ever arrive in your faith. It will grow your entire life if you're willing to let it. The minute we think we know everything about God is when the rug gets ripped out from underneath us. That's when we become even more susceptible to believing the lies that are thrown at us." Joanna watched as Nora fingered the crystal at the end of her necklace.

"There may be some more work we need to do in cleaning out your house of spiritual evil. I can come over later tonight to help you? Maybe around 7:30?"

Nora nodded her head in approval. "I have so much to learn. I'm feeling a bit overwhelmed."

Joanna patted Nora's hand. "That's understandable. But you're not alone." Joanna's gaze drifted out the window and she pondered aloud. "So, I'll fast and pray for the rest of today, and then for dinner I'll eat a very high protein meal for emotional strength. I'll ask a few people to be in prayer for us as well. I'll let the prayer team know when we head over to your house, so that they can pray for us specifically when we tell the demons to leave."

Sitting with her feet pulled up and her wet hair French-braided, Nora swallowed the last of her drink and reached for her purse.

"Hon, before you go, I wanted to give you this." Joanna handed Nora a small Bible. Nora's fingers traced the floral pattern on the navy leather cover. She smiled up at Joanna with gratitude.

"God's words are comforting and informative. I know you said your dad was dying. My guess is that you're going to have to wrestle with some painful emotions, wondering what will happen to his soul. All I can say, dear, is that we aren't the final judge. And thank heavens for that!

"All you need to know is that Christ is in control, and you shouldn't think that the God of the universe doesn't understand your emotions or see the worry and conflict in your mind. He does. You let your father go. Pray over him as best you know how, and don't let doubt about our just God creep into your mind because it will try hard to do just that.

"You will deal with anger at some point, regret and mourning too. But anything is possible with God. Remember that; let that bring comfort to your troubled heart." Joanna finished up her advice with a hug.

I feel like I have always known Grandma Joanna. She's going to be my family.

She knew, sitting in this modest little kitchen, that she was going to find herself here often, pretending this dear woman was her own grandmother. It just felt right.

People don't have to be blood-related to be considered family. Family means caring about each other. From what I've observed, for many people, blood-relation doesn't mean anything. True family means those who care for you and welcome you and share life with you.

"Thank you, Grandma J." Nora's cheeks turned pink as the nickname slipped out. "Um—is it okay if I call you that?"

"Of course, you may, dear." The lovely older lady smiled and patted Nora's back.

Nora had been through the wringer during the last few days, both in body and in spirit. Like anyone who goes through something new and terrible, she was sure life couldn't get any worse. But, life doesn't care about what we think. It unfolds itself the way it sees fit and expects us to adapt whether we think we can or not.

- Twenty-Four -

The Final Farewell

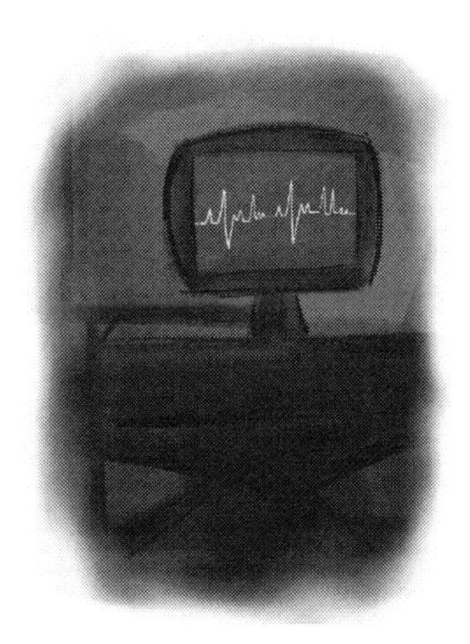

"For nothing will be impossible with God."

~Luke 1:37 (ESV)

NORA PULLED UP to Green Acres and turned off her rig. She paused before opening the truck door.

I don't want to do this again… No, be brave Nora. It doesn't matter what you're feeling, you have to do the right thing.

She didn't want to think about her father on his deathbed, not having lived for Christ. What would that mean for him? Or for her late mother?

Nora found herself in the dim room where her father lay still. Outside, the cloudy sky was threatening to rain. Thunderstorms had been forecasted for the next few days. Nora set up her tiny portable speaker, playing some soft, soothing music, and then pulled out the Bible that Grandma J had sent with her. She found the ribbon in the foreign book marking a page titled PSALMS. She began there. A book of worship and prayer, Psalms spoke what her heart felt. She read it aloud and felt peace there in the hospice room. Gently holding her father's hand, she begged the Lord to forgive him, to spare him.

Joanna's words echoed in Nora's mind all throughout the long day. "Anything is possible with God." Though the words weren't a concrete answer to her questions about her dying father's spiritual destination, somehow, they delivered hope.

Nora was at her father's bedside all day. At about 4:30 PM alarms began to sound, and a few nurses rushed into the room. They allowed Nora to hold his hand as they checked him over and then stood quietly to the side as his heartbeat went silent. One nurse flipped a switch on the monitor to turn the alarm off, quietly announcing the time of death. The nurses covered his face with a sheet and left the room.

She sat there alone, having seen her father's body give up his spirit.

I have no more tears to shed. My ducts are dry.

"Farewell Daddy. I'm going to miss you something terrible," she spoke aloud.

A sense of peace overcame her. Her father's body was done suffering, and now it was up to the Lord to decide his spirit's fate. In order to maintain her newfound loyalty to Christ, she knew she must trust in the sovereignty of his love and justice.

Lord, please help me through this. I'm an emotional wreck. Like it says in Psalms, shelter me with Your wings.

She picked up her purse and left the room where her father's body lay lifeless.

Nora signed some paperwork at the front desk and was finished by early evening. It felt to her like midnight, rather than 6:00. Getting back into her truck, she warmly received Mr. Cooper's enthusiastic welcome, scratching his ears, then let him out for a potty break. Sitting in her cobalt rig, Nora texted Trey to let him know about her father's passing. She didn't have much to say about the event, but she wanted to be sure she let Trey know when important events occurred in her life from now on. He clearly cared, and having proven his trustworthiness, she wanted to confide in him more. She texted Joanna to let her know that she was on her way home, then called Cooper back into the truck, and started it up.

As Nora's truck rumbled up her gravel drive, she looked around and saw that Joanna hadn't yet arrived. Nora got out of her truck hesitantly and let the dog run around and stretch his legs. Nora walked over to Fran's patio chair and sat down in the dark. She held still and listened as the breeze gently picked up momentum through the clump of evergreen trees nearby. Leaves pulled away from the alder trees, and in between little cloud lanes in the sky, the moon's light dimly lit Nora's surroundings. Nora knew Mr. Cooper was busy sniffing around, reading doggy news, so she assumed that the sounds in the bushes were coming from him.

Nora turned her attention to her side of the duplex. No porch light beamed over the humble home's meager cement porch. She thought about what had transpired today and how much her mind just felt overloaded—with her becoming a believer in Christ, her father's death, and now (hopefully) eradicating demons from her residence. It was a lot for anyone to take in all at once. She was bushed and weary, but even through all of it, she somehow still had a surge of adrenaline, equipping her for what she knew lay ahead. She was optimistic.

Nora welcomed the sight of approaching headlights. Joanna put her car in park and opened her car door slowly. As she stepped out, Nora briskly walked over to her and gave her a hug.

"How are you doing, dear?" Joanna asked Nora.

"Well, I feel ready to do this, despite what a huge day this has been." Nora tightened her ponytail as they walked to her front door. She fumbled for the silver house key as Joanna held her phone's flashlight over the slightly rusted lock.

As Nora began to turn the door knob, Joanna placed her hand gently on Nora's hand, stopping her. "Before we go in, I'm going to pray. And then when we go in, I'll ask you to bring to me anything that was taken from the last residence or given to you by your previous landlords. Everything must be destroyed and removed from this house that came from that place. I want you to think about whether you have any other objects that might be occultic in nature—hard rock records, pornographic books or movies, weird idols, masks, souvenirs from foreign countries, or any strange symbolic-type things.

"These types of things can open doors and turn loose trouble within your living space. I know this sounds kind of unbelievable and quite obtuse. But people have no clue what dangerous things they unknowingly drag into their homes. I want you to be aware that demons can attach themselves to objects. We may not find everything tonight. However, you need to watch and pay attention to the things in your home. The Holy Spirit can help you see objects that aren't right, if you tune yourself in to His leading."

Nora nodded in the dark and chirped, "Okay."

Joanna prayed before entering the apartment. She asked everything in the name of the Lord Jesus Christ. There was the sound of something breaking inside the apartment as Joanna continued her prayer of asking Christ to remove the demonic spirits. Opening the door, Joanna held Nora to the side as if she expected something to come through the doorway. Something did come through, bashing the ladies into the screen door, causing the screen to bend a little too far backward.

"Demons headed out," Joanna said coolly.

Walking toward the kitchen, the ladies viewed the pieces of broken plates on the floor that hadn't been completely cleaned up. Nora flipped on the light and grabbed the broom.

Joanna put a hand over the broom to motion for her to stop. "We need to finish this before anything else. Go and retrieve any items I just talked to you about. If you're unsure, bring them to me, and I can help you figure out if they should be burned or not. Meanwhile, I'm going to start flushing the demons out by prayer and marking the doorways with oil."

Nora flipped on the lights in every room in the house. She encountered a few lights flipping themselves off again. Nora felt the demonic oppression more than ever. Since this morning, it was like she had a new-found Spidey sense to this evil.

Nora remembered the Dez Crosser book—the one about witchcraft—that Victor had loaned to her. She located it on her small bookshelf and brought it into the kitchen. Then Nora remembered the crystal keychain Stella had given to her inside the gift basket when Nora had first moved in. She found that in the kitchen drawer, attached to an extra truck key. Removing the key, she set the crystal keychain on top of the book. The gift basket Stella had given her was holding extra toilet paper in the bathroom. As she retrieved the basket, she remembered that she had accidentally taken one of the mugs from the last apartment. Bringing her coffee to go one rushed morning, she had left it in her truck. She now found it in the cupboard, pulled it out, and set it in the growing pile. Glancing at it again, she realized that it was the Wiccan Haven mug.

Nora had never been to any third-world countries and didn't do a lot of shopping, so most of what she owned was from her parents' home. And that wasn't much.

"I don't watch porn, I don't travel, don't do much shopping, don't get many gifts, so this is all I can think of at the moment," Nora said to Joanna.

"What about the necklace you're wearing? Where did you get that crystal?" Joanna asked, eyeing the pendant Nora wore.

"Oh, yeah, this too."

Nora quickly reached to unclasp the silver chain from around her dainty neck. It made a clunking sound against the Wiccan mug as she threw it onto the heap of items from Deape Woods.

"That was a gift from Stella. She said it would ward off evil spirits. But you're saying these things could be cursed and demons are actually *following* these objects?" Nora asked, with a little disbelief in her tone.

"That's exactly what I'm saying. Many people bring an item into their home not knowing there are demonic entities following it or attached to it. It's sort of like a Trojan horse. Unfortunately, many people who say they are Christ-followers don't know anything about these little satanic traps because they aren't educating themselves, nor getting educated by their churches.

"I don't think the good majority of preachers, teachers, and church leadership have the foggiest idea of the power and tactics the enemy uses. Members of church leadership don't seem to know much at all about the very being they have devoted their lives to war against. I suppose it's Satan's prerogative to bog down the church with taking potshots at the issues and distracting them from understanding why the issues are there in the first place. Yes, I can see why the enemy keeps them quite distracted, keeps them from staring the ugly truth in the face. If the enemy can keep our leadership from confronting and realizing the ugly reality and tangibility of his claws in everything, he can keep the 'sheeple' in the dark as well."

Joanna seemed to trail off in thought and then came back to her original comment about the junk people haul into their homes. "So, honey, these items can't be cleansed; they must be destroyed. They shouldn't be given away because you'll just be sending trouble to someone else. Also, try not to buy any souvenirs from other countries that are connected with witchcraft and voodoo. Many of those objects come with their own free curse," Joanna said. She swept the mound of things into a box and set it outside the house. "I'll take them and destroy them for you," she told Nora.

Joanna propped open the front door, then brought out her phone, plugged it into Nora's small speaker, and blared some uplifting Christian music. "Demons hate worship music. That's one good reason to play it often in your home," she said.

Joanna started from the back of the apartment and prayed over each room, closet, and open space, commanding the evil spirits to exit in the Lord's name. "You have no right to be here any longer—you must leave this home! I am a child of the Most High God; it is with His authority I command you to go!" While she spoke over the apartment, she dabbed oil on furniture and in doorways and over windows.

When she had made it through the entire house, she made a request: "Holy Spirit, come and dwell within this home. Fill it up with what is of You, Lord, and let it be dedicated to Your service." She looked at Nora and explained, "What we have emptied of evil we must fill up with good, or it will come back, most certainly in a larger force."

Nora felt peace when Joanna finished. Her fear wasn't eradicated completely, but she sensed a calmer atmosphere. Nora and Grandma J sat at the tiny table, eating cheese and crackers in silence as the Christian music played in the living room.

"Who sings these songs, Grandma J? I want to look them up on Spotify. I'm going to hit *replay* and let it go all night."

"Oh, it's a mix of Chris Tomlin, Kim Walker, MercyMe, and when I'm feeling a little daring—some Kirk Franklin." Joanna smiled, but her face quickly grew serious. "Honey, you need to know that you may still have some trouble with these spirits. The enemy is relentless. They cannot rob you of your gift of the Holy Spirit, but they most certainly are outside watching you, like rabid dogs ready to shred you up one side and down the other.

"Worship music is a great deterrent, but you must also become active in prayer, in reading the Bible, in surrounding yourself with other believers who are trustworthy. You must put on the full armor of God. Just because you became a believer doesn't mean they won't come after you and do everything in their power to cause you grief—"

"What's the armor of God?" Nora interrupted.

Joanna picked up the Bible she had brought with her. "It's spiritual armor. It's right here in the book of Ephesians, chapter six, verses ten through eighteen. We can study this more in depth later, but for now, I'll just tell you—it's invisible armor every Christian needs to be aware of in order to fend off attacks.

"While you're learning—and dear, that's all the rest of your life—don't underestimate the power of the enemy. Don't get arrogant, independent and haughty, thinking that you have more power than Satan. You don't, only Christ does. Educate yourself. Be aware that, as a Christian, you will now be at war for the rest of your life. There will never be a time when you will not be at war.

"Guard yourself well, and never take Christ's gift for granted. He will never leave you, but you most certainly can decide to reject the gift He gave you. I believe He gave us a choice and free will." Joanna hugged Nora goodbye and asked her to call in the morning.

Nora showered, then cautiously peered around the curtain to look at the mirror. Nothing. Just your average humid film.

Relief.

This is a good start to a new life.

By the time she crawled into bed, it was late—1:00 AM. The new sound of worship music softly playing from her phone in the other room gave her an odd feeling of protection. She picked up her journal, suddenly realizing that she must record the events from her day, before the memory was no longer fresh in her mind. She spent a long time writing down her thoughts, her story, and her feelings about the last twenty-four hours. Before turning out the light, she prayed. She felt somewhat strange speaking to an unseen Being in an adoring fashion. But she knew—as is the case when forming any new habit—that she would eventually get used to it. Nora decided to take another day off of work, a day to repair herself a little.

A peaceful sleep came easily to Nora that night. A mighty angelic being made sure of that. It was requested from the top that he guard the tiny home from the dirty vermin that had been harassing Nora for a while now. The guardian angel stood tall and alert with his jagged-edged sword gleaming at his side. He took his job assignments seriously. There was no atonement for angels gone rogue.

The next morning, Nora made a call to the office, texted Trey and Jessa, then checked in with Grandma J.

Nora stayed in her jammies until after lunch—she had more important things to do than get dressed. That day, she jump-started her education about each of the million questions she now had. Joanna had told her it would take a lifetime of learning, and even then, she still wouldn't have everything figured out. That was okay with Nora. She loved to learn and wasn't afraid to ask about things she didn't know.

Sipping tea near the front window, Nora jumped when a bird flew into the window. Generally, she would consider that occurrence just a random, unfortunate accident. Today, she wasn't sure of that. Breathing big and sitting up straight, she prayed out loud again for the demons to be bound.

Nora checked in with her older neighbor, Fran, asking if she would mind if Nora prayed through her house. The deaf woman grinned and nodded her approval as Nora went through her home as she had seen Joanna do, anointing the doorways with oil, doing her best to flush out anything dark hiding there as well. They had a conversation on a paper pad for a while, then Nora walked the cracked cement path back to her side of the duplex.

A wave of exhaustion swept over Nora. Laying her head on her pillow that night, she sorted out the last few days in her head. Mr. Cooper licked her hand to show his devotion to his master, and Nora patted him with affirmation. Life hadn't been easy since she had moved, and somehow, she knew that her experiences during the last few months were going to take her down a hard and narrow road. This battle didn't feel quite over.

A dread overcame her as she considered the power she was up against. Then, from somewhere inside herself, she felt a wave of peace that surpassed all understanding. The Holy Spirit gave a shot of encouragement into her faith as He reminded her of His powerful force, and that He was not to be reckoned with.

Good old-fashioned rest came to Nora, healing her body. She would need to be sufficiently stocked up for what lay ahead. She had thought the worst was over… The next few days would prove her wrong.

- Twenty-Five -

The Missing Coworker

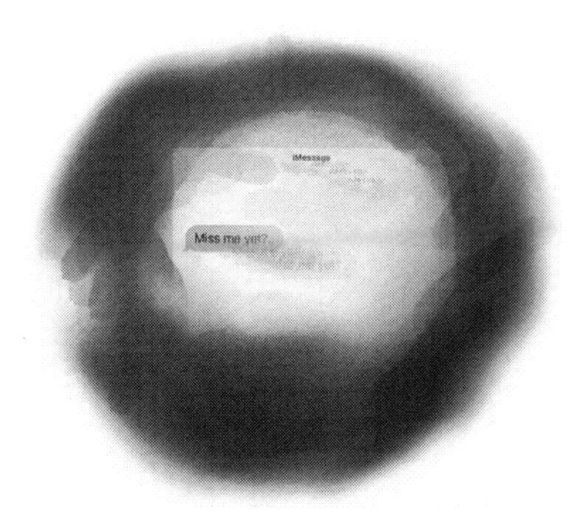

"Ideas pull the trigger, but instinct loads the gun."

~Don Marquis

THURSDAY MORNING ushered in torrents of rain to the typically drier climate. Coming into the office, Nora felt different. The way she saw people, herself, her job. She had only been gone a few days, but it felt like she had been on some strange adventure. Trey greeted her at her desk with coffee from an espresso shop and a lemon muffin in a brown paper bag.

"How are you this morning?" he asked, smiling at his lovely lady friend.

"Thanks for the coffee and the treat! You're a sweet man. I'm feeling a little worn out, but I'm here this morning and going to make the best of things," Nora said, sipping the mocha and scanning the office for her workmates. Trey and Nora talked for a few minutes, and then he headed off to his department.

After a couple hours of code-writing and working out the kinks in their newest software platform, Nora checked her watch. It was nearing 10:00 AM, and Camilla was still not at her desk. Nora left her own desk and located Jessa, who was finishing up a meeting.

"Hey Jessa, do you know if Camilla is coming in today? I need some information about a project she's heading up, and I was wondering if you knew if she was sick or something?"

The blond girl stopped and tapped the ink pen to her lips, "You know, I don't think she has been in the office for the last two days. Did you check with Randy?"

Nora shook her head no. "I'll go find him and ask."

Nora arrived at Randy's office just as he was hanging up the phone. "Hello Nora, welcome back! My condolences on your father passing away," the balding man said, without much emotion.

"Thank you, sir, I appreciate that," Nora replied. "Hey, I was wondering if Camilla was coming into the office today; Jessa told me that she hasn't seen her in two days."

Randy chewed his lip, scratched his neck, and wheeled his squeaky chair over to his computer. "Let me double check the employee system here… I don't remember her not coming into work, but maybe I missed something." As he tapped away endlessly on his keyboard, Nora eventually began to preen her nails.

"Nope, I don't have any notes here about her not coming into work. You have her number, right? Want to give her a call and find out what's going on?" Randy asked Nora.

"Yes, I have her number, I'll call her. Thanks!"

Nora left his office and headed back to her desk. She found her coworker's number and dialed. Pacing in front of Camilla's workstation, she listened to the phone ring. For every ring that went unanswered, Nora's stomach tightened a little more. An automated message told her the voicemail box was full. Nora hung up and texted Camilla, asking her to please call her back.

Nora walked over to Camilla's desk and pulled out some stacks of papers, looking for any information that might help Nora with her overdue project. Shuffling through a few things, Nora came across a sticky note stuck to a drawing, with the name and phone number for a tattoo parlor scrawled on it. Staring at the picture, she didn't quite understand what it was. Using her phone, she snapped a photo of the paper and restacked the paper pile.

It was about 4:00 PM when Nora received a text from Camilla's phone.

MISS ME YET?

Nora stared at her phone. She had just had a conversation with Camilla on Monday; nothing had seemed out of sorts with her. In fact, she remembered Camilla telling her that she was out of vacation days, and that if she was gone from work and wasn't home sick, Nora should "send a search party..."

This smells fishy. I should check in on her.

Nora informed Randy of the strange message she had received from Camilla.

Randy, eyes on his computer screen, told Nora to give it until Monday, and then he would decide what to do.

"Can I have Camilla's address in case I want to go by and check on her?" Nora asked him.

The manager leaned back in his chair. "We're normally not supposed to give out private information like that... but I don't have the time to check up on her, and I guess it wouldn't hurt, since you're her direct manager." He turned back to the computer, locating Camilla's contact information. "It *would* be good to know why she hasn't shown up for a couple of days, and get her back here ASAP so she can pull her weight on your team projects. Goodness knows you're already short-handed with those other two ladies out…" He jotted down some sloppy writing on a post it and handed it to Nora. "Keep me informed on anything you find out."

Nora thanked him and returned to her desk. She finished up her last project of the day, then went to dinner with Trey. They discussed the strange case of the missing coworker, the text, and the last conversation Nora remembered having with Camilla. Trey agreed that it wouldn't hurt for Nora to check up on Camilla. It was 7:30 PM when Nora headed home, but not before stopping by Camilla's house. Patting the Glock 42 under her full skirt, she walked up to the old house in the dark and cautiously knocked.

The man who came to the door was only partly dressed. "Yes?" he said through the cracked door.

"Hi," Nora stammered, "I was wondering if Camilla's home?"

"Camilla? There isn't a Camilla here. I think you have the wrong place, girly." And with that, he shut the door in her face.

Nora stood there a little stunned. It was hard enough knocking on people's doors uninvited, but getting the wrong address on top of it—that was even worse!

"Oh! Randy's sloppy handwriting!" she mumbled, fishing through her purse for the sticky note and her phone, then turning on the flashlight to check the house number again.

Maybe the one was a seven?

Nora walked along the street until she found another home with what she thought might be the right address. Knocking on the door, she hoped this was the correct place. As she waited, the wind blew the bamboo chimes around, and the white wooden porch swing moved in the soft porch light. She waited a long while and then knocked again, hoping it wasn't too late in the evening to be knocking.

The door opened, and this time a middle-aged woman with short curly hair answered. She waited for Nora to speak.

"My name is Nora, and I work with Camilla—do I have the right house? Is this where Camilla lives?" Nora said in an uncertain tone.

The woman nodded and said, "Yes, this is where she lives, but she isn't here right now."

Nora told the woman that Camilla hadn't shown up for work in a few days, and then when she had texted her, Camilla had responded with an odd message. "I just wanted to make sure she was all right. It didn't seem like her to just quit cold turkey like that."

"You're saying she hasn't been in to work?" The woman paused and invited Nora inside. "Camilla can throw temper tantrums. She got quite angry at us a few days ago. She told us (her father and I) that she was going to her friend Nora's house—I'm assuming that was you? It isn't unlike her to leave the house for several days at a time when she gets mad. So we haven't been worried about her. She usually comes back home after a few days of venting. You *are* her friend, Nora, right?" The woman asked, a little worried.

"Uh, well, I don't know that I'm close enough to her to be called her *friend.* We work together, and I'm one of her managers. She hasn't been to my house, and we haven't been out socially with each other. Although we were once at a party at the same time." Nora's thoughts began to drift back to the harvest party at Deape Woods.

"Well, that's a little worrisome. I don't know where Camilla is, then," the lady said sharply, tripping on her slipper as she shuffled over to the landline phone. Picking up the black receiver, she dialed a few numbers. "I'm calling the police. This doesn't feel right."

Nora sank onto the couch as the woman called to file a missing persons report.

An hour later, Nora watched as the woman—who must have been Camilla's stepmother—gave the report to the policeman. "We argued over money a few days ago. She wanted to get herself a new tattoo, and we said no. 'You want to do that, you pay for it, but we aren't allowing you to skip this month's rent to pay for it!' She got so angry she picked up a vase off the table and threw it against the pantry door—shattered the glass in the door and the vase." The woman pointed to the broken door, and as she continued talking, Nora's mind drifted to the drawing she had found on Camilla's desk earlier that day. Nora had taken a picture of it. She pulled up the picture on her phone and brought it to the attention of the police officer and the woman. The cop merely grunted.

The woman said, "That would be a hideous tattoo. I hope she didn't actually go through with it." Then they continued to discuss other details of Camilla's absence.

How could these people not think this drawing is important?

"Okay, I'm gonna leave, but here's my name and number in case you find her or need anything else from me." Nora scribbled out the info on a notepad, and then she left the house.

Nora went home and sat for a good long while, just thinking. She was concerned about this young woman and colleague who apparently was missing. Nora thought about the party at Deape Woods that both she and Camilla had attended. Could she be at another similar party tonight?

Wait… Halloween seems like a big deal to people who are into all that weird, creepy, spiritual stuff that Camilla is into… Stella had even said they would have a big Halloween celebration. When is *Halloween anyway?*

Nora checked her calendar—today was the 30th.

I wonder if maybe Camilla went to Deape Woods for their party. Oh, I don't want to go looking. No, I do not.

Nora's nerves were frayed.

Can a girl just get a break here? … but this is important. Camilla might be in trouble. Maybe the tattoo parlor is a good place to start.

◆ ◆ ◆

The next day, on Nora's lunch break, she located the tattoo parlor from the information on Camilla's desk. Putting her truck in park, she slowly headed into the shady-looking building. A man with a completely shaved head, except for a long dark braid at the base of his skull, walked slowly from the back room and greeted Nora at the counter. He bore so much ink that Nora wasn't sure what color his skin had been originally. Trying not to just stare at the man, she pulled out her phone and showed him the photo of the drawing, explaining to him that Camilla was missing.

"Can you tell me if you have done any tattoos that look like this picture, this week, on any young Latino women, with long dark hair, with bright-purple highlights?"

The man was slow to speak.

This guy knows more than he's letting on. He's trying to decide how much he should say…

The man's eyes blinked several times over the picture. "The ink in that picture looks like a type of occultic branding mark. I don't believe I've done that particular ink on anyone this week." He handed the phone back to Nora and stood looking at her intently.

Well, at least I have an idea of what this tattoo is, I guess. That's a start.

There was nothing left to say, so Nora thanked him and left as quickly as she could manage. There was a heaviness in that parlor. It reeked of incense too.

Nora stopped in at the teashop to grab a quick bite and to say hi to Grandma J. After they had talked for a few minutes, an idea popped into Nora's head. She showed the picture of the tattoo design to Joanna, hoping she might know what it was, and a solemn look came across her face.

"Unfortunately, I do know what this is. This mark is traditionally put on girls who are to be sacrificed to Satan or other demons. It's typically forced on them, or in some cases, they willingly get one—thinking they are just a member of some classy coven—in obedience to the master of the group. It's almost guaranteed that they will die within a short time after getting this tattoo. Generally, they don't know what it represents, unless they are forced into it. Where did you get this picture?" Joanna asked.

Nora explained about her missing coworker and how the police officer hadn't seemed to think the information about the tattoo was worth anything.

Joanna was silent for a few minutes. "You know, we have a lot of this kind of activity here in town. We had this girl…" Joanna said as she walked over and pointed to the missing poster on the cork board. "She went missing not even six months ago. The police try hard to solve these cases, but they don't believe in a lot of spiritual stuff because it's not logical, hard to prove and hard to find and, therefore, don't actively search in the right spots. I have my suspicions about who could be responsible. I have told the police multiple times about them. I think they consider me a religious nut who is off her rocker because they have never researched the places I've told them about, due to lack of evidence."

Nora gave the older woman a hug and headed for the door; it was time to get back to the office. But she just couldn't stay focused the rest of the day. Her mind kept drifting to the missing coworker; staring at Camilla's empty seat was a big distraction. Nora's gut was telling her something was wrong. She wasn't one to over-dramatize things. She was also not used to the out-of-control imagination she was dealing with about what could have happened—or might be happening—to Camilla.

Nora forced her eyes away from Camilla's desk, and her gaze fell on a group of employees chatting near the kitchen. Most of her coworkers had decided to dress up for Halloween. Many of the women in the office took the opportunity to dress in less-than-adequate clothing. Some men went full garb with their movie character costumes; there were lots of ugly, dark imitations of things mostly not human. Nora saw a man in a little, cloth dresser with a lampshade on his head—he was a "one night stand." There was a mobster, several Marvel characters, a few inflatable costumes, and several women had on tiny dresses, exposing body parts that shouldn't be shared in an office.

One whole department came in dressed as zombies and annoyed the rest of the office all day, moaning and groaning and chasing other coworkers. They even dimmed their lights and dressed up their area with fake bloody legs and other nasty things hanging on the walls and ceiling. Upstairs, a secretary was using an evil clown puppet to do all her talking. Mr. Cooper was apparently confused about all the strange characters in the office that day. His demeanor was restless. Nora was sure the whole office got nothing done all day. The employees were given permission to leave work an hour early. Apparently, the management had decided it was a lost cause. Nora was more than happy to escape.

Trey was busy that night, helping his dad work on a car project. Neither of them had felt that it was important to make special plans for Halloween.

Nora returned to her apartment and was greeted with a stench that smelled like something rotten. The smell hadn't been there before she left for work. Nora checked in on her neighbor Fran to make sure she was okay. The nasty smell appeared to only be on Nora's side of the duplex.

Nora checked over her fridge, pantry, trash cans, and bathroom cabinets—then walked outside to see if it might be coming from something outdoors.

Nope, it was definitely coming from the inside of her house. Puzzled and frustrated, Nora dialed Joanna, the person she trusted most when she needed wisdom about anything—spiritual or sanitary.

"Hey Grandma J, I have this awful smell coming from my house. I can't find the source of it anywhere. I checked outside and with Fran next door. It has to be coming from inside my place. I just wanted to ask your thoughts on this… Do you think it's something that died under the foundation? Should I call the landlord?" Nora waited for Joanna's reply.

"Well, hon, this sounds a little like it could be demons in your place again. Demons can smell bad. I don't know the science behind it all, but there's a reason why many people in demon-filled spaces burn incense and candles and such. They have to cover up the demonic stench. Open your front door, then starting at the back of your house, cleanse your place with prayer again, and turn on some more worship music—see if that clears it up."

"Okay, I'll do that." Nora thanked her and hung up the phone. Nora spent a while following Joanna's instructions and eventually the smell began to dissipate.

Nora opened a can of soup and had a quiet dinner, the dog watching her take every bite. She couldn't help but keep thinking about the conundrum of the day.

Where is Camilla? Maybe she's at Deape Woods... Why do I keep coming back around to this idea? Lord, are you trying to tell me something? I should drive there and sneak in and see if I can spot her. Oh, you're nuts, Nora! You don't want to go back there again. But, what if she's there? I know the property pretty well. I could stay in the shadows of the trees. I'm sure they're having a big, weird shindig tonight—if people are walking around drugged, they won't have any idea who I am.

Nora made her decision. She changed out of her business-casual dress into dark pants and a black coat. She wound her hair into a tight, high bun and covered her head with a dark-gray knit hat. She pulled out her Glock and checked the ammo, making sure it was loaded, and grabbed an extra magazine just in case, zipping it into a pocket on her lower leg. Nora checked the battery of her phone and charged it for ten minutes before adding that to her growing pile of spy gear. Locating a headlamp and a tiny flashlight, she set those down on the counter and went back into her room for a small knife in a sheath, which she had bought for camping. The last item was a head camera that clipped onto her headlamp band. Whatever she saw tonight, she was planning on recording it. Nora didn't know what to expect, but when it came to that particular place, she decided to prepare for the worst. She clipped the knife to her side and adjusted the green headlamp on her hat-covered head.

Scanning the old, chipped-up Formica counter, she decided she was ready. A look at the clock told her it was 8:32 PM. She loaded Mr. Cooper into the cab and climbed behind the worn-down steering wheel of her truck. Switching on the big, round headlights, she slowly backed out of her driveway, trying really hard to talk herself out of this insane idea as she drove back to the property that she—at one point—had been so desperate to get away from.

- Twenty-Six -

The Sacrifice

"In life there can be no victor, for death comes to all and smites them."

~J. R. R. Tolkien

NORA DID HER BEST to not allow fear to creep into her mind as she drove the fifteen minutes to the entrance of the property. Coming around the last corner, Nora found a few cars parked along the entrance of the driveway. She knew the crunch of gravel under her tires along the driveway would openly announce her presence—she planned to park here and enter the property on foot, through the woods. She parked the truck on the other side of the road, away from the other cars, backing into a little nook. She wanted to be ready to speed out if the need arose. Sitting in the cab, she cracked the window an inch and heard the rumblings of drumming and chanting in the distance. Looking at the dog, she decided it was best for Mr. Cooper to stay right there and wait for her. As much as she wanted him by her side, she knew he could give her position away or get hurt.

This was Deape Woods, a place wild dogs called home.

Getting out of the truck, she heaved the heavy door shut and locked the cab. Mr. Cooper began to bark immediately. He was obviously upset at her leaving him. Nora ignored his barking and walked across the dark street to the driveway's gravel entrance. The evening's clouds were moody. The wind was strong and the low clouds rapidly covered and uncovered the almost-full moon. The thick woods talked tree language, swishing its sea of limbs to and fro. Nora kept her eyes wide open and prayed for God's protection as she slowly put one foot in front of the other.

What am I doing? Why am I here alone? Whose idea was this? Yours, Nora, ya dope.

Nora did her best to push aside the fear and doubt and kept going. Keeping her headlamp off, she did her best to listen for sounds in the woods through the gusts of wind. A tree let loose of an old limb and it came crashing to the ground, causing her heart to skip a beat. Nora paused briefly and looked towards the noise. Clicking on her headlamp, she aimed the beam in the direction of the sound. Remembering her head camera, she reached up and pressed the record button. Nora saw nothing unusual. She clicked her lamp back off and readjusted to the dark before continuing.

Nora walked along the edge of the woods, just off the gravel where the dirt was softer and quieter. She had worn a pair of tennis shoes in case she needed to pick up speed. Nora was halfway there now, and she cringed when she heard a dog howling in the darkened woods.

Was that Cooper? No. I locked the cab; there's no way that could be him in these woods…

Nora turned in the direction she had just come from and listened. The dog howled again, and she decided that it didn't match Mr. Cooper's voice. Nora picked up her pace and swiveled her head to and fro to watch for danger. The muffled drums—which had previously stopped—now began again, joined by chanting.

Out of the corner of her eye, Nora saw movement to her right.

That could just be deer. There are tons of those out here.

As she pointed the lamp again into the darkness, her beam fell on a set of golden-yellow eyes reflecting back at her. She couldn't quite make out what it was; it was too far away. The eyes did not move.

Maybe it's just something in the forest these people set up as a joke.

Nora clicked her lamp off and back on to see if the eyes were still there. The glowing yellow globes were gone. Nora swept her gaze over the entire area and found nothing. A dog's howl sounded again, but this time it was closer, and on the other side of her. She looked toward the sound and drew her gun. Slowly moving the light, she saw what looked like a wolf's backside disappear behind some brush. The yellow eyes glowed again; however, this time the light was masked through a bush. Nora guessed the animal was a couple hundred feet away.

She swallowed hard. She was now being stalked. Nora began a light jog, still heading toward the farmhouse in the belly of the woods. She could fire her weapon to scare off the animal, but that would also alert the party-goers to her presence. If she could just get to a more populated, well-lit area, she might be in a safe zone from whatever was out there hunting her.

Nora decided to just run as fast and as quietly as she could, praying that the Lord would protect her. The only sound she heard was the wind in her ears as she bolted ahead, goose bumps rising on her arms, trusting that she would make it without becoming wolf dinner.

Coming up to the clearing where the big barn, house, and other outbuildings were located, Nora slowed to catch her breath. She stood behind a batch of old tree stumps as she scanned the place and considered what to do next. Many parked cars lined the gravel road, but there were not a lot of people roaming freely. Nora wondered if the party was inside the house or in the garden area. She held her breath and listened, straining to hear anything that would give her more information.

It sounds as if the drumming might be coming from inside the barn. It should be easy to peer in through a cracked door or one of the windows.

Walking in the dark along the edge of the woods, Nora carefully crept up to the end of the barn she thought safest for spying. Peeking around the corner, she saw someone leaving the exact spot she had planned to use. She held her breath and waited a few minutes. Seeing that the place was still vacant, she walked up the to the end of the huge red barn, toward the little window. It was a bit too high for her, so she used a metal bucket nearby as a step.

Peering in through the dirty window, she saw that there were many people in the barn. Some wore costumes or robes, and many had tribal marks or strange signs printed on their faces. There were a big circle of candles and some sort of white powdery substance outlining a large pentagram on the ground. Within the star, there appeared to be a wooden altar surrounded by big, brass candelabras and burning candles. Behind the altar was a figure in a pointy-hooded black robe. Nora couldn't make out the face under the full, dark hood.

The black-robed figure held its hands to the sky; one hand held a shiny, jagged-edged dagger about a foot long. A liquid substance dripped from the end of the blade. Nora looked more closely at the altar—there was some sort of animal lying there, still and lifeless. Nora's heartbeat was loud. She now knew something horribly evil was going on here. Many people were bowing down, hands outstretched toward the altar, and some of them were dancing to the drums. The faces Nora saw looked stoned or otherwise drugged.

Nora stepped down from her bucket and retreated into the woods. She pulled out her cell phone to dial 911. Whatever was going on here was not legal. Her fingers hesitated over the numbers, and she dialed Trey instead.

"You went where?" Trey asked Nora, incredulously.

"I don't have time to explain. Just make sure the police come. I'm calling them next, but just make sure they come!" Nora said in a voice quivering with fear.

After explaining to the 911 dispatcher where she was and what she was seeing, she went back to the bucket and again peered in through the dirty window. This time, the limp animal that had recently been stabbed to death on the altar had been removed. Now a woman was being placed on the altar. She was clothed in drapey red material; her hands and feet were bound in shackles. She lay still, unmoving. Her long, dark tresses hid strands of fluorescent purple. Nora's stomach dropped down into her knee caps.

I think that's Camilla! It looks like she's next for some kind of ritual sacrifice! I have to move fast, or she's a dead woman for sure. Think, Nora, what should I do now? What's my next step? I'm freaking out. What will they do to me if they catch me?

The black-robed figure was now waving its arms and splashing something wet onto Camilla's limp body. The group of people grew louder in their chanting, dancing with their arms in the air.

Nora got down off the bucket. The police weren't going to make it in time. It was up to her to save this girl's life. She didn't have time to consider the implications of coming out of hiding.

The decision to intervene sometimes has to be made within seconds of whatever you're faced with.

Who else is here to do this job? It's just me. Lord, please guard me!

She knew courage was being asked of her. She may die trying to save someone else, but she knew she wouldn't be able to live with herself if she didn't act in this moment of need. Nora held her gun in tight fists and squeezed her eyes shut, asking the Holy Spirit to guide her weapon and quiet her fear. Nora opened her eyes, took a huge breath, and moved along the building toward the entrance. She yanked on the massive barn door, throwing her body weight into it. Sliding it open as fast as she could, she stood in the doorway, pointing her pistol directly at the figure holding the dagger.

The hooded figure—who now seemed unnaturally tall—had the knife in both hands, poised to kill. All at once, the drums halted in anticipation. The worshipers turned from the altar as the sound of the large door being flung open alerted them to the young woman standing firmly in the door's wake. Silence hung in the air.

As if in slow motion, Nora took aim and squeezed the trigger. The bullet left the barrel as requested, smoky residue curling in the air. The small silver bullet moved through the air faster than the speed of sound, hitting the black-robed figure. The figure crumpled to the ground.

The large crowd of people went running in all directions. Nora stood still amongst the commotion and chaos, watching the party disperse. Her eyes widened at the unmistakable roar of growling, snarling animals rushing across the gravel from a distance. Her weapon still tight in her grip, she turned under the single light bulb illuminating the barn doorway. Fog encroached on the dimly lit area.

Uh oh. I just know whatever's in that darkness is headed for me...

"Lord, I need You now! Where are You?" she screamed, fear seeping throughout her body.

Back turned to the now nearly empty barn, Nora raised her weapon toward the thickening fog and the increasingly louder snarls, and waited for the worst.

Six wolves stepped out of the light fog. Eerily they slowed and stopped, like a truck revving its engine in preparation to run someone down. Nora flipped her headlamp on, her fingers feeling like rubber. In fight-or-flight mode, her fear was so excessive that her hands were shaking and beads of sweat were rolling down her eyelids. She didn't know which one to shoot first. She was outnumbered. This was not good; there was no way she could escape or outrun the wolves. There were too many. One alone would have been hard to get away from, let alone six. Nora thought rapidly about the number of bullets she had left. She had used one on the hooded figure, which meant she had five rounds left, with six extra bullets in her leg pocket. Discreetly reaching down, she unzipped the pocket, pulled out the extra magazine, and stuffed it in her coat pocket. How much damage could her little bullets inflict on these rabid beasts?

This is it. I am about to die. I never dreamt my life would end by being torn to shreds by wolves. Lord, where are You?

As she backed up slowly in the barn entrance, the wolves began to charge her. *Bang!* Her gun sent a lead bullet into one wolf with a yelp. The wolves kept coming. *Bang! Bang, bang, bang!* Nora's weapon finished emptying itself, smoke curling around the barrel. Time slowed as Nora released the empty cartridge onto the barn floor with a clank. As quickly as she could, Nora grabbed the full magazine, but her hands were shaking so badly that she dropped it. The ammo fell, ricocheted off her foot on the way down, and slid across the floor into the shadows.

Suddenly, a black and white dog came running out of the darkness. Moving at full speed, his body rammed the pack of wolves from the side.

"Cooper!" she screamed in absolute terror. Over and over she screamed, horrified. She knew he was no match for the wolves; they would shred him in seconds. She grimaced at the horrid sound of the dog and wolves fighting, and sank to the ground. This distraction would give Nora the time she needed to reload her gun.

Nora, now on her hands and knees—furiously feeling around for her lost magazine—glanced back at the battle. Just then her hands landed on something hard, and quickly, with one smooth motion, she slid the magazine into her gun. Nora didn't want to shoot; she was afraid of hitting her pet. But she had no other choice. She pointed her gun, eyes open wide, and took the shot, nailing one wolf. The wounded beast yelped and dragged itself off into the shadows. Aiming the barrel again at the pack of fighting animals, she pulled the trigger and hit another—it dropped, lifeless. The third and fourth gave up, turning and running off into the woods. Wolf number five stood still, one paw raised, glaring at Nora. Hearing sirens from afar, it turned and ran off with the others.

Nora's brown eyes scanned the mess of bloody animals in the cloudy light. She looked in horror as the last wolf dropped the limp border collie from its jaws and stared her down, its yellow eyes full of seething hate, its rabid jaws shaking in anger and frothing bloody saliva. The wolf snarled angrily as it picked up speed, charging at Nora. All in one fraction of a second, she sucked up her fear, held her breath, and pointed her gun at the charging black wolf. She closed her eyes and fired the last two rounds at what she hoped was directly into its thick skull. Opening her eyes, she watched the sixth wolf drop to the ground just three feet in front of her.

Nora dropped her gun and ran to cradle her dog, tears streaming uncontrollably down her face, as he lay dying in her arms. She applied pressure on two wounds where her precious pet had been torn wide open. The animal had offered his life to save her. Mr. Cooper whined softly in pain and didn't try to get up or even move. His body was filleted like a fish; he was losing blood fast.

The sound of sirens got louder as the emergency vehicles hastened up the gravel driveway and eventually came to a stop right in front of Nora. The bright headlights of three police cars—followed by two ambulances and a fire truck—were blinding in the foggy night. A policeman ran over to Nora, and seeing the injured canine, immediately called the emergency vet to prepare for their arrival. Three men scooped up Mr. Cooper, loaded him into a car, and left the scene.

Nora was in shock. She couldn't fully process everything that had just transpired. It had all happened so incredibly fast. With bright headlights in her face, Nora saw the silhouette of a tall young man running towards her through the fog. Trey trotted up to her and said nothing, wrapping her in his freckled arms as her body went limp from trauma.

After a few minutes had passed, Trey helped Nora stand up. A young police officer approached them.

"Are you the one that made the call?" he addressed Nora.

"Yes," Nora managed.

"Can you tell me what happened to these men here?" As the officer pointed his flashlight into the dark, Nora turned to follow his gaze. There in the shadows where the wolves had dropped from her bullets were three naked men lying gravely still as the medical responders attended to them.

"What the—they were wolves! They attacked me! They changed! They were wolves, and now they're men?! I… I shot at the wolves… those men weren't there before!" Nora was astounded. She knew she must sound crazy, but she also knew that what she had seen and experienced was real. At that very moment—though she was certain she wasn't insane—she didn't know how to prove her sanity to the others.

The officer looked at her from behind his notebook with unbelief. "Okay, so that's what you want me to write down? That these three men were wolves and attacked you and your dog?" The officer raised his brows, shook his head, and wrote out Nora's testimony. "We should probably get a drug test done…" he mumbled.

Another cop, standing nearby listening to their conversation, asked the note-taking officer, "Jack, you don't believe in shape-shifters? I've seen a lot of strange things in my career. I'm going to go on record and say that this shape-shifting stuff is absolutely possible." The two officers debated amongst themselves as they looked over the report.

As Nora crept a little closer to the wounded men, she recognized two of them. Victor and his brother John. She didn't know the third man. She shuddered as she heard a faint howling come from the woods. Nora asked the officers if anyone had been killed, or just wounded. Checking with the paramedics, an officer replied that both Victor and John were dead, but the third man should recover.

Nora looked back at the barn; the door had swung closed and remained unnoticed by the police officers. Nora cautiously walked to the massive, sliding red barn door, and for the second time that night she heaved it open with a resounding clunk. A waft of incense hit her nostrils. Orange and white candles were still lit all around the area, flickering innocently amongst all the chaos and confusion. A still life form lay listless on the wooden platform. Seeing Camilla through the now open barn door, the paramedics rushed to the frail girl, quickly moving her onto a stretcher and into a waiting ambulance. She was still breathing, but barely. She had been heavily drugged and thoroughly abused. She was taken to the hospital along with the man suffering from a gunshot wound.

Nora walked behind the tall altar and found the black-robed figure on the ground, the large, baggy hood still covering its face. The person was camouflaged against the dark, dirty floor.

An officer approached and removed the hood from the figure. Her face crumpled in pain, her silver hair in a bun, tiny neck wrapped by a gaudy silver choker with a large red stone set in the center—it was Stella.

Death was hovering, waiting to collect Stella's soul, ready to squeeze her in its bitter clutches. Stella had been unable to finish giving the gift to her malevolent master. Nora and Trey looked on with conflicting emotions as the paramedics loaded her onto a stretcher and into an ambulance.

The large, jagged knife Nora had seen in Stella's hands was nowhere to be found. There were bloody remnants of previous animal sacrifices discovered in and near a large fire pit that was beginning to die down.

Most of the people who had been in the barn had scattered after Nora shot Stella. A few were so drugged that they lay incoherent in corners of the barn, unable to attain consciousness. They were rounded up and taken to a police facility to sober up and to be questioned.

The young officer approached Nora again. "I'm sorry ma'am, but you'll need to come down to the police station for further questioning."

Nora's eyes widened as the officer ushered her into the back of the police car.

"Hey—what's going on?" Trey let out a strangled sound. "Is she under arrest? It was self-defense!"

The cop shut the door and turned to Trey. "That's yet to be determined. We'd like to ask you a few more questions, too. But you can drive yourself to the station."

Trey anxiously ran his hands through his hair and jumped into his van.

As the police car drove away from Deape Woods, Nora gazed out the window through tears. She took a deep breath and prayed.

Jesus… I need You right now. Please, help me.

Back at the police station, Nora was escorted into a small interview room. A detective explained that they had confiscated her weapon, and he asked her to recount her story. She showed him her concealed carry permit and turned over her head camera, which was still fastened around her beanie. Another detective entered the room and asked her more questions about why she had brought a gun with her and how many shots she had fired that night and why. Nora explained her rental history at Deape Woods, her suspicions about the landlords, and her concern for the missing Camilla. Nora was then taken to a holding cell.

As the hours ticked by, images from the evening's events haunted her thoughts. Knees pulled up under her chin, Nora shuddered and hid her face in her little cocoon. All she could manage was a weak, repetitive, desperate prayer. Nora's mind turned to her wounded, brave animal friend.

Oh, Jesus. Please let him be okay. Please save Cooper.

"Nora."

Nora looked up to see Trey walk into the room, accompanied by a deputy. Trey clasped her hands through the steel bars.

"They're going over the evidence and I heard they called in an occult specialist. I don't know how long you'll have to stay here… I'm so sorry…"

"Oh. Okay. I guess that makes sense. How can they believe my story? When there's two dead men and two other wounded people, and obviously I shot them…" Nora swallowed, trembling. "But what about Cooper?"

"I called the vet before they let me back here to see you. They have him on an IV and antibiotics. They stitched him up—it was really bad. They said it's the worst they've seen. Surgery took a few hours. They said if he makes it through the night, he'll have a pretty good chance of surviving. They'll know more tomorrow."

Nora took another breath, trembling, and nodded to Trey. Trey explained that his dad's lawyer had agreed to defend her when the case went to court.

"Sorry, sir. Time's up." The deputy held the door open for Trey to exit.

"I'll be praying, Nora. I'll stay here until they let you go, okay?"

Nora nodded again, eyes glued to Trey until he was out of sight. She sat on the little bench and closed her eyes. Out of sheer exhaustion, she fell asleep.

"Ma'am? Ma'am?"

Nora squinted up at the stranger touching her arm.

"You're free to go."

Nora looked around. She remembered where she was. It was around 4:00 PM. The police officer explained to her that the occult specialist had finished going over evidence and had deduced that—though the case was indeed strange—the evidence proved that Nora had not shot and killed the men in cold blood.

Though the specialist couldn't completely explain it, the head camera proved Nora's innocence. It had captured footage of her weapon firing at the wolves, and each bullet had been accounted for. The timestamp on the camera footage lined up with Nora's testimony. She had a valid alibi.

Trey was waiting outside the holding cell and embraced Nora as soon as he saw her. He led her to his van, keeping her close as they walked. He opened the passenger door for her and closed it behind her gingerly. As he sat in the driver's seat and started the engine, he asked her, "Are you up for going to get your truck from Deape Woods?"

Nora nodded numbly.

Trey shifted gears and left the police station parking lot. He stayed silent for a few minutes.

"Oh!"

Nora jumped.

"Sorry—I didn't mean to scare you. I just forgot to tell you—good news! Cooper made it through the night. They called earlier this afternoon. He's doing a lot better. It's pretty much a miracle, they said."

Despite all she had been through in the last twenty-four hours, a smile crept upon Nora's lips as she heaved a sigh of relief.

"Thank God."

Trey smiled and adjusted the rearview mirror. "Yes; thank God."

Dusk was rolling in as Trey pulled up next to Nora's Ford at the gravel driveway entrance. Nora didn't want to go back to her apartment. She just didn't think she could handle demons messing with her while she sorted through her own shock. Trey helped her gather a few things from her home, and then took her to Grandma J's house, where the two ladies sat on the couch with cups of tea, talking through Nora's unwanted adventure the night before.

"Nora," Joanna took a breath and cleared her throat. "I need to tell you something. The partner I told you about the other day? It was Victor Woods. And Stella Deape was the girlfriend I mentioned. I didn't know when would be the right time to tell you. You said the other day that you had been renting an apartment from them, and I was sickened when you said it," Joanna told Nora. "For years, I've prayed for them, and have also told the police of my suspicions, of their possible part in kidnappings or strange, unexplainable things that have happened around here."

"Grandma, I… I'm so sorry…" Nora whispered humbly.

Joanna waved her hand. "No, you did what you had to do, to try to save someone's life, and your own. They made their choice; this is not your fault in any way. The whole incident is awful, from the horrible rituals of the occultic group right on down to the fact that all those people don't call Jesus their Lord. If only they could see the light of the truth…

"Listen, I know you've been through so much these last few months, and now adding this to your experience is enough to send anyone into a fit of despair. God is preparing you, dear, for things yet to come. These trials and rough patches are shaping you into a new person. If you allow Him to, He will use you in situations and ways that you didn't know you were capable of. Just trust Him and follow the breadcrumbs He sets out for you"

Nora no longer had the strength to hold open her eyes. She wanted so desperately to soak in what Grandma Joanna was speaking to her, but the rest would have to wait until tomorrow.

- Twenty-Seven -

THE PASSING OF TIME

"Forgive yourself for not knowing what you didn't know before you learned it."

~Unknown

THE NEXT MORNING ushered in the month of November. Nora sat quietly in the kitchen, sipping hot coffee and petting Grandma Joanna's kitty, Moses. Joanna entered the kitchen and greeted Nora with a hug.

"I called the vet today already. I'm going to go down and see Mr. Cooper this afternoon. I also called the police and learned that Camilla's in a coma. They don't know when—or if—she'll ever wake up." Nora looked out the window with a far off look on her face. "The shape-shifter, however, is recovering well. The police are going to question him later today."

Nora felt awful. Her body ached from the stress and adrenaline that had been pumping through her veins.

She decided to visit Camilla on her way to see Mr. Cooper. Trey, Jessa, and Nolan joined her. The four of them stood looking through the window of the intensive care unit, watching a machine push air through Camilla's limp body. They briefly talked to a nurse, but due to confidentiality, she wouldn't say much about Camilla's condition. The nurse didn't seem very optimistic about Camilla's recovery, stating that she had come in with a broken body that was one breath away from death.

"I have never seen someone so broken and still breathing!" the nurse quipped.

Nora's first visit with Mr. Cooper was difficult. She had to hold back tears as she gently caressed his stitched-up body. After four days of healing, he was released from the vet. He limped and was in obvious pain, but he was so happy to be with Nora again, that—in his meager doggy mind—he didn't care what condition he was in, as long as he had his master near him. Returning home together for the first time in a week, Nora sat down on the living room floor, taking some time to cuddle her beloved canine.

Thinking back to the Halloween night at Deape Woods, Nora couldn't figure out how the dog had gotten out of the truck in the first place. She had locked the doors. It was a complete mystery. Would she have survived if he hadn't been there in time? She was sure she wouldn't have. He had literally saved her life.

The black and white face looked up at her and held her gaze.

"Oh, fine, you can have a treat!" Nora broke off a piece of a jerky dog treat, and tossed it into his mouth. He didn't even pause to taste it, he just swallowed it right down. Over the course of the next month, Mr. Cooper continued to recover and was soon almost as good as new.

Nora had visited Camilla every day during the first week of her stay at the hospital, even if only for a few minutes. Later Camilla was moved to a different room that was more accessible to visitors. She still had machines keeping her alive, and the doctors were basically waiting to see if she would wake up. It turned out that Camilla *had* gotten a tattoo like the drawing she had on her desk. The tattoo artist was questioned by the police, but he wouldn't admit his involvement. No one knew if the tattoo was forced on her or not.

Nora came and visited Camilla a few times a week, talking as if Camilla could hear her. Nora talked about everything, right on down to Jesus Christ. Nora also began praying over Camilla. Being somewhat of a novice at prayer, she sometimes wondered if her prayers were good enough to be heard.

Grandma J had told her that it didn't matter how eloquent her prayers were, the Lord knew her heart. He was the Heart-Reader, the Soul-Whisperer, and the Mind-Consoler. If a person had only groans to give, He would understand. Nora had so much to learn and was planning on spending the rest of her life uncovering the mystery of who He was.

◆ ◆ ◆

The red and orange fall froze into a blue and silver winter, and the winter melted into a green spring. Tiny white and pink buds were born on the brown branches of shrubs and trees yet again. Rainbows in all their splendor smiled across the sky amongst the dense clouds of water droplets, and the winds began to turn warmer. Easter dresses were put out on the racks in stores, and sandals in the shoe department. Nora never understood why the fashion world thought anyone would be wearing sleeveless dresses and sandals in the moody, wet, chilly weather. But, she supposed, it went along with spring. The idea of early budding and early summer clothes didn't make sense logically, but perhaps it represented hope for the sun to come and warm the frigid world.

The police questioned all of the party-goers they had caught at the scene, regarding that Halloween night at Deape Woods.

Everyone was quite tight-lipped. The shape-shifter laughed when he was told that Nora claimed he had been a huge wolf. He decided to play it out as a joke and basically accuse her of shooting him and the others because she was delusional. He said he would press charges against her. His lawsuit wish and nasty little smirk faded quickly when he learned that Nora had been wearing a head camera along with her headlamp—and had indeed filmed six giant wolves in attack mode, along with her gunshots.

Stella's dagger was never found. The specialist believed the knife had been taken by another member of the party who hadn't been caught, eventually to be used in another ritual, as it probably had unique curses attached to it. The police had suspicions that the missing girl from the poster in Grandma J's teashop might have been abducted and used as a sacrifice in an earlier occult party. But they couldn't get anyone to divulge any information, and they had no way of tying the missing girl to anyone involved at this particular party.

Nora remembered hearing the fire trucks' sirens as they screamed down the road that night. Later, she was told that every single building on the Deape Woods property had been set on fire—they all burned to the ground. The investigation of who started the fire was ongoing.

Summer busted through spring's defenses, and once again the earth heated up to bring popsicle season. Nora, Jessa, Trey, and Nolan sat in the shade of a striped blue and white umbrella, sipping cold drinks with ice cubes clinking as they awaited their food. They reminisced about the year that had passed and the discoveries and trouble it had brought. Jessa wore a shiny, diamond engagement ring that Nolan had given to her just two months prior. Their wedding would be in October. Nora was looking forward to making new memories this fall—what a fantastic way to do that with a wedding to anticipate!

"I'm going to be wearing my grandmother's wedding dress," Jessa said. "That will be my something old. My something new will be my veil, and the something borrowed will be a necklace from my mother. Something blue… haven't decided on that yet."

The guys scratched their heads, looking at each other with confusion.

Nora smiled. "Sounds like the plans are coming along! I can't wait to go shopping for my bridesmaid dress!"

Nora's phone buzzed. Getting up to answer it, she saw that Camilla's dad was calling her.

"She's awake! Camilla's awake!" His elation was evident, even over the phone. After making plans to visit Camilla within the coming weeks, Nora hung up the phone and returned to the table to tell her friends the great news.

Later that night, Trey and Nora walked along the lake's edge, their dogs running on ahead, sniffing the ground and chasing tiny animals. They stopped and watched as fish jumped up out of the water for bugs. Standing at that lake where they had both made the decision to seek Jesus, they felt a connection deeper than anything they had ever felt toward any other human. The small spark of connection between them had caught fire, fanned by the profound experiences they had been through. Silently, their bodies communicated to each other, his hand holding hers. In this moment, the world seemed like an alright place to be. Nora and Trey were both learning that it was okay to "check out" when they needed to, but that they always had to be on guard spiritually. There was never the right time to be lazy and take it easy when it came to standing firm in their faith. They knew the enemy was constantly waiting for them to allow their defenses to fall.

The dark powers may not always be harassing, but they are always watching and probing, ready to pounce upon our weak areas and take advantage of our feeble human nature. They are always tricking and deceiving and lurking around ignorant, unsuspecting people. The evil resistance works to keep people from the truth, to prevent their eyes from being opened, to entrap them in constant chaos and busyness, and sometimes entrap in absolute terror and fear. If distraction doesn't work, then allowing them to taste power will. There is an angle to be worked on every single person. Male and female. Old and young.

◆ ◆ ◆

October's colored brilliance made a beautiful backdrop for the wedding nuptials of Nolan and Jessa. The weather was perfect —not too hot, not too cold—and sunny on that Saturday afternoon. In the bridal suite, Nora laced up the back of Jessa's strapless dress with a satin champagne ribbon. She smiled in the mirror at her glowing friend. Jessa nervously grabbed the edges of her true-white gown and fluffed it, the taffeta underneath supporting the shape of her full, ball gown skirt. She smoothed the beaded waistband and looked in the mirror.

"Aw, Jessa!" one of the bridesmaids squealed. "You look like a real princess!"

Jessa's smile was almost too broad for her pretty face. She adjusted her delicate tiara, allowing Nora to pin a stray curl back into place. Finally, Nora handed Jessa her bouquet and prepared to head outside with the other bridesmaids. They had practiced the processional three times yesterday, but still, they all had butterflies in their stomachs.

Looking radiant, Jessa held onto the arm of her proud father as he walked her down the grass path to a long road of commitment in marriage. How blessed Jessa was to have her father and mother present on one of the most memorable days of her life. Nora was slightly envious but very happy for Jessa—it was with joy and confidence that she supported Jessa's choice to enter this lifelong bond with Nolan. Nora, Jessa, Nolan, and Trey had been through a lot together. Nora knew that Jessa and Nolan weren't entering marriage lightly, but that they were seeking this partnership as a means to an end—that of worshiping the Highest Power—the Most High God. As they had grown in their faith together over the past year, they grew closer to each other, and knew that they wanted to choose one another again each day for the rest of their lives, spurring one another on toward Christ.

Nora stole a look at Trey, standing beside Nolan, whose eyes were fixed upon the beauty walking towards him. Trey's eyes met Nora's and the two of them shared a moment of wordless love and mutual hope for their own soon-to-be wedding. They too, like Jessa and Nolan, understood the profoundness of committing to someone for life. Having experienced the death of Nora's father, a terrifying haunting, a journey in uncovering the mysteries of the unseen world, and the discovery of the most powerful Love that saves—they knew they could get through anything together. They had seen tragedy and horror, as well as joy and laughter. They would always be deeply connected by their history, their shared quirky sense of humor, and their commitment to follow Jesus Christ. They knew life wouldn't be easy, and they knew they wanted to take on life's challenges together.

◆ ◆ ◆

January brought snow flurries and a trip to the Bahamas for Trey and Nora's tropical wedding ceremony. They bought plane tickets for Jessa, Nolan, Grandma Joanna, and Trey's parents so they could join them in celebration of the two lives becoming one.

The warm salty breeze of the ocean complemented the smell of the fresh island flowers encircling Nora's brown, loosely braided hair. Nora's simple, pure-white dress with an overlay of lace trailed to the ground with a short train. Around her neck was a strand of uneven saltwater pearls that had belonged to her mother. Her island bouquet paired nicely with her fuchsia-pink lips. Trey, in cream-colored linen slacks and a pink floral-print bow tie, smiled at his bride as she clasped his hands, standing in front of the officiant. With their vows recited to each other for better or for worse, richer or poorer, in sickness and in health, Trey and Nora made the decision to do life together forever.

These memories were captured not only on cameras, but etched into the hearts of those closest to them.

Life isn't perfect. There is no such thing as perfect humans living perfect lives. But there are moments within those lives that can feel perfect. And those little moments of perfection are what we yearn for. It's those moments that make everything else completely worth the struggle. Those moments inspire hope. And hope propels us forward towards the treasure that awaits us.

Our world, it seems, is only capable of manufacturing an overwhelming amount of bleak interference. Yet within it, light dwells. The light is always here with us, and no matter how much the darkness wants to hide it, cover it, and snuff it out—it will always triumph.

Truth is always waiting to be discovered and it longs to set us free. All too often, we only accept the truth when there is nowhere else to go, no one else to turn to, and no more excuses left to use. And then we see Truth standing there in her raw honesty, and she is standing where she has always been. Truth didn't move—we did.

Here on earth, we live within a constant, exhausting battle of power and will, with the persistent war of righteousness and evil playing out daily. We swim around in our imperfection, drowning in our vast selfishness and praise to false gods. You see, we were designed to worship. Worship is natural for humans. Making poor choices in what we worship is what we gravitate toward.

Ultimately, we get to choose what—or Whom—we worship. We alone make that choice. Let us choose wisely, for our destinies depend on it.

JOIN RAPHA HOUSE IN FIGHTING DARKNESS

Every single copy of Deape Woods sold helps support a very important organization called Rapha House.

Their mission is to end the trafficking and sexual exploitation of children through education, prevention, and aftercare for survivors. You can learn more about this incredible organization at http://raphahouse.org.

Why support an organization like Rapha House with sales from a fiction novel like Deape Woods?

That's a good question! While the connection may not seem obvious at first, Prudence and the Contagious Vision Publishing team understand that the sex trafficking industry is a very complex and evil world. There is a profound darkness interwoven throughout every aspect of it. We believe Satan is hard at work in this industry, and his ultimate goal is always destruction.

While the story of Nora Miller is fiction, there are many stories just like hers that are very real. Darkness oppresses humankind in many ways, every day, all over the world—sometimes in your very own hometown. It's often easy to put these horrible atrocities out of your mind when you aren't dealing with them directly.

In this way, child sex trafficking is similar. It's dark. It's oppressive. It's evil. It's common, it's real, and it's often utterly ignored.

The Rapha House is doing the challenging and desperately needed work of loving, rescuing, and healing the victimized. It's our hope that, through the sales of Deape Woods, we might help them further their endeavors and work toward the greater mission of ending the exploitation of the most vulnerable in our community and around the world.

If you have any questions about Rapha House and our involvement with them, please don't hesitate to reach out to us directly at info@contagiousvision.com.

About the Author

Prudence O'Haire is a quirky woman with a lot of passion and creativity wrapped up in a tiny package with big hair and big ideas. A wife and a mother of two girls and two boys, she loves to write and enjoys infusing truth, wisdom, and humor into one bag.

Prudence and her family live in the Pacific Northwest and enjoy the four seasons of the year—but fall is her favorite. She believes that written words are our very souls stamped tangibly for all to absorb and that everyone has a calling whether they are aware of it or not.

Prudence believes we all can learn something from one another and that fear is a driving force that must be squelched daily through God's power.

She believes the truth sets us free, no matter how ugly or unimaginable it can be, and that all of us need to make the effort of going from knowing what others believe to knowing what we believe.

It's her hope that you've enjoyed this story straight from her imagination to yours.

Made in the USA
Columbia, SC
05 May 2022